'I thought I was going to die that night,' she confessed.

Trahern took her face in his hands, touching his forehead to hers. 'But you found the strength to live.' For a long moment he stood with her face close to his own. Her scent entranced him like summer dew.

And when she lifted her face he needed to kiss her again. His mouth covered hers, soothing away her pain. Offering her the broken pieces of himself.

When she broke free her lips were swollen, her cheeks bright, as though she were too embarrassed to mention what had just happened between them. He didn't know what to say.

She seemed to sense his reticence, but before she could pull her hands away her hips accidentally bumped against his. She paled, realising what reaction she'd evoked.

'Morren—'

She stepped back, covering her face with her hands. She had gone pale, but took a deep breath. _____ o kiss me, so you _____ This was my faul

AUTHOR NOTE

Sometimes there are difficult books which demand to be written. I knew at the end of TAMING HER IRISH WARRIOR that the character of Trahern MacEgan would need his own story. As a bard and storyteller, Trahern has always had the love and support of a strong family, despite his travelling nature. When tragedy strikes his heart, he turns inwards and loses sight of the man he is. Though his compassionate spirit is buried, he finds a woman who awakens him to love.

Morren Ó Reilly is a heroine who has made difficult sacrifices to save her sister. When Trahern rescues her, they find healing in each other. He is the strength she needs, and Morren becomes his steadfast rock when unexpected secrets unfold within Trahern's past. Their love story is filled with emotional obstacles, but even in the darkest shadow lies hope for the future.

This was one of the most challenging books I've ever written, but I believe deeply in this story. I hope that you will enjoy the journey of Morren and Trahern as they find happiness together.

This is the last book in the MacEgan Brothers series. Other titles include: HER WARRIOR SLAVE (prequel to the series), HER WARRIOR KING (Patrick); HER IRISH WARRIOR (Bevan); THE WARRIOR'S TOUCH (Connor) and TAMING HER IRISH WARRIOR (Ewan). As a special bonus in this book you will find a short story—*Voyage of an Irish Warrior.* I first wrote this story for eHarlequin.com's website.

Visit my website at www.michellewillingham.com for excerpts and behind-the-scenes details. I love to hear from readers, and you may e-mail me at michelle@michellewillingham.com or write to PO Box 2242 Poquoson, VA 23662, USA.

SURRENDER TO AN IRISH WARRIOR

Michelle Willingham

MILLS & BOON

First published in Great Britain 2011
by Mills & Boon, an imprint of Harlequin (UK) Limited,
Eton House, 18-24 Paradise Road, Richmond, Surrey TW9 1SR

© Michelle Willingham 2010

ISBN: 978 0 263 88294 0

ROM
Pbk

Harlequin (UK) policy is to use papers that are natural,
and recyclable products and made from wood grown in
forests. The logging and manufacturing pro
legal environmental regulations of the coun

Printed and bound in Spain
by Blackprint CPI, Barcelona

Michelle Willingham grew up living in places all over the world, including Germany, England and Thailand. When her parents hauled her to antiques shows in manor houses and castles Michelle entertained herself by making up stories and pondering whether she could afford a broadsword with her allowance. She graduated *summa cum laude* from the University of Notre Dame, with a degree in English, and received her master's degree in Education from George Mason University. Currently she teaches American History and English. She lives in south-eastern Virginia with her husband and children. She still doesn't have her broadsword.

Visit her website at: www.michellewillingham.com, or e-mail her at michelle@michellewillingham.com

Previous novels by this author:

HER IRISH WARRIOR*
THE WARRIOR'S TOUCH*
HER WARRIOR KING*
HER WARRIOR SLAVE†
THE ACCIDENTAL COUNTESS**
THE ACCIDENTAL PRINCESS**
TAMING HER IRISH WARRIOR*

**Also available in eBook format in
Mills & Boon® Historical *Undone*:**

THE VIKING'S FORBIDDEN LOVE-SLAVE
THE WARRIOR'S FORBIDDEN VIRGIN
AN ACCIDENTAL SEDUCTION**
INNOCENT IN THE HAREM
PLEASURED BY THE VIKING

The MacEgan Brothers
†prequel to *The MacEgan Brothers* mini-series
**linked by character

Dedication:

To Chuck, my wonderful husband, who challenged me
to break the rules.

Acknowledgements:

With many thanks to my editor Joanne Grant
and my agent Helen Breitwieser for believing in me
and encouraging me. You are both such
a wonderful support, and I can't thank you enough
for everything you do.

Chapter One

Ireland—1180

The autumn wind was frigid, cutting through his cloak in a dark warning that he needed to seek shelter. Yet Trahern MacEgan hardly felt the cold. For the past season, he'd felt nothing at all, his emotions as frigid as the surrounding air.

Vengeance consumed him now, along with the fierce need to find the men who had killed Ciara. He'd left his home and family, returning to the southwest of Éireann, where the Ó Reilly tribe dwelled at Glen Omrigh.

His brothers didn't know of his intent to find the raiders. They believed he was travelling again, to visit with friends and tell his stories. As a bard, he rarely stayed in one place for very long, so they weren't at all suspicious.

But for this journey, he'd wanted to be alone. His brothers had their wives and children to guard. He'd never risk their safety, not when they had so much to lose. He had no one, and he preferred it that way.

The land was more mountainous here, with green hills

rising from the mist. A narrow road snaked through the valley, and misty warm clouds released from his horse's nostrils. The emptiness suited him, for he'd never expected to lose the woman he'd loved.

Earlier in the summer, Ciara's brother, Áron, had sent word that the *cashel* had been attacked by Viking raiders. Ciara had been caught in the middle of the battle, struck down and killed when she'd tried to flee.

The devastating news had kept him from Glen Omrigh for months. He didn't want to see Ciara's grave or hear the sympathy from friends. More than anything, he needed to forget.

But time hadn't dulled his pain, it had only heightened it. He shouldn't have left her. The guilt consumed him, eating away at the man he was.

Hatred flowed within his veins now, suffocating the pain of loss. The anguish had been replaced with rage, a sense of purpose. He was going to find the raiders, and when he did, they would suffer the same fate Ciara had endured.

When the sun had grown lower in the sky, he set up a fire and unpacked the tent. Though he could have finished his journey to Glen Omrigh, had he continued to ride for another few hours, he preferred to spend the night alone.

The flames licked at the wood, flaring bright orange against the night sky. Tomorrow, he would reach the *cashel* and begin tracking his enemy.

Trahern stretched out upon his cloak, watching the fire and listening to the sounds of the evening while he ate. In the distance, he heard the faint rustling of leaves against the forest floor. Likely animals. Even so, he reached for his blade.

The movement was heavier than a squirrel or a fox. No,

this was human, not an animal. Trahern clenched his sword, waiting for the person to draw closer.

Abruptly, a figure emerged from the trees. It was a young maiden, perhaps thirteen, wearing a ragged white *léine* and a green overdress. Dirt matted her face, and she held out her hands near the fire. She was so thin, it looked as though she hadn't eaten a full meal in weeks. Long brown hair hung to her waist, and she wore no shoes.

Jesu, her feet must be frozen.

'Who are you?' he asked softly. She kept her gaze averted, not answering his question. Instead, her cheeks flushed with embarrassment before she beckoned to him.

'Come and warm yourself,' he offered. 'I have food to share, if you are hungry.'

She took a step towards the fire but shook her head, pointing to the trees behind her. Trahern studied the place, but saw no one. Although the girl raised her hands to warm them in front of the fire, her expression grew more fearful. Again, she gestured toward the trees.

'What is it?' he asked.

Coughing, she moved her mouth, as though she hadn't spoken in a long time. 'My sister.'

Trahern rose to his feet. 'Bring her here. She can warm herself and eat. I've enough for both.' It wasn't true, but he didn't care if they depleted his supplies or not. Better to let the women sate their hunger, for he could always hunt.

The girl shook her head again. 'She's hurt.'

'How badly?'

She didn't answer, but beckoned to him as she walked back into the forest. Trahern eyed his horse, then the wooded hillside. Though it was faster to ride, the trees grew too close for a horse.

He had no desire to venture into the woods, particularly when it would be dark within another hour. But neither could he allow this girl to leave with no escort. Grimacing, he fashioned a torch out of a fallen branch. He slung his food supplies over one shoulder, not wanting to leave them behind.

The girl led him uphill for nearly half a mile. The ground was covered with fallen leaves, and he was careful to hold the torch aloft.

They crossed a small stream, and not far away, he spied a crude shelter, built from the remains of an old roundhouse. When they reached it he followed the girl inside.

'What is this place?' he murmured. Isolated from anywhere else, he couldn't imagine why it was here.

'A hunting shelter,' she answered. 'Morren found it years ago.'

Inside, the hearth was cold, the interior dark. Then, he heard the unmistakable moans of a woman. 'Build a fire,' he ordered the girl, handing her the torch.

Then he leaned down to examine the woman lying upon the bed. She was racked with shivers, clutching the bedcovers to her chest. Her legs jerked with pain, and when he touched her forehead, she was burning with fever.

Trahern let out a curse, for he wasn't a healer. He could tend sword wounds or bruises, but he knew nothing about illnesses that ravaged from inside the body. The woman was in a great deal of pain, and he didn't have any idea what to do for her.

He eyed the young girl who was busy with the fire. 'Your sister needs a healer.'

'We don't have one.' She shook her head.

Trahern sat down and removed his shoes. Though they would never fit her, it was better than nothing. 'Put these on. Tie them if you have to.'

She hesitated, and he gentled his tone. 'Go back to my camp and take my horse. If you ride hard for the next few hours, you can reach Glen Omrigh. Take the torch with you.'

Under normal circumstances, he wouldn't even consider sending a young girl out by herself in the dark. But between the two of them, he had a greater chance of sustaining the wounded woman's life until help arrived. Trahern had no doubt that the Ó Reilly men would accompany the girl back with the healer, once she made it there safely.

'If you can't make it that far, seek help at St Michael's Abbey.'

The girl started to refuse, but Trahern levelled a dark stare at her. 'I can't save her alone.'

He wondered what had become of their kin. Had they been killed during the raid? Since the girl had not mentioned anyone, Trahern suspected they were alone.

Reluctance coloured her face, but at last the girl nodded. 'I'll find someone.' She tied his shoes on, using strips of linen. Without another word, she seized the branch he'd used as a torch and left them alone.

It would be hours before the girl returned, and he hoped to God she wouldn't abandon them. Trahern struggled to remember what his brother's wife, Aileen, would have done, when healing a wounded person. He recalled how she examined the wounded person from head to toe.

'Sometimes, you'll find an injury where you least expect it,' she'd said.

Trahern moved beside the woman. Her eyes were closed, and she shuddered when he touched her hand, as though his fingers were freezing cold.

'It's all right,' said softly. 'You'll be safe now.' He studied her closely. Though her face was thin from hunger, her lips were full. Long fair hair lay matted against her cheek. He sensed a strength beneath the delicate features, and though the fever was attacking her body, she fought it back.

She wore a ragged *léine* that covered her torso, and the thin fabric was hardly enough to keep anyone warm. Trahern brought his hands gently down her face, to her throat. Down her arms, he touched, searching for whatever had caused the fever.

'Don't,' she whimpered, her hands trying to push him away, then falling to her sides. Her eyes remained closed, and he couldn't tell if his touch was causing her pain or whether she was dreaming. He stopped, waiting to see if she would regain consciousness.

When she didn't awaken, he pulled back the coverlet. It was then that he saw the reason for her agony. Blood darkened her gown below the waist. Her stomach was barely rounded from early pregnancy, and she tightened her knees together, as if struggling to stop the miscarriage.

Jesu. He murmured a silent prayer, for it was clear that he'd arrived too late. Not only was she going to lose this child, but she might also lose her life.

You have to help her, his conscience chided. He couldn't be a coward now, simply because of his own ignorance. Nothing he did would be any worse than the pain she was already suffering.

Reluctantly, he eased up her *léine*, wishing he could protect her modesty somehow. 'It's going to be all right, *a chara*. I'll do what I can to help you.'

Morren Ó Reilly opened her eyes and screamed.

Not just from the vicious cramping that tore her apart,

but because of the man seated beside her, his hand holding hers.

Trahern MacEgan.

Panic cut off her breath, seizing her with fear at his touch. She wrenched her hand away from him, and thankfully, he let go. The fever still clouded her mind, and she had no memory of what had happened during the past day.

Mary, Mother of God, what was Trahern doing here? Not a trace of softness did she see in his face. Though he was still the tallest man she'd ever seen, his appearance was completely changed. He'd shaved his head and beard, which made his features stark and cold. Stone-grey eyes stared down at her, yet there was emptiness in his gaze, not fury.

Beneath his tunic, tight muscles strained against the sleeves, revealing the massive strength of a warrior. Morren's heartbeat quaked, and she dug her hands into the mattress, wondering if Jilleen had brought him. She saw no sign of her sister.

'The worst is over,' he said. His voice was low, emotionless.

But it wasn't. Not by half. Morren curled her body into a ball, the dull pain sweeping over her. Her rounded stomach was now sunken and flat. From the pile of bloodstained rags nearby, she suspected the babe was gone.

It was her punishment for all that had happened. Hot tears gathered in her eyes. No, she hadn't wanted the child, not a permanent reminder of that awful night. But now that it was gone, she felt emptiness. A sense of loss for the innocent life that had never asked to be born from a moment of such savagery.

I would have loved you, she thought, *in spite of everything*.

She buried her face into the sheet, suddenly realising that

she was naked beneath the covers, except for the linen between her legs.

Humiliation burned her cheeks. 'What have you done?' she demanded. 'I want my clothing.'

'It was covered in blood. I had to remove it, to help you.' His voice was heavy, as though weighted down by stones. 'I'm sorry I could not save your child.'

The words cut through her, and she wept for the loss. A warm hand came down upon her hair as she hid her face from him. Though she supposed he'd meant to comfort her, she couldn't bear anyone touching her.

'Don't.' She shrank back from Trahern, binding the covers tightly to her skin.

He lifted his hands to show he meant no harm. 'I've sent your sister for help.' Studying her, he continued, 'Until she returns, I'll find something for you to wear.'

He rummaged through her belongings, and though Morren wanted to protest, she held her tongue. Another cramp rolled through her, and she couldn't stop the gasp. The room tipped, and she lowered her head again, fighting the dizziness.

'I've seen you before, but I don't remember your name,' he admitted, finding a cream-coloured *léine* within the bundle. He tossed it to her, turning his back while she pulled the gown over her head. 'I am Trahern MacEgan.'

It disappointed Morren to realise that he didn't recognise her at all. But then, his attentions had been focused on Ciara and hardly anyone else.

She knew Trahern well enough. During the months he'd spent living among her tribe, she'd listened to countless stories he'd told. It wasn't often that a bard could captivate an audience, weaving a spell with nothing but words, but Trahern was a master.

'Morren Ó Reilly is my name,' she answered at last.

He didn't show any sign that it meant anything to him, and she accepted it. Another dull cramp gripped her, and the pain threatened to sweep her under again.

'Is your husband alive?' he asked, a moment later. He'd phrased the question carefully, as though he already knew the answer.

'I have no husband.' And never would, God willing. Her sister, Jilleen, was the only family she had left. The only family she needed.

Trahern's gaze met hers, but he offered no judgement. Neither did she offer an explanation. 'When did you eat last?'

'I don't remember.' Food was the very last thing she'd thought of when the pains had come upon her. The idea of eating anything made her stomach wrench. 'I'm not hungry.'

'It might help.'

'No.' She buried her face on the ragged cloak her sister had used as a sheet. 'Just leave me. My sister will return.'

He dragged a stool nearby and sat beside the bed. 'I can see that you're hurting,' he said. 'Tell me what I can do for you.'

'Nothing.' She bit her lip, wishing he would go, so she could release the tight control she held over the pain.

Trahern crossed his arms over his chest. 'Your sister will return with the healer soon.'

'No, she won't.' Morren couldn't stop the gasp when another wave of pain struck her. 'Our mother was the healer. She died last year.'

Trahern leaned in, frustration lined upon his face. 'Then she'll go to the abbey and bring someone back.'

'I don't know if anyone will come,' she answered honestly.

The monks at St Michael's would tend anyone brought to their abbey, but she doubted if any of the elderly brethren could make the journey here.

Trahern's grey eyes were nearly black, his mouth taut with anger. Morren had never seen him this furious, and she tried to retreat as far away from him as possible. She closed her eyes, focusing on enduring one breath at a time.

'Don't blame Jilleen,' Morren insisted. 'She might still bring back someone to help.'

But even as she spoke the words, she suspected they were untrue. Her sister had gone, and there was no way of knowing if she would return. Ever since the night of the attack, Jilleen had not been the same.

Neither had she.

Morren gripped her arms tightly, not wanting to think of it again. *Let it go*, she told herself. *The sacrifice was necessary*.

'Are there many survivors left at Glen Omrigh?' he asked.

Morren shook her head, not knowing the answer. 'I don't know. We left, and I don't know where the others fled. Possibly to other clans.'

'How many of the *Lochlannach* attacked that night?'

Morren didn't speak, the dark fear washing over her. She clenched her teeth, fighting to keep herself together.

But Trahern wouldn't let it go. 'How many, Morren? Did you see them?'

Staring directly into his face, she said, 'I know...exactly how many men there were.'

She could tell from the look on his face when he understood her meaning. Trahern expelled a dark curse, his gaze crossing over her broken body.

She said nothing more. There was no need.

When his hand reached out to touch hers, she pulled it back. And this time, when the darkness lured her in, she surrendered.

She'd started bleeding again.

It bothered Trahern, having to care for Morren in such an intimate manner. She was a stranger to him, and he knew nothing about how to fight the demons of sickness. Though he did his best to help her, he wondered if it would be enough.

God help her, she was still burning with fever. Trahern gave her small sips of water and did his best to tend her. But he did not reach for her hand, nor touch her in any way. It wouldn't bring her comfort anyhow.

His rage against the Vikings heightened. The *Lochlannach* had done this to Morren, and worse, he feared they'd also violated Ciara. He renewed his vow of vengeance against the raiders. They would suffer for what they'd done. If what Morren said was true, that the tribe had scattered, then she might be his best hope of learning more about these raiders.

The hours stretched onward, and Trahern kept vigil over Morren. In the middle of the night, she started shaking. Terror lined her face, and he wished he had some means of taking away her pain. But he knew nothing of plants or medicines. And he didn't want to leave her alone, not when she'd lost so much blood.

Helplessness cloaked him, and he wondered if Ciara had suffered like this or whether she'd died instantly. Had anyone taken care of his betrothed during her last moments?

He stared down at his hands, wishing there was something he could do. There was only one thing he had left to offer—his stories. Though he'd been a bard for as long as he could remember, not a single tale had he uttered since Ciara's death. He hadn't been able to find the words any more. It was as if the stories had dried up inside him. Bringing laughter and entertainment to others seemed wrong, not when the woman he'd loved was gone and could no longer hear the legends.

But now, while Morren was fighting for her life, he saw it as a way of bringing comfort without a physical touch.

The story of Dagda and Eithne flowed from inside him, the way he'd told it to others, year after year. Morren's trembling grew calmer when he used his voice to soothe her.

'Dagda was a god who invoked goodness among the earth and in the fields,' Trahern murmured. 'But one day he saw a beautiful woman whom he desired as no other before. Her name was Eithne.'

Trahern wrung out a cold cloth and set it upon Morren's forehead, careful not to touch her skin. He told the story, using every nuance of his voice to capture her attention.

He spoke of the god who seduced Eithne and gave her a son. Trahern continued until his voice was nearly hoarse, stopping just before dawn.

Morren shuddered, struggling as the fever drew her deeper. She thrashed on the small pallet, her face tight with pain.

'Don't,' he ordered her. 'You're not going to give up now.'

'I've no wish to die,' she whispered, leaning forward when he offered her another sip of water. Her skin was flushed hot, her body limp and weakened. 'I have to look after my sister.'

She lifted her eyes to his. They were a deep blue, the colour of the sea. Within them, he saw a rigid strength to match his own.

'You're going to live,' he insisted.

Her expression was glazed with fever, but she pleaded with him, 'Trahern, when my sister returns, don't tell her about the child.'

Whatever he'd expected her to say, it wasn't that. His mouth tightened into a line. 'How could she not already know?'

'I...hid it from her. Jilleen knows what happened to me on the night of the raid. She doesn't need to know about the child—she's only thirteen.'

'She's old enough. And it will fall to her, to take care of you after this.' He couldn't stay with her indefinitely.

'Please,' she whispered. 'Say nothing.'

His hand clenched into a fist. 'I can make no such promise.'

Chapter Two

The next morning and afternoon went by with still no sign of her sister. Worries eroded her conscience, and Morren tried to convince Trahern to leave.

'Jilleen is just a girl,' she argued. 'She shouldn't be travelling alone.' Her own wild fears came back to haunt her, of all the things that could happen to her sister. 'You have to bring her back.'

'One more day.' Trahern folded his arms across his chest. 'I won't leave you behind when you're still unwell.'

'I'm afraid for her, Trahern. Please.'

'Not until you're strong enough.' He held out a plate of food, but Morren could hardly bring herself to eat any of the dried venison or the tart apples he'd brought. 'Try to eat.'

She forced herself to pick at a piece of the venison. 'Why did you come back?' The meat tasted bland, and she struggled to chew it.

'I came to avenge her death.'

She knew he meant Ciara. 'How did you hear of it?'

'Her brother sent word. I want to know the rest.'

She saw the terrible expression on his face and held her tongue. Some things were better left unremembered.

'Tell me,' he ordered. 'You were there.'

'No.' She saw no reason to torment him. It wouldn't change Ciara's fate.

Irritation flashed over his face. 'I've the right to know what happened to her. We were betrothed.'

She kept silent, meeting his gaze with her own stubbornness.

'I want to know everything,' he insisted. 'And I will revisit the same upon my enemies tenfold.' The ferocity of his glare left her no doubt that he meant what he said.

'Tomorrow,' she murmured. 'Take me back to Glen Omrigh, and help me find Jilleen. Then I'll tell you what you wish to know.'

'You'll tell me now.'

'Or what?' she taunted. He could say nothing to threaten her. The worst had already happened.

Fury flashed over Trahern's face and he strode outside, slamming the door behind him. When he'd gone, Morren drew her knees up. The pain had abated, though the dizziness remained. She reached for another piece of meat, forcing herself to choke it down.

You have to live, she told herself. *For Jilleen.*

Her hands moved to her midsection once more, and the soft, sunken skin bruised her spirits. After the massive bleeding, she didn't know if she would ever be able to bear another child.

It didn't matter. No man would want her, after what had happened, and she had no wish to let anyone touch her.

Slowly, Morren eased her feet to the side of the bed, wondering if she had the strength to stand. She set both hands on the edge, gingerly easing her feet down.

The door opened, and Trahern stopped short. 'Don't even consider it. You're too weak.'

He moved towards her, and out of instinct, Morren shrank from him, pulling her legs back onto the bed.

'I won't hurt you,' he swore. 'But you'll never make it back to Glen Omrigh if you exert yourself too soon.'

He moved over by the hearth, adding more wood to the fire. His shoulders flexed with hardly any effort at all as he arranged the oak logs into a small stack.

'It's just a fever,' she said. 'It will go away in a few days.'

He crouched by the hearth, eyeing her. 'You said your mother was a healer. What would she have done for you?'

'Raspberry-leaf tea, I suppose. Or willow bark, if the fever got too hot.'

He shrugged. 'I saw neither when I was out getting water. I'm sorry.'

'It doesn't matter.' She would find them herself, if the bleeding continued. It seemed to be lessening.

Trahern stopped arranging the wood for a moment. The firelight gleamed against his head, and she wondered why he'd shaved his hair and beard. The clothing he wore was hardly more than a slave would wear, as though he cared nothing for his appearance.

He grieved for Ciara, she realised. He'd loved her.

Morren studied him, not understanding how such a fierce, hot-tempered man could stay at her side all night telling stories. Amidst the smothering fever, she'd heard his deep voice. It had reached within her, giving her something to hold on to. She let her gaze fall over his face, noticing the worn lines and exhaustion. He hadn't slept at all, using the captivating tale to ease her pain. And something within her was grateful for it.

'Where are the others?' he asked. 'Your kinsmen?'

'Jilleen and I have no one else. Our parents are both dead.'

He returned to her bedside, holding out the food once more. 'How long have you been living here?'

She took one of the apples, with no true intent of eating it. 'Since the attack happened, in early summer.'

'And you've been here alone since then?'

'Yes.' Morren's gaze fixed upon his. 'I don't know how many of the Ó Reillys are left.' The only person she'd wanted near her, after that night, was Jilleen. She hadn't returned to the *cashel* after they'd fled, nor to St Michael's Abbey. She hadn't wanted anyone to know of her shame.

'After we find your sister, you should stay at Glen Omrigh,' Trahern said quietly. 'It isn't right for the two of you to be alone.'

She rolled the apple between her palms, not wanting to think about the future. Enduring each hour at a time was all she could manage. 'I'll find a place for us. Somewhere.'

He studied her, as if trying to ascertain her worth. 'Do you know enough of your mother's healing? Your skill would hold great value with another clan.'

She shook her head. 'I know the plants and trees and their uses. But I'm not a healer.' More often than not, her kinsmen had asked for her guidance when the crops were failing. Her talent lay in making things grow.

Outside, the wind shifted through the trees. Morren huddled beneath the coverlet, sensing what was to come. A change in the weather was imminent.

'You should put on your cloak,' she advised. 'It's going to rain.'

As if in answer to her prediction, she heard the soft spattering of droplets. Minutes later, the thatched roof began leaking, the water puddling upon the earthen floor, transforming it into mud. Trahern grimaced and lifted up his cloak to shield his head from the water. The rain felt cool upon her face, easing the fever.

'Take the other end of this,' Trahern said, holding out his cloak. 'We'll share the shelter until it stops.'

She made no move to take it. 'I don't mind the wetness.'

'It's not good for you. You'll catch a chill and get even weaker than you already are.' He sat down beside her on the bed, offering her the other end.

Morren scooted far away from him. Trahern's head towered over her, making her feel uncomfortable.

'I'm not planning to touch you,' he said gruffly. 'There's no harm in both of us using the cloak for shelter.'

Without waiting for her argument, he tossed the end over her head. She lifted the wool from her face, shielding her head from the rain.

The heavy cloak held his scent, masculine and safe. She could feel the heat of his body within the cloth, and her cheeks warmed from more than the fever.

Trahern wasn't looking at her, but he stared at the fire sputtering on the hearth. Rain dampened his face, and she saw the light stubble of beard upon his face.

She'd thought him handsome before, when his dark hair had touched his shoulders, his beard masking his features.

Now, he'd stripped away all traces of that man. Cold and hardened, he wasn't the same at all. And yet, he'd stayed up all night at her side. He hadn't abandoned her, not once. It wasn't the demeanour of a monster, but of a man she didn't understand.

Morren shivered, thinking of his devotion to Ciara. It was as if no other woman in the world had existed. Certainly, he hadn't noticed her.

'I remember when you first came to our *cashel* last year,' she said. 'You stayed up all night, telling your stories.'

He sobered, and she wondered if she shouldn't have spoken. 'I used to be a bard, yes.'

'And you stayed with us all winter long. Because of Ciara?'

He gave a nod. Drawing his knees up, he discarded the cloak and sat up. She noticed his bare feet and wondered what had happened to his shoes.

'Get some sleep, Morren. If you're well enough, we'll find Jilleen in the morning.' Trahern laid down again, drawing the cloak over both of them. In his eyes, she saw his own exhaustion. He hadn't slept in two days.

When he caught her staring, he added, 'I promise, I won't touch you.'

Strangely, she believed him. He had no interest whatsoever in her, and she felt herself relaxing in his presence.

'You should sleep, as well,' she offered. 'It was my fault that your rest was disturbed last night.'

He cast a wary look. 'You needed someone to watch over you. And there's no threat from me, I promise.'

When she rolled to the other side of the bed with his cloak shielding her hair, the anxiety that clenched her nerves tight seemed to soften.

Perhaps he really could keep her safe.

Trahern heard the sound of muffled weeping, a few hours before dawn. Morren remained with her back to him, the cloak draped over her. Her shoulders trembled, and his body tensed.

'Morren?' he whispered. 'Are you in pain?'

She remained far away from him, but her sobs grew muffled. 'A bad dream. That's all.'

He didn't know what to say. Words were meaningless after what she'd suffered. It was no wonder nightmares bothered her.

'And your fever?'

She rolled over to look at him. Her wheat-coloured hair hung against her face, and she looked as though she'd endured a gruelling night. 'It's better.' He didn't believe her and reached out to touch her forehead.

Morren cowered from him, and he let his hand fall away. A tightness formed within him, that she was unable to bear even a simple touch.

'I'll be all right,' she insisted. 'We need to find Jilleen today.'

Though her colour had improved, he wanted her to remain abed for at least another day. She might worsen if she pushed herself too hard. 'I know you're feeling better, but I'd rather you stayed here. I'll leave you with food, water and firewood before I search for your sister.'

Morren sent him a steady look. 'If you go without me, I'll follow you as soon as you've left. She's my sister, and I need to know that she's safe.' With a firm stubbornness, she raised her chin and began to sit up. 'I'm going to search for her. With or without you.'

Trahern sat up on his side of the bed, suddenly realising that his feet were beneath the sheet. Some time in the middle of the night, Morren had covered them. He hadn't expected the kindness.

He got up and returned to the bundle of clothing he'd found earlier. From within it, he found an overdress. The colours were dull, the wool coarse and prickly, but the material would keep her warm.

Once he helped Morren to find her sister, he would bring them somewhere safe. Perhaps to another clan, if the Ó Reillys hadn't yet rebuilt their *cashel*.

A cold fury spread through his veins once more, as he imagined the devastating attack the Ó Reillys must have suffered. He simply couldn't understand why the *Lochlannach* had tried to destroy an entire clan. A cattle raid was one matter, but this killing went beyond all else.

He needed to understand why. And after he'd found his enemies, he vowed to avenge Ciara's death and bring both Morren and Jilleen to safety.

Picking up his pouch of supplies, Trahern used his knife to slice through the leather. He made crude shoes out of the material, insulating them with straw. He gave Morren one set and offered the laces from his tunic to tie them on. He nodded at his cloak. 'Wear that. You'll need it to stay warm.'

'It's too cold,' she argued. 'You'll need to use it yourself. And I can use the cloak that was on the bed.'

'Take both of them. You need to stay warm more than I do.' When she was about to protest, Trahern picked up the garment and tossed it to her. If he had to fasten it himself, he'd make her wear it.

'St Michael's Abbey lies a few miles to the west,' he continued. 'We'll stop there to rest.'

'There's no need to stop on my behalf.' Morren eased to the end of the bed and stood. The woollen clothing hung against her thin body, and Trahern knew in his gut that she would never make it to Glen Omrigh. For that matter, he wasn't certain she would reach the abbey without collapsing.

He suspected she would push herself beyond all endurance to help her sister. He couldn't blame her for it. For his own brothers, he'd do the same. It didn't matter how far or how weakened he was. If a family member needed him, he'd drag his body halfway across Éireann.

'I'll arrange to borrow horses from the monks,' he said, concealing his irritation about losing his own mount, Barra. With luck, he'd get the horse back. 'That will make it easier on you.'

She seemed to accept it, and started towards the door. Trahern stopped her by offering her a cup of water and food. 'You're not leaving until you've finished this.' Though the dried meat wasn't appetising in the least, the fare was better than nothing. After today, he'd have to hunt for more.

Morren drank and nibbled at the venison. Though she didn't eat enough, in his opinion, at least it was a start. When they'd finished, he walked alongside her. 'If you start to feel weak, tell me. We'll stop and you can rest.'

'I'll be fine,' Morren insisted.

Trahern wanted to take her hand, to offer her support, but he knew she'd refuse. They travelled downhill, and he could see her breath in the cold autumn air. Morren stepped carefully through the fallen leaves, grasping at tree trunks for balance.

Her pallor matched the grey sky, and more than once she stumbled. When they reached the edge of the forest, where he'd made his camp two nights earlier, she looked ready to collapse.

'Do you want to go on?' he asked.

'I've no choice.'

Her answer didn't suit him at all. Without asking, he lifted her into his arms. 'Pretend you're walking.'

She looked panicked and struggled to get away from him. 'Put me down.'

'If I do, you'll faint. And we'll travel faster this way.' They would have to stop at St Michael's. Already he'd abandoned the idea of travelling to Glen Omrigh. There was no chance Morren could make the journey.

He stopped walking when he saw the tension in her body. 'I know you don't want me to carry you. But if you can endure this for another hour, we'll be at the abbey.'

Her gaze wouldn't meet his, but she didn't protest again. Fear was etched within her posture, in the way she tried to distance herself.

She weighed hardly anything, and Trahern found that it was no hardship at all to carry her. How any man could attack a woman as vulnerable as Morren was beyond his comprehension.

She had a face that most men wouldn't notice at first, soft, with unremarkable features. But her blue eyes surprised him. Although they were weary, there was strength and determination in them, despite her physical weakness.

'Was the abbey attacked by the *Lochlannach*?' he asked. If there were other threats lingering, he needed to know of them.

'As far as I know, our *cashel* was the only victim.' Morren turned her gaze to the horizon where the rolling hills merged into the mountains. 'I still don't understand why we were attacked. We've lived in peace among the *Lochlannach* for so long. Some of our women married among the Norse.'

Trahern walked through the tall grasses, holding Morren

close. She couldn't seem to relax, though he'd done nothing to threaten her.

'Tell me the rest of the story,' she asked quietly. 'About Dagda and Eithne.'

It was natural to slip into the tale, spinning a distraction that both of them needed. Trahern continued where he'd left off, and in the midst of his storytelling, the strained tension in her body seemed to relax.

'The god Dagda wanted to grant his son a piece of land, when Oengus grew to manhood. But the land that Dagda wished to offer was held by a man named Elcmar. Oengus did not want to kill Elcmar, and so it was that he and his men attacked during the celebration of Samhain.

'When Oengus conquered Elcmar, he asked to rule the land, for one day and a single night. Afterwards, both would go to Dagda and ask who should rightfully possess the land.'

Though Morren remained silent, he saw her face softening as he wove the story. Her lips tilted upwards, when he spoke of Oengus's trickery.

'When both men came to Dagda, the god proclaimed that it now rightfully belonged to Oengus. For Samhain is a feast where time holds no meaning. And ruling it for a day and a night during that time of celebration is to rule it for eternity.'

When he'd finished the story, the stone walls of St Michael's emerged over the horizon, less than a mile away. Trahern set Morren down, asking, 'Do you want to walk the rest of the distance, or shall I carry you?' He doubted she'd want to appear like an invalid in front of the monks, but if she lacked the strength, it was no hardship to continue the rest of the way.

'I'll walk,' she answered.

Made of stone, the abbey stretched high above the landscape, flanked by a round tower. Arched windows, as tall as an ordinary man, encircled the structure, but he could not see any of the brethren at first. At the bottom of the hill, a silver strand of water wove through the countryside.

Morren held the edges of her cloak around her body, to guard against the cold. 'You're planning on leaving me here at the monastery, aren't you?'

'You're not strong enough to reach the *cashel*.' It was best to grant her the protection of the Church. In this way, he could ensure her safety. 'I'll find your sister and bring her back to you.'

'I want to believe you. But I don't.'

'You think I'm the sort of man who would leave her there alone?' His temper flared that she would think such a thing. 'I'm the one who sent her for help. It's my obligation to bring her back to you.'

'Jilleen is just a girl, a stranger to you.' She exhaled a breath, still not trusting him. 'What if the *Lochlannach* found her?'

'Stop thinking like that. We don't know why she didn't return. But I promise you, I'll find her.'

'You're a bard, not a warrior.'

Trahern took a step forward, using his height in an unspoken warning. Morren met his gaze, and he rested his hand upon his sword. 'Be assured, Morren, I know how to fight. And defend.' He'd spent years of his life practising with his brothers. Though he might be older than many, he hadn't lost any of his abilities. If anything, his instincts were sharper.

Morren's blue eyes faltered, and she looked away. Good. He wasn't used to women doubting him.

'If I had been there that night,' he vowed, 'each and every

one of the *Lochlannach* fighters would be dead. They'd not have laid a hand upon you or Ciara.'

Morren's shoulders lowered. 'Would that it were so.' She didn't look at him, and he saw that words would not convince her. She picked up the long hem of his cloak and continued walking.

They travelled on in silence until they reached the stone chapel. Trahern was about to enter when he sniffed the air. The acrid scent of smoke suddenly permeated the landscape.

Morren moved to the crest of the hill, and Trahern spied billowing smoke clouds rising in the distance. From his vantage point, he saw flames rising from the fallen *cashel* in the distance.

'They're back.' Morren's hands moved to cover her mouth, and her face went white.

Trahern half-pushed Morren towards the chapel. From within, he heard the plain chant of the monks echoing. 'Stay here with the brethren. I'm going after them.'

'You have no horse,' she protested. 'They'll cut you down.'

'They won't touch me.' Trahern checked his weapons and cast her one final look. 'I'm going to find out why they've returned. And what it is they want.'

'Be careful,' she urged.

He caught her hand in his. 'Wait for me, Morren. I'll be back by sunset.'

Chapter Three

The remains of Glen Omrigh were ghostly, with charred grasses surrounding the *cashel*. The wooden palisade wall was blackened and ruined in sections, the air heavy with smoke.

Trahern crouched low in the tall grasses, watching the silhouettes of two horsemen. It had taken him nearly an hour to reach the fortress, due to the hilly terrain, and the afternoon sun had already begun to drift downwards.

The invaders wore the clothing of the *Lochlannach*, Viking raiders by the look of it. Their long cloaks were fastened with large bronze brooches, and although the taller man wore no armour, Trahern sensed he would make a formidable opponent. His companion was shorter, with darker blond hair. Trahern grasped the hilt of his sword, while he pondered whether or not he could defeat them alone. It would be dangerous.

One of the huts was still burning, the thatch bright orange with flames. Smoke rose high into the air, the acrid scent smothering the *cashel*.

Trahern watched the two men as they patrolled the remaining huts, inspecting the contents. Not a single other person did he see. Any Ó Reilly survivors had abandoned the *cashel*.

Trahern kept one hand on his sword hilt when the men rode closer. Their faces showed displeasure, and he overheard them arguing in the Norse tongue.

They weren't here to attack, it was clear, nor to steal the tribe's valuables or supplies. Instead, the men's expressions were grim, as though dissatisfied by what they saw.

Trahern moved in closer, keeping his body pressed to the ground. Dry grass tickled his face, the cold earth damp with frost. When he reached the outer palisade wall, he crept nearer to a burned section to get a better look.

One of the riders was on a familiar mount. It was Barra, the destrier that he'd paid a damned fortune for. The black horse was nervous from the smoke, prancing his feet. If the *Lochlannach* thief didn't control Barra, he'd find himself on his backside.

Though Trahern wanted to attack the two men and regain his horse, logic forced him to hold back. He needed answers, and these men would lead him to them.

Within a few more minutes, the Vikings left the settlement and rode west. Trahern was torn between following them or entering the *cashel* to search for Jilleen Ó Reilly. Though he believed they'd taken her, he couldn't be certain.

He cast a backward glance at the men before racing inside the *cashel*. Heavy smoke choked the air in his lungs, and heat blazed from the burning hut. He had only a few moments to spare before he had to follow the men.

Fate blessed him, for near the outer gate lay one of the shoes he'd given to Jilleen. Whether the girl had dropped it on purpose or whether she'd lost it didn't matter. It confirmed that she was here. And he knew who'd taken her.

His fist curled around his sword hilt. The *Lochlannach* would answer for this.

Trahern picked up the shoe and ran back to the trail, running behind the men. He found a second shoe only a mile further, on the same path travelled by the riders.

When he reached the top of the next hill, he dropped low to study the men. They were travelling towards the Viking settlement along the coast. He'd seen it before, but knew he couldn't make it there by nightfall, not without a horse.

He cursed, for he had no alternative except to turn back. He needed to borrow a mount from the monks.

Frustration shredded his patience, and he began the walk back to the abbey. Donning his own shoes once more, he imagined exactly how he would break through the Viking forces.

The abbot granted Morren the hospitality of St Michael's, and an older monk, Brother Chrysoganus, led her to the guest house adjoining the monastery. He offered her a kindly smile and began filling a basin with water. When Morren realised he meant to bathe her feet as a gesture of welcome, she interrupted.

'Forgive me, Brother Chrysoganus, but I would prefer to wash my own feet.' She couldn't bear the idea of anyone touching her just now, even if it was a tradition.

The older man appeared surprised by her declaration, but he deferred. 'If that is your wish.' Offering her the basin, he added, 'I must join the others for *none*. If you have need of anything afterwards, you've only to ask.'

Morren nodded, unwrapping the leather shoes Trahern had made for her. She rested her bare feet in the warm water.

'Thank you, Brother.' After he'd gone, she bathed her feet and let them sit in the warm water for a few minutes.

The bells sounded for *none*, and she heard the monks' voices rising and falling in plain chant. The simple tones were soothing, but when her hands moved over her skin, she started to tremble.

Dark memories pulled her down, the men's faces taunting her. Morren tried to block it out, but the nightmare of the attack returned. She lowered her head, nausea forming in her stomach. God help her, she couldn't bear this. Her hands moved to her empty stomach, and the coldness seemed to envelop her, drowning her.

Don't think of it, she warned herself. *Forget.*

Closing her eyes, she removed her feet from the basin and sank to her knees. The haunting voices of the monks echoed within the stone chapel, their prayers rising into the air. The coldness swallowed her up, taking her back into the numbness that she needed to survive. There had been no one to save her, no mercy. She didn't know what she'd done to deserve such a fate.

Worse, there had come a time when she'd stopped fighting. She'd lain there, staring at the dark sky, waiting for it to be over. Shame swelled up inside her, for she should have struggled. Used her fists, her teeth—anything.

Instead, she'd prayed to die.

Her gaze fell upon the crude shoes lying beside the basin. Trahern had fashioned them for her, not wanting her to suffer from the cold. A hard lump formed in her throat at his kind gesture.

She suspected he wasn't coming back. Though he'd sworn he'd return at sunset, she wasn't certain he would keep his word. Her hands clenched together, and Morren forced herself to rise. Leaving the guest chamber behind, she stumbled to the one place that would offer sanctuary to her troubled thoughts: the garden.

Inside the monks' small courtyard there were neatly tended plots that had not a single weed. A few heads of cabbage were left behind, along with herbs. In the corner, tucked away behind one of the apple trees, she saw an abandoned garden.

It was covered in dead weeds, left alone to grow over. Perhaps the monks no longer had a need for it, but she longed for something useful to do.

Over the next few hours, Morren busied herself clearing out the waste, working the good nutrients back into the barren soil. Perhaps, in the spring, they might find a purpose for the bed. The soil needed to rest through the winter, but in spring it would yield a good harvest if someone tended to it.

The distraction did nothing to cease her worry for Trahern. Likely another attack was happening at the *cashel* right now. He was alone, and though his strength was undeniable, if the *Lochlannach* found him they would kill him.

The thought made her nerves constrict tighter, and Morren voiced a silent prayer for his welfare. Though Trahern was hardly more than a stranger to her, he'd saved her life. If she hadn't been there to tend her, she'd have bled to death.

She only wished he hadn't sent her sister for help. Jilleen was her only family, her only companionship. Without her, Morren had no one.

She ripped out the weeds from the roots, as though she could tear out her own frustrations and fears. She longed to return to the *cashel*, to see for herself the extent of the damage, but her body couldn't endure it. Even now, she fought the dizziness that threatened her vision with bright spots.

* * *

She didn't know how many hours had passed, but in time Brother Chrysoganus brought her a simple repast of bread and cheese. 'I thought you might like something to eat.'

'Thank you, Brother.' She wiped her hands on her skirts, realising she was hungrier than she'd thought. 'I hope you don't mind I spent my time working.'

Chrysoganus leaned heavily upon his walking stick, inspecting her efforts. 'Not at all. I fear we've let that particular plot go fallow, but now that you've cleared it back, we'll find a use for it. Thank you for your labour.' He peered closer at the earth. 'My hands can't pull the weeds as easily as I'd like. Often the gardening falls to the younger brethren.'

Morren softened at his thanks, offering a tentative smile. Since she had no silver or possessions to offer the monastery in return for their hospitality, her skill was all she could give.

'I've saved the weeds in a small pile over there,' she said. 'Cover them with leaves, and in the spring till the mixture into the soil, along with animal droppings,' she advised. 'Your garden will give you a good harvest.'

His craggy face formed an amused smile. 'Will it, now?'

She rested her dirty palms on her lap and nodded. Broaching the subject she feared, she asked, 'Have the fires in the *cashel* stopped?'

Chrysoganus's smile faded, and he sat down upon a large, flat stone near the edge of the garden. 'No, not yet. We don't know who started them, but it must have happened early this morning.'

'Not everyone died in the attack,' Morren said slowly. 'Why didn't the survivors come here?'

He shook his head. 'I can't be certain. We prepared the

guest house, in anticipation of their arrival, but you and your companion have been the only folk we saw.'

How could it be that not a single person had taken sanctuary in the abbey? The fear she'd held back was starting to intensify. She'd wanted to believe that she could bring Jilleen back home, that they could find their place again and start over. But it was more likely that everyone was gone.

She looked into Brother Chrysoganus's sympathetic brown eyes. 'My travelling companion, Trahern MacEgan, went to look for my sister. He promised to return at sunset.'

'I will see to it that accommodation is prepared for him.' The monk inclined his head in a silent farewell as he took his leave.

After he'd left, Morren rose. Though her body ached and she still felt weak, she forced herself to walk to the tallest point of the abbey grounds. She needed to see her home, though it had been destroyed.

Each step was a struggle, and when at last she reached the topmost point of the hill in front of the abbey, she peered down and saw a rider approaching, a spear in his hand.

But it wasn't Trahern.

Gunnar Dalrata knew he'd been followed. It was only out of sheer luck that he'd happened to see the grass ripple before his eyes, otherwise he'd not have seen the intruder watching them from outside the *cashel*.

He gripped his spear tighter and eyed his brother. Hoskuld didn't seem to notice, but Gunnar remained a few paces behind. Glancing backwards, he spied the runner.

An Irishman. Had he been one of the Ó Reilly survivors? Gunnar thought about alerting Hoskuld, but for what purpose? The Irishman had done nothing, except observe. He might have been looking for the girl they'd taken yesterday.

They crested the hill, and still the man pursued them. Was he planning to follow them to the settlement on foot? With another glance, Gunnar saw that the intruder had stopped at the top of the hill. Moments later, the man turned back.

Gunnar brought his horse alongside Hoskuld's. 'Someone was following us. I want to know why.'

'Do you want me to come with you?'

'No. The man is on foot and unarmed from what I can tell. I want to question him.'

'Bring him with you,' Hoskuld suggested.

Gunnar's expression turned grim. 'I might.' He quickened the pace of his mount, riding hard. He was about to overtake the Irishman when he happened to look up. The man was moving in the direction of St Michael's Abbey, and in the distance, he saw the reason.

A woman stood at the top of the hill in front of the abbey. She was waiting for the man, and as Gunnar rode past, he saw the sudden fear and fury overtake the man's expression.

It intrigued him. Perhaps the best way to get his answers was to await the man at the abbey. With his spear gripped in his hand, he rode up the hill to St Michael's.

He saw the woman at closer range then. With fair hair and a quiet sort of beauty, her face would make any man want to fight for her. But when she caught sight of him, she fled.

Gunnar wheeled his horse back, keeping his spear aloft. When the Irishman arrived, he would be waiting.

Trahern tore up the hillside, his legs taking long strides. Anger gave him a speed he normally wouldn't have. By God, he'd murder the Viking where he stood if he laid a hand on Morren.

It was the longest mile he'd ever run in his entire life. Fear punctuated his stride, along with guilt at having left her. Jesu, he shouldn't have let Morren remain behind.

As he reached the top, he saw Morren disappear towards the chapel. Thank God, she'd had the good sense not to remain. He hardly felt his own exhaustion as he lunged towards the waiting rider. Energy roared through him as he seized the man's spear and tossed it aside, dragging the Viking from his horse.

His enemy weighed nearly as much as he did, and Trahern grimaced when the man used his own strength to knock him to the ground.

'I don't like being followed,' the man remarked, his voice heavy with a Norse accent. He twisted, wrestling Trahern to the side.

'Neither do I.' Trahern grunted, throwing the man off him. When the Viking stood up straight, he was startled to realise that they were the same height. Few men were as tall as himself, and even fewer possessed his strength.

The man's gaze narrowed, and both of them saw the resemblance at the same time.

'You're one of us, aren't you?' the foreigner murmured. 'I didn't expect it.'

Trahern unsheathed his sword. 'I'm not a damned *Lochlannach*, no.'

'Then you haven't looked at yourself recently.' The man drew his own sword. 'Why were you following me?'

'Where is the girl?' Trahern countered, swinging his weapon hard. The Norseman met his blow, blocking it.

A long blade came arcing towards his head, and Trahern

sidestepped to avoid it, deflecting the slice with his own weapon.

'I suppose you mean the one we found at the *cashel* yesterday,' the man replied. 'She's at our settlement. But I don't know if I'll let you follow us there. Not with the kind of welcome you've given me.' He lunged forward, his blade thrusting at Trahern's gut in a physical challenge.

Trahern parried it, steadying his balance before he renewed the attack. He focused upon the fight, letting his training flow through him, meeting blow for blow. Sweat gleamed upon his skin, but he drove the man back.

When his blade nicked his opponent's shoulder, satisfaction rippled through him. He'd been waiting half a year for this. He only wished he could fight against the other invaders, killing all of them.

He poured his rage, his grief, into the fight. It didn't matter to him that they were standing upon holy ground, that it was a sin against God to fight here. This man had slaughtered innocents, like Ciara. He'd violated women, and he deserved to die.

Behind the Viking, he spied Morren walking slowly. The folds of her gown draped over her thin body, and she gripped the edges of the borrowed cloak. The hood had slid down, revealing her golden hair. Fear and horror washed over her face.

It renewed his strength, and Trahern slashed a brutal blow toward his enemy's blade, sending the weapon spinning until it landed in the grass. The man's look of surprise changed to grim acceptance, when Trahern grasped him by the hair, fitting his sword to his enemy's throat.

Staring hard at Morren, Trahern demanded, 'Did this man dishonour you?'

Chapter Four

All the blood had left her face, and Morren knew without question that the Viking was going to die at Trahern's hands. His life depended upon her answer.

'No,' she whispered. Then louder, 'No, he wasn't one of them. He wasn't there that night.' She kept her voice steady, hoping he would believe her.

Trahern's iron gaze pierced her. 'Don't lie. He deserves to die for what he did.' The blade remained tight at the Norseman's throat.

'I'm not lying.' Though she didn't want to draw closer, she forced herself to intervene. When she stood within an arm's length of them, she pleaded, 'Let him go, Trahern.'

It was clear he didn't want to. She took another step closer, but he snarled, 'Stay back.'

There was no mercy on his face, and she feared he wouldn't listen to her words. She looked into his grey eyes, waiting. Letting him see that her words were true. The wildness in his demeanour was hanging on edge, as if he were fighting against the instinct to kill.

'Let him go,' she repeated.

Moments seemed to border on eternity. After a long pause, Trahern lowered his blade. Shoving the man away, he sheathed his weapon.

Morren breathed a little easier. The Viking wiped at the blood on his shoulder, and sent her a grateful look. 'Thank you for my life, fair one.'

She recognised the interest behind his compliment. With dark grey eyes and blond hair, many women would call the *Lochlannach* handsome.

Not her. She had no interest in any man, especially not a Viking.

'Who are you, and why were you at the *cashel*?' she asked.

'I am Gunnar Dalrata. And we were obeying the orders of our chief.' He cast a glance at Trahern, wiping the blood at his shoulder. The wound didn't appear deep, and the man hardly paid it any more heed than a scratch. 'We were looking for more survivors, like the girl we found yesterday.'

'Jilleen,' Morren breathed, her heartbeat quickening. 'Where did you take her?'

'We took her to our *longphort*,' Gunnar said. 'You are welcome to join her. I'll provide you with an escort.'

'Morren will go nowhere with you.' Trahern moved beside her, like a silent shield. His hand rested upon his sword hilt, poised to defend her. He looked as though he'd rather tear the Viking apart rather than release him.

'The girl you found is my sister,' Morren told Gunnar. 'Please, let her go. She's done nothing wrong.'

'She is not a captive,' Gunnar argued. 'But we didn't want her wandering out alone. We brought her with us when she asked for our healer.' He studied her, his grey eyes narrowing with concern.

Morren held on to her waist, refusing to explain. Though the bleeding had nearly stopped, she didn't feel like herself any more. It was as though she were hollowed out inside, with hardly anything left.

The day had taken its toll upon her, and though she didn't want to feel any sort of weakness, she hadn't recovered as quickly as she'd wanted to. And worse, Trahern seemed to sense it.

He kept his gaze fixed upon Gunnar, but his words were meant for her. 'We'll go to the settlement at dawn and bring back Jilleen.'

'We should go with him now,' Morren insisted.

'You're too weak to make the journey. Give it one more night.' Trahern sent Gunner a dark look. 'Unless you want me to go back with him.'

She hesitated. A part of her resisted the idea of leaving Jilleen for one more night, especially when she didn't know whether or not her sister was all right. Then again, she hardly trusted Trahern not to get himself killed on account of his temper.

'She's unharmed,' Gunnar said. 'I promise you that.'

Morren stared at the *Lochlannach*, but he didn't appear to be lying. His grey eyes held sincerity, and he added, 'The rest of the Ó Reilly tribe sought sanctuary with us.' He sent a distasteful look back towards the church.

The monks had begun returning from prayer, and the abbot quickened his pace at the sight of them. His face curdled with unspoken anger, and he reached for the long cross hanging around his neck as if warding off demons.

A grim expression formed upon his face when he reached

them. Several of the other monks flanked him, as if in silent protection. Morren took a step back, distancing herself from the men.

'I'll return to the *longphort* and let them know to expect you,' Gunnar said, whistling for his horse. He spoke not a word in greeting to the abbot, but gave a cold nod.

Before he could mount, Trahern interrupted. 'I'll be wanting my horse back.'

The edges of the Norseman's mouth curved up. 'Come and fetch him, then.'

A cloud drifted across the afternoon sun, shadowing the abbot's face. Trahern inclined his head. 'My apologies, Father.'

The abbot folded his arms. 'To shed blood upon holy ground is a sin.'

The chastising tone in the priest's voice seemed to stoke Trahern's anger. Morren took another step away while the two men confronted each other.

Trahern's height towered over the diminutive abbot. His grey eyes turned to granite. 'I granted him mercy.'

The two men locked gazes, with the abbot making the sign of the cross. It seemed less like a blessing and more like an absolution, Morren thought.

'There is still hatred in your heart.'

'And there it will remain, until every last one of them is dead.' When Trahern turned back to her, she saw the pain cloaked behind his anger.

It frightened her to see him so intent upon vengeance. She doubted if he cared anything at all for his soul.

He's as lost as I am.

Trahern hardly spoke to Morren the rest of the night. God above, he didn't know what was happening to him. It was as if he'd stepped outside himself, becoming a man who cared about nothing. He'd almost murdered the Norseman, simply because of the man's heritage.

It didn't seem to matter that Gunnar Dalrata hadn't been there on the night of the attack. Everything about the man grated upon him, like sand in an open wound.

Innocent women had suffered and died on the night of the attack, due to men like Gunnar. The blood lust had seized him with the need to avenge, the need to kill. But Morren's voice had broken through the madness, soothing the beast.

He moved to sit at the low wooden table at the centre of the room. The interior of the guest house was not large, but there were six pallets set up within the space, three on either side with the table to separate them.

The remains of their meal lay upon the table, and Trahern frowned at how little Morren had eaten. It was hardly enough to keep a child alive, much less a woman.

He'd wanted to pursue the *Lochlannach* tonight, but there was no chance Morren could endure the journey. If he ventured further than five miles, no doubt she would collapse.

She stepped quietly to a pallet on the far side, lying down with her back to him. Delicate and fragile, he didn't miss the worry that burdened her. Despite her physical weakness, there was no doubt of her determination to reach her sister.

Trahern poured water into a wooden bowl and splashed it on his face. Water trickled down his stubbled cheeks, and he felt the prickle of hair forming on his scalp and beard. Though most Irishmen prided themselves on their hair and beards, he wanted to strip it all away.

He didn't want warmth or comfort—only the cold reminder of what he'd lost.

With his blade, he shaved off the hair, never minding the

nicks upon his flesh. Without it, he appeared more fearsome. Different from the others, a man not to be trusted. If changing his physical appearance kept others away from him, so be it.

When it was done, he set the knife back on the table, a flicker of light gleaming off the blade. There were traces of his blood upon it, but he didn't care.

He poured more water into the wooden bowl, using his palms to spill more of it over his head, the droplets washing away the blood. The remaining water in the bowl rippled, then fell still. In the reflection, he saw his angry features, the monster who lived for violence. A man who no longer cared if he lived or died.

A man who looked like one of the Vikings.

Trahern wanted to hurl the bowl across the room, because he wanted nothing to do with them. They were savage murderers, not men. He loathed the fact that their appearances were similar.

It shouldn't have surprised him, for his great-uncle Tharand had been a *Lochlannach*, as well as his mother's father. Even so, he'd never truly compared himself to the foreigners. But when he'd battled against Gunnar, for the first time he'd not looked down upon his enemy. They were the same height, the same build. It bothered him more than he cared to admit.

Jesu, how could he even consider bringing Morren into their settlement? She'd endured enough suffering. It was best to leave her here, where she wouldn't have to face the men who had harmed her.

But then he'd never know who the raiders were. Without her, he couldn't identify them. Trahern gritted his teeth, fingering his dagger before sheathing the blade. There was no choice but to bring her.

He risked a glance at her sleeping form on the opposite side of the guest house. Like a ghostly spirit, Morren appeared caught between the worlds of the living and the dead. Though she claimed she wanted to live, to take care of her sister, after the horror she had endured he wondered if she would ever find contentment in her life.

She rolled over, her golden hair veiling one cheek. She slept with her hands clenched on the coverlet, as though she were still trying to defend herself.

He wondered if she preferred him to sleep far away from her. Or was it better to remain nearby, to keep her safe, if any other guests arrived at the monastery?

To avoid making a decision, he spent time clearing away the dishes and leftover food. Silence descended over the abbey, with all the monks asleep until *vigils*, which would begin in a few hours.

He chose the pallet furthest from Morren, deciding it would make her more comfortable. Stretching out on the fur coverlet, he closed his eyes and tried to sleep.

In his mind, he saw Ciara's face. Her spirit haunted him, with a smile that tore him apart.

I love you, she'd whispered in his ear on the morning he'd left. He'd kissed her goodbye, never suspecting that it was the last time he'd ever hold her in his arms. So many things he'd never said. He hadn't told her that he'd loved her. And now, she'd never know it.

He shifted restlessly on his pallet and turned to find Morren watching him.

'I can't sleep,' she confessed. 'I've tried, but I'm too worried about Jilleen.'

Trahern stood and crossed the room, sitting down upon one of the pallets close by. He stretched out beside her, careful to keep a physical distance from her. He propped up his head on one elbow, watching her. 'Are you afraid of visiting the *Lochlannach*?'

Her mouth tightened, and she nodded. 'Yes. I know Gunnar said she wasn't a captive, but if that were true, why didn't she come back? Why didn't they send their healer?'

'I don't know. But we'll find out tomorrow.' He studied her, and her blue eyes filled with worry. 'If you'd feel safer staying behind, I promise I'll bring her back to you.'

Morren sat up, drawing her knees close. 'You shouldn't go alone.' Her arms tightened around her knees, and she lowered her forehead. He suspected she didn't trust him to keep his word from the way she wouldn't meet his gaze.

'I wish I were stronger,' she continued. 'I'm afraid that the longer I wait, the more danger Jilleen faces. If it weren't for me, she wouldn't have left.'

'Tomorrow,' he promised. 'We'll get her back.' A grim feeling slid over him, and he added, 'I suppose we should have kept Gunnar as a hostage.'

'No. You were right to release him.' She met his gaze. 'And I rather doubt the monks would have allowed it.'

He shot her a sidelong smile. 'No? Perhaps with a generous gift to the monastery, they would turn a blind eye.'

Morren shook her head, her mouth softening. Clearly she thought he was teasing, and though that wasn't entirely true, it eased the tension. 'Gunnar owes you a debt now,' she added. 'It may keep us both safe.'

'The *Lochlannach* have no honour.'

She started to speak, but fell silent, almost as if she wanted to argue with him but had changed her mind.

Trahern leaned back, staring at the ceiling. 'I don't like

bringing you there. I think you should stay here at the abbey.'

'I'll be all right. With each day, my strength improves.'

He didn't think it was enough. 'We'll borrow horses. And if there's any sign of danger, I'm sending you back.' He could defend them long enough for her to get to safety, of that he was certain.

Morren laid back down, and he wondered suddenly why the monks had left them alone in the guest house. In an intimate space such as this, it seemed too close. He could smell the fragrance of Morren's skin, like crushed rosemary. It intrigued him, and he found himself staring at her. Her features were soft, with clear blue eyes and fair hair that fell below her shoulders, as though she'd cut it a few years back. Her nose had a slight tilt, an imperfection that drew his attention to her mouth.

He forced his gaze away, rising from the pallet and stalking towards the fire. He added more peat, regaining control of his errant thoughts. What was the matter with him? He supposed his response was because he hadn't been with anyone since Ciara. He wasn't a damned monk, able to shut out his body's instincts.

'Are you all right?' Morren asked, sitting up again.

'Yes.' He poked at the fire, though it needed no tending. 'I wanted to ensure that the fire would last for the night.'

He returned to the pallet, rolling onto his stomach. He did his best to shut her out, but he sensed she was still awake.

'I'd ask you to tell me more of your story,' she murmured, 'but I can see that you're tired.'

Sleep was the furthest thing from his mind. 'In the morning, perhaps.' He could easily have continued the tale of Eithne and Dagda, but telling stories would only intensify the connection with her. And the truth was, he didn't want her watching him with those blue eyes. Though he had no intention of laying a finger upon her, he couldn't deny that she was beautiful.

'It was a sword,' she said softly.

'What was?'

'Ciara. You asked me how she died, and I promised to tell you if you helped my sister.'

His fingers dug into the pallet, his lungs tight. He couldn't speak, feeling as though a stone were crushing him. But the need to know was greater than his desire for secrets.

'She was cut down by one of their swordsmen,' Morren said. 'I don't think he meant to strike her, but she was fleeing behind the man when he swung his weapon.'

'Did she suffer?' He couldn't stop the question, though he feared the answer.

'It was quick.'

The words granted him a slight reprieve, but he didn't release his tight grip upon the pallet. Though he'd give anything in his power to have Ciara back, if she'd had to die, at least she hadn't lingered.

'Thank you,' he said. And meant it. He'd tormented himself with images of her death, wishing to God he knew what had happened. Hearing the truth made it somewhat easier to bear.

'She was a friend,' Morren added. 'And you gave her happiness. She often spoke of how much she loved you.'

The invisible grip around his heart squeezed tighter. A thickness rose in his throat, and he felt the need to leave.

Without a word of explanation, Trahern threw open the door and strode outside. He stumbled through the darkness, the night enfolding him. A lonely cross rested upon the hillside, shadowed in the moonlight.

He fell to his knees before it, the pain of loss suffocating him. He might die tomorrow, killing the bastards who'd taken her life. And God help him, he didn't care.

Whether minutes or an hour passed, he didn't know. But he sensed Morren's presence standing behind him. Her hand settled upon his shoulder in a gesture of comfort. He knew what it cost her, to reach out with a physical touch.

'Go back to the guest house,' he said. 'I'll join you later.'

Her fingers squeezed his shoulder, and she obeyed.

In the distance, Trahern heard the faint sound of the monks' footsteps as they returned to the chapel for *vigils*.

In the morning, Morren was feeling better, and she had no doubt she could finish the journey this time. Trahern had arranged to borrow horses from the monks, with the promise to return them within a few days.

They rode south, and along the way, she saw Trahern's face tighten with restrained anger. He didn't speak to her; outwardly, it appeared that countless plans and strategies consumed his mind.

In his expression, she saw vengeance. He believed he would find the *Lochlannach* who were responsible for the attack, and that she would be able to identify the guilty men.

A shiver passed over her. Although the men deserved to die for what they'd done, she'd never wanted to be an executioner. Morren slowed her pace, torn between wanting her own vengeance and wanting to forget.

Trahern drew back, turning concerned. He handed her the water bag. 'You're looking pale. Would you rather go back?'

'No. I'm all right.' It wasn't physical weakness that bothered her; it was her own fear of what would happen when they reached the *longphort*.

After a drink, she handed back the water bag and took the reins again. 'It's not far. We'll be there in less than an hour.' Before Trahern could argue, she urged her horse into a walk, forcing him to follow. No matter what the danger was, she couldn't leave Jilleen alone.

Trahern brought his horse alongside hers, and though he didn't protest, she caught him watching her. A few cuts marred his chin and scalp where he'd shaved the hair off again. With his size and fierce appearance, she had no doubt he would intimidate many of the Vikings.

Yet she'd seen a different side to him. Last night, he'd remained outside until *vigils* was finished. Gone was the hardened warrior and in his place was a man consumed by grief. A part of her had wanted to bring him peace. Without thinking, she'd touched his shoulder.

His skin had been warm, the muscles tight and knotted. He'd flinched with shock, but then relaxed when he saw that it was her.

She'd almost pulled back her hand but didn't. Instead, she'd squeezed his shoulder. It had been an impulse, born from a fleeting moment when he'd needed comfort. When she'd returned alone to her pallet, her cheeks had burned with embarrassment. Would he understand that it was friendship she'd offered, nothing more?

Bitterly, she turned her head against the wind, staring into the empty horizon. She knew full well that she was forever damaged, a woman no man would ever want.

Her hand moved to her barren stomach, and a tendril of sorrow took root. Once, she'd dreamed of becoming a mother.

Of feeling soft arms wrap around her neck, a child's cheek resting upon hers.

The ache of emptiness became a physical pain within her womb. And then it rose into anger.

Those men had taken away the promise of any other children. Never before had she thought of it in that way.

Her knuckles tightened upon the reins, the unfettered rage battering against the shield of calm she'd wrapped around herself.

Don't think of it. Put it in the past, where it belongs.

But when she met Trahern's dark gaze, she saw the reflection of herself in his eyes.

Chapter Five

The *longphort* rested a few miles inland from Beanntraí, along the river and facing the south-west coast. Vivid blue water nestled against the shoreline, while in the distance, shadowed mountains hovered. Although the structure had been built centuries earlier, the Vikings had continually expanded, adding stone outbuildings to the settlement.

Trahern examined the *longphort* with the eyes of an invader, looking for flaws. From their elevated vantage point, he could see inside the fortress. Three circular outer walls formed multiple layers of defence, with deep gullies between each fosse. The interior longhouses were arranged in quadrants, each set of dwellings forming a square. Most rested on raised platforms to avoid flooding.

At a closer look, Trahern saw at least a dozen men stationed at all points around the outer palisade. It would not be easy to infiltrate.

But then, they wouldn't have to. Gunnar had invited them here, presumably to join the survivors. Trahern's suspicions sharpened. He'd promised himself that if any danger threatened Morren, he'd send her back to the abbey without hesitation.

He brought his horse alongside hers. 'Are you ready?'

'I am.' Upon her face, he saw a renewed willpower. Though she still hadn't fully recovered, Morren looked ready to do battle on behalf of her sister.

Before she could ride forward, Trahern rested his hand upon her horse. 'Stay close to me. I don't want you endangering yourself. If you see one of the raiders, tell me. I'll take care of him.'

He shielded her as he took the lead, riding inside. Though it was brutally cold, he was numb to the elements. Vengeance warmed his blood as he thought of the men who had murdered Ciara and violated Morren. They would answer for their crimes with their lives.

When they reached the first outer wall, armed men held their spears aloft in a silent threat. Trahern met their guarded gazes with his own. But when they spied Morren, there was hesitation in their stance.

He stopped at the first gate, knowing that word would spread of their arrival. He kept his hand firmly upon his sword, waiting quietly. The enemy guards never broke eye contact, and neither did he.

Nearly a quarter of an hour passed before he spied Gunnar striding towards them. The Viking kept one hand upon his sword, seemingly unconcerned that he was on foot while Trahern and Morren had the advantage of being on horseback.

'I see you decided to join us,' he greeted them. With a glance at Morren, he added, 'Your sister awaits you within my brother's house.'

Morren's mouth tightened in a line, as though she wanted

to run Gunnar through with a weapon of her own. 'I want to see Jilleen now.'

'Follow me,' Gunnar bade them. He gestured to two older boys, ordering them to come and take the horses.

Trahern dismounted and reached over to help Morren down. He didn't keep his hands at her waist any longer than was necessary, and Morren's face showed relief when he released her from his touch.

She kept his cloak tightly wrapped around her, as though she could shut out all the bad memories. Not once did she look at him.

Trahern didn't like seeing any woman retreat inside herself this way, and it renewed his anger. He remained beside Morren, ignoring the silent stares of those they passed. No one else spoke to them, and tension coloured their arrival.

'Morren.' A young man approached, nodding his head in greeting. It was one of the Ó Reillys, Trahern guessed.

Morren started at his voice, her face flooding with embarrassment. She kept her gaze averted, as though afraid of what else he might say to her.

Trahern led her away, following Gunnar deeper into the *longphort*. Other clan members spoke to Morren as she passed, and most appeared surprised to see her. Did they know what had happened to her on the night of the attack? It didn't seem so.

Trahern planned to speak with the survivors in private, to determine why they had come to dwell among the Vikings. The lack of fear or anxiety among the people was startling. They behaved as though they were among family and friends, not the enemy.

He couldn't understand it. Distrust curled up inside him,

and he stared at the Ó Reillys, wondering what had led them here, of all places.

When they reached one of the longhouses within the centre of the *longphort*, Gunnar led them inside. A fire warmed the interior while the yeasty scent of bread emanated from a covered pan. Two other men were engaged in conversation, and an older woman sat with Jilleen, her watchful gaze unmistakable.

When Morren saw her sister, she ran forward, embracing her tightly. Jilleen held still at first, but then gripped Morren hard. Silent tears streamed down her face.

'Are you all right?' Morren demanded. 'Have they taken care of you?' Jilleen nodded, her face pale.

Trahern moved closer, keeping a close watch on the older woman. 'What happened?'

'Gunnar found her wandering around Glen Omrigh,' the older woman interrupted. Her eyes flashed with anger. 'How could you have let a young girl go off traveling alone? Don't you know what might have happened to her?'

He knew the risk, but there had been no choice. Morren would have bled to death, had he left her alone. He had no intention of justifying himself to a *Lochlannach*, however, and he bit back his own retort. 'Who are you?'

'I am Katla Dalrata,' the woman answered. Fine lines etched her eyes, and he guessed she was slightly older than himself. She reached out to touch Jilleen's shoulder. 'You should be thankful that we found her.'

He recognised the scolding for what it was—concern over Jilleen's welfare. For that reason, he took no offence and refused to respond to the chastisement.

'I'm sorry, Morren.' More tears welled up in Jilleen's eyes. 'They wouldn't let me leave.'

'Hush. It's all right. I'm fine now.' Morren pulled her sister back into a hug, soothing her. 'Trahern took care of me.'

Her gaze met his in a silent plea not to say anything more. He wasn't about to make a thirteen-year-old girl feel any guiltier than she already did. With a slight nod of his head, he gave Morren his promise.

The fierce loyalty she felt towards Jilleen was something he understood. The bond between family was unbreakable. But even as Morren murmured to her sister, stroking her back in comfort, her eyes didn't leave his.

There was thankfulness there, a softness he hadn't seen before, lining the curve of her jaw. Without meaning to, he found himself studying her mouth. The barest flush of rose tinted the skin, her lips unremarkable, yet they drew his attention.

He snapped his attention back to Gunnar, feeling his own cheeks grow warm. 'Why did the Ó Reillys come here? I can't imagine that they would want anything to do with the *Lochlannach*.'

Gunnar's stance turned defensive. 'We offered to help them rebuild after we learned what had happened. Most of their homes were destroyed by fire, and we gave them a place to stay.'

Trahern didn't for a moment believe that was true. 'I saw you at the *cashel* yesterday. You set the remaining homes on fire, didn't you?'

The Viking didn't deny it. 'It's easier to rebuild when the old wood is gone. Our chief ordered us to burn the remains in order to clear out the rest.'

It seemed entirely too convenient. 'If that were true, why wouldn't you have done it months ago? Why wait until now to rebuild?' There was no conceivable reason to wait.

Gunnar's expression tightened. 'There weren't enough of the Ó Reillys at first. Only three, before the other survivors joined us.' He looked angry at having to explain himself. 'We've gone back every day, and more of them are returning.'

'How many Ó Reillys are there now?'

'About a dozen.' Gunnar's gaze turned hard. 'Whether or not you believe our intentions doesn't matter. The Ó Reillys are here, and we've chosen to help them.'

'They could have gone to the abbey,' Trahern argued.

'True enough,' Gunnar acceded, 'but they chose not to. They preferred not to be indebted to the abbot.'

'Why?'

'More tithes,' was all Gunnar would say. His hand moved to the battle-axe slung at his waist. 'Enough questions. You've found the girl, and if that's what you wanted, you can take her and leave.'

'What I want is to find the men who attacked and bring them to justice.' Trahern let his own hand drift down to his waist, settling upon the hilt of his sword. 'If they are among your kinsmen, be assured, I'll find them.'

Or Morren would. Inwardly, he tensed at the thought of her having to face her attackers. She shouldn't have to.

'Our men were not responsible,' Gunnar insisted. 'And we've already sent men to investigate the settlements nearby.'

'Why would you? If what you say is true, it's not your affair.'

'It is, when my kinsmen are accused of trying to annihilate an Irish clan. The peace between us is fragile enough.'

'With reason.'

Gunnar shook his head in disgust and pushed the door open. 'The Ó Reillys trust us to help them. You should do the same.'

He wouldn't trust a *Lochlannach* with a dog, but Trahern

didn't say so. As it was, he intended to take Morren and her sister away from this place as soon as possible.

'I'm beginning to wonder if Gunnar was telling the truth,' Morren whispered to Trahern, as they shared a meal that night among the other *Lochlannach*. 'I haven't seen any of the men who were there on the night of the attack.'

She'd studied each of the Vikings, but none of the men had the faces that haunted her dreams. The survivors of her clan appeared unconcerned, which reassured her. Enough of her people had seen the raiders with their own eyes, and it was doubtful that the enemy was here.

Even so, she found it hard to relax. She kept searching the unfamiliar faces, the hard knot of fear tight within her stomach, mingled with hunger.

Trahern had hardly touched any of his food. He eyed the Vikings as though expecting them to attack at any moment. 'I don't trust them.'

He picked at a bit of fish with his dagger, but his grip remained tight on the weapon. 'This is the closest *Lochlannach* settlement, Morren. Someone here was involved.'

His dark insistence sent a chill over her, for a part of her wanted to believe that she might be safe here, with her people.

'I hope you're wrong.' She turned her attention back to the food, his black mood shadowing her own. To distract herself, she finished the remainder of the fish and drank the sweetly fermented mead.

Jilleen sat beside her, hardly speaking at all. Though they had spent several hours together, her sister had remained quiet and had withdrawn inside herself, like a shadow.

Not once did Jilleen make eye contact with anyone, and

Morren realised she'd been wrong to hide with her sister. By isolating both of them, she'd made it even harder for her sister to rejoin the Ó Reilly survivors.

Regrets filled her up inside, but she couldn't dwell upon them. She had to look after Jilleen and give both of them the best possible life. Their parents were dead, so it fell upon her shoulders to plan their futures.

The very thought was overwhelming. To distract herself, Morren reached for a honey cake that was topped with dried apple slices. The flaky crust melted on her tongue, the apples mingling with the sweetness of the honey. She closed her eyes, licking her fingertips and savouring the intense flavours. It had been so long since they'd had good food.

When Morren opened her eyes, Trahern's expression had transformed suddenly. His mouth formed a tight line, his grey eyes hooded. He gripped the edge of the low table, and an unexpected flush crossed over her. 'What is it?'

'Nothing.' He turned away, and anger lined his face again.

Morren supposed it was his bad mood tainting his enjoyment of the meal. She glanced around at the people and she saw Katla watching her. Though the Norse woman had been infuriated with Trahern earlier, she offered a warm smile, her grey eyes softened with friendliness. She wore a crimson gown with a fawn-coloured apron fastened with golden brooches at the shoulders. A grey shawl hung across her arms.

Katla approached them, her expression contrite. 'I was upset earlier,' she apologised. 'I want to welcome you and your sister to our home. You may stay with us, if you wish.' A bleakness crossed over the woman's eyes, as if in memory of the attack. But she forced the smile back again, her eyes resting upon Jilleen. 'Your sister was glad to see you, I know.'

Morren gave a nod. 'Thank you for looking after her.'

Katla's smile grew strained, but she looked upon Jilleen with fondness. 'She reminds me of my daughter.'

There was pain in Katla's voice, but Morren didn't press for answers. It explained why the woman had taken such an interest in looking after Jilleen. Despite the reasons, she was grateful for the woman's care.

Katla tore off a piece of bread and added it to Jilleen's plate without asking. Her eyes didn't miss much, and no doubt she'd noticed the young girl's thin frame. 'You should have joined the others sooner,' Katla scolded gently. 'It's not safe for women to be alone.'

Morren hesitated, not knowing what to say. Excuses faltered on her tongue. No one knew what had happened to her on the night of the attack, except Jilleen. And only Trahern knew of her miscarried babe.

'She had no desire to live among the enemy,' Trahern interrupted, his tone cool.

Katla uttered a laugh. 'The enemy, are we? And who provided food and shelter for the Ó Reillys, these four months past? Who sent men to Glen Omrigh every day, helping to clear it out for rebuilding?'

'Are we expected to believe that you're overly generous?' Trahern asked. He didn't bother to keep the sardonic tone from his voice.

Katla rested her palms on the table, meeting his accusatory look with her own indignant glare. 'Who are you to doubt us, Irishman?'

To distract Trahern, Morren placed a goblet of mead into his hand. In the midst of the argument, Jilleen had shrunk back, leaving her own food unfinished. She stared down at the table, as though she wanted to disappear.

'I've no reason to trust you,' Trahern responded. 'Your people killed the woman I intended to marry.'

Katla's face turned scarlet. 'You're wrong.' She reached out and snatched his food away. 'And if you won't believe that, then you can leave.'

'Katla,' another man said softly. He came up behind her and replaced the food. 'Leave him be.'

From the protective way the man rested his hands upon the woman's shoulders, Morren suspected he was her husband. Katla didn't apologise, however, and Trahern stood. He ignored both of them and strode out of the longhouse.

Morren cast a glance at Jilleen, who still hadn't looked up from her food. 'Wait here,' she advised her sister. 'I'll be back.'

Trahern's restless energy, his caged anger, made him a threat to anyone who came too close. Soon enough, someone would provoke him, and she didn't know if she could calm his temper. Perhaps it would be best if he left.

The thought was strangely disappointing. In the past few days, Trahern had taken care of her, protecting her from harm. His steady presence had silenced her fears. If he went away, she would have to face all the questions that she didn't want to answer.

Outside, the wind whipped at the thatched roofs. The night sky was dotted with stars and all around them were the mingled voices of Irish and Viking.

Trahern stood with his back to her, his tall form silhouetted in the darkness. The outdoor fires cast a slight glow, barely enough to see. An invisible weight bore down on his shoulders, and, like her sister, he appeared to stand apart from the others.

Moreen stepped nearer to him, keeping her tread loud

enough to be heard. There was a restlessness brewing within him, of a man who didn't want to be here. He needed his freedom, and she had no right to ask him to remain.

'You don't have to stay on my behalf,' she offered gently. 'There's nothing to keep you here.'

He turned, his massive height overshadowing her. His grey eyes locked onto hers, and the fury seemed to drift away. With each breath, he grew calmer. 'That isn't true.'

Colour rose to her cheeks. Though she knew she meant nothing to him, his tone suggested otherwise. 'We'll be all right.'

'I left Ciara behind, thinking she would be safe.' He took a step forward. 'I said goodbye to her, believing that the others would protect her.'

The night air prickled the back of her neck, and she took a step backwards. 'You couldn't have known what would happen. They set our homes on fire in the middle of the night. No one was expecting the attack.'

'You're asking me to do the same thing again. To leave you and your sister behind, at the mercy of these *Lochlannach*.'

She drew the edges of her *brat* tighter. His face was determined and fierce, his entire body rigid with pain. 'It's not the same. Some of my cousins and friends are here.'

'I promised your sister I wouldn't let any harm come to you.' Trahern reached out and drew her *brat* over her head for warmth.

Morren wanted to step back, but she found herself unable to move. Something about his protective air held her locked in place.

'Do you want me to escort both of you to the abbey instead?' he asked.

She knew Trahern meant to bring her to safety, but she

couldn't hide among the monks forever. She had to return to her clan, for the sake of Jilleen. And that meant staying here.

'Thank you,' she told Trahern, 'but no. It's best for my sister if we remain among our people here. When the rest of the Ó Reillys return to Glen Omrigh, we'll go with them.'

'I don't like it, Morren.'

'My kinsmen trust the Dalrata people well enough, and they've been here for months.' Beyond that, she saw no other choice.

'What happened to your chieftain?' he asked.

She lifted her shoulders in a shrug. 'Lúcás died, I suppose. I don't know which of the men is leader now.'

'And neither do they.' Trahern pointed back to the dwelling. 'Haven't you seen the way they look to each other, waiting for someone else to lead? Were Lúcás's sons also killed?'

'I don't know. They aren't among the survivors. But even so, there are a few men who might fill Lúcás's place.'

Their chieftain had not been the strongest leader, often preferring to let the others make decisions. Morren had never particularly cared for him, though she couldn't say why. For now, perhaps it was best if her clan remained blended with the *Lochlannach*.

Trahern led her across the *longphort*, towards the gates. 'Until someone becomes the chieftain, your tribe has essentially fallen into the hands of the *Lochlannach*.'

'The Dalrata weren't our enemy,' she pointed out. 'Several of our women married them. It isn't as though we have no ties.'

Trahern stopped and surveyed the entire structure, which dominated the landscape. Easily as large as his brother's kingdom, the Viking holdings stretched out to the western sea.

'I wouldn't trust them. And neither should you.'

She crossed her arms and regarded him. 'You don't trust anyone any more.' She exhaled, not understanding what had happened to him. Had one woman's death affected him this profoundly?

She remembered his laughing demeanour, the way he'd always had a story to tell. The way he would swing a child up onto his shoulders, teasing and joking with others. That man was now gone.

'I've reason to be angry,' he responded. 'Until I've had my vengeance, I don't care how I appear to others.'

'You're letting it destroy the man you were.'

'And are you the same woman you were?' His words cut her down, and she looked away in shame.

'Neither of us will ever be the same. But I've chosen to bury my feelings about what happened. I can't indulge myself in anger or weeping. I have a sister to take care of.'

'Do you really believe that you can simply forget about what happened?'

'I don't have a choice.'

His tone altered, turning gentle. 'It's a poison, Morren. It festers inside you, until you think you're going to go mad.'

She shivered, for there was a truth to his words. Every time she pushed away the nightmares, they only returned stronger than before.

'I tried to forget and go on with my life,' he continued. 'I have a family. Four brothers, all married with children of their own. And every time I looked at them and saw their happiness, I thought of Ciara. She was taken from me, and I'll be damned if I'll let the raiders find happiness of their own.'

She pulled away, feeling even colder. 'Your need for revenge has changed you. Ciara wouldn't have wanted that.'

Turning her back on him, Morren strode back to the house where she'd left her sister. The autumn air shifted against her hair, sending the cold onto the back of her neck. Behind her, she heard Trahern's footsteps trailing her. He wouldn't let her alone, not even for a moment.

Before she reached the house, he said, 'Morren, wait.'

She stopped walking, but didn't move to face him. He could say what he wanted, but it wouldn't change anything.

'If you intend to stay among the *Lochlannach*, then I won't leave. Not until I know you'll be safe.'

His sense of honour was so strong that she suspected it would be some time before he'd leave her. The thought made her feel even more like a burden. 'I'm not your obligation. If you stay, it's for your own reasons. Not because you feel some need to guard me.'

She kept moving forward, but Trahern intercepted her, standing in her path. He looked into her eyes, folding his arms across his chest. 'You don't believe you need protection from them?'

'Not if it's given by a man who will brood and sulk the entire time. Or tell me that I'd be better off taking my sister some place isolated from everyone.'

The corner of his mouth twitched. 'I'm not brooding.'

'You are. And I've no doubt that you'd complain at every moment.'

He seemed taken aback, but she didn't apologise for the truth.

'You think I'm behaving like a child.' Without warning, his mouth curved upwards. It was the first time she'd seen him smile, and it transformed him from an angry warrior into a man.

A handsome man, if she were honest. She'd never really

thought about it, but Trahern MacEgan was a man who had captured the attentions of many women in her clan, not just Ciara. Months ago, he'd worn his hair and beard long, but now, his shaved head and face were a stark contrast to his grey eyes. The smooth skin sharpened his features, like a honed blade.

And right now, he was staring straight at her with amusement. She didn't know whether he was silently laughing at her or whether he'd recognised his own faults.

'I promise not to sulk or complain,' he said, gesturing for her to walk in front of him. 'But I still won't trust the *Lochlannach*.'

She didn't doubt that. 'You have the same purpose, the desire to find those who were responsible for the attack. Despite your suspicions, I know there are men who want to find the raiders, the same as you.'

'They'll have to prove themselves first.' When they returned to the longhouse, he pushed open the door, waiting for her to enter. Morren glanced back at him. Although Trahern was no longer smiling, at least he seemed more relaxed and less likely to kill the next man he saw.

'Where will you sleep tonight?' she asked, before they rejoined the others. She saw her sister seated near the *Lochlannach* chief, but Jilleen appeared uncomfortable. As she walked to them, Gunnar rose to his feet. The Norseman offered an open smile of interest.

Trahern's hand came down on her shoulder in an unmistakable message. She forced herself not to pull away, though she wanted to. 'I won't be leaving your side, Morren. Tonight, I'll sleep wherever you are.'

Chapter Six

Jilleen Ó Reilly was a coward. A weak-minded, self-centred coward, and she hated herself for it.

Though she'd been with the Dalrata people for several days now, she'd allowed them to treat her like a small child. Katla had given her clothes and although she'd brought her among the other girls her age, Jilleen knew she didn't fit in with them. She was an outsider. Different.

Already they'd branded her as a stranger, and though they'd said nothing impolite, she sensed their distance. And why would they want to befriend an Irish girl? She wasn't one of them and never would be. Although there were some ties among the married women, it didn't matter so much now. After the raid, few of her people lived. Hardly more than a dozen, it seemed.

The horror of that night washed over her, and her stomach wrenched into twisted knots. She wished she could just close her eyes and shut out every memory. She'd seen what the men had done to her sister, and hatred burned through her veins while she'd watched.

Not just for what they'd done to Morren, but also hatred at herself. She'd hidden in the trees, instead of going for help. She'd done nothing to stop the men, and that made her the worst coward of all.

Tonight, seeing Morren among the others, she knew that her sister had changed. Still shy, of course, but Morren no longer smiled. Jilleen couldn't help but blame herself. If she hadn't allowed herself to be caught, none of this would have happened.

She would make up for it somehow. The fervent need to atone for Morren's suffering overshadowed everything else.

Jilleen's gaze settled upon Trahern MacEgan. The giant had frightened her at first, the night she'd found him. But she'd remembered his storytelling, and the kind way about him. From the moment she'd seen him, she'd known he could help Morren with the fever.

And so he had. He'd protected her, and she saw the way he watched over Morren, even now.

Though Jilleen had never been much of a matchmaker, if she helped put them together, there was a strong chance that Trahern would take care of Morren.

Maybe that would make up for her cowardice.

Maybe.

'We're going to meet tonight to discuss the attack,' Gunnar said, when the crowd had begun to dissipate. 'Áron thought you would want to attend.'

At the mention of Ciara's brother, Trahern tensed. He hadn't seen Áron, hadn't known that he'd returned. Áron wasn't among the other Ó Reillys, and it struck him as strange that the man hadn't greeted them.

He glanced back at Morren, who answered his unspoken question. 'Go with Gunnar. I'll be fine with Jilleen.'

'I don't want you unguarded.'

'She can stay with Katla,' Gunnar offered. 'My brother's wife will keep her safe.'

Trahern had no doubt of that. He imagined the Norsewoman would wield a spear against any man who threatened someone under her protection.

'It's all right, Trahern. You may as well go with them and find the answers you're seeking.'

He would have preferred it if Morren came with him, but she was looking pale. It was best if she got some rest. He also wanted the healer to look over her in the morning, to be sure she hadn't suffered unduly from the miscarriage.

'I'll be back later tonight,' he promised.

'I know you will.' She lifted her eyes to his, and they were a steady, deep blue. Although she didn't appear confident, she put on the appearance of bravery.

Without thinking, his hand reached out to her cheek. He touched it with his palm, and she flinched. The reaction was so fast, he dropped his hand away.

'I'm sorry,' she murmured. 'I know you didn't mean any harm.'

He mumbled that it didn't matter, but inwardly it bothered him to think that any unexpected touch would have such an effect upon her. He left without another word, following Gunnar outside the house to another rectangular structure. The air had turned even colder, hinting at a freezing rain or snow.

The Norseman stopped before the entrance, eyeing him thoughtfully. 'Have you claimed Morren as your woman?'

'Not in the way you're suggesting. But I won't allow you or any other man to bother her. I've sworn my protection.'

'Selfish bastard.' Gunnar pushed open the door. 'You don't want her, but you don't want anyone else to have her.'

'You're right.' He offered no excuses, for Morren had endured enough.

When they reached the interior of the dwelling, Trahern saw five men seated. Ciara's brother, Áron, was there with a resigned expression. The man looked as though he'd given up hope.

He's avoiding me, Trahern realised. But why? Was it sorrow at losing Ciara…or guilt?

'This is our chief, Dagmar,' Gunnar said. A taller, older man, the chief wore costly gold rings and a band around his upper arm to denote his rank. Shrewd brown eyes stared into his own, as if assessing his measure. Trahern didn't falter, but stared back, daring the man to voice a protest.

'I know you believe we were behind the attack that night,' the chief began, 'but it isn't true. We're trying to learn who was.'

Trahern chose a seat beside Áron, studying each of the *Lochlannach* men. A man's posture and demeanour would often proclaim his guilt when he spoke false words. But so far, he had found nothing.

The chief spoke the Irish language, out of courtesy for himself and Áron. Trahern had learned a bit of the Viking tongue from his grandfather as a child, but his abilities were limited.

'A runner returned last night from Corca Dhuibhne,' the chief said. 'The Irish and Ostmen are essentially one tribe there. They had no reason to attack Glen Omrigh.'

Trahern could have told them that, for his own grandfather

Kieran had spent a great deal of time in Corca Dhuibhne with the Ó Brannon family.

'What about Port Láirge?' he ventured. 'There's a large settlement along the river.'

The chief looked doubtful. 'It's a good distance from here, but possible.' He shrugged as if it were no matter to him. 'Gunnar, see to it.'

Then he turned to the others. 'It's turning colder, and it will be more difficult to rebuild when the ground freezes. We'll need a group of men to start working on the foundations tomorrow. The sooner we rebuild, the sooner the Ó Reillys can return to their own *cashel*.' The conversation turned towards the needs of the Irish clan and whether or not all of the survivors should make the journey.

Trahern watched the men, feigning his attention, but his true interest was in learning just why they wanted to help the Ó Reillys. Though it was common for one Irish clan to assist another, there was no discussion of what would be given to the Dalrata in return. Finally, after the men ended the meeting and began leaving for their own houses, he asked Áron.

'They are planning to expand their own territory,' Áron answered. 'We've granted the Dalrata people some of our land in return for their help. With fewer clan members, we don't need the space.'

Trahern didn't like it. 'How much land?'

'Not as much as you might think.' Áron sent him a warning look and lowered his voice to a whisper as they returned to the center of the *longphort*. 'Trahern, if it weren't for them, we'd be dead. We lost most of our harvest in the fires, and they've invited us to stay with them through the winter.'

'I wouldn't trust them if I were you, Áron.'

'We've no choice.' He stopped walking and shook his head.

'You might be suspicious, but I am grateful. You're welcome to come with us on the morrow, when we rebuild the *cashel*.'

'I might.' The more time he spent with the men, the more he could learn about what had happened that night.

'Why did you come back, Trahern?' Áron asked suddenly. His face tightened with wariness, as though he didn't want Trahern to be here.

'I intend to avenge Ciara's death. I'm going to find the men who were responsible for the attack.'

Áron seemed unsettled, his gaze shifting back to the *Lochlannach*. More than ever, Trahern was convinced that the man knew something.

'I know you cared for my sister,' Áron admitted. 'I would have been glad to call you brother. But nothing will bring her back. Finding the men won't change that.'

Trahern took a step closer, revealing the icy anger he'd caged. 'I *will* find them, Áron. And they will answer for her death.'

Áron nodded, but refused to make eye contact. He cast a glance at the Viking dwelling where the women slept. 'How did you come to travel with Morren? We never knew what had happened to her.'

Trahern held back, not wanting to reveal too much. 'I found her and Jilleen in an abandoned hunter's cottage in the woods. I brought them to the abbey first, but then learned you had come here.'

'We searched for them, but thought they were both dead.' Áron's expression grew pained. But Trahern sensed that it was false, that no one had searched for the women. His uneasiness trebled.

'When I saw the men going after Jilleen,' Áron continued, 'I feared the worst.'

'And you did nothing to help her?' His fist curled over the wooden door frame. 'She's a girl, for God's sakes.'

'You weren't there that night,' Áron responded, his voice growing cold. 'All the homes were on fire and the fields, too. We were trying to get the children out. We weren't prepared for the attack.' He reddened, staring off into space. 'When Morren and Jilleen didn't return over those few months, we assumed they were either dead or prisoners.'

'You left them behind. No one searched,' Trahern accused.

'I lost my sister and my parents that night,' Áron said. 'I had enough of my own dead to bury.'

It didn't assuage Trahern's anger that the clan was so caught up in their own problems, they'd ignored two of their own kin. 'What happened to Morren's family?'

'She and her sister were already alone. Their parents died last year, and if they had uncles or aunts, we never met them.' Áron thought a moment and added, 'There was a man who courted Morren, I think. Adham Ó Reilly was his name.'

That brought him up short. Trahern tried to remember if he'd seen Morren with anyone, but to be honest, he'd spent so little time with the rest of the Ó Reilly clan, he didn't know.

'What happened to Adham?'

'He is still here.'

Trahern didn't respond, but it was as though a strand of tightened steel had pulled through his stomach. Though he'd never met Adham, he had little faith in any of the Ó Reilly men.

There had been no reason for the clan to abandon Morren, despite the danger.

'I'll come with you when you leave,' Trahern said. 'And I intend to take my horse back from Gunnar.'

Áron ventured a smile. 'I'll arrange it.'

The two men crossed through the *longphort*, but Trahern departed Áron's company, continuing on to Katla's dwelling, where Morren was staying. The tall woman intercepted him at the door and nearly shoved him outside again. 'You cannot come inside. Only the women may stay.'

Trahern ignored her. 'Your husband is here, is he not?'

Katla planted both hands on her hips. 'I trust Hoskuld with my life. I don't, however, trust you.'

'I swore to Morren that I'd keep her and Jilleen safe,' Trahern argued. 'If it bothers you to have a guard, then I'll take them somewhere else.'

'You aren't her family,' Katla argued. 'You haven't the right.'

'I'm the only man who's shown any concern for them, so aye, I have the right.' He wasn't going to let a sharp-tongued Norsewoman badger him.

'Stubborn brute of an Irishman,' she cursed, trying to shut the door on him.

'That, and more.' He didn't back down, but met her fierce brown eyes with his own, keeping the door open with the strength of one thigh. 'No harm will come to them.'

Morren had risen to her feet, sleepy-eyed, her fair hair neatly braided. 'It's all right, Katla. He can stay.'

'And what about the others? They've no need to be bothered by a man such as him.'

Morren touched Katla's shoulder. 'Trahern would do nothing to hurt any of the women. But if you'd rather, I will go elsewhere to sleep.'

Something knotted up inside him at her quiet offer to stay at his side. Her trust in him was unexpected, humbling even.

Katla stared at both of them, sending Trahern a heated look

of disapproval. Pointing to the far end of the longhouse, she ordered, 'Stay on that side, then.'

Trahern waited until the woman had reached the opposite side before approaching Morren. He eyed her carefully, wondering if she wanted him to leave. 'I didn't mean to wake you.'

'I wasn't truly sleeping,' she admitted. 'I don't like to dream.'

He didn't press her to answer why. 'Do you want me to go? I'll sleep outside if it would make you more comfortable.'

'Don't be foolish. It may freeze tonight. And what good are you, if you're dead?'

Her macabre remark made it hard not to smile. 'Are you certain?'

She nodded and patted the ground beside her. 'Sit with me and tell me what you learned from the others.'

In a low voice, he relayed all of the information to her, but left out any mention of Adham. Though he didn't know the man, he distrusted him for leaving Morren behind. He also wondered what feelings she held for Adham, if any.

'They're going back to the *cashel* in the morning,' he told her, 'to rebuild the homes. Do you want to come?'

Morren hesitated. 'Will you go?'

He gave a nod. 'I had planned to, yes. I want to speak with the other Ó Reilly men about the attack.' He softened his tone, suddenly aware of the dark memories Glen Omrigh would hold for her. 'But if you'd rather remain here—'

'No, I need to return.' She looked over at her sleeping sister. 'I think it would be best for Jilleen, as well.'

She leaned back, her spine resting against the wall of the hut. With their voices lowered, she had to lean closer to him to hear. He wondered if it made her fearful, being so near to him.

'Trahern, how long will you stay?'

Until I know you're safe, he almost said, but stopped himself. She might misunderstand the words.

Protecting Morren and her sister was a way of atoning for his mistakes with Ciara. He wanted to be certain that her clan didn't fall victim to the Vikings or be absorbed into the Dalrata tribe. And that would take time he didn't have.

Though he didn't like the idea of wintering amongst the *Lochlannach*, soon enough it would be too dangerous to travel. 'Long enough to help your clan rebuild,' he admitted. 'I want to know why the *Lochlannach* are so interested in your land. I suspect that there's more that the chief isn't telling us.'

He cast a look over at Katla, who had gone to sleep. 'Among the Ó Reillys, I may learn more about the attack. And, if we work hard, you might spend the winter in your own homes.'

Morren shook her head. 'Even if we rebuild, we don't have the supplies we need to last through the winter. Not unless any of the harvest was spared.' A despondent look crossed her face. 'I doubt if anyone tended the fields.'

'There's time enough to hunt. If everyone works together, we could preserve enough meat.'

'But we've no grain.' She drew her knees up, growing quiet for a time. 'And it's too late to plant.'

'We could trade for what you need,' he offered. 'There's always hope.' He opened his palm to her.

She looked into his eyes, and he saw softness mingled with determination. Tentatively she lifted her hand and placed it in his. 'You're right. There's hope.'

He curved his fingers over hers, knowing what it had meant for her to reach out to him. The serene beauty of her face caught him like a spear between the ribs. For Morren Ó Reilly was more than what she seemed, with a strength veiled beneath the delicate features. Her wistful blue eyes had seen too much horror. He found himself wanting her to find happiness again.

But not with Adham Ó Reilly.

He didn't know where these possessive thoughts had come from. She needed a steady man to take care of her, to push away the nightmares of her past. Why should it matter if it were Adham, or Gunnar, or any other man?

Because those men didn't know what she'd suffered. They hadn't held the body of her child in the palm of their hand, nor did they know the unimaginable torment that she'd locked away.

She shouldn't have to reveal it. They didn't need to know.

Morren's gaze fell to his feet. The ties of his shoes were loose, the leather stiff from the cold. She reached out to his feet, meaning to bind them.

The light brush of her hands against his feet sent a rush of blood through his body. Though she did nothing more than adjust the ties, the gesture was unexpectedly arousing.

He couldn't have stopped the reaction if he'd tried to stop breathing. The light scent of her hair, the fragile air about her, made him want to pull her close.

What in the name of God was wrong with him? Was he so desperate for a woman that he'd consider touching Morren? He loathed himself for the betraying thoughts that desecrated Ciara's memory.

He jerked away from Morren and stood. 'Go to sleep. We'll leave in the morning.' Without a word of explanation, he moved as far away from her as he dared.

But as he tried to force sleep, all he could think about was her.

* * *

At dawn, Morren rode back with the others toward Glen Omrigh. She hadn't been back in so many months, she was almost afraid of what she'd find.

Trahern had sent two of the Vikings back to the monastery to return the ageing horses they'd borrowed. Now that he was riding his own mount once again, he appeared more relaxed.

And yet, not once had he spoken. His cool demeanour unnerved her. Last night, he'd treated her like a vial of poison, after she'd mistakenly touched the ties of his foot coverings. She'd done it without thinking, the way she would adjust a child's laces.

But Trahern had behaved strangely ever since. He'd not spoken to her this morn, nor had he met her gaze. If it weren't for his protective guard, she'd have thought he was avoiding her.

He must have thought she was reaching out to him, wanting him in the way a woman desired a man. That wasn't true at all. Her cheeks flushed red. But even if it were, he'd treated her like discarded goods, a woman contaminated.

It cut through her, reaching down to the pain she'd tucked away, flaring the anger back. *It wasn't my fault. I'm not to blame for it.*

She knew that, in her heart, but she forced her emotions back, burying them deep. *Don't think of it.* She clenched the reins of her horse, fighting back tears that she refused to shed. Although Trahern had saved her life, she suspected he viewed her as a burden.

And why? Had she ever demanded anything of him? The more she thought of it, the more resentful she grew. He treated her like a younger sister or a child he felt responsible for. But she was a grown woman, more than capable of surviving on her own. She didn't need Trahern.

Morren closed her eyes, willing herself to be strong. She would be no man's inconvenience, nor would she let her fear transform her into a shadow. She had to think of Jilleen.

As she continued on the journey, she found herself staring at the small group of Ó Reilly survivors. One familiar face caught her eye. It was Adham, a man who had once shown interest in her.

He'd spoken to her when she'd arrived at the *longphort*. She hadn't replied, not wanting to face him. Silently she'd hoped that he would abandon his courtship efforts. She didn't want to be noticed by any man at all. Not any more.

Steeling her posture, she rode at Trahern's side. It was strange to be surrounded by so many people, and yet she'd never felt more alone.

The morning was cool, with low clouds shifting around the skirts of the hills. They rode north-east for over an hour before they passed the abbey, tucked high upon the hillside. After riding north for another half an hour, they reached the ruined *cashel* of Glen Omrigh.

The acrid scent of smoke struck her as they neared, the odour clinging to the ashen remains. Morren sobered at the destruction, but her gaze was drawn to the blackened fields, rather than the burned fortress. The raiders had set fire to the grain that night. The green barley shouldn't have burned so easily, but they'd been fighting a drought. Within minutes, the parched stalks had caught fire and burned brightly.

She doubted if any of the grain could be saved now. Their homes could be rebuilt, but it would take more time to heal the scarred land.

The men were already dismounting, and Morren led her

horse to the stream that swelled around the edges of the *cashel*, dismounting and letting the animal drink.

She wouldn't let herself look at the far exterior of the fortress, where the men had attacked her. The blunt memories were too raw to bear. Instead, she stared at the ground, forcing herself to concentrate on the land.

When the others went inside, she remained behind. Trahern accompanied Jilleen to the outer gate before he stopped, waiting for Morren to join them.

Though she knew it was foolish, she needed a few more moments outside. She signalled for him to go on, but Trahern didn't move. Instead, he watched over her, like a silent sentinel.

She walked through the blackened barley field, kneeling down as she examined the damage. Somehow, amid all the destruction, some of the stalks had survived. The golden colour contrasted against the ashes, offering a glimmer of hope. With nothing but the rain and the sun to nourish it, the barley had fought to live, in spite of being abandoned.

She lost track of time, but eventually, a movement caught her attention. Trahern now stood at the edge of the field, though he hadn't spoken to her. He watched over her, his hand resting upon his sword hilt.

The wind caught at his cloak, the dark mantle shrouding his form. Morren forced herself to leave the charred grain behind, walking toward him. When she stopped a few feet away, he held out his hand.

She hesitated, remembering how she'd held his palm last night. It had been a simple gesture, but one that still made her uneasy. The physical touch of his hand had sent a shiver of awareness within her. Not threatening, not forceful. But the warmth of his fingers closing over hers had been like an embrace, a reassurance that he would be there for her.

But that wasn't true, was it? Their paths were separate, and nothing would change that.

Trahern saw her discomfort, and he lowered his hand. She was afraid she'd offended him, but he shielded his thoughts and emotions.

'Come,' he said gruffly. 'There's something I want you to see.'

Chapter Seven

'What is it?' Morren followed Trahern inside the *cashel* where she found Jilleen waiting. Her sister had a nervous expression on her face, but she gave Trahern a brief nod.

'It's something Jilleen discovered,' he admitted. 'I thought you might like to go with us.'

Something about his tone made her sense her sister's fear. 'All right.'

There was almost a visible relief on Jilleen's face, and Morren followed the pair further inside. Several men had begun clearing away the burned wood, while others worked on cutting timber for new framing. A few of the Viking women had come along and were gathering thatch to repair the roofs. Katla was directing the process, as though she were personally trying to rebuild every house. The men appeared irritated, and Morren hid a smile at the woman's forceful presence.

Jilleen continued leading them to the far side of the fortress, and Morren slowed her steps. If they continued, she would have to walk past the place where —

She shut out the thought. Jilleen was guiding them to the

souterrain passage. She reached out and took Trahern's hand, keeping her eyes averted. She didn't want to look at the trampled grasses or remember anything at all.

His strong hand guided her away from it, in a steady grip that reassured her. She only wished he could protect her from the nightmares, as well as the strangers here.

Jilleen held back the underbrush, revealing the entrance to the *souterrain*. The underground tunnel was used for storage and as an escape route during times of need. On the night of the attack, the raiders had set fire to the hut that covered the *souterrain* entrance, making it impossible to use the passageway.

'Why are we going here?' Morren couldn't understand the purpose or why her sister had led them this way instead of using a ladder within the *cashel*.

Trahern squeezed her hand. 'Go on, Jilleen. We'll follow.'

Once they were inside, Morren could see nothing in front of her. The stale interior smelled of earth and rot. She held her breath, following the pair deeper inside. Trahern's hand pulled her forward into a shaft of light that shone down from above.

Jilleen pointed to a pile of shattered clay vessels. 'Look.'

Morren caught her breath when she saw what her sister was pointing towards. A handful of silver coins were scattered over the ground, as if gathered in a hurry. 'Where did it come from?'

Trahern picked up one of the coins and held it to the light. 'I suspect it was payment,' he answered. 'Given to the *Lochlannach* raiders.'

Looking back at Jilleen, he added, 'You were right to lead

us this way, so the others wouldn't follow.' He reached down and poured a handful of coins into Morren's palm.

She couldn't repress an inadvertent shudder when the cold silver slid through her hand. 'How do you know they belonged to the *Lochlannach*?'

'Because these coins are older. Do you see the long cross? They're not Irish. Possibly a hundred years old.'

He held one out to her, and she examined it. He was right. She'd never seen coins such as these.

'Should we show them to the Dalrata chief?'

He opened her palm and placed a handful inside. 'No. Don't speak of it to anyone, and we may learn more. After the *Lochlannach* have returned to their settlement, you can use them to buy more grain and supplies for the winter.'

He didn't trust Dagmar, Morren realised. But she was less inclined to believe that the chief had anything to do with the attack. If he'd been responsible, why would he expend so much effort on rebuilding?

The warmth of Trahern's hand lingered a little longer than was necessary. Her skin prickled, and she didn't understand her response to his touch. It wasn't fear, but something else. Something unexpected.

She broke free, kneeling down to pick up the remaining coins. It gave her a means of hiding her embarrassment, and she placed them inside a clay vessel.

'I'm going back,' Jilleen said, 'before Katla notices.'

'We'll follow you in a moment,' Trahern promised. Jilleen left the *souterrain* through the tunnel, while Morren finished gathering the coins.

When she stood, a gust of wind brought flakes of white drifting down the opening from above. 'Snow?' She couldn't believe it, not this early in the season. It rarely snowed in this part of Éireann, and she was more accustomed to cold rain.

Trahern held out his palm, and the flakes melted upon them. 'It's early for it.' A hint of a smile played on his features.

'When I was a lad, I used to fight with my foster-brothers in the snow. We'd pack it into balls and throw it at each other.' His mouth softened at the memory.

'The boys used to run from me,' Morren admitted. She reached up and another flake faded upon her fingertips.

'Why would they run?' He led her outside the tunnel, taking her in the opposite direction, to the barley fields.

Morren breathed an inner sigh of relief that he hadn't led her back the way they'd come. 'Because I could hit any of them with a ball of snow. Jilleen used to taunt them, and I had to defend her.'

He gazed at her with an intrigued expression. 'Having good aim is a useful skill.' His grey eyes softened with interest, and she felt her cheeks redden. It wasn't the first time a man had looked upon her in that way, but she'd never expected it from Trahern. Especially not after the way he'd been distant earlier.

She tore her gaze away and moved toward the entrance of the *cashel*. 'Let's go and meet the others.'

Lacy flakes swirled in the air, but most disappeared as soon as they touched the ground. When she walked inside again, she took time to examine the damage.

Charred wood and fallen stones were everywhere. The destruction made her throat ache as she remembered the families who'd lived here. She turned in a slow circle, her eyes burning with unshed tears.

Such violence that night. For no reason at all, save the pieces of silver.

Trahern came up behind her. He said nothing at first, letting her grieve. She turned and saw her own pain in his eyes. The snow cut through her skin, the frigid air as cold as her heart. Her fingers tightened into a fist, as she understood his need for vengeance.

Friends, distant family members…gone now.

Her hands tightened upon the clay container, as though she could shatter the earthenware under the pressure. She handed it to him, closing his fingers around the open container. 'Find the men who did this, Trahern. Please.'

'I will.' Trahern's vow was quietly spoken, but there was intensity beneath it.

She believed him. He wasn't a man who would give up, not until he'd brought the raiders to justice.

'You'll need the coins to buy grain for your people,' he said.

It made her skin crawl to even think of touching the coins that had paid for the lives of her kinsmen. But he was right. She would have to use them, and even then, it might not be enough.

'Keep them for me,' she pleaded. 'For now, at least.'

He emptied the container into a pouch at his waist. 'They are yours, whenever you need them.'

Morren turned back, walking slightly faster than Trahern. She didn't want to believe that one of her own clansmen might have hired the men, but it was possible. She watched a group of Vikings working alongside Áron and a few of the other survivors. They'd finished a rough framing of two huts, and no doubt within a few more days, the shelters would be finished.

Gunnar was balanced atop one of the walls, hammering the

wooden frame supporting the roof. Jilleen had joined Katla and some of the other women, bundling the thatch.

When she passed her own clansmen, Morren caught Adham watching her, a slight smile on his face. It was a questioning look, as though asking whether she would speak to him. She turned away, her stomach uneasy.

The truth was, she didn't want to face him. He'd done nothing that night to protect her. And, as far as she knew, he hadn't searched for her either. She couldn't quite let go of the resentment.

Trahern caught her hand in his once more. Though he masked the gesture as a way of leading her away from the men, she sensed his impatience. 'What is it?'

'You're pale.' He led her inside one of the half-finished shelters and dragged a sanded tree stump for her to sit upon. 'I don't want you to push yourself too hard.'

'Stop treating me like I'll shatter,' she protested. 'There's nothing wrong.'

'It's only been a few days,' he reminded her quietly. 'And there's nothing wrong with taking a moment to rest.' His eyes passed over her in a silent inspection. 'You haven't seen the Dalrata healer yet, have you?'

'No. There was no need.' Did he truly believe she'd reveal her shame to a stranger?

He sat across from her. 'Morren, you need time to recover. You lost a great deal that night.'

The words sliced through her at the mention of her child. Her eyes welled up, though she managed to hold back the tears. 'I'm all right.'

But she wasn't, not truly. Even so, she forced herself to say, 'You needn't treat me like I'm weak.'

'Allowing yourself time to heal isn't a sign of weakness.

It's good sense.' He studied her face, and his expression was haggard and grim. 'I shouldn't have brought you here.'

'I needed to come.' She rested her wrists upon her knees. 'And in a moment, I'm going back outside. There's a lot of work to be done.'

'Not by you. The others are stronger.'

'I can't sit and do nothing, Trahern.' She gripped her hands together. 'Otherwise, I'll start to remember it. I need the work. It makes it easier to bear.' She stood and crossed the hut to stand before him. 'Can't you understand that?'

A glimmer of sorrow passed over his hardened face. 'I understand the need to forget, yes.'

'Then let me work. I want to tend the burned fields and do what I can to make things right again.'

His palm reached over to her hair, with the lightest touch. It was the sort of gesture a parent might grant to a child, to lend comfort. No longer did she fear his touch, but the simple caress unnerved her. She found herself wanting to rest against his broad chest, to feel strong arms around her. To draw strength from him, for she had nothing left inside.

'I'll work alongside you,' he offered. 'And if you start to tire, you're going to stop.'

The hint of a smile faltered upon her mouth. 'Is that a command?'

'Aye.' He walked outside again, waiting for her to follow.

When they approached the others, Jilleen walked towards them. Her sister's tangled brown hair hung against her cheeks, and Morren reached for a strand, tucking it behind one ear. Though she'd slept beside Jilleen last night, her sister had hardly spoken to her.

'I'm going back into the fields with Trahern,' Morren said. 'Come and help us.'

A strange look crossed Jilleen's face. Her gaze shifted to Trahern's face and then back again. 'No, I don't think I should.'

Morren frowned, not knowing whether her sister was afraid of Trahern or was simply trying to avoid the labour.

'Why not?' she probed. 'Did something happen?'

'No, nothing.' Jilleen blushed. 'But Katla asked me to help her and the other women with the thatching. We're working to get it ready for the rooftops.'

Morren hesitated, and her sister begged, 'Please? It's dull working in the fields. And besides, the crops are all burned anyway. Can't I stay here?'

The fervent tone sounded a little *too* enthusiastic. Jilleen didn't even know the *Lochlannach* women, so why was she trying to remain with them?

'Trahern would be more help than me.' Her sister shot the man a faltering smile. 'He'd do whatever you asked him to.'

Morren doubted that, but it was starting to become clear what her sister's intentions were. The faint colour in Jilleen's face made it even more apparent.

'I'd like to speak to my sister alone for a moment,' she asked Trahern. Thankfully, he looked grateful to escape.

'I'll go and help with the wall,' he said, pointing to a group of men who were dry-fitting limestone into the stone palisade.

When he was out of earshot, Morren leaned over to her sister. 'Jilleen, what is going on in that head of yours?'

Her sister shrugged. 'He watches over you. And you need someone to take care of you now.' Jilleen glanced up at the sky, where it had stopped snowing. 'He would protect us.'

Morren put an arm around her sister, in a half-embrace.

'We're going to be safe,' she promised. 'I won't let anything happen to you again.'

'But what about Trahern?'

'He saved my life, and that's all.'

Jilleen didn't look convinced. 'He likes you, and I've never seen him leave your side.' With a hopeful look, her sister added, 'He could be handsome, if he grew back his hair.'

Morren couldn't believe they were having this conversation. Was her sister honestly trying to make a match between herself and Trahern? 'No. It's not that way.' Trahern was still in love with Ciara, and she had no desire to form a match with any man. 'It won't happen,' she insisted.

'Not if you don't try.' Jilleen turned her attention back to the men who were rebuilding the outer wall.

Morren stared at her sister. 'Why would you think I'd want to "try", after all that's happened?'

Her sister held herself motionless for a long time. When Morren was about to repeat her question, she saw the stricken expression on Jilleen's face. She opened her arms, and Jilleen gripped her tightly, her voice trembling.

'It's my fault, Morren. All of it. And I don't want you to be so alone any more.'

'No, it wasn't your fault.' Morren stroked her sister's hair, murmuring words of consolation. 'It wasn't.' She held her sister's face between her palms, trying to make her sister see that she didn't hold her to blame. 'What happened that night is over. I'm all right.'

She repeated the words, meaning to make Jilleen feel better. But they seemed to slip down inside her, like a fervent wish for herself.

She caught Trahern watching her, his face concerned. He

saw the way she was holding on to Jilleen, and his silent question was evident.

Morren gave him a faint nod of reassurance, waving her hand for him to go on with his work. He held back a moment, his steady expression reminding her that he was there for her.

A faint warmth spread through her skin, with the trust that he would. His abrupt behaviour last night was starting to become clear. She'd trespassed, behaving like a wife instead of a friend. It wasn't her place to take care of Trahern.

But he took care of you.

She released Jilleen, her feelings tied up into knots. Her sister meant well, but there could be nothing more between herself and Trahern.

Not if you don't try, Jilleen had said.

Morren walked alongside her sister, braving a confidence she didn't feel. She planned to lose herself in tending the fields, using the numbing work to forget the dark memories. And perhaps, one day, she'd lock them away forever.

The men were hauling more stones from the opposite side of the *cashel*, building the wall higher than it was before. Though it was beginning to resemble the height of the *Lochlannach longphort*, she didn't like the look of it. 'They're piling the stones too high,' she murmured to Jilleen. 'It's not stable.'

Should she say something? Then again, the men knew what they were doing, didn't they? The chief's expression remained determined, and she doubted if the leader would listen.

But Trahern might.

She walked towards the wall, hoping to warn him. When she reached his side, the world seemed to stop. The pile of rocks shifted, and Trahern lunged, pushing her forward.

'Get back!' he roared. He struggled to keep the stones from

falling onto her, just as Gunnar ran forward. Together, the two men leaned against the weight of the wall.

Morren scrambled away, and seconds later, the rest of the balanced stones began to tumble.

Chapter Eight

Gunnar tried to block the stones, but Trahern strained hard, ordering, 'Let them fall! It's not worth breaking an arm.'

The two men moved away at the same time, the wall collapsing without their weight to hold it.

Trahern stumbled forward, leaning to kneel beside Morren. Her face was ashen, horrified. His own heartbeat shuddered within his chest, and he struggled against the instinct to pull her into an embrace. Instead, he touched her cheek. 'Are you all right?'

She nodded. 'I didn't mean to be in the way. I saw the unbalanced wall and wanted to warn you.' She reached out to his arm and he noticed the smear of blood. 'You're hurt.'

'It's nothing.' He helped her rise, wiping the blood away.

Her hand closed over his, her blue eyes filled with worry. Though she was still pale, relief had replaced the earlier horror. He squeezed her fingers, and was startled when she returned the gentle pressure.

'I'm glad you're all right.' With a half-smile, she released his hand and walked to the gates, her sister beside her. He knew she planned to take a closer look at the fields, to see if any grain could be salvaged.

'You missed an opportunity, Irishman,' came an accented voice beside him. He glanced at Gunnar, who was eyeing Morren. 'You should have told her that you needed her to tend that wound. Nothing like a woman to make a man feel better.'

The teasing in the Viking's voice reminded him a little too much of his brothers. Trahern sent him a glare. 'I wouldn't lie to her.'

'Maybe one of the stones should have knocked your skull. Use a little sense, Irishman.' Gunnar lifted some of the fallen stones aside. 'Take advantage of what's offered. Haven't you seen the way she watches you?'

'She trusts me. I've promised to take care of her, and that's all.'

'And if one of my kinsmen wanted to "take care of her", I suppose you wouldn't mind?'

Trahern glared at Gunnar, but it did nothing to dim the man's amusement. 'I'd tear his arms off.'

'Open your eyes, Irishman. She's a fair woman. You should do more than take care of her.'

He couldn't do that. Morren had been hurt too badly, and he couldn't betray Ciara by replacing her with another.

Shaking his head, he told Gunnar, 'I only met her a few days ago.'

'Sometimes a few days is enough.' Gunnar took a stone from him. 'We'll finish up here. Go and help her in the fields. She shouldn't be alone, anyway.' The Viking gave him a brief shove. 'If she spurns you, we'll drink a barrel of mead tonight.'

'I tried to kill you, two days ago,' Trahern pointed out.

'Why in the name of Belenus would you want to drink with me?'

'I'd drink with Loki himself, if the drink is good enough.'

A flicker of a smile pulled at Trahern's mouth, though he couldn't quite understand why Gunnar was able to forgive him so easily. With a single slice of the blade, he might have killed the man.

'There may come a time when I'm sorry I didn't kill you,' Trahern remarked. 'For now, I'll say that I'm glad Morren intervened.'

'I'll agree with you on that.' Gunnar picked up one of the smallest stones and tossed it in the air. 'When she turns you down, you'll want that drink.'

Trahern didn't respond, but helped the other men push the remaining stones aside. They stared at the wall, debating the best way to rebuild it. 'We need mortar,' Gunnar pronounced.

'Leave it,' a voice interrupted. It was the Viking chief, Dagmar. 'I've decided that we'll stay through the night instead of going back.' Dagmar pointed at the dwellings that were nearly finished. 'We'll need to finish two shelters: one for the men, and one for the women.'

Trahern glanced toward the fields where Morren and her sister had gone.

'Go with her, Irishman.' Gunnar nodded at him. 'Or I'll go in your place.'

'Not if you want to keep your arms attached,' he retorted.

The Viking gave a knowing smile and pointed to a row of iron tools. 'You might need those.'

Trahern picked up two of the scythes, heading outside the

cashel. He didn't care about the remaining work. The two shelters were nearly completed, and there were enough men to finish them. He didn't want Morren to be alone at any moment.

Especially not here, when he wasn't certain whom he could trust.

Morren walked through the burned barley field, past the charred grain. Fragile golden stalks struggled against the freezing weather, their heads lowered. Though it was late for harvesting, there might be some way of saving some of the grain. They would have to begin cutting it today, if possible.

After a few minutes of walking around the perimeter, Jilleen mumbled an excuse about speaking to Katla about the thatching. Morren didn't pay much heed to it, until she looked back and saw her sister returning inside the *cashel*.

She thought about calling her back, but changed her mind. Maybe it was for the best, having Jilleen work alongside the other women. It wasn't good for her sister to be so isolated from the others.

Morren folded her arms and stared at the barley, trying to determine where to start. The east section seemed to have the least amount of damage, whereas the portion closest to the *cashel* was burned into ash.

'Do you need help?' a voice interrupted. She turned and saw Trahern standing before her. In one hand, he held two iron scythes.

She sent him a grateful smile. 'I'd be glad of it. It seems my sister is finding other things to do.'

His mouth gave a slight upward curve. 'When I was her age, I did whatever I had to, to avoid work.'

'I can't imagine you as a lazy boy.' She meant the words as teasing, and Trahern returned a slow smile.

'I used to charm the girls into doing my share of the work.'

'You couldn't have charmed me.'

He seemed to take the words as a challenge, and suddenly, his expression changed. The look in his eyes was the sort that would make younger girls blush and older girls flirt. He was looking at her as though nothing else in the world mattered. Like he wanted to drop the scythes and pull her close, kissing her. And she had a feeling, she would like it. A lot.

A flood of embarrassed warmth seized her, as she forced the vision away. To distract herself, Morren took the scythe from him, testing its weight in her hand.

Her gaze moved toward the first row of grain. 'We'll cut the barley that's ready. But if you see any with a grey rot, leave it. I want nothing to contaminate the good grain.' She walked forward, tracing her fingertips over the golden spears.

'Where do you want me to start?' he asked.

'Take that side of the field, and I'll work over here,' she directed.

Trahern unfastened his cloak and spread it on the ground. 'We'll bundle it with this.'

Though she didn't like the thought of him working in the cold with no outer garment, they had nothing else. And he seemed to understand that this was important to her.

He moved to the edge of the field and grasped a handful of grain, slicing it with the scythe, near the ground.

He'd done this before, Morren realised. Someone had taught him to gather and slice, preserving the stalks that would be used to feed the livestock over the winter.

She remained a few paces to his left, picking up the blade and cutting the grain. Handful after handful fell beneath the scythe, and she created a small pile upon his cloak. It was a welcome respite, losing herself in the mindless monotony.

'I used to have a small garden outside my home when I was fostered,' she confessed, when Trahern came to drop his own bundle of grain on the cloth. 'As a child, I loved watching the seedlings grow. My grandmother once told me that the faeries blessed the land and the harvest.'

Trahern moved in front of her, to a new section. 'I believed in magic, as a child. It's why I taught myself all the stories from the poet who used to visit our ringfort.' He met her gaze, and his eyes held remembrance. 'I thought, by learning the tales, I might learn the magic, too.'

He gripped his scythe with the ease of a weapon. Once more, he swung at the grain, slicing the stalks. Morren kept parallel to him as she worked. 'Your stories have a magic of their own. They bring comfort to the people.'

He looked slightly embarrassed at the compliment, but nodded his thanks. They worked alongside each other for the next hour, and only when her arms began aching, did she stop to rest.

Trahern continued wielding the scythe, his muscles flexing as he cut away the ruin. She'd known he was strong, but she found herself entranced by the way his arms bulged against the sleeves of his tunic as he swung.

He'd kept the wall from falling on her, shielding her with his own body. It humbled her to realise that he'd protected her without thinking, out of instinct.

A light shiver tingled through her skin as she watched him. Though she lowered her head, pretending to cut more of the grain, she couldn't stop herself from watching Trahern's movements.

His shoulders tightened, the blade moving steadily. She

couldn't hope to keep up with his punishing pace. Instead, she worked slowly, sneaking glances at him with her peripheral vision.

Despite his physical strength, his soul seemed caught up within the past, clinging to the memories of Ciara. She wondered if he would ever find another woman, someone to soothe the raw wounds no one else could see.

He caught her looking at him when he'd reached the middle of the third row and lowered his scythe. Colour stained her cheeks, and she looked away.

'Is something wrong?' He approached, and she saw a line of sweat sliding down his throat beneath his tunic. He drew closer, and Morren lowered her own scythe. She was embarrassed that she'd managed to cut only half of what he'd accomplished.

'No. I'm fine.' She tucked a strand of hair behind one ear, adjusting her *brat* over her head to keep it warm. 'My arms were tired.'

'You shouldn't be working this hard,' he said. 'It's too soon.' Guilt coloured his face, as though he'd forgotten about her injuries.

When he moved closer, she started to feel lightheaded. His height towered over her, and her grip tightened upon the handle of the scythe. 'It needs to be done.'

'But not by you.' Trahern took the scythe from her. 'Go back with the others. I'll finish here.'

'You can't possibly finish it today. Not alone.' She wiped her palms upon her skirts. 'Besides, it's getting late. We'll go back together.'

Trahern strode back to the bundle of grain lying upon his

cloak. He helped her gather up more of the barley, using the cloak to wrap the grain into a large sheaf.

She struggled to lift the bundle, which was far heavier than she'd imagined. He tried to take it from her, but Morren refused to allow it. 'I can manage.'

'If you want to try.' He waited as she adjusted the sheaf, her cold fingers trembling on the knotted wool that bound it. The bundle was awkward and slipped from her hands several times. She tried again to hoist it onto her shoulders, because she wanted to prove to him that she'd regained her strength.

'It weighs half as much as you do,' he said quietly. 'And you may as well bring back the tools.'

'I'm being foolish, aren't I?' Morren sighed and set down the barley.

Trahern lifted the bundle onto his shoulder with no effort at all while she retrieved the two iron scythes. 'Not foolish. Over-ambitious, perhaps.'

They returned to the *cashel*, but just before they reached the gates, Adham Ó Reilly approached. His brown hair was damp, as though he'd taken the time to smooth it before coming to see her. Trahern moved beside her, his posture guarded.

'Morren,' Adham greeted her. 'I'm glad to see you're unharmed.'

She set down her scythe, returning the greeting. 'Adham.'

Why had he come to speak to her? Was he hoping to renew his courtship? She didn't want that at all.

'I thought you might need help.'

Two hours after they'd been working? She doubted if that was his intention.

'We've finished for the day,' Trahern remarked. 'Morren has no need of your "help".' MacEgan's height towered over

Adham by a full head, and he openly glared at the man as he set down the bundle of grain.

'I'd rather hear her own wishes,' Adham said, his eyes meeting hers.

Morren knew that, with a word from her, Adham would return to the others. He wasn't the confrontational sort. But she wasn't certain how to send him away without sounding rude.

When Adham stepped closer, Morren shied away. Her hand brushed against Trahern's without really meaning to. His strong fingers closed over hers in a silent promise to guard her. Adham saw her response and frowned.

'I'll be fine with Trahern,' she said. 'You needn't worry about me.'

'But—'

'Go back with the others,' Trahern ordered. He kept his grip firm upon her palm, and reached for the scythe with his other hand, grasping it like a weapon.

'I'm sorry, Morren,' Adham blurted out. 'I couldn't find you afterwards, and...' He lowered his gaze with regret. '...I thought you had died that night.'

His brown eyes never left hers, as though asking for forgiveness. She saw him as the awkward, quiet man he'd always been. A man who would sooner hide from an attack than grab the nearest weapon. It disappointed her, realising that she'd considered him as a suitor once.

'You shouldn't have left her alone, to protect herself and Jilleen,' Trahern admonished. 'Aye, she's alive, but no thanks to men like you.'

Morren didn't like them fighting over her. She felt like a scrap of meat, caught between two dogs. But Trahern was right. Neither Adham, nor any of the other men, had done anything to look after her and Jilleen. They'd been left to fend for themselves.

Adham sent her a wary look, as though he didn't want her alone with Trahern. She didn't yield, but sent him a steady gaze.

In the end, he lowered his head in farewell. 'Perhaps later we can talk.'

'Perhaps.' But she gave no commitment. Right now she couldn't unravel the tangled thoughts inside. Trahern was still holding her hand, and even after Adham left, he didn't let go.

She wasn't sure she wanted him to.

Nonetheless, Trahern handed her the scythe again and picked up the bundle. 'Did you want to speak to him?'

'Not really.' She started walking back to the *cashel*, not meeting his gaze. 'I know I shouldn't be angry with him, but I am. If he'd truly cared about me—'

'Nothing would have stopped him from reaching your side.'

She lifted her eyes to Trahern's. The fierce intensity made her flush. For a moment, it was as if he were speaking of himself. And though they were virtual strangers to one another, she sensed that Trahern was a man of strong passion. A man who would love a woman with every breath in his body.

She caught the hint of pain beneath his words, the memory of Ciara. No doubt if he'd been there that night, he'd have protected his betrothed with his life.

Morren ached for his loss, and wished she had the words to say it. In the end, she touched her fingertips to his face before leaving him.

When they reached the interior of the *cashel*, Morren could smell a rich stew bubbling on one of the outdoor fires. Her stomach was roaring with hunger, and it was all she could do not to run towards the food.

Two of the huts were now completed, with a third begun. At this pace, the *cashel* would be rebuilt within another week or two. Morren replaced the scythes they'd borrowed and nearly bumped into Gunnar.

He eyed the pair of them, but Morren didn't quite understand the look he flashed at Trahern. 'You've been busy.'

'We managed to save some of the grain,' she explained.

'Good.' Gunnar pointed towards one of the newer huts. 'We're using that shelter for tools and food. The women will sleep there, and the men in the hut we just finished.'

Trahern went to place the bundle inside the hut Gunnar had designated. Even though he left her for only a brief moment, she noticed that he kept glancing back at her.

Ever vigilant, she had no doubt that Trahern would never let anything happen to her. Today, he'd let down his guard, showing her traces of the man she'd once known. The afternoon they'd spent together, though tiring, was one she'd remember. It felt good to be useful, to bring back an offering that would help her people.

And somehow, when she was around Trahern, she managed to find a part of herself she'd lost. He made her forget the darkness.

But how long would he stay?

'Your sister is with Katla,' Gunnar was saying, as Trahern returned to them. 'They're preparing for the meal tonight.'

Morren didn't understand why her sister had abandoned the fields, to work among strangers, but at least she hadn't been alone. 'I'll join her and help. I understand we're not returning to the *longphort* tonight?'

'No,' Gunnar said. 'It will be crowded, but Dagmar wants

us to spend the night here and continue working in the morning.'

'Why not travel to the abbey?' she suggested. 'It's not a far ride, and they have more space.'

Gunnar's smile grew strained. 'We're not friends with the brethren. The abbot believes we should be granting more of our land to the Church.' With a grimace, Gunnar added, 'It isn't enough that they've claimed a large portion of the Ó Reilly lands.'

Morren wondered if there had been animosity between her people and the abbot. It would explain why they were reluctant to stay at St Michael's, though their chieftain had never spoken of any disagreements between them.

Could the abbot have had anything to do with the attack? She found it difficult to believe that a man of the church would do such a thing. Brother Chrysoganus had made her feel welcome at the abbey.

But if her people were dead, the church could lay claim to the land. So could the *Lochlannach*, for that matter.

Trahern seemed to share her thoughts, for he addressed Gunnar. 'Haven't you done the same, claiming Ó Reilly land in exchange for your labour?'

'Some of our men are wed to Ó Reilly women. It's not the same at all. The land will be shared between us.'

'Will it?' Trahern's tone grew cold. 'Or will you take what rightfully belonged to them?'

He didn't wait for a reply, but strode off to a group of ruined huts. Morren didn't follow at first, but turned to Gunnar. 'He's restless,' she apologised.

'Frustrated, I suspect.' Gunnar sent her a teasing smile, and Morren suddenly caught his innuendo.

'No. That isn't it.' She glanced back at him, before

confiding, 'His betrothed wife was killed by the raiders. He's angry about it.'

The smile faded from Gunnar's face. 'I didn't know.'

Morren rubbed her arms, suddenly feeling the cold. 'I need to speak with him.' Trahern's anger went deeper than an argument over land. And she wanted to know why.

Gunnar murmured a farewell, adding, 'You could do much to console him, Morren. A woman with your beauty would make any man forget his sorrow.' With a nod, he turned away.

She eyed Trahern, standing alone by the palisade wall like an outsider. The wind whipped across the *cashel*, cold and biting. A low fog had descended over the land, encircling the walls so that she could hardly see the abbey on the hillside. Light flakes of snow swirled in the air, and when she reached his side, Morren adjusted the cloak over his shoulders to shield him from the wind.

Trahern muttered his thanks beneath his breath. A melancholy mood had settled over him. She studied his grey eyes, and asked, 'What is it?'

He shook his head. 'I shouldn't stay here through the winter, as I'd planned. Rebuilding this *cashel*, living amongst the *Lochlannach*…it feels like I'm forgetting my purpose.'

She could see that the bitterness was eroding his heart, taking away the man he'd been. 'And what is your purpose? Vengeance?'

He gave a nod. 'I'm losing time. I need to find them.'

His restlessness was rigid in his posture. Morren didn't know what to say, but she understood his frustration. 'I want you to find them, too.'

She moved to his side, and her fingers inadvertently touched his. She expected him to pull away, but he didn't. 'But I fear, even if you do find the men who attacked that night, it won't bring you the peace you're seeking.'

'Vengeance is all I need.'

'I don't believe that.'

His hand curled over hers, and a pained expression came over his face. 'Don't try to save me, Morren. It's already too late.'

Chapter Nine

Trahern didn't move, though he should have. Right now, he despised himself for being so aware of Morren. Her dark golden hair hung against her face, her blue eyes filled with uncertainty. She deserved his trust and protection, not the unholy thoughts coursing through his undisciplined brain. Somehow, she'd kindled feelings that he'd thought were dead, long ago.

Nothing in the world could have been more wrong. He needed to get away from her, to get out of this place. With every moment he spent at her side, his vengeance was becoming less about Ciara and more about Morren.

God above, what was the matter with him? He pulled his hand free of hers, furious with himself. Though he would never hurt her, right now, he didn't understand the strange pull between them.

'Are you hoping to die,' she asked, 'after you've faced your enemy?'

He didn't answer. The truth was, he didn't know. Living each day was a torment in itself. Being here, around Ciara's kinsmen, dredged up older memories that he didn't want to face.

Morren reached out and quietly touched his shoulder. Her blue eyes met his with iron determination. 'You're strong enough to overcome your grief over what happened. Just as I am.'

His hand dug into the wooden palisade wall so hard, splinters pierced his flesh. She'd seen past his fury to the aching centre of pain in his heart. And with a light touch, she brushed her fingers against his shaved head, then down his bare cheeks, in a reminder that he couldn't strip the last part of himself away.

He caught her hand in his, meaning to push her away. But the warmth of her palm seemed to ease the chill in his skin. He clung to her fingers, not knowing why.

Abruptly, she pulled back. 'I should go.'

Before he could blink, she'd fled his side, and he was left standing like a fool.

What in the name of Belenus had just happened? He watched her from the doorway, walking apart from the others. She glanced over at her sister, but made no move to join Jilleen.

Gunnar's words came back to prod him. *'You should do more than take care of her.'*

But there was nothing between them. Trahern took several steadying breaths, gathering up his resolve. He'd speak to the other Vikings and find out what he could.

He spied Morren ahead, leaning her hand against the stone wall they'd been repairing earlier. Her face had gone pale, and she remained frozen in place. Was she in pain? Had the bleeding begun again?

But then he saw the cause of her anguish. Seated near one

of the outdoor hearths was a young woman, an Ó Reilly who had wed one of the Dalrata men. Her husband stood beside her, and in her arms the woman cradled an infant.

Morren never took her gaze from them, and Trahern released a curse. The raw pain in her eyes was unmistakable, as if she knew she would never again bear a child of her own. He wanted to offer her comfort, the hope that perhaps one day she would.

If he had half a brain, he'd speak to Adham and get the man's promise to look after her. But the thought of any man getting close to Morren made him want to snarl.

She's not yours, he reminded himself. *She needs someone else to take care of her.*

As if in response to his thoughts, Morren looked back at him, seeming to draw strength. The rest of the people seemed to fade into the background, and he looked past her fears and pain. Aye, she was hurting. But beneath it all, there was still hope.

Trahern crossed the *cashel*, no longer caring that it was growing dark. He needed her to understand that her life wasn't over. And an idea came to him, something that would make her feel better.

'Walk with me,' he commanded, extending his hand.

Morren sent him a confused look, but placed her palm in his. 'What is it?'

He led her back outside, taking a torch from one of the iron sconces. 'You'll see.'

She followed him, back to the fields where they had worked together. Although the vast majority of the earth was blackened from fire, the small section where they had cut away the ruin could be ploughed under in the spring.

'Why did you bring me here?'

His fingers remained laced within hers, trying to offer her reassurance. 'I saw you looking at the babe.'

She gave a slight nod, her face reddened against the glow of the torch. 'I shouldn't have. It only makes it harder to endure.'

'I wish I could have saved your child,' he said.

'It wasn't meant to be.' Her shoulders lowered, but he wouldn't allow her to pull her hand away. Not yet.

'There may be other children for you, one day,' he offered, squeezing her fingertips. 'Your life isn't over, Morren, because of that night.'

'No man here would want me. Not after what happened.' A tired smile crossed her face. 'You're the only one who knows the truth. Even if it weren't for Ciara, admit it—you wouldn't want a woman who was used like that.'

He lifted his hand to her cheek, warming it. 'You're wrong.'

The words came forth, intending to reassure her. But it startled him to realise that it wasn't a lie. Something about Morren Ó Reilly had slipped past his shielded anger.

Her fair hair gleamed in the firelight, her lips slightly parted. He wondered what it would be like to kiss a woman like her, to satisfy the human need to touch.

Gods, it had been so long since he'd embraced a woman, and despite the protests rising in his brain, his body began to respond. He wanted to jerk his hand away, but if he did, she would misinterpret the reason.

He saw the uncertainty on her face, the way she blamed herself. 'You're not to blame for what they did.'

She shook her head. 'Yes, I am.'

'How can you say that?'

'Because it was my choice.' She stepped back from him,

tightening her arms around her waist. 'I told the men that I wouldn't fight them. That they could do as they wished to me.'

Trahern felt as though a barrel of ice water had been poured over him. He couldn't believe the words she'd spoken. But the calm serenity on her face revealed the truth of Morren's words. And suddenly, he understood why.

'It was for her, wasn't it? They were going to hurt your sister.'

'I took her place so Jilleen could escape,' Morren admitted. 'By the time they'd finished with me, they'd forgotten about her.' A brittle strength tightened in her face. 'I don't regret my choice.'

He didn't know what to say. Her bravery and sacrifice were greater than anything he'd ever heard of. Few women would do such a thing, surrendering their virtue for a loved one.

His silence made her turn away. 'And now you understand.'

'I do.' But he wouldn't let her denigrate herself any more. 'And I still don't blame you for it.' He pointed out to the fields, lifting the torch higher to reveal the remaining grain that stood undamaged, amid the ashes. 'Sometimes that which has been ruined can be rebuilt. And new life can emerge.'

When she turned back to him, he saw the tears on her face. 'I want to forget what happened to me.'

He looked into her eyes, trying to offer comfort. 'You will.'

The look in her eyes said she didn't really believe it. With one hand, he wiped the tears away, sliding his fingers into her hair. He lowered his forehead to hers, and in the silence he could hear her breathing.

The warmth of her skin against his own seemed to push

away his common sense. He acted on instinct, and seconds later, his mouth brushed against hers in an unexpected kiss.

Light, unthreatening, he'd done it without thinking. It was meant to comfort her, nothing more. But the soft warmth of her mouth had evoked an unexpected connection with her. For a single, frozen moment, she'd filled up the emptiness.

Morren pulled away from him, her face pale.

'I'm sorry,' he said. Without another word, he took her hand and began leading her back to the *cashel* with the others. Inside, his mind was roaring with self-condemnation. She'd given him her worst secret of all, and he'd undermined that trust by forcing a kiss she hadn't wanted.

It was tempting to go and bash his own head against a wall. Fool. Idiot. He should leave right now, before he did anything worse.

As she joined her sister at the fire, he kept himself apart, granting her space. She sat beside Jilleen, hardly touching the stew Katla gave her.

She didn't meet his eyes, and he hung back, not knowing what to say or do. It took the greatest restraint he possessed, to remain seated when Adham Ó Reilly approached her.

'May I sit with you?' Adham asked.

Morren hesitated, but could see no reason why she shouldn't speak to him. He'd done nothing wrong. With a quick glance over at Trahern, she saw that he was no longer watching her. Her cheeks warmed, and she nodded to Adham. 'If you like.'

Right now, she needed a distraction. Anything to take her mind off the stolen kiss. It had happened so quickly, she was certain Trahern had done it without thinking. It was a gesture meant to comfort, the same as the embrace a friend would offer.

But something had changed between them. The kiss, as light as a snowflake, had melted into her skin. Her lips felt warm, even now, remembering the brush of Trahern's mouth upon hers. Undemanding, as though she were a woman to be savoured.

He'd awakened feelings that had lain dormant for so long; she hadn't realised she was still capable of feeling the faint stirrings of desire.

A part of her wanted to cry right now. She hadn't believed Trahern when he'd said her life wasn't over because of that night. For so long, she'd felt the chains of her shame weighing her down. He knew everything now, her most ragged secrets bared before him.

And yet, he'd understood why she'd protected Jilleen. It was something she'd never expected.

Morren wrenched her attention back to Adham, who had chosen a seat beside her. He held an empty bowl that had once contained stew, and it appeared he was rehearsing his speech, trying to decide what to say.

Finally, he admitted, 'MacEgan was right. I should have searched for you.'

I'm glad you didn't, she thought to herself. She didn't want anyone to know about her pregnancy or what she'd endured.

Instead, she replied, 'It's all right. I'm here now, and the past will stay forgotten.'

He looked relieved and set the bowl down on the ground. 'Good. I was hoping…that you would stay here with us while we rebuild.'

His eyes lingered upon her, and his intentions were clear. Morren fought the urge to shudder. The question irritated her, for where else could she go? Either here, with her kinsmen, or she could possibly go back with Jilleen to the Moriartys, where her sister was fostered. The idea of becoming a burden on another clan didn't appeal to her.

And Trahern was going to leave, soon enough.

She risked a glance back at him. There was a tension in his body, as though he wanted to come over and drag Adham away, yet he didn't move.

He was the one who'd wanted her to begin anew. No doubt Adham was a reliable man, one who would ensure that she had everything she needed. But if he learned anything about her past, he'd be appalled. He wouldn't understand the reasons for what she'd done, whereas Trahern didn't blame her at all. He knew everything, and he hadn't turned away from her. That was the difference. Being here with Adham felt like a lie, and the longer she endured his company, the worse she felt.

The women had begun to clear away the evening meal, and Morren bid Adham goodnight, excusing herself to work alongside Katla and Jilleen. She lingered among them, falling into their shadow. But she was aware of Trahern's presence and the way he kept a close watch over her.

When she followed the women back to one of the completed shelters, she saw Trahern leave his place by the fire. The men went to the other hut, speaking of their plans to start repairing a third shelter in the morning.

He started to walk towards her, but stopped short. For a brief moment, he met her gaze. She wanted to follow the women, to hide from his notice.

Instead, he approached her, keeping a safe distance away. 'I'm sorry for what I did earlier. I never meant—'

'It's all right.' She didn't want to hear regrets, nor excuses for why he'd kissed her.

'It wasn't all right.' His grey eyes darkened with remorse. 'And I want you to know, it won't happen again.'

The frost in his tone was bitter, like the night air. She didn't know how to respond, so she simply nodded. An unexpected bleakness filled up inside her. Though days ago he'd been a stranger to her, there was now a bond between them of shared grief.

'I know…it's difficult for you to be here,' she murmured. 'Remembering Ciara.' She looked into his eyes, hoping he would understand the regret she held in her heart.

When he turned away, she couldn't stop the tear that slid from her eye.

Morren was crying again. Jilleen wondered if her sister even knew that it happened every night. Or at least, it had for the past few months. Though Morren was curled up on her side, her cheeks were stained with wetness, her arms clenched around her waist.

Would she have been like this? Jilleen wondered. If her sister's fate had happened to her, would she suffer such grief, night after night?

The guilt crossed over her like a dark shadow.

My fault, she thought. None of it would have happened to Morren, if Jilleen had managed to escape her captors.

That night, flames had soared into the night sky, tearing down the huts. The choking scent of smoke and death surrounded the place. And the screams of the dying had drowned out her own cries for help.

But Morren had heard her. Weaponless and unprotected, she'd faced the men and made the ultimate sacrifice. Because of Morren's choice, Jilleen had escaped unharmed.

Her own tears dampened her cheeks as the self-blame

descended. She'd been such a coward, failing her sister. If only she could go back and change things, she'd have done something. Maybe stolen a weapon and attacked while they weren't looking. Something.

Reaching out to her sister, Jilleen held Morren's hand. Morren's eyes flickered open, worry filling them up when she saw Jilleen's tears. 'What is it?'

'You were crying.' Jilleen squeezed her fingers, then wiped her own tears away. 'Another nightmare?'

Morren nodded. 'Did something happen?'

'No. I'm all right. Just…worried about you.'

Morren pulled her into a fierce hug. 'You don't worry about me, Jilleen. Everything will be well now. We're safe.'

But Jilleen knew that wasn't true. Until her sister's nightmares stopped, nothing would be well. And if there was anything she could do to make the past go away, she'd do it. Without question.

A strange sense of power filled her up inside, replacing the fears. Maybe being brave wasn't the lack of fear, but the determination to act, instead of running away.

Jilleen laid down beside Morren, feeling better. She couldn't change what had happened in the past. But perhaps she could change her sister's future.

That night, Trahern couldn't sleep. Inside the men's hut, he'd stared at the walls for hours, his thoughts in pieces. He was haunted by Morren. He wanted her to find peace, after what she'd been through.

Needing fresh air and a chance to clear his head, he donned his shoes and stepped outside. He walked through the quiet ruins, the moon sliding out from behind a cloud. The crisp, cool air still held traces of charred smoke, but the odour was beginning to lift.

When he reached the furthest edge, a sound caught his attention—a horse whinnying from outside the *cashel*.

No one should be outside at this time of night. It sounded like a single rider, which could mean one of the brethren from the abbey. Yet his instincts suspected it was an intruder.

Trahern returned to the men's hut, where he retrieved his sword. If the visitor meant no harm, he'd learn that soon enough.

The motion made Gunnar stir. 'What is it?' the Norseman asked, rising to his feet.

'A rider is outside.' Trahern kept his voice low, so as not to disturb the others. 'I'm going to find out who it is.'

Gunnar reached for his own weapon, a lighter version of a battle-axe. 'I'm coming with you.'

Trahern led him back to where he'd first heard the sound. They stared out into the darkness, listening for the sound of an intrusion.

Time inched forward, and it wasn't until Trahern heard a light scraping noise that he realised where it was coming from.

The *souterrain*.

A ruthless anticipation flowed through him, overshadowing the danger. Likely the intruder had come for the coins that had once been hidden there. He lit a torch at one of the fires and moved toward the interior entrance of the *souterrain* pit. Usually it was hidden within one of the dwellings, but there was nothing but fallen debris and ashes surrounding the ladder that led below.

'Wait here,' he whispered to Gunnar. He preferred to face his enemy alone, but the *Lochlannach* could back him up, if need be.

Trahern climbed down the ladder into the *souterrain*.

Gunnar held his battle-axe in one hand and took the torch. He backed away, keeping the light away from the passage.

The frigid interior of the underground passage was much colder, and Trahern felt ice upon the stone walls. He kept his back pressed to the shadows, his sword ready.

Footsteps crept closer, the intruder nearing the storage containers. No light permeated the space, and Trahern waited until he heard someone reaching for one of the containers. Though he didn't know who the man was, he was sure the person was connected to the attacks.

He threw himself at the intruder, slamming the man against the wall. A grunt expelled from his enemy's throat, and clay containers shattered beneath his feet. Trahern punched hard, his fist clipping the man's jaw, dropping him to the ground.

'Bring the torch,' he called out to Gunnar. 'I want to see him.'

The torch flared above, illuminating the passage. Trahern grabbed his attacker by the hair, jerking the intruder's face up into the light to see who he was.

It wasn't one of the Ó Reilly men, nor one of the brothers from the monastery, but he was undeniably a Viking.

Trahern hauled the unconscious man over one shoulder and struggled to climb up the ladder. The added weight put additional stress upon the wood, and one of the rungs cracked.

'Take him,' Trahern ordered, and Gunnar grasped the man beneath his arms, dragging him away from the *souterrain* entrance. 'Do you know who he is?'

Gunnar laid the man out on the ground, exposing his face. 'I've never seen him before. He has the look of one of the Danes.'

A quiet voice interrupted. 'I've seen him.'

Trahern climbed the ladder and saw Morren standing on the threshold of the women's hut. Her face had lost all colour.

He knew what she would say, even before she spoke the words.

'He was one of the raiders.' She clenched her arms around herself, looking as though she wanted to flee. 'He was there that night.'

Chapter Ten

Trahern shoved the man onto his stomach, pinning him down. Morren remained in place while they lashed the raider's hands behind his back, tightening the ropes. Blood stained his nose, and when the Viking regained consciousness, his efforts to fight back were quickly subdued.

Though she didn't know his name, she recognised the man's face. She felt hollow inside, as though she'd left her body standing there while her mind was screaming. For months, she'd tried to block out all thoughts of the attack, pretending as though it hadn't happened.

But as soon as she saw the raider, it came flooding back.

Bile rose up in her throat, and Morren struggled not to be sick. He'd been one of the men to hold her down, grinning as the first had violated her.

She tasted blood in her mouth, biting her tongue in an effort to hold on to her control.

Trahern forced the man to walk towards one of the fallen beams, where he secured the man's bindings, imprisoning him.

'I've done nothing wrong,' the raider protested. 'I was lost and came seeking shelter.'

Liar. She tried to protest, but no words came. She couldn't speak. Couldn't breathe.

'You were sneaking around in the storage chambers.' Trahern reached into the pouch at his waist. 'Looking for these.' He allowed the coins to slip back down through his fingers.

Morren didn't want to move any closer, but her feet were driven forward with the need to face him. To prove to him that she was strong enough for this.

When she emerged in front of the flickering torches, he saw her at last. A light smirk pulled at his mouth, an unspoken taunt.

'Where are the others?' Trahern demanded. The man gave no answer, and his silence earned him another punch and a split lip. 'Tell me.'

Morren took another step forward, though it pained her to be anywhere near the man. Her stomach roiled inside, but she fought the nausea. Her hands clenched at her sides, her nails digging into her skin.

Trahern saw her coming closer and held up his hand to stop her. 'You don't have to watch.'

And she knew then that the raider was going to die. He would suffer as they questioned him, and upon Trahern's face she saw no emotion. He didn't care what happened to the prisoner. His moment of vengeance was here, and he would glory in it.

Gunnar moved forward. 'Go back and fetch the chief,' he ordered her. 'He'll decide what's to be done with this man.'

'No,' Trahern said. His voice was fierce, and she heard the undertones of grief within it. 'For all I know, it was this man who killed Ciara.'

It wasn't. But Morren couldn't bring herself to speak. Her numbing fear was transforming, building up inside, until it became something else entirely.

Rage. Cold fury at this man who had hurt her, not caring that she had never been with a man before. He, along with the others, had made her endure the worst nightmare of her life.

He didn't deserve to live.

She wanted to strike out at him, to make him suffer as she had.

'Where are your people?' Trahern demanded. Blood streamed down the raider's throat, but still, there came no answer.

With a glance back at Morren, Trahern kicked between the man's legs, and his enemy cried out in pain. He'd deliberately chosen to emasculate their enemy, avenging her in a way that would torment the raider.

'Gall Tír,' he gasped, doubled over with pain.

The settlement was nowhere near here; rather, it was close to Trahern's home at Laochre, near Port Láirge.

Strange. Why would the man be so far from his own clan? Morren couldn't understand it.

Trahern stepped away, letting the raider catch his breath. Several of the others had awakened from the noise, and they gathered around the small space. Morren heard the murmurings of her clansmen who had seen the intruder.

They knew who he was, but not why he was here. Was he alone or had the other raiders returned as well? Trahern seemed to read her thoughts, for he spoke with Gunnar, who ordered several Vikings to scout the territory nearby.

Morren's nerves drew tighter when she saw Jilleen. Her

sister stared at the man, recognition dawning. Tears filled Jilleen's eyes, and she moved closer to Trahern.

It happened so fast, Morren didn't even realise her sister's intent. In a flash, Jilleen seized Trahern's knife from his belt and darted towards the bound raider.

Trahern reached out to stop her, but it was too late. The knife lay embedded in the man's throat, his last breaths gurgling away.

Morren could only stare, shocked as Jilleen ran back sobbing. Her sister flung her arms around her waist, trembling violently. 'I'm sorry, Morren. It was my fault that night. I'm sorry.'

She held Jilleen tightly, her fingers stroking her sister's hair.

And moments later, the raider slumped forward. Dead.

'What will happen to her?' Trahern asked the chief quietly. Jilleen had committed murder, in front of several witnesses. He didn't know if the Vikings would honour the Brehon laws of the Irish. Under them, Jilleen would be required to compensate the raider's family with a body price.

But given the raider's crimes, that might not be necessary. There wasn't a man among them who hadn't wanted him dead. After the number of lives the raider had taken, the penalties would cancel one another.

'Her actions were clear,' the chief remarked. 'She committed murder.'

'The man was one of the attackers that night,' Trahern said. 'There are several who can testify to it.'

'That may be. We will hold an assembly in the morning and decide her penalty. For now, she will remain confined with the women and guarded.'

'She's a girl,' Trahern snapped. 'Not an adult. A girl of thirteen who saw more violence that night than she should have.'

He said nothing about Morren's suffering, though he wanted to. The truth was, if Jilleen hadn't killed the raider, he would have. Without a second thought.

'It's late, MacEgan. As I've said, we will gather everyone in the morning and decide what to do.'

'We bury him,' Trahern remarked, 'and we'll take a group of men to Gall Tír to find the other raiders and bring them to justice.'

'This isn't our battle,' the chief remarked.

'I didn't say your men, did I?' Before he lost the tight control over his temper, Trahern turned and left. Though it was only hours before dawn, he felt nothing but raw madness coursing through him.

When Morren had looked upon the raider, horror had washed over her face, as though she were reliving the nightmare all over again. He'd wanted to go to her, to reassure her of his protection. But at that moment, his greater focus had been on getting information.

The raider had come from Gall Tír, a Viking settlement only miles from his family lands. Why had the men travelled so far? Someone had hired them, but who?

He needed those answers. And he had every intention of tracking the men down. Though it was not the best time to travel, there was still time before winter struck.

He could recruit men from among the Ó Reillys, men who wanted vengeance as much as he did. Perhaps Ciara's brother, Áron, would come. He visualised the men to ask, his mind spinning with plans.

As he turned to walk back to the men's hut, he saw Morren

standing near the palisade wall. Her back faced him, and from the trembling in her shoulders, likely she was weeping.

Trahern didn't think about what he was doing. He simply closed the distance and took her into his embrace. She wept shuddering sobs, her tears dampening his tunic.

'What will happen to Jilleen?' she asked at last, lifting her tearstained eyes to his.

'Nothing.' His voice was hard, confident. 'I'll let nothing happen to her.' He stroked her hair, fitting Morren's slender body against his own.

'She's all I have left, Trahern. I can't let anyone harm her.' She pulled back and wiped her eyes. 'They wouldn't let me close to her, she's so heavily guarded.'

'I'll speak to them.' He took her hand in his, leading her back to the women's hut. 'Trust me.'

'I don't know why she did it,' Morren confessed. 'She would never hurt anyone. Jilleen is the most soft-hearted person I know.'

The anguish in her face pierced him through the heart. He stopped walking, his fingers caressing hers. 'She loves you, Morren.'

'And I love her. But I would never have asked her to do something like that.'

'You sacrificed yourself for her. Don't you think she would do the same?' He touched her damp cheek, and her blue eyes grew solemn. His thumb brushed against her temple, and her cheek warmed against his palm. 'She wanted to punish the raider for what he did.'

'I was so angry,' she admitted. 'I didn't know how much until I saw him.' She touched his hand, gently moving it away. 'I'm not sorry he's dead.'

'Neither am I.'

After a few moments passed, she seemed to realise that she was still holding his hand. Her blush darkened in the torchlight, and she dropped her fingers from his.

But she didn't leave him.

'You're going after them, aren't you?' she guessed. 'To Gall Tír.'

He inclined his head. 'As soon as I can gather men to join me.'

'I want to go with you.'

He'd sooner cut off his legs than put her in danger. 'No. The other men can identify the raiders. There's no need.'

'Can they?' She shook her head. 'I doubt it. It was dark that night, and they struck so quickly, everyone was trying to put out the fires.' She squared her shoulders, as if trying to reassure herself.

'Stay here with the others, and rebuild your *cashel*. Let a man like Adham look after you.' The words he spoke were the right ones. She should remain safely within her clan, protected by a man who cared about her.

But in his gut, he knew that Adham Ó Reilly didn't have the courage or the ability to appreciate a woman like Morren. The man would never understand the kind of hell she'd been through.

And if he dared to blame her for the attack, or treat her like an outcast…

Trahern's fingers curled into a fist, his mouth set in a dark line.

'I'm not going to marry Adham. Or anyone.' She took a deep breath, cutting off his arguments before he could voice them. 'I'll go with you to Gall Tír because I want justice, the same as you. I've been cowering for long enough.'

She crossed her arms and looked him squarely in the eye.

'I want to look upon their faces and let them know that they didn't defeat me. And when I've done that, the nightmares will stop.' Her hands moved down to her mid-section. 'They took everything from me. I'll have no children because of them.'

He wanted to deny it, but the words were trapped in his throat. His own memories came back, of the night she'd lost her child. Grief caught him like a blade between his ribs, along with the need to share the truth with her.

'You had a son that night,' he said.

Morren looked stricken, and her eyes filled up with tears again. He felt his own eyes burning, but he continued on. 'He was too small to live, hardly larger than my palm. I baptised him with a little water and said a prayer for his soul.' He took a breath, finishing with, 'He's buried outside the hut.'

Silent tears ran down her cheeks, and he took her into his arms again, letting her weep. Though death had taken the lives of many, and certainly enough women had suffered the same loss as Morren, he felt her pain as his own.

'I thought I was going to die that night,' she confessed.

Trahern took her face in his hands, touching his forehead to hers. 'But you found the strength to live.' For a long moment, he stood with her face close to his own. Her scent entranced him, like summer dew.

Morren's arms moved around his neck, returning the embrace. She held tightly to him, as if drawing strength only he could give to her. And though a part of him hesitated in offering comfort, this was no betrayal of what he'd had with Ciara. Morren needed him right now, and there was no sin in it.

The longer he held her, the more something within him began to shift. He didn't want to let go. He wanted to keep her within his arms, for she'd given him a chance at redemption.

She was a beautiful, desirable woman who had lost as much as he had. Perhaps more.

And when she lifted her face, he needed to kiss her again. His mouth covered hers, soothing away her pain. Offering her the broken pieces of himself.

She was hesitant, unsure of herself. But a moment later, her lips moved upon his, kissing him back. Light as rain, her cool mouth quenched a thirst he didn't know he had.

His body responded to her, and though their hips were not touching, he prayed she was unaware of her effect upon him.

Though he'd promised her it wouldn't happen again, this wasn't meant to be an act of desire—it was reassurance. Comfort and healing.

His mind was ordering him to end the kiss before he lost his head even more. But if he pushed her back now, she'd think it was because she repulsed him.

Far from it. He angled his mouth, tasting her lips, the sleekness of her tongue. So long it had been. Ciara hadn't been much for kissing. She'd tease him, taking a quick kiss before holding him tight. She'd wanted his strength, and she delighted in it when he'd carry her off, bringing her some place where they could be alone to love one another.

Morren was different. She seemed to need the kiss, as though she were pushing away the darkness she'd suffered. And he let her kiss him as long as she wanted him to, his mouth moving against her hesitant lips.

Her hands moved to his head, touching the prickled scalp where his hair was growing back. She broke free and said, 'It's softer than I thought it would be.'

Her lips were swollen, her cheeks bright, as though she were too embarrassed to mention what had just happened between them. He didn't know what to say.

She startled him, by bringing her hands over the hair he hadn't shaved. 'You should grow it back, Trahern.'

He wasn't certain he wanted to. Not until he had his revenge and completed the task he'd set for himself.

She seemed to sense his reticence, but before she could pull her hands away, her hips accidentally bumped against his. She paled, realising what reaction she'd evoked.

'Morren—'

She stepped back, covering her face with her hands. Her face had gone pale, but she took a deep breath. 'Don't say it. I wanted you to kiss me, so you didn't break your promise. This was my fault.'

'No.' He met her gaze. 'But it's another reason why you shouldn't come with me. It's better for both of us, if we go our separate ways.'

The longer he spent time with her, the more she evoked a desire he didn't want to feel. He might inadvertently forget himself and frighten her.

Morren paled, but didn't move away. 'You make me feel safe, Trahern. When I'm with you, I can forget about my past.' Her gaze moved down to the ground. 'But I understand why you wouldn't want me. Those men—'

Anger lashed through him. 'Is that what you think? Do you believe that I hold you responsible for what those bastards did?'

'No, but—'

'I kissed you because you were hurting. Because I wanted you to know that, in spite of everything, you're a beautiful woman who deserves to have a future with a family of your own.'

He raked a hand over his head. 'I'm angry at myself because I came here intending to avenge Ciara. But with each day that

I spend with you, she's fading from my mind. I don't like it. I feel like I'm betraying her, because I can't think of her when you're here.'

She stared at him, taken aback by his words.

Gods, he was behaving like an ass. Why would she care about any of that?

'I'm sorry,' she whispered. Reaching up, she ran her fingers over his rough skull, down his bristled cheek, to his lips. 'For both of us.'

He caught her hands, choosing his words carefully. 'So am I.'

'I haven't kissed a man in nearly a year.' She looked uncomfortable, but forced herself to continue. 'And until now, I couldn't bear to be touched.'

Until now? The words sent up a flare of warning within him. But before he could think of what to say, she pulled back from him. 'I'm grateful to you for that.'

She adjusted the *brat* across her shoulders. 'Will you help me to see Jilleen? I want to be there with her tonight.'

And just like that, the moment was over, as though it had never happened. Trahern gave a curt nod, escorting her back.

He didn't look at Morren again, nor did he dwell upon the unexpected kiss. It meant nothing.

But he sensed the faith she held in him, the confidence that he would make things right again. And without knowing why, he took her hand in his, in a silent promise.

Chapter Eleven

She didn't know how he'd done it, but Trahern had kept his word. With Katla's help, they managed to get past the guards to see Jilleen. Morren held her sister tightly in her embrace, while Trahern remained at the doorway.

They stayed together through the remaining hours, though Morren knew Jilleen wasn't sleeping. Before dawn filtered through the hut, her sister raised up to face her.

'I don't regret what I did.'

'Shh—don't speak of it now.' She took Jilleen's hands. 'Try to get a little sleep, if you can.'

Jilleen's eyes no longer held the innocence of a thirteen-year-old girl. She drew her knees up, meeting Morren's gaze. 'I'm glad he's dead.'

Morren smoothed a lock of hair away from her sister's face. 'He won't trouble us again.'

Jilleen's mouth trembled, her hands clenching together. 'I should have run faster that night. If they hadn't caught me, we'd both have been safe.'

Morren's eyes burned, her heart aching for her sister. 'It wasn't your fault.'

'It was. And now I've done something to make amends.'

From across the room, she saw Trahern approach. His height overshadowed the young girl, and he stood over her. 'It was not your task to kill him,' Trahern said. 'Though I understand your desire to avenge Morren.'

Jilleen jerked her attention to Trahern, her face colouring. He dropped to one knee, so as not to intimidate her. When he glanced at Morren, she saw that he was trying to help.

'When my brother Ewan was a young lad, he followed my brothers and me everywhere,' Trahern said. 'No matter whether it was a ride across the fields or on a dangerous cattle raid, he wanted to be there.

'We're more than brothers,' Trahern admitted. 'Friends, even.' His voice had drifted into storytelling, and Morren saw that he'd captured Jilleen's full attention. 'We became closer, after we all returned from our fostering. One night, almost ten years ago, we faced a Norman attack. Dozens of archers and riders in full chainmail armour attacked us. Our eldest brother, Liam, was killed that night.'

The catch in his voice was hardly noticeable, but Jilleen heard it.

'You tried to save him,' her sister said softly.

'We did. And we weren't fast enough to stop the sword that struck him down.'

Morren hadn't known of his personal tragedy, for he'd never spoken of an eldest brother. She knew of his other four siblings, for he'd mentioned them a time or two.

'You wanted to kill the Normans,' Jilleen predicted.

'Yes. And my older brother Bevan wanted them dead most

of all, for he was the closest to Liam. For a long time, he kept the vengeance in his heart.

'He let it grow, filling him up inside, for he not only lost his brother, but also his wife in that battle.'

A tear had slid down Jilleen's cheek, and she hugged her knees tighter. Morren felt her own eyes sting, for it seemed that Trahern was no longer speaking about his brother.

'He lived each day, consumed by grief. And we all blamed ourselves.' Trahern lowered his voice to almost a whisper. 'But in the end, we had to keep on living. We had to go on with our lives, for that was what Liam would have wanted.'

Morren tightened her arms around Jilleen, the story reaching down inside her. She stared at him, his grey eyes meeting her own. There was sadness in them, and resignation.

'Get some sleep,' she told her sister, easing Jilleen down so that her sister's head rested on her lap.

Morren lifted her palm to Trahern, offering a brief touch of thanks. She only wondered if, after so much loss, he could let go of his pain and go on living.

Or if she could.

The *Lochlannach* chief, Dagmar, held the assembly at dawn the next morning. Morren hadn't let go of her sister's hand, and Trahern saw the shadows under her eyes.

The gathering was held in the centre of the *cashel*, and the body of the raider was laid out with his face revealed. One by one, the men and women passed by the man to identify him.

And every last Ó Reilly agreed that the raider had been one of those responsible for the attack. Before the raider's body was covered once more, Trahern saw Gunnar removing something from the man's belt. A dagger, possibly.

'He deserved what he got,' Adham Ó Reilly pronounced, as one of the witnesses. 'And were he alive, he'd have to pay restitution for the damage he did to our homes.' His gaze fixed upon Morren. 'And he'd pay the body prices of our family members.'

Trahern stood, waiting until the angered voices grew hushed and fell into silence. His expression softened when he regarded Morren's sister. When he spoke, he used the power of his voice to reach out to the people.

'Jilleen Ó Reilly should not have murdered this man, true enough,' he began. 'But there is not a man here who didn't consider taking the raider's life'

'I believe there should be a penalty,' the chief interceded. Morren gripped Jilleen harder, and Trahern was prepared to argue, before Dagmar added, 'But a minor one.'

Rising to his feet, the chief gestured towards the ruined homes. 'Over the next month, Jilleen must work with her kinsmen and women, helping to repair the damage. Her restitution will atone for the raider's death.'

'She shouldn't have to lift a single stone,' Trahern argued.

'Are you questioning my judgement?' The chief stood and walked to face him. Eye to eye, the Viking leader saw the argument as a personal threat.

Trahern didn't care. 'A girl of thirteen years is not the same as a murderer. We may not know why the raider joined in the attack, but his crimes were clear.'

'It's all right, Trahern,' Jilleen interrupted. Stepping between the two men, she looked at one, then the other. 'I accept my punishment. I'll help them rebuild.'

The girl slipped her hand in his, to reassure him. The chief stared hard at Trahern. At last, he gave Jilleen a nod of dismissal, turning his attention back to the matter of sending supplies and more men and women to the *cashel*.

Jilleen broke free and went back to Morren. A few minutes later, Katla approached. For a long moment, she studied the two women, saying nothing. Morren drew her sister closer, not meeting the woman's gaze.

As if a silent question had been answered, Katla turned back to Trahern. 'I will look after them, when you leave. You have my word.'

The woman's face was grim, filled with understanding. But, to her credit, she said nothing more.

It was an opening, a way of leaving them both behind with the reassurance that Katla would watch over them. As a married woman, Katla could open her home, and he felt certain that Morren and Jilleen would be all right.

Still, he felt hesitant. There was a sense that he was abandoning Morren, just as he'd left Ciara behind. And try as he might, he couldn't seem to push away the feeling of uneasiness.

The crowd began to disperse, the chief returning with several men back to their own *longphort*. Trahern accompanied Morren and Jilleen, and for the next few hours, they joined the others, working on one of the new huts.

But even the distraction of building couldn't stop him from catching glimpses of Morren. Her wheat-coloured hair was braided, and she kept her *brat* wrapped closely around her shoulders. Last night, it had rained, and the *cashel* was sodden with puddles and mud.

Morren kept guard over her sister, but he suspected she yearned to be back in the fields, from the way she kept casting glances outside the *cashel*.

'Do you want to go and cut the rest of the barley?' he asked her. It would take a few hours, but they could finish. 'We could get a few of the others to join us.'

'I don't want to leave Jilleen,' she admitted, glancing at her sister.

'I'm not a child, Morren,' Jilleen insisted. 'You don't need to watch over me.' Morren's face showed her doubts, but her sister waved her on. 'I'll be fine. And I'd rather work here with the others than out in a muddy field. Go with him, if that's what you want.'

Jilleen's words did little to convince her, and it was only Katla's faint nod of reassurance that made Morren change her mind. 'All right. But only for a short while.'

She lifted her *brat* over her head to shield against the wind. Trahern picked up the scythes when he accompanied her and tried to encourage a few of the clan members to help. Not Adham, however. He couldn't bring himself to invite the man, not after the coward had abandoned Morren.

Despite asking several of the folk, none of the clan members wanted to venture forth into the fields, since there was so much labour to be done within the *cashel*. Were it not for Morren's fear that the grain would rot, he'd have been tempted to let it be.

But this was important to her. There was a connection between Morren and the land, one he couldn't deny. Upon her face, he'd seen the dismay at the burned grain, and the faint hope when they'd saved some of the barley yesterday.

As they walked together outside the *cashel*, he wondered if it was a mistake to be alone with her once more. The kiss last night had startled him. He'd dreamed of her that night, of her soft mouth and the taste of innocence. Despite the horror she'd known, Morren was a beautiful, desirable woman. And he wanted her far more than he should.

When they passed beyond the boundaries of the *cashel*, the ground was less treacherous, with grass to help them keep their footing. They chose a place near the remainder of the grain, cutting on opposite sides.

'Thank you,' Morren said suddenly. 'For letting me see Jilleen.'

'She's going to be all right,' he reassured her. 'The others are looking after her. Even Katla treats her like a daughter.'

Morren sent him a soft smile. 'I know Katla lost her own daughter. I think taking care of Jilleen has given her a new purpose. It's as if my sister has a foster mother and a home once again.'

'And you? Do you think you've found a home once more?'

Her smile faded away. 'No.' She reached for a handful of barley, slicing it low. 'Not really. They think I'm the same woman I used to be. But I'm not.' She set aside the grain and reached for another handful.

'You're stronger than that woman,' he said, 'because you survived.'

Her blue eyes met his. 'Sometimes, I think a part of me did die that night.'

He leaned upon his scythe, studying her. She was struggling, not really seeing herself as he did. He searched for the right way to explain himself, wanting to help her overcome the past.

'Did I frighten you last night, when I kissed you?'

She stilled, and the grain fell from her hands. 'A little.'

'Did you believe I would force myself on you?'

She shook her head silently.

'Because you know I wouldn't. And when a man comes along who cares for you—' he reached out and rested his hand upon her shoulder '—you'll know that there's nothing to fear. When love is there, it's about offering yourself. Not taking.'

Her palm covered his hand, the sudden warmth permeating his own skin. His desire to hold her, to feel the comfort of a woman's touch, was making itself known again.

He drew back slowly, so as not to give her the wrong impression. Suddenly, his feet slipped out from beneath him, and he landed hard on his backside.

'Damned mud.' He regained his footing, not missing Morren's stifled laugh. 'Watch yourself, or you'll end up—'

Morren skidded forward, laughing as she landed face down in the grain. She rolled over, her arms and cheek covered with the slimy mud.

'Oh, this is terrible. We look like we've been bathing in it.' She wiped her face on the sleeve of her gown, wincing at the mess.

'It's slick.' He reached down, bracing himself to help her up. 'Be careful.'

'My hands are covered with muck.' But there was a light in her eyes, a humour at what had happened.

'I'm not certain today is the best day for cutting grain,' he said. 'I think we've got most of it, anyway.' He realised that this part of the field was sparser, unprotected from the mud.

'Weakling.' Morren took a careful step, reaching for her scythe. 'You're afraid of getting your clothes dirty, aren't you?'

'They're already soiled. And I've nothing else to wear.'

'I think Katla has an extra gown,' she teased.

'I'd rather go naked than wear women's clothing, *a chara*.' He saw the sparkle in her eyes, and her spirits seemed to lift.

She continued to cut the remaining grain, taking careful

steps. 'I'll finish this, and you can go back and labour with something more strenuous, if you must. I'm certain there are stones that need to be broken or heavy timbers lifted.'

A split second later, her feet slipped out from under her again, and she fell backwards. The scythe came spinning out of her hand, heading straight towards him.

'*Jesu,*' he breathed, dodging the blade. 'Were you trying to kill me, then?'

She got onto her hands and knees, horrified by what had just happened. 'I'm sorry, Trahern. I never expected—'

'I know I need to shave my head again, but not in that way.'

She sat back, resting her dirty hands on her knees. 'I apologise again. It really was an accident.'

Trahern took a careful step, not bothering to pick up her fallen scythe. 'You're not going to be wielding blades again today. I value my life.'

Morren struggled to get up, but her heels slid out, and she toppled onto her back. 'This is hopeless,' she complained. 'I don't know how I'm going to get back to the *cashel* without crawling on my hands and knees.'

Trahern's hands were muddy as well, but he adjusted his footing onto a patch of grass, to steady himself. 'I'll help you.'

He lifted her into his arms, carrying her with careful steps across the field. 'I don't trust you not to fall again. Once we're on the grass, I'll put you down.'

Her arms held tight to his neck, the cool mud warming upon his skin. 'I should have known the ground would be too muddy.'

'You like working in the dirt, don't you?'

'Dry dirt, yes. Mud, no.'

He managed to bring them both to safety, letting her down. Morren stared at him in horrified wonder. 'We both need to bathe or they'll never let us in the *cashel*.'

His gaze moved past her face, and heat flared up at the sight of her body. The mud had plastered her thin gown to her skin, outlining the generous curve of her breasts. One sleeve hung down, baring a shoulder. Her hair hung in muddy ropes across her skin, tendrils that flirted with her tight nipples.

He remembered kissing her, and how it had felt when the warmth of her tongue slid within his mouth. She was as desirable now as she had been yesterday. More so, with the way she'd smiled at him.

Trahern spoke not a word, but headed straight across the meadow towards the river. It wouldn't have mattered if the water held a film of ice. Right now he wasn't thinking of cleanliness, only drowning out the maddening lust that was rippling through him. He dove off the edge of the bank, breaking through the frigid water, and swimming long strokes to clean off the mud.

Morren watched him swim, not knowing what had caused him to go so swiftly. One moment, he'd been standing before her, and the next, he'd all but pushed her away.

She eyed the water, knowing how cold it had to be. But the mud was beginning to dry upon her skin, and if she didn't clean it off, it would cause her skin to itch.

Did she dare join him in the water? It looked terrifyingly cold.

'How bad is it?' she asked him, when he surfaced. Droplets of water slid over his skin, down to his mouth.

'Too cold for you.' He strode out of the water, his clothes completely sodden. Though the remark was probably true, she didn't like the way he assumed she was unable to handle the temperature.

It couldn't be that bad, could it?

Before she could lose her courage, she dropped her *brat* and ran off the edge of the bank, plunging into the water feet first. The shock of the cold river was like a blade through her spine, numbing her. She surfaced again, her teeth chattering.

'What in the name of Danu did you do that for?' Trahern demanded. He strode back into the water, reaching out to hold her steady.

'I n-n-needed to wash my hair.'

'The water is so cold, there was likely ice on it this morning,' he argued. 'You could have drowned.'

'I'm t-t-tall enough to stand in it.' She reached back, trying to wash the mud from her hair. Trahern held her neck, quickly rubbing her scalp until the long strands were clean.

'We could have heated a tub of water. You didn't have to do this,' he chided, lifting her out of the water. When the cold outside air hit her skin, she started trembling even more. Trahern wrapped her in the long *brat*, but the woollen wrap did little to warm her icy skin. Only Trahern's body heat made it bearable.

'I didn't think it was that bad,' she admitted. 'You took a swim and didn't seem affected.'

'I'm larger than you, and the water isn't as cold against my skin.'

Trahern carried her back to the *cashel*, his long strides crossing the grass without any effort. Morren clung to him tightly, as if trying to absorb the heat of his skin into her own.

Trahern was nearly at the gates when suddenly he stopped. He let her down, and her knees nearly buckled.

'I'm sorry,' she said. 'I shouldn't have gone into the water.' She held tightly to her shoulders, shivering. But it wasn't just the cold that made her shiver.

It was the dark look in his eyes, the look of a man who wanted her. He was giving her the chance to walk away, and she knew, without a doubt, that he wouldn't lay a hand upon her.

But his restraint was taking a toll. His gaze was smouldering, like a fire that began upon her skin, working its way over her breasts, down to her thighs. Her nipples tightened beneath the wet wool of her gown, and Morren flinched as something unexpected began to warm between her legs.

Desire. Something about Trahern MacEgan was stirring up buried feelings she'd never expected to feel.

Perhaps she wasn't quite as broken as she'd thought.

Right now, she wanted to move back into the circle of his arms. She wanted him to warm her up, to feel safe. Because she knew he would never, ever hurt her.

'I'm sorry,' Trahern murmured, taking a step closer. His head gleamed with water, his skin pale from the cold. But as soon as he was within a hand's distance, she found herself staring at the prickles of hair upon his face, the unyielding strength in his arms.

'Sorry for what?' Her voice didn't break a whisper, and her breath seemed trapped within her lungs.

'For this.' Trahern captured the back of her neck and pulled her into a hard kiss.

Chapter Twelve

Need and primal hunger rushed through Trahern as he captured her lips. He wasn't thinking clearly, and he knew on the deepest level that this was wrong. But she was so damned beautiful, and seeing her smile had made it impossible to ignore the desire he was feeling.

He expected Morren to push him away. Right now, his guilt roared at him not to do this. He was behaving as badly as the raiders who'd attacked her.

But feeling her mouth against his, and the soft way her arms wound around his neck…it was like a balm upon his spirit. Her body fit against him, and she was kissing him back.

Her freezing skin had begun to warm, and he held her tightly against him. At last, his common sense won over, and he ended the kiss.

She was staring at him, her blue eyes mirroring his own desire. But there was fear beneath it, and shame. She held herself tightly, rubbing her arms.

'Trahern—'

'Don't. I lost sight of myself for a moment.' He raked a

hand over his head, feeling like a criminal. Not at all sorry that he'd broken the rules, but sorry for the consequences. 'Perhaps Katla will have some dry clothes, and you can sit by the fire to get warmer.'

The truth was, he wanted to wrap Morren up in a blanket, letting his body heat warm her skin. In his mind, he imagined them near a fire, with her naked body lying atop his. He'd caress the curve of her hip and her smooth skin.

The tendrils of anger snaked through his mind as he thought of how he was betraying Ciara with those very thoughts.

'I'm going back to get the grain,' he told Morren, needing the brief escape. He was grateful for the heavy bundle, for it kept his hands occupied. When he reached her side again, she cast an uncertain glance at him.

'You're looking as though you want to set the *cashel* on fire again,' Morren remarked, glancing at him. 'What's the matter?'

Everything. I'm a bastard who needs to go and soak his head.

'Nothing. I'm just cold.'

She nodded, pulling her wet clothes tighter against her body. 'I'm dreaming of that fire right now. But none of us has any extra clothing, and I know the chief hasn't sent the supplies yet.'

But as they entered the *cashel*, they discovered Morren was wrong. Supplies were there, but not from the *Lochlannach*.

Instead, a group of four monks had arrived from St Michael's Abbey, along with the abbot. The abbot himself was directing the brothers on how to dispense the food and clothing.

Trahern's suspicions prickled, though Morren appeared glad to see them. Why had the monks ventured forth now, after the death of the first raider? Had they learned of the man's demise? He couldn't quite bring himself to welcome them.

Morren left his side to greet Brother Chrysoganus, and Trahern left to put the grain away with the harvest from the previous day. He returned to the men's hut, intending to warm himself by the fire. His clothing had turned clammy, and he saw Ciara's brother, Áron, taking a drink of ale from one of the skin containers.

He didn't speak any greeting, though the sight of Áron sobered him. It was as if the man had guessed what he'd been doing with Morren, only minutes ago.

Áron came to stand by the fire, his expression tight. 'I heard you're leaving us.'

'I'm going to Gall Tír,' he admitted. 'To find the rest of them.'

'Are you taking her with you?'

He knew Áron meant Morren. 'No. I was hoping you or some of the Ó Reillys would come with me.'

'I'll go,' came a voice. Gunnar Dalrata stood at the entrance, and his expression furrowed when he saw Trahern's soaked appearance. 'What happened to you?'

'I went for a swim.'

Gunnar's face lightened with amusement. 'On purpose?' He paused in thought, then added, 'I suppose if I spent the morning with Morren Ó Reilly, I would need a cold swim.' His eyes were teasing, and Trahern didn't miss the way Áron's anger heightened.

'Close your mouth, *Lochlannach*. You're revealing your lack of brains again.'

No sooner had Áron spoken the words than Gunnar's arm shot out and took him by the throat. He gripped Áron hard and pressed him up against the wall of the hut. 'I could squeeze yours out, Irishman.'

'Let him be.' Trahern moved beside Gunnar in a silent warning. Though Gunnar appeared unwilling, eventually he released Áron. The Norseman had a hot temper, one that could get him into trouble or be useful under the right circumstances. It was a risk, but Gunnar had proven himself to be a strong fighter already.

'You can go with us,' Trahern said to Gunnar, 'as long as you keep your aggression aimed only at our enemies. I don't need you practising on the Ó Reillys.'

'I don't know why you'd want one of them to go with us,' Áron said, coughing and rubbing his throat. 'He'd turn traitor at the first opportunity.'

Though once he'd have agreed with Áron, Trahern couldn't count Gunnar among the enemy. He ignored Áron's prediction and asked again, 'Are you coming with us?'

'I am, yes.' Áron rubbed at his throat again, coughing as he regarded the two men. 'I suppose I shouldn't be surprised that you'd want Gunnar to come along. Too much blood in common.'

'What do you mean?'

Áron moved towards the entrance. 'Look at yourself, Trahern. You're one of the *Lochlannach*, whether you'll admit it or not.'

'I'm a MacEgan. And there may be Norse blood on my grandfather's side, but—'

'No.' Áron paused at the doorway, and Trahern saw that it had begun to rain. Water spattered against the doorway, and an earthen smell rose up from the ground. 'You're a bastard son.'

Before Trahern could seize him, Áron had already ducked outside into the rain.

Trahern knew he could pursue the man, but what good would it do? It was nothing but words, and he refused to let them bother him. There were enough MacEgans who were descended from and had intermarried among the Vikings. He didn't question who he was.

Yet he was still tempted to go after Áron and deny it, knocking some sense into the man. He glared at the rain, even knowing they were better off without him. When he turned around, Gunnar was staring at him.

'What?' Trahern demanded. 'You don't believe what he said, do you?'

'No.' Gunnar met his gaze, eye to eye. 'Not really.'

'Then why, in God's name, are you staring at me?'

Gunnar gave a shrug. 'Nothing, MacEgan.' Though the *Lochlannach*'s tone was casual, there was a glint in his eye. 'It's nothing that would concern you.'

But now, Trahern sensed that Gunnar was lying. And he didn't know what to make of it.

The rains came down that evening, soaking the ground and the fields. Morren had remained in her wet clothes, for the monks had nothing for her to wear. Still, they were grateful for the bread and fresh meat. Brother Chrysoganus had blessed the meal, offering prayers for the rebuilding. The abbot had already returned with one of the other monks, leaving only two behind.

When the evening rain continued to pound, Chrysoganus attempted to entertain the folk with tales of crusaders who had gone to Jerusalem.

'They prayed to God for victory against the Turks,'

Chrysoganus explained. 'And many fell in battle, to join their Eternal Father.'

As the monk expounded upon the virtues of dying for the faith, lecturing on ways that men could devote their lives to God, Morren saw Trahern shifting in his seat. Several of the older adolescent boys were growing restless, staring outside as if pleading for an escape.

When the monk paused to drink a sip of ale at the end of one of his tales, Morren moved towards Trahern and leaned to whisper in his ear, 'Why don't you tell a story of your own? I remember how you used to make us laugh, last winter.'

He started to shake his head, but she leaned down to whisper again. Her cheek brushed against his, and the warmth of his skin seemed charged with an unexpected intensity. 'Please, Trahern. I think we're all tired of hearing about dying pilgrims.'

Before he could say no, she rose to her feet. If Trahern needed prodding, she was glad to do it.

'Thank you, Brother Chrysoganus. I'm certain you must be hungry after so many tales. Why don't we have another story from Trahern, while you go and enjoy your own meal?' She reached out and offered the monk a bit of bread.

The older man's face creased into a smile. 'That's kind of you.'

Trahern eyed her as though he didn't care for her actions. She knew it had been many months since he'd told stories to a crowd. But surely they were still there.

When she'd been hurting that night, he'd eased her pain with the power of his voice. He'd made her forget about her loss, weaving a spell around her grief.

The people needed an escape right now. She settled back down, gesturing for him to sit in the centre of the crowd.

When he rose to take his place, he studied the group as if determining the type of story that was needed.

Trahern began with a tale of Lugh of the Long Arm, his rich baritone voice filling up the small hut. He described the journey Lugh travelled on his way to greet King Nuada. And with his words, he drew everyone into his story, letting them envision the young Lugh who longed to enter the kingdom.

'Before they would allow him entrance, Lugh had to demonstrate a skill.' Trahern unsheathed his sword, brandishing it in the air like a champion. His muscles flexed, and a few of the *Lochlannach* women cheered. Morren kept silent, but she stared at Trahern's strong arm. She'd felt those same arms around her, shielding her.

Though she'd been cold before, now a warmth began to rise up beneath her skin. She leaned closer to hear his tale better.

'Now it was that Lugh intended to show his prowess with his blade,' Trahern continued. 'He offered his skill to the guard, and was denied entrance. "We have swordsmen more skilled than yourself," said the gatekeeper.' Trahern sheathed his sword, sitting down once more.

'Not to be deterred, Lugh offered his skills as a harpist. Then a poet. And once more, as a sorcerer. When he was turned away each time, he was despondent, for he could think of no other skill that would get him inside. He had seen the fair maiden Nás at a distance, and longed to be with her.'

His gaze settled upon Morren, his low tone enfolding her like a caress. As he spoke of Nás's virtues, Trahern didn't take his eyes off her. He focused upon her mouth, and Morren brought her hands to her lips, remembering the dizzying kiss and the way Trahern had made her feel.

She wondered…what it would be like if he touched her elsewhere. Would she fall beneath his spell, enchanted like one of his stories?

As Trahern continued the tale, describing all of Lugh's efforts to gain entrance to the palace, Morren found herself caught up in the story. She wrapped her arms around her knees, watching the way Trahern had restored the good humour of the tribe.

He was meant to be a storyteller, she realised. A man who could command a group to join in his vivid imagination, bringing them entertainment in the midst of such ruin.

She found herself leaning forward to hear the end of the tale. 'And finally, when Lugh approached for the last time, the guard reminded him that they had someone who could perform each of the talents. "But do you have one who can perform them all?" Lugh responded. The guard could think of no man with such power. And so Lugh was allowed to enter the kingdom of Tara.'

Trahern left his seat to loud cheering and applause, and he inclined his head. Though he remained quiet, there was a satisfaction on his face, almost as if he'd missed storytelling.

The rain had softened enough for the women to return to their own hut, and before Morren followed them, she stopped to speak with Trahern.

'You've a gift, Trahern MacEgan. I've missed your stories.'

He answered her smile, and when she saw him without the mask of anger, returning to the good-hearted man he'd once been, she felt warm from the inside.

After he'd gone, she held the story within her, as if holding a part of the man himself.

* * *

Although an hour had passed since the storytelling, restlessness gripped Trahern. He moved to the far end of the *cashel*, his mind filled with errant thoughts.

He'd met Ciara on a night such as this. He'd told her stories, watching her face light up with interest. And their friendship had gradually transformed into a love that had filled him up inside.

He leaned back, sitting against the palisade wall in the shadows. Remembering her didn't hurt as much as it once had. He could still see her smile, almost imagine her arms around him. She'd been a woman like no other, one who had laughed and brought her warmth to those around her.

But she wasn't coming back. He didn't want to accept it, but he understood the truth. He closed his eyes, letting the grief wash over him and through him. Morren was right. If she were here now, Ciara wouldn't like the man he'd become. He'd let the hatred shape him, and he'd lost all sense of himself.

Tonight, when he'd told the story of Lugh, he'd resurrected a piece of his spirit. He'd felt content. And when he'd watched Morren smile, it had made him grateful. She'd been through so much darkness, he wanted to give her more.

The kisses they'd shared were unlike anything else he'd known. Even with Ciara. The way Morren clung to him, the way she opened up to him with such trust…it was humbling.

He didn't want to leave her, though he had to. Like before, he'd make the journey alone.

And will she die, while you're away? an inner voice taunted. *Will she truly be safe?*

He wasn't certain. Though he tried to convince himself that Morren belonged here, among her sister and kin, the truth was, he wanted her at his side.

He wanted her for himself.

His hand curled into a fist, angry with himself for even considering it. *She doesn't want you or any man. And never will.*

The pain she'd suffered went too deep. Wanting to be with her, as a lover, was asking too much.

A faint noise caught his attention, and Trahern remained still. Against the flickering torches, he spied a hunched figure searching among the huts. He couldn't tell who it was, so he crept closer.

The man was cloaked in dark wool, with a roped belt around his waist. He leaned heavily upon a walking stick, and when the moon slid out from behind a cloud, Trahern recognised Brother Chrysoganus.

Now what was the monk searching for, so late at night? The *souterrain* entrance, perhaps? Fallen coins, left behind?

Trahern moved swiftly, catching the monk unawares. Brother Chrysoganus jerked backwards, shivering with a nervous laugh. 'Why, Trahern. You startled me.'

'Were you looking for something?' He didn't bother to hide the edge in his voice. The monk was trespassing where he shouldn't, and he wanted to know why.

'No. Well, yes, I suppose. It's probably nothing, but I thought I'd help them search.'

Trahern moved close enough to rest his hand upon his sword. 'And what were you looking for?'

'It wasn't a what, my friend. It's a who. Katla alerted us and asked for help.' The monk cleared his throat and wiped at his forehead with his sleeve.

Trahern felt a sense of dread creeping over him, even before Brother Chrysoganus finished.

'Morren Ó Reilly's gone missing. And no one has seen her.'

Chapter Thirteen

It wasn't at all what he'd expected the man to say. 'How long has it been?'

'Half an hour, so she said. Katla claimed she left the hut and hasn't returned.' The monk shrugged. 'I was speaking with her sister, Jilleen, beforehand, and when we returned, Morren was gone. I thought I'd join in the search over here. I suppose you haven't seen her, either?'

Trahern shook his head. Without bothering to say farewell to the monk, he ran back towards the women's hut. When he saw Jilleen's stricken face, his fear trebled, for nothing would make Morren leave her sister.

'I only left for a few minutes,' Jilleen wept. 'I wanted to see Brother Chrysoganus, to seek penance for—for…what I did. And when I returned, Morren was gone.'

Trahern studied each member of the clan, Irish and Viking alike. When he realised that Adham was also gone, a tight rage settled in his stomach.

While he'd been mourning Ciara, the bastard had taken her.

He allowed the fury to flare within, along with the unfailing vow to find her.

And God help Adham Ó Reilly, when he did.

'Where is Jilleen?' Morren muttered to herself, her worry knotting within. Her sister had slipped away during the storytelling, and no one knew where she'd gone. Morren had left the women's hut to look for her, and Adham had offered to accompany her. When her efforts came up fruitless, he'd promised to walk back with her.

'Do you think she could have fallen into the *souterrain* passage?' he offered. 'It may be that she lost her footing and fell into the pit.'

'No.' She shook her head 'Jilleen had no reason to be near the *souterrain*.'

'We've searched everywhere else,' he said, shrugging. 'And what if she struck her head or harmed herself? She wouldn't be able to cry out for help.'

Though it seemed doubtful, Morren supposed they shouldn't leave the *souterrain* without searching. 'All right.'

She went down the ladder first, shivering at the cold. Adham followed, bringing the torch. Though it cast a small heat, she couldn't stop the chill flooding through her. 'She's not here.' The unbearable pressure of fear heightened. 'Where could she have gone?'

'We'll find her, Morren,' he said. 'Don't be afraid.' He put his arm around her shoulders, and she flinched.

You're being foolish, she told herself. *He's just trying to offer you warmth.*

But she couldn't bear the thought of his body so close to hers. And wasn't that unreasonable, given that she'd huddled so near to Trahern?

She pulled back, about to climb the ladder. 'Wait, Morren.'

Adham reached out to touch her hair, and a cold wave of revulsion shuddered through her. 'You're so beautiful. I wanted to tell you that.'

Ice crawled over her skin, but she managed to pull away once again, touching the first rung of the ladder. 'Th-thank you.' Her teeth were chattering from the cold, but it wasn't merely the frigid air.

He stopped her from climbing the ladder, his hand snaking around her waist. With a smile, he said, 'You spent the entire night staring at MacEgan. I was hoping for an opportunity to speak with you myself.'

With a step closer, she could smell the fermented mead upon his breath. No doubt it gave him the courage to be so bold.

The world seemed to hold still when his mouth moved closer to hers. She wanted to run, but she froze. His kiss wasn't meant to threaten her, but at the unwanted touch of his mouth, she shoved him.

Memories shattered inside her, of the men hurting her. Of the searing pain and humiliation. The wild anger burning up inside suddenly broke free like an unstoppable wave. Though she knew she was behaving as if she'd gone witless, she couldn't stop herself. Adham tried to soothe her, touching her shoulders, and again she pushed at him. 'Don't touch me! Please, just don't!'

He mumbled through an apology, but she couldn't seem to stop the torrent of rage pouring through her. Not again. Never again would she allow a man to take what she didn't want to give.

When Adham gaped at her, she seized the torch from his

hand and pointed to the ladder. 'I don't want you. Get out, and don't come near me again.'

He took a hesitant step away, and she waved the torch at him. Struck senseless, he climbed the ladder, and it was then that she heard the voices.

Trahern was there. She caught angry words and the sound of a fist hitting flesh. Seconds later, he climbed down to her. She was shaking, the torch casting erratic shadows on the wall.

'He's gone,' Trahern said softly. 'I sent him away.'

The torch fell from her hands, dropping to the ground. She sobbed, clutching her middle while she sank against the wall.

'Did he hurt you?'

'He tried—tried to kiss me.' Lowering her head to her knees, she poured out her fury. 'I know it was just a whim. He didn't plan any of this, but I didn't want him to touch me. I couldn't—I just couldn't. Not again.'

Her words weren't making sense, but Trahern mumbled something about flaying the skin from Adham's body. 'No.' She took a deep breath, trying to steady herself. One breath, then another.

Gradually, the rage disappeared, and embarrassment came over her. 'He only thought to steal a kiss. He doesn't know what happened to me. I suppose he thinks I've gone mad.'

Grey eyes regarded hers with seriousness, but Trahern bade her wait a moment. He climbed the ladder, and she heard him ordering the people back to their huts. 'She's fine,' he said. 'I'll bring her back in a few minutes.'

When she heard her sister's voice mingled with Trahern's, relief broke through her. Trahern climbed back down to her and sat beside her. 'Jilleen went to give her confession to

Brother Chrysoganus, during the storytelling. She never left the *cashel*.'

'She's safe?'

Trahern nodded. He drew up his own knees, resting beside her.

'You don't have to be here, you know.' She wiped at her eyes, knowing that she must look like a mess. 'I've created more trouble than I intended.'

He waited for her to continue, offering no judgement. The tears stopped, and she felt drained. Tired.

'I wouldn't let him touch me,' she said at last. 'I fought back. The way I wanted to fight that night.' She shivered, and he set his cloak across her shoulders. Not once did he touch her, respecting her need for physical distance.

'I was afraid,' she admitted. 'And angry with him. I never knew I could feel that way. And now—' she rubbed her arms, drawing his cloak tighter around her '—now, they'll talk about me. They'll know what happened that night. I can't bear it.'

'It wasn't your fault.'

'I know.' Though she uttered the words without thinking, a part of her wondered if it was true. If she'd fought back against the men, as she had tonight, could she have escaped? Would everything be different?

'I want to ease your fear,' he said quietly. 'But I don't want you to be afraid of me.'

She lifted her face to his. In the flickering torchlight, his grey eyes were filled with compassion. His chiselled jaw was strong, but there was no condemnation against her.

When he opened his arms, she went to him. His strong embrace pushed away all else, and she gripped him hard, sitting upon his lap. He'd come for her, and she realised that she'd wanted that.

She'd hoped that he would come. This man, who drove away her demons and kept her safe. The barriers seemed to fall away, and she breathed in his scent, letting him hold her. How could she let him go, after all this? It hurt, just thinking of it.

'Trahern,' she whispered. *I care for you in a way I don't understand. I need to be with you.*

'What is it, *a chara*?'

My friend, he'd called her. Not his love or his dear one. A piece of her heart cracked apart, for how could she reveal her longing? His heart had been given to another. Not her.

Instead, she hugged him harder, not letting him see the emptiness that stretched before her. 'Just hold me. For a little while longer.'

He did, without questioning why. And though she needed him this night, not a word did she speak about the desires hidden within her heart. Time was slipping away, and she feared she wouldn't see him again, after he left.

'Trahern is leaving today,' Jilleen predicted. 'Isn't he?'

Though it was dawn, her sister hadn't missed the preparations and the group of men gathering with Trahern.

'He said they would.' Morren donned her overdress, wishing it weren't in such poor condition. She needed a new one, but there was no spare wool to be had.

'Why aren't you going with him?' Her sister drew near, her soft blue eyes filled with worry.

Morren didn't answer, but simply shook her head.

She embraced her sister, stroking Jilleen's hair. 'He doesn't want me to come. And besides, I can't leave you.'

Jilleen hugged her tightly. 'Don't worry about me. I'll be all right here.' A choked sob rose up, and her sister gripped her as though she didn't ever want to let go. 'Those men don't deserve to live, after what they did. It was supposed to be me that night, Morren. Not you.' She wiped at her tears. 'I wish to God I'd been brave enough to endure what you did.'

'You are thirteen. Not a grown woman.' She didn't regret her choice for a moment. There was no doubt in her mind that Jilleen wouldn't have survived the attack, had she not intervened.

'I'm not sorry I killed that man,' Jilleen said. 'And I want the others brought to justice. If I could go, I would.'

Thankfully, the Dalrata chief wouldn't allow it. But Morren didn't like the idea of Jilleen being alone, even though there were other Ó Reillys here. 'I won't leave you behind. And that's that.'

'You're falling in love with him, aren't you?' Jilleen said wistfully. 'He rescued you last night. I thought he was going to murder Adham for stealing a kiss. He—'

'You're wrong. I don't love him.' Her face turned crimson, for that wasn't at all what she felt. She didn't—that is, she couldn't—

Her muddled thoughts made no sense, even to her.

'Go with him, Morren,' Jilleen urged. 'Even if you don't find the raiders, he's a good man. He'll take care of you.'

The door opened, and Katla came inside. In her arms, she carried a small bundle of clothing. The troubled expression on her face suggested that she'd overheard more of the conversation than she should have. 'I don't blame you for killing the raider, Jilleen.' Her eyes narrowed. 'Anyone who threatens family deserves to die.'

She reached out to Morren, her face ravaged with frustration. 'And though I suppose I shouldn't have been eavesdropping, I believe Jilleen is right. Someone needs to bring the rest of them to justice. They don't deserve to live, after...what they did.' The older woman's voice broke, and she rested both hands upon Jilleen's shoulders. Her hand patted the young girl, as if trying to replace the daughter she'd lost.

And when her gaze fastened upon Morren, the flush of shame returned. Katla knew what had happened to her. Somehow she did. Possibly Jilleen had admitted the truth.

'Go with them,' Katla urged. 'Trahern needs your help.'

'He doesn't want me to go.' Morren drew closer to her sister, her heart aching already.

'You're wrong.' Katla offered a sympathetic smile. 'You mean a great deal to Trahern. All of us see it. He would have torn the *cashel* apart last night, just to find you.'

The Norsewoman walked across the room and lifted a small bundle wrapped in wool. 'Here is an extra gown and supplies for your journey. You have my vow that I'll watch over Jilleen like I would my own daughter.'

Morren's hands closed over the bundle, her throat closing up. Though she wanted to remain with Trahern, the fear of her past was far too daunting. She wasn't sure she could face the men, even if it was to bring them to justice.

And as for Trahern... Her stubborn heart beat far too quickly at the thought of him. He'd brought her back last night, his hand holding hers. And before he'd let her go, he'd embraced her, as if it were the last time.

'He won't let me go,' she repeated. 'It's not possible.'

'Ask,' Katla said simply. 'There's no harm in it.'

She started to find another excuse, but Jilleen took her hands. Steadily, her sister looked into her eyes and pleaded, 'Bring them to justice, Morren. Not just for me, but for yourself.'

Trahern readied his horse, tying the supplies of food and drink from the Dalrata tribe members, after the chief had provided the promised goods. Four men, including Áron and Gunnar, had elected to join him.

It was mid-morning, but he was surprised to see Morren approaching with a horse. From the reins she held in her hands and the pack of supplies loaded on the animal's back, he recognised her intentions.

He crossed over to her, taking the reins of her mare. 'No.' There was no chance he'd allow Morren to travel with them. It wasn't safe.

She ignored him and boosted herself up onto the horse's back. 'These men can't identify the other four. I can.'

'Do you believe I'll let you come to harm by travelling with us?'

'No, I don't. I know that you'll guard me. And once I've helped you find the men responsible, I'll return home.'

He saw no point to her defiance, and he reached up to lift her down again.

Morren gripped his hands to stop him. 'I'm a grown woman, Trahern. I make my own decisions.'

He lifted her down anyway, keeping his hands around her waist. Leaning in, he said, 'You've a sister to look after. Or have you forgotten?'

'Katla has promised to guard her. I believe she will.' Morren rubbed her arms. 'And Jilleen wanted to remain behind with the others.'

He was about to deny it again, but she touched her hands to his. 'You're not the only one who wants vengeance, Trahern.' Her voice had grown hard, reminding him of her rage last night. Lowering her voice, she said, 'Every time I see a child's face, I think of those men. They stole that from me.' Her blue eyes stared into his. 'I don't sleep at night, because I see their faces. I remember what they did, and I relive it every day. I want it to end. I've had enough.'

When he looked into her blue eyes, he saw the same darkness that had haunted him over the past few months. The same despair that had torn him down, breaking his spirit into pieces.

He didn't want that for Morren. He wanted her to remain with her family, safe from harm. But then, hadn't he tried that himself? He'd lived with his brothers, trying to forget about Ciara. All it had wrought was madness.

Morren returned to her horse. She mounted the mare, sitting squarely upon the saddle. Her expression held determination and not a trace of fear.

Trahern swung up onto his own horse, Barra, and brought the animal alongside her. Morren stared straight ahead, pretending as though he weren't there. 'You're going to stay with me,' he said. 'In my tent. I won't allow any of these men to come near you.'

She paled, but jerked her attention to him, suddenly realising what he meant.

'They're going to think we're lovers,' he said sharply. 'And even if I deny it, it's what they'll believe.'

'I don't care what they believe,' she insisted, her voice almost inaudible. 'I trust that you'll keep me safe. And that you won't…touch me, either.' She looked away, an awkwardness suddenly lacing her tone.

He rested his hand upon Barra's mane. Though he wanted to make the promise, to vow that he wouldn't set a finger upon her, he couldn't speak the words.

In the end, he admitted the only truth he could. 'I would die before hurting you.'

Chapter Fourteen

They travelled from dawn until dusk that day, hardly speaking. Morren kept to herself, half-afraid Trahern would change his mind about bringing her along. The other men stayed away from her—partly out of respect, but mostly because of Trahern's fierce glare.

She studied him closely, realising that he hadn't shaved his head since they'd left the abbey. A light layer of hair was beginning to cover his scalp, and it was dark in colour, likely even softer now.

She shook the thoughts away, warning herself not to think of him in that way. They were friends. Barely that, for Trahern kept his emotions and thoughts so tightly guarded, she hardly knew him. The only time he released a part of himself was through his stories.

He became a different man, then. Teasing, soft-hearted. A kindly giant of a man who knew how to make a crowd of people leave with a smile.

He brought his horse closer to hers. 'You're staring at me. What is it?'

She shook her head. 'Nothing, really. I was wondering if you would tell another story tonight.'

The shield came down over his face. 'Not tonight.'

And just like that, he'd grown distant again. Her attempt at friendship seemed to shrivel up in the face of his cool demeanour. Morren gripped the reins of her mare, pretending as though it didn't bother her one way or another.

But the truth was, it did. She couldn't stop thinking about his promise to share her tent. Her mind filled up with thoughts of his kiss. Though he'd conquered her mouth, there was nothing forceful about it. Despite the dizzying sensations he wrought inside of her, beneath it all, she sensed his restraint.

I would die before hurting you.

She believed it. And his intensity, his protective nature, seemed to draw her closer. Would he sleep beside her tonight, letting her draw comfort from his presence? Or would he turn back, as though she disgusted him?

Her heart turned cold at the thought. Though he'd insisted that she could leave her past behind, she didn't really believe him. Broken and violated, there was hardly anything left of the woman she'd been.

Yet, when she was with Trahern, he made her feel safe. When he'd kissed her, she'd forgotten about everything else.

She turned away, suddenly aware of what she was doing. There was no chance that a man like Trahern would heal her invisible wounds. He had his own cross to carry, of Ciara's death.

And perhaps that would never change.

Disappointment cloaked her as they stopped for the night. Morren sat beside him while they ate, but he didn't look at her. She was like a shadow, hardly noticed by anyone.

The men discussed their plans to travel to Laochre, a castle belonging to Trahern's brother, King Patrick. 'You can stay with my brother and his wife and lend your testimony if we bring the men to trial,' Trahern said.

In other words, she would not go to the Viking settlement. Gunnar seemed to guess her dissatisfaction. While Trahern continued to speak of their plans, the Viking drew closer and sat on the opposite side of her. Trahern frowned, but he was busy drawing a map of the region in the dirt.

'I know you have a reason for coming with us,' Gunnar murmured to her, beneath his breath. 'I suspect you were a victim, weren't you?'

Her words froze up in her mouth, and she couldn't bring herself to admit anything.

'Don't worry, Morren,' Gunnar said. 'We all have our secrets to bear. And I have my own reasons for going to Gall Tír.' A dark look crossed his face. 'Reasons that have nothing to do with the raiders.'

He was prevented from offering any further explanation when Trahern strode across and took Morren by the hand. 'Go to our tent, Morren. It's late.'

He might as well have growled at Gunnar like a dog. But she was weary of listening to battle plans and had intended to sleep anyhow.

As soon as she reached the tent flap, she glanced back at Trahern. His expression softened in a silent apology, and she understood that his disgruntled mood was aimed at Gunnar and not herself. He didn't seem to trust the man, even now.

After hearing Gunnar's remark about having his own reasons for travelling with them, she was beginning to wonder if Trahern was right.

Inside the darkened space of the tent, she found a sleeping fur and a rough woollen blanket that he'd brought along. She took off her shoes and laid down upon the fur, pulling the wool coverlet over her. It was only a few minutes before the tent flap opened, and Trahern ducked inside.

'Goodnight,' he mumbled, rolling as far away from her as he could. He had no coverlet, and he was resting on the cold ground.

'Take this,' she offered, handing him the fur. 'It will keep you warm.'

He didn't move, and she felt foolish holding it. Finally, she let it fall onto the ground in front of him. 'Trahern, what is it? What's troubling you?' She sat up, facing him.

'This was a mistake.' He held out the fur again. 'I shouldn't have agreed to share a tent with you.'

His frustration seemed to fill up the tiny space. She couldn't understand his reluctance. Was she that abhorrent to him?

'I'm sorry. If we stop somewhere on the morrow, I'll try to trade for another tent,' she said. Rolling over, she huddled in a ball to try to keep warm. It also hid her embarrassment, for how could she have known he would behave like this? 'I didn't realise it would bother you to be near me.'

'Morren,' he said quietly, 'you misunderstand me.' He reached out and touched her shoulder. She found him stretched out on his side, propping his head on one hand as he regarded her. 'It's nothing you've done wrong.'

'Then what is it?' She sat up and wrapped her arms around her knees, as if trying to retreat within herself. 'I don't understand.'

A faint smile cracked across his mouth. 'If anything, it's my own fault.' He reached out and touched a lock of hair that had fallen across her shoulders. He lifted it to his face, breathing it in.

'You look upon me as if you believe I could slay dragons.' His hand moved down her cheek. 'I'm no saint, Morren.'

A strange prickle of longing tugged at her. She wanted to go to him, to feel his arms around her once more. But a moment later, he rolled away from her, facing the opposite side. It hurt to see it.

Maybe he was right. Maybe it wasn't safe to remain this close to him, after all. She'd only get her heart broken.

An eerie cry broke through the stillness of the night. Trahern awoke and heard Morren tossing against the fur he'd laid over her. Though he couldn't see her face, her breathing was unsteady.

'It's a dream,' he said gently. But his voice did nothing to break through the nightmare. Fear ripped through her voice and she cried out, 'Run, Jilleen!'

Trahern sat up and tried to rouse her from sleep. Seconds later, she was in his arms. Her skin was frigid, her body shaking. He held her as close as he could, with her seated in his lap. He stroked her hair, and his own heartbeat responded to her nearness.

'Why won't it stop?' she wept. 'Why do I have to relive it, night after night?' She clung to him, her tears dampening his tunic.

'You're stronger than that. You can conquer your fear.'

She kept her hands around his neck, and in time, her body began to warm. It was torment to hold her this closely while instinctive needs pulled at him.

He wanted to wrap both of them in the furs, holding her skin against his own. Somehow, Morren Ó Reilly had slipped through his defenses. She needed his protection, nearly as much as he needed her.

Her fingertips pressed against his nape, her breathing slowly growing steady. 'Sleep beside me,' she begged. 'Please.'

To rest beside her would drain him of any remaining restraint. He couldn't do it. To feel her soft body pressed against his own, sleeping with her scent so close…it was unbearable.

But the need to comfort her was greater. He laid down beside her, keeping her in his arms. She nestled close to him, and he gritted his teeth, praying he could hold back any physical response to her nearness.

'Thank you,' she breathed. When her bottom pressed against his groin, he hardened. Damn it. He couldn't stop the reaction, no matter how he tried.

'It's all right,' she managed. Her voice held fear he hadn't meant to cause, and he suppressed a curse. It had been so long since he'd been with any woman, the frustration of celibacy was starting to take its toll.

'As I said before. I won't bother you.'

He started to leave her, but she took his hands and returned them around her waist. Snuggling against him, she said, 'Stay. Please.'

He wrapped the fur around her, pulling it over both of them. But then, without warning, she rolled over to face him. Her mouth hovered near his, and the invitation to kiss her was intoxicating.

'Tell me another story, Trahern,' she pleaded.

He shut his eyes, struggling to think. They both needed the distraction, before he did something he'd regret. But her mouth was so close to his, and his body was fighting against the urge to lose himself in her kiss.

'There was a warrior named Tristan who loved an Irish princess named Iseult.' He touched Morren's hair, sliding his fingers down her cheek. 'She was a woman he couldn't have. A woman he should never have desired.'

His thumb moved down to her lips. Her breath caught, her eyes staring into his.

'But he loved her, didn't he?' Morren whispered. 'Even though it was wrong.'

'Yes.' His hand moved to her face. 'He loved her.'

Morren touched her mouth to his, and the sweetness of her lips turned into desire he'd never expected. Every thought of vengeance, every memory of Ciara, seemed to dissipate. There was only Morren.

Fragile and soft, her body moulded to his, her arms pulling him closer. He was careful not to rest on top of her, keeping her at his side.

The kiss turned hungrier, slashing him with the need to remove the barriers between them, to feel her skin against his own. His body ached to be inside her, to push away the loneliness.

Instinctively, his hand moved to her breast, gently cupping the weight, his thumb caressing her nipple. The tip grew erect, but when he stroked her, she moaned and pulled back.

'I'm sorry.'

She turned her back on him, curving her body with her knees up. Her shoulders caved inwards, and he cursed himself for pushing her too far.

'Morren, I never meant for this to happen.' He sat up, wondering if he should leave.

'No,' she whispered. 'I just thought…that I might be able to overcome my fear. I wanted to know what it would be like, if a good man touched me.' He heard the soft shudder of her voice, but she wasn't weeping. There seemed to be an uneasiness, mingled with self-degradation.

'I blame myself,' she whispered. 'Not you.' She reached out to him and he held her close, stroking her back. She rested her head upon his chest, as if absorbing comfort from him. And he began another tale, this one of his own making.

'There was a sultan, long ago,' he began, 'who had a hundred concubines.' He paused, waiting for her to respond. Hoping he could distract her with a story, easing the physical tension in her body.

She waited for long moments, then asked, 'Tell me.'

Trahern lifted the fur coverlet over her. 'Each night, he took a different lover. But no matter how beautiful the women were, he was unsatisfied. And one day, he met a young maiden in the market place. She was fleeing from a man who wanted to claim her.'

Morren curled both palms beneath her cheek, listening to his story. She looked innocent, and her lips were parted with interest.

Trahern found himself wanting to kiss her again, to touch the curves of her body and awaken her to a sensual pleasure. One that would help her to see that lovemaking could be breathtaking.

'The sultan reached down and lifted the maiden onto his horse. He carried her to safety.'

'He protected her,' she whispered. She leaned on one arm, still watching him.

'The sultan was captivated by her beauty, though he knew no man had ever touched her. He wanted to keep her for himself.'

'He wanted to gift her with the finest silks and jewels, using whatever means he could, to win her heart.'

'And did he?' Morren reached out and touched his chest with her hand. When she did, it was as if she'd reached inside him, to take his own heart. The past crumbled away, leaving room for nothing else but her. This frightened woman, who needed him as badly as he needed her. It shook him to the core, when he realised what had happened.

'Did he win her love?' Morren whispered again. Her hand fell away from his chest, and Trahern felt as though someone had poured mud into his veins, choking out everything. He couldn't think right now.

'I'll tell you the rest of the story tomorrow,' he promised. He laid down with his back to her. With every last fibre of determination, he forced the desire back.

And just as he closed his eyes, trying to grasp at sleep, he felt the warmth of a fur coverlet that she'd slid over him.

Trahern avoided her for the next several days. He'd kept to his side of the tent, while Morren remained on hers. From time to time, she would awaken at night to feel his warm body pressed against hers. Though she'd shied away at first, in time, she'd grown accustomed to it.

He never intentionally slept beside her. It was simply that the tent was too small for a man of his size to avoid her. Any slight movement would bring him close. In time, she felt the need to sleep in his arms.

On the last night, after she was certain he was asleep, she'd moved beside him to share in his body warmth. The nights had grown so much colder, it made it easier to endure the frigid ground. And there was something reassuring about having his large form beside her. She'd snuggled close to him, her mind drifting back to the night when he'd touched her more intimately. His hand had caressed her nipple.

Her first reaction had been to push him away. But just thinking of him, remembering the feelings of arousal, made her wonder if she'd been too quick to deny him. Trahern wouldn't have hurt her; she knew that.

What would have happened, if she'd allowed him to continue? She closed her eyes, trying to imagine his broad hands sliding over her skin. Awakening her.

When she was growing up, she'd overheard her friends gossiping about being with a man. They'd flushed and giggled, laughing about how it was to take a lover. There had been no pain in their experiences, no feelings of being abused. She felt cheated, for her only carnal knowledge was of being punished and discarded.

She tucked her head beneath Trahern's chin, curling up into his body. In the midst of his sleep, a heavy arm came down around her. He encircled her in an embrace that warmed her, holding her close.

And a secret smile curved over her mouth as she succumbed to sleeping beside him.

Chapter Fifteen

~~~~~~

Just before dawn, Morren had moved back to her side of the tent, saying nothing to Trahern about sleeping beside him. They'd continued their travels, but that morning, he'd seemed edgier than usual. Once or twice, she'd caught him looking at her, but she couldn't guess at his veiled thoughts.

It was mid-morning before they reached Laochre, the home of Trahern's brother, King Patrick. Once they reached the land boundaries, Morren noticed an immediate transformation in Trahern. He quickened the pace of his mount, as if eager to see his family. She followed beside him, craning her neck to look at the stone castle.

It reminded her of the Norman castles she'd seen in the north and those from England. Powerful and imposing, the structure would keep away any coastal invaders.

When they reached the interior, a woman came forward to greet them. Her veiled hair was covered with a silver circlet and a matching torque at her throat. With a warm smile and brown eyes that revealed happiness at Trahern's arrival, the woman embraced him. 'Trahern, I'm so happy you're home.'

She drew back to look at him, examining him with critical eyes. 'You're looking better than the last time I saw you.' When she risked a glance at Morren, the woman's expression turned curious.

Trahern ignored the unspoken question, saying, 'My Queen, you look as beautiful as ever.'

Her mouth twisted in an amused smile. 'Why are you still calling me Queen, Trahern, when you know full well that I prefer Isabel?'

'*Queen* Isabel,' he said, emphasising her title, 'this is Morren Ó Reilly.' He introduced the remaining men, but Morren didn't miss the note of distrust when he offered Gunnar's name.

The Queen's gaze narrowed at the sight of the Viking, but a moment later she seemed to dismiss her suspicions. She offered Morren a smile of welcome, but it was guarded. The Queen would ask questions, Morren knew, and she didn't know if she was prepared to answer them. She hadn't really thought of explanations or what she would say to Trahern's kin about why she had come.

'I'll send servants to prepare your chamber, Trahern,' the Queen offered. 'Morren, you may stay with my ladies.' She let her gaze linger a moment before she enquired, 'How long will you stay, Trahern?'

'Until I've finished what I came to do.'

The Queen issued orders to a servant, and then took his arm, walking alongside him. Morren followed behind at first, but then Trahern extended his other hand. She took it, her heart warming at his effort to include her.

'Patrick is with Ewan now,' the Queen explained. 'They're working on Ewan's ringfort. I imagine he'll want to build a castle as grand as Laochre.' With a smile to Morren, the

Queen said, 'Ewan married his Norman bride only a few weeks ago. They're planning to live a few miles inland from here.'

She brought them inside the castle, leading them up the stairs to the hall. The interior walls were thick, perhaps the length of her arms. Morren lifted the hem of her skirts, but Trahern still didn't let go of her hand.

'You're in time to join us for the noon meal,' Queen Isabel offered. 'Morren, if you'd like to change your gown or bathe beforehand, you are welcome.'

Morren's smile grew strained, for although Katla had given her an extra gown, the Viking woman was taller. The hemline needed to be adjusted, but she hadn't had time. In the meanwhile, she had no other gown but the one she wore. It embarrassed her, thinking of how she must appear to the Queen.

Trahern caught another servant and spoke to him beneath his breath. Morren couldn't make out what he'd said, but the servant raced away to do his bidding.

The Queen led them inside the Great Chamber, and Morren saw two men seated with their wives and several children running around, chasing the dogs. There was an air of contentment, and the blond man scooped a toddling child out of harm's way, just as one of the dogs skidded to a halt.

A pang caught Morren's heart at the sight of another woman seated near the fire, nursing a newborn infant. The woman's hair was veiled, and a dark-haired man eyed her with a protective air.

Two of the men came forward, and from their resemblance to each other, Morren guessed they were brothers. 'These are my brothers Bevan,' Trahern introduced her to the dark-haired man, 'and Connor.' He pointed to the blond man.

'My God, he has hair again,' Connor teased, as he pounded

Trahern on the back. 'As old as you're getting, I wasn't sure it would grow back.'

'You're only a year younger than me,' Trahern pointed out. 'And as for my hair, the nights were growing colder. It was time to grow it out again.'

But Morren wasn't so certain that was the true reason. Her hand bumped against his and she whispered, 'I like it better this way.'

Bevan gave a nod of agreement. 'You're looking more like your old self. I'm glad of it.'

Trahern's expression grew uncomfortable, and he turned his attention back to introductions, leading Morren forward to the veiled woman who held the infant. 'This is Bevan's wife, Genevieve.'

Another woman approached to welcome her, and Trahern introduced her as Connor's wife, Aileen. 'She's the most skilled healer I've ever known.'

After greeting Aileen, Morren turned back to Genevieve. The woman smiled, but there was exhaustion in her features, as though she'd been up all night. 'I would stand to welcome you, but I'm afraid my daughter, Alanna, would protest.'

'It's all right.' Morren managed a smile, but inwardly, her thoughts went back to her own lost pregnancy. The hollow ache hadn't faded, despite the weeks gone by. She marvelled at the tiny fingers of the babe, the head so delicate that she could hold it in the palm of her hand.

Genevieve patted a seat beside her. 'Come and join me, if you'd like to warm yourself by the fire.'

Morren sat with the woman, and moments later, one of the children came to inspect her. The young boy strode over with a confident air. 'I'm Liam MacEgan. Who are you, and are you going to wed my uncle Trahern?'

Morren blinked at the direct question. She gave her name and said, 'No, I'm not going to marry your uncle.'

'Then why are you here?' Liam planted his hands on his hips.

Beside her, Genevieve's mouth tightened to avoid a smile. 'Liam, it's not polite to ask so many questions of someone you've just met. Tell her you're sorry.'

'I'm sorry,' he repeated. But in his eyes, she saw that he wasn't sorry at all, only curious.

Morren folded her hands in her lap, not bothering to hide her own smile. She'd always liked children, and Liam had a smile that was every bit as captivating as Trahern's. She realised he'd been named for the eldest MacEgan brother, who had died years ago.

Abruptly, the boy reached for her hand and dropped a kiss on the back of her wrist.

'Liam…' Genevieve warned. 'What did you do that for?'

'My Uncle Ewan said that when you want something from a lady, you're supposed to kiss her.'

'Oh, did he?' Genevieve rolled her eyes. 'Ewan would say that, wouldn't he?'

'Does it work?' Trahern interrupted, a gleam in his eyes.

Liam frowned, staring at Morren's hand. 'Not yet. But I would like a honey cake or a sweet. If you have one.' He sent Morren a broad smile, and she couldn't help but answer it.

'I'm sorry, but I don't have any food with me.'

Trahern nodded to Liam. 'You'd best go to the kitchens, lad. Practise your kissing on one of the maids, and perhaps you'll get your honey cake.'

The young boy took the hint. Isabel leaned down and kissed his forehead, before the lad scampered away. 'Liam is my eldest son,' the Queen explained. 'He's being fostered with

Bevan and Genevieve and is here to visit for the Samhain festivities.'

'You still celebrate the old ways?' Morren knew that many clans held on to the ancient traditions, though most of the churches frowned upon it.

'I see no harm in celebrating with family and friends. Any excuse for food, drinking and storytelling is welcome here.' Isabel's gaze turned to Trahern in an unspoken hint.

'There is no greater bard than Trahern,' Morren said. 'I've always loved his stories.'

Trahern appeared pleased at the compliment, and his eyes softened upon her. Morren's gaze travelled to his mouth, remembering the feel of his lips.

Connor elbowed his brother, his grin light-hearted. 'Liam's right, you know. Kissing a woman is quite good for getting what you want.' With a knowing smile, he leaned down and kissed his wife, Aileen. 'If you know how to kiss. But you may be out of practice, Trahern.'

Morren's face turned crimson, and Connor didn't miss her blush. 'Or perhaps not.'

'Stop your teasing, Connor.' The Queen swatted at him and offered, 'Morren, if you'd like to escape their company, I'll take you above stairs now.'

She followed the Queen and a maid up the winding stairs and down a narrow corridor. The maid opened the door to the solar, and Isabel gestured for Morren to enter.

'Genevieve will join us, once she's finished feeding Alanna,' Isabel said. She ordered the maid to bring a basin of warm water and a clean *léine* and overdress. 'She'll want to hear about everything.'

'Everything?'

A secretive smile crossed the Queen's face. 'Trahern has

never brought a woman to Laochre before. You must mean a great deal to him.'

Morren shook her head. 'No. We're friends, nothing more.'

'He never took his eyes from you. Not even once,' Isabel pointed out. 'It may be that you're friends now, but perhaps later—'

'No.' Morren cut her off. 'That's all there is between us.' She decided to give the Queen a shortened version of her story. 'Our *cashel* was attacked, and Trahern's betrothed wife, Ciara, was killed. I survived the attack, and I've promised to help identify the raiders. We think they were among the *Lochlannach* who dwell at Gall Tír, not far from here.'

Isabel frowned. 'That can't be true. The Hardrata tribe members are our allies. Patrick's Great-Uncle Tharand lived there, long ago. Their men have no reason to attack a settlement so far from here. Are you certain it's them?'

Morren nodded. 'Trahern can tell you more.'

Isabel seemed to sense her reluctance, and she offered, 'My maid will help you dress for the meal. You are welcome here at Laochre, and if you've the need for anything, simply ask.'

'Thank you,' she murmured. After the Queen had left, the maid helped her into the borrowed green *léine* and overdress. Thankfully, the gown fit her better than the one Katla had given.

Morren sat down while the maid helped comb the tangles from her hair. The relaxing motion made her close her eyes for a moment. Trahern's family had a boisterous air that made her feel welcomed.

The door opened a few minutes later, and she saw the dark-haired healer, Aileen, standing there, with Trahern behind.

Morren couldn't understand what they wanted, but when she saw the devastated expression on Aileen's face, she knew.

Trahern had told the healer.

Morren looked away, her face crimson with shame. She didn't want anyone scrutinising her, nor had she wanted anyone else to know.

Aileen dismissed the maid, and Morren sent a hard look towards Trahern. Why had he told a stranger of her dishonour? There was no need for it. She'd healed well enough.

'I asked Aileen to come and look at you,' Trahern said. 'I thought that after the birth—'

Anger rose up from inside her, betrayal that he'd told another woman of her shame. 'No. I'm fine.'

'Trahern said that you lost your babe, a few weeks ago,' Aileen said gently. 'He wanted to ensure that you've fully healed.'

'I have,' she snapped. 'And I need no one to examine me.'

She knew she sounded ungrateful and harsh, but she couldn't understand why he'd revealed her secret.

'Trahern, leave us,' Aileen ordered. Though her voice was calm, there was a firm tone to it. He looked as though he didn't want to, but in the end, he obeyed.

Aileen closed the door behind him. After long moments passed, she admitted, 'He's afraid.'

'Afraid of what?'

'He tended you that night, and he's afraid he did something wrong. He wanted to be sure that you were all right.'

'I am.' Morren gripped her arms, rubbing them for warmth.

'I know what it's like, to lose a child,' Aileen said. Upon her face were the lines of sorrow, the unspoken pain. 'I went through six years of being childless. And I've miscarried several times.' She pulled up a chair and sat down. 'I won't ask you questions you don't want to answer. But know that you've a friend to speak with, if you have the need.'

Morren's chest ached, and she clenched her teeth together. No, she didn't want to talk about it. She wanted to forget all about the pain and devastation of that night.

But she answered, 'That's kind of you.' She met Aileen's gaze, adding, 'The bleeding stopped several days ago. I'll be all right.'

'If you start to feel feverish, or if you have any more cramping, please tell me. I'll do what I can.' Changing the subject, Aileen said, 'Would you like to help with the preparations for Samhain? I'm certain Isabel would be glad of an extra set of hands.'

Morren nodded, grateful for a means of occupying herself.

'We're helping the children to make masks this afternoon,' Aileen said. 'They usually wear them on Samhain Eve, but the adults also wear their own masks. After the children have gone to sleep, we have our own celebration. The masks can make the evening more adventurous.'

Aileen began to lead the way down the stairs. Halfway, she stopped and regarded her. 'He cares about you, Trahern does. If you're wanting more than friendship, you've only to reach out to him.'

Morren said nothing, for she didn't know what to think any more. She was still upset with him for telling Aileen about her lost child.

He wanted to be sure you were all right, Aileen had said. Had he told Aileen about that night? Did the healer know more than she should?

Though he'd intended to ensure that she was all right, it felt like a betrayal. Her stomach hurt when she walked downstairs with Aileen.

Inside the Great Chamber, long tables were heaped with food. Freshly baked fish, meat pies and boiled goose eggs were offered for all to share. Aileen brought her to sit with the family, and Morren saw that Trahern had also changed his clothing. Unbidden, she found herself staring at him.

He truly was a handsome man, with sharp features. There was a great deal of his grandfather's blood within him, for now that she could see him among his brothers, she realised that he didn't resemble them much at all. Only their eyes were similar in colour.

When Trahern caught sight of her, he crossed the room to take her palm in his. He led her to sit beside him, murmuring, 'You look beautiful, *a chara*.'

His compliment was unexpected. Beautiful wasn't the word she'd use to describe herself. She murmured her thanks, but didn't meet his eyes.

He leaned in, his breath upon her ear. 'I told Aileen nothing, except that you lost your babe. That's all.'

He'd sensed what was troubling her. She couldn't stop the relief, knowing that her terrible secret was safe. She rested her cheek against his. 'I wish you hadn't said anything.' Her loss was still too raw, and she didn't want to think of it.

'I want you to be all right,' he said, his hand reaching around to touch her neck. 'I couldn't do much for you that night. And when you refused to see the *Lochlannach* healer, I thought you might agree to let Aileen help you.'

'I'd rather not,' she said, pulling back. Forcing herself to look into his eyes, she added, 'I'm sorry I snapped at you earlier. I thought you had told Aileen…everything.'

'I wouldn't do that to you.'

She squeezed his hand in silent forgiveness, and he walked her toward his family, who were seated at a long table upon a dais. They were prevented from further conversation when they sat among the other MacEgans.

Liam MacEgan kept coming to ask her questions, and Connor's twin boys followed their cousin everywhere. The noise and bustle of the large family was infectious, and by the end of the meal, Morren found herself holding Genevieve's baby daughter, Alanna.

The baby's blue-grey eyes were serious, her tiny mouth pursed up like a rosebud. She was perhaps three months old, and when Morren lifted the babe to her shoulder, Alanna opened her mouth and began rooting against her neck.

It was bittersweet, to feel the warm baby skin against her own. If she hadn't lost her child, she'd have a rounded bump now. Perhaps she'd even have felt a kick or two.

'I haven't anything to feed you, little one,' she apologised.

'She's just been fed,' Genevieve offered. 'She'll be fine.'

A moment later, Alanna stuffed a tiny fist into her mouth and began suckling it. Her downy head pressed against Morren, and within moments she was asleep.

'Do you want me to take her?' a voice asked. Turning, she saw Aileen. The healer's tone was gentle, knowing how difficult it was.

But Morren couldn't bring herself to let the child go. 'Not yet.' She cupped the baby's head, smoothing at the downy hair on Alanna's scalp.

Trahern sent her a smile, and there was a softness beneath it. He looked for all the world like a man who was meant to be a father. Though he was older than many of his brothers, there was a yearning in his face.

A part of her ached, knowing that another woman would have to give him that, for it wouldn't be her.

Shakily, Morren offered Alanna back to Genevieve. She picked at her food, finding it hard to concentrate.

Beside her, Trahern's leg pressed against her own. Hard and muscled, she remembered the touch of his body. But instead of frightening her, she was drawn to him.

If you're wanting more than friendship, you've only to reach out to him. Aileen's words resonated in her mind, making her wonder.

Several of the men rose, after their meal. She spied Connor and Bevan talking together, before Trahern leaned in. 'We're going to Gall Tír.'

'When?'

'Now.' His expression darkened, and she felt the urge to shiver.

'Do you want me to come with you?' Though she knew it was necessary, a coldness slipped down her body, flooding her veins.

'Not this time. We're going under the guise of a visit. If you go with us, it may alert the raiders.'

'Be safe,' she said, gripping his hand. A prayer came to her lips, for he and the men to return unharmed.

His hand squeezed her fingers. 'I'll come back tonight.'

Morren didn't miss Isabel and Aileen's knowing looks, but she said nothing. She didn't want to think about what was happening between herself and Trahern. Something had shifted, somehow. Now that he was among his family, his anger was softening. Moment by moment, he was starting to return to the man she'd known.

It unsettled her. As long as his focus was upon avenging Ciara's death, he hadn't looked upon her with anything but friendship. But more and more, she felt intertwined with Trahern, bound to him in a way she didn't understand.

He started to walk towards his brothers, but stopped suddenly. She waited to see what it was he wanted. Before she could take another breath, he pulled her close and kissed her hard.

'Until tonight, *a mhuirnín.*'

Later, Morren joined Isabel, Genevieve and Aileen in helping the children to make their masks for Samhain. The activity brought back moments of her own childhood when she and Jilleen had laboured over their own masks.

Made of wood bark and pitch, the fragile masks wouldn't last more than a single night or two. Liam was seated away from his cousins with his completed mask drying upon the table. He laboured over a turnip, scraping out the insides.

'It will be a lantern,' he promised. 'And Cavan and I will try to catch one of the *sídhe* on All Hallow's Eve.' He beamed at the thought. 'Maybe we'll find one of the dead.'

'You're the one who will be a dead man if you and Cavan leave this ringfort after dark,' the Queen warned.

Though Liam sent a contrite look to his mother, Morren didn't miss his impish wink. After he'd finished hollowing out the turnip for his lantern, Liam brought her a piece of birch to decorate as a mask.

'I have one made of silver that you may borrow,' Queen Isabel offered. 'After the feast, we'll have dancing, games, and perhaps we can convince Trahern to tell stories.'

'He might,' Morren said. Studying the fragile birch, she

reassured Liam, 'I think this mask will do nicely. I won't need another.'

A boyish smile creased his face. 'I'll find goose feathers for you. You can decorate the mask with them.' He hurried off in search of them.

But though Morren continued working on the mask, as time crept on, she found herself worrying more and more about Trahern. She wasn't the only one who was restless. After another hour, the boys began chasing each other around the chamber.

'Outside,' Queen Isabel ordered, when Liam started racing across the floors, skidding into a sliding position to see how far he could reach.

'I love my son,' she remarked, 'but there are times when I'm glad Bevan is fostering him, else I might murder the lad.'

Genevieve laughed. 'I'm certain you feel the same way about Duncan and Cavan.'

Isabel sent Morren a mischievous look. 'Not at all. Genevieve's sons do nothing wrong.' Even as she spoke the lie, the two boys raced across the Hall, colliding with Liam before they all went outside.

When the room had emptied of the boys, the Queen invited the women near the hearth. 'Shall we have a bit of sport?'

Aileen spied the pile of hazelnuts and shook her head. 'Isabel, that's nothing but nonsense. You cannot determine a woman's fortune with a handful of nuts.'

'Oh, but it's fun,' Genevieve insisted. 'Come on, then, Isabel. I'll go first.'

Morren had heard of games such as these, and she saw no harm in it. Genevieve cast two nuts near the hearth stones. As they grew warm from the fire, the pair of nuts seemed to grow closer to one another.

'It seems that you and Bevan will continue to be happy together,' the Queen pronounced. 'Now me.'

She cast two more nuts upon the hearth, and Morren gathered with the others to watch. As the heat intensified, Isabel choked out a laugh when both nuts burst into flames.

'Someone will be enjoying a passionate night tonight,' Aileen predicted.

'Patrick *has* been away a good deal.' Isabel blushed. 'Well, I won't argue that one. He's always a bit eager whenever he comes back from a journey.'

From the pleased blush on the Queen's cheeks, it appeared that she wasn't at all unhappy about the prediction of passion in her future. Morren's own cheeks warmed, though she had never experienced pleasure with a man. In spite of herself, she thought of Trahern's warm body and the touch of his tongue against hers. Her breasts shifted against her gown, and she crossed her arms to hide the tightened nipples.

'Now Morren,' the Queen said. She handed Morren the nuts, with the instructions to toss them upon the hearth. She did, wondering to herself what prediction would come true.

The nuts rolled together at first, but as they heated, one rolled in the other direction.

The mood grew sombre, and Morren already knew the meaning. She and Trahern would part ways.

'It's only a game,' Isabel reassured her.

She knew that. And it shouldn't bother her at all, for she'd always known she would return home. But the strange ache of discontent wasn't easily brushed aside.

'Trahern will return with the others,' Aileen reassured her. 'The Gall Tír settlement isn't far. I've no doubt they'll be back within another hour or two.'

Morren tried to venture a smile but was unsuccessful. 'I'm sure they will.'

Genevieve offered her the sleeping Alanna. The tiny babe was warm and soft, and Morren knew she'd meant the child as a distraction. But it was like holding a lost piece of her heart.

As the time crept onward and Trahern still hadn't returned, her spirits sank even further.

*Did you know you could
have received this book
before it hit the shops?*

Visit www.millsandboon.co.uk

MILLS
BOON

www.millsandboon.co.uk

**PLUS, by ordering online you
will receive all these extra benefits:**

- Be the first to hear about exclusive offers
  in our eNewsletter

- Try before you buy! You can now browse
  the first chapter of each of our books online

- Order books from our huge back list at
  a discounted price

- Join the M&B community and discuss your
  favourite books with other readers

Chapter Sixteen

Trahern slipped inside the room Morren was sharing with the other unmarried women. He awakened her with a touch on her shoulder. Leaning down to her ear, he whispered, 'If you want to hear about my encounter with the *Lochlannach*, come with me now.'

Morren nodded and got out of bed, reaching for her over-dress. Trahern turned his back while she dressed, and when he felt her palm in his, he led her down the stairs. Past the sleeping men and outside to the inner bailey, they walked hand in hand.

He led her to Isabel's herb garden and Morren sat upon the ground, her gaze assessing the plants without really meaning to. Though she didn't ask him, he knew what she wanted to know.

'We think they were there,' he admitted. 'Áron Ó Reilly swears he saw one of them.'

'Did you confront the chief?'

He shook his head. 'Not yet. I want to speak with my

brother Patrick first. As King of Laochre, he'll know the best way to seek justice.'

After seeing the fortified settlement, he'd had second thoughts about his plans. Though it was a blended tribe of both Irish and Viking, Gall Tír was heavily guarded with trained fighters to defend it. Despite his need for vengeance, to see the men punished, Trahern couldn't risk his family's safety by causing a war. It was best to visit them again with his brother, the King, at his side.

A large granite rock stood in the garden, coated lightly in moss. Trahern sat down on the ground beside her, resting his back against the stone. Morren had neglected to bring her *brat*, so he gave her his cloak to wrap around herself.

She huddled within it and moved beside him. 'Share it with me. We'll both keep warm.'

He opened his arms and pulled her next to him, draping the cloak around them. 'I would take you inside, but I'd rather not disturb the others, nor have listening ears around us.'

She shivered, and he did his best to warm her. 'Do you still want to go to the settlement?'

'Yes.'

But her voice was hardly a whisper, and he sensed more that she wasn't telling him.

'If you feel uncertain about it, you don't have to go. I wouldn't ask that of you.'

Morren rested her head against his chest. 'I'm going with you, Trahern. Tomorrow, if you want.'

'Not until the King returns. And we need to plan this carefully.' He gathered her onto his lap, pulling her close. The softness of her hair tickled his nose, and he breathed in her scent. It felt right, holding her like this.

Her hand moved in slow circles over his chest, and the

gentle caress brought him a peace he hadn't known in a long time.

'Morren,' he murmured, catching her hand. He drew her back to face him, and in the faint moonlight, her face was shadowed. 'I should tell you…that when I want these men punished…it's not only for Ciara. It's for you.'

Morren didn't speak, but moved her palm to touch his face. The bristles of his growing beard abraded her hand, and she moved it across the new growth of hair. A faint smile tilted her mouth, and he inwardly vowed not to shave it again.

The softness of her fingertips held him captive. Did she know that she'd brought him back from the edge, transforming the beast into a man once more? She'd taken away the emptiness, making him feel emotions again.

'You loved Ciara, I know.' Her voice remained quiet, but her hand was stoking another kind of warmth. He wanted to taste her mouth again, to forget the empty months of loneliness.

'I did.'

'Do you miss her?'

Ciara's presence wouldn't easily be forgotten. But there was a goodness in the bond between himself and Morren. Something that was soothing the raw scars, healing the pain of loss.

'Aye. But it's not as bad as it was.' He drew his hand down to her nape, bringing her closer until her forehead touched his. 'You bring me solace.'

There was a slight hitch in her breath, and her trembling no longer seemed to be from the cold.

'Every moment I spend with you, it gets a little easier.' His mouth moved so close to hers, it was almost a kiss. Against her lips, he murmured, 'I'm thankful for it.'

When he took a kiss from her, she opened to him. Like

a seedling, thirsting for water, she drank from his lips. And though he longed to deepen the kiss, he didn't push her, keeping it as nothing more than an offering.

'Once this is over, I'm returning home,' she said, breaking away from him.

She was poised as if ready to flee. Her fear was written upon her face, and she turned her face to his shoulder.

'I know. But is there harm in wanting to be with you? To see what happens?' He rested his palm upon her back. 'Unless you'd rather I left you alone.'

'Trahern, I held Genevieve's babe in my arms today.' Her voice held the weight of unshed tears. 'It made me think of my son.'

His answer was to pull her into his embrace, holding her. Her arms wound around his neck, and it consoled him to know that she wasn't pushing him away.

He kept his voice steady. 'I wish I could have saved him.'

'It's just that—you were meant to be a father one day. I can see how much you love your nieces and nephews. And I can't give you that.'

'Don't think about what might or might not happen in the future,' he said, running his hand down the length of her hair. 'One moment at a time.'

She grew still within his arms, and he cupped her face in his hands. 'Unless you'd rather I didn't touch you at all.'

Morren didn't know what to say. Right now, being in his arms, she could feel the desire he was trying to hold back. And her own skin was growing hotter, despite the crisp autumn air. She couldn't deny the things he made her feel. They were at a crossroads, and though her mind was warning her that she couldn't possibly consider anything more with Trahern, her body was responding to him.

Her hesitation brought back the guarded expression on his face. By remaining silent, she'd made him believe that she wanted nothing to do with him.

He helped her rise to her feet. 'I'll escort you back to your chamber.'

But she didn't want that. She didn't want him to distance himself, not now. When she was with Trahern, the past didn't seem to matter any more. He didn't look upon her as a damaged woman.

'Wait.' She took his hand in hers. Though heat rushed into her cheeks, she wanted him to know that she cared for him. Guiding him to the stone, she exerted a gentle pressure on his shoulders. 'Sit down for a moment.'

He obeyed without question, and Morren stood before him. She rested her hands on his shoulders, and forced herself to move closer. Lifting his palms, she set them about her waist.

She didn't know if she had the courage to reach out to him in this way. But she couldn't say what was inside her heart, for she didn't really understand the feelings. All she knew was that she needed him. His presence steadied her, and she didn't want to lose that.

Slowly, she bent down and touched her mouth to his. It was the only offering she could give, and he took it, meeting her kiss. He brought her closer, opening his mouth and touching her tongue with his own. The shocking sensation sent a tingling shudder through her body, until her nipples strained into tight peaks.

But it wasn't from the cold.

Trahern kissed her as though she were the only woman in

the world, the one who had brought him back from the edge of madness. The heat swirled through her, dampening the place between her legs. She ached there, and it startled her to think that she could ever welcome a man in that way.

'Come here,' he whispered. 'Sit with me.'

She thought he would pull her onto his lap, but instead he lifted her to straddle his muscled thigh. Her instinct, to pull away, was so strong, she almost did. But he didn't move at all, only resting his hands at her waist. He massaged a soft circle over her spine, and she began to relax.

The pressure of his leg against her centre brought another rippling sensation. She didn't understand it, but before she could protest, he captured her mouth with his.

His tongue nudged hers, sleek and wet. A moan caught in her throat as he kissed her. He shifted his leg in the barest movement, and her breathing quickened. The sensation of his thigh pressed against her sent a tightness swelling up in her centre.

She yearned to run from it, for she didn't want this feeling. Fear washed over her, but she forced the memories away. She trusted Trahern never to hurt her. And in his dark grey eyes, she lost herself.

'Don't fight it,' he said gruffly. 'Let me give this to you. Just let go.'

He shifted his leg again, sliding her against the thick muscles. She could hardly breathe as his mouth took hers in a kiss that pushed away all the darkness. In a rhythm that tantalised and terrified her, he moved his thigh, while his tongue slid inside her mouth.

A strange yearning began to fill her, and she strained against his leg. Swollen and burning with need, she nearly tried to move away from him, but he held her fast.

'Let it happen,' he urged again. And with another nudge of motion, she felt herself trembling on the brink of something. His mouth captured hers, and abruptly, her body erupted with a shimmering pleasure that rocked through her. She gasped against his lips, and her nipples rubbed against the fabric of her *léine* while she rode out the intense sensations.

She melted against him, holding fast to his neck while her heartbeat raced.

'What happened to me?' she whispered. 'Just now when you—' Her words broke off when he pressed his leg between hers again. 'Sweet Virgin, don't.'

His hand stroked her back, and he drew her to him with a wicked smile. 'That's what lovemaking is about, *a stór*. Giving a woman pleasure.'

Her mind went back to Queen Isabel's earlier remark about her husband and the passion they shared. The happy blush on the woman's face hadn't been at all fearful. Was that the way it was meant to be?

She searched Trahern's face, trying to understand. Beneath his lazy smile, she saw a hint of physical frustration. 'What about you?'

'Don't worry about me. This was for you.'

She brought her mouth to his and kissed him with a gentle brush of her lips. He returned the light kiss and stood, easing her down. 'I'll escort you back.'

She could hardly walk, and delicious sensations thrummed within her body. But even so, she didn't miss the caged hunger in his demeanour, nor the way he watched her from the corner of his eye.

His heated gaze made her recall the fierce, soaring pleasure. She was attuned to him in a different way, and she wondered why he'd awakened this within her.

When they stood before the chamber she shared with the rest of Isabel's ladies, he touched her face. 'Sleep well, *a mhuirnín.*'

A blush warmed her cheeks, but she nodded. 'And you.'

'In a few days more, we'll return to Gall Tír,' he said. 'After Samhain and the King's return.'

A cold chill spiralled through her. Though she understood that she had to go to face her attackers, another part of her wanted to hide from it.

'You won't be alone,' he assured her. 'The King and our men will be there. I'll guard you myself.'

She knew it, but it didn't diminish her consternation. Nor the fear that, once she faced the men, she would retreat back inside herself again.

Trahern hardly saw Morren the rest of the following day. After King Patrick returned with their youngest brother, Ewan, all of them gathered to discuss the raiders.

'They were mercenaries,' Trahern told them. 'Hired by someone to kill as many of the Ó Reillys as possible.'

'But even if you do find the mercenaries among the Hardrata tribe, can it be proven?' Patrick asked. 'It's your word against theirs.'

'We have multiple witnesses who can identify them. And surely they would have been gone from Gall Tír at the time of the attack.'

'Where does Morren fit into this?' the King asked suddenly. Trahern saw the knowing look in Patrick's eyes. There was more to the question than simple curiosity.

He could try to hide the truth from them, but they knew him too well. If they believed she was simply the victim of losing her home or kin, they might not understand his deep need for justice.

He wanted those men dead. And they'd never understand why, unless they knew the real reason.

'She is one of the witnesses,' he answered. His voice hardened, and his knuckles clenched. 'She can identify the men better than any of the others. Every single one.' He stood from the table and regarded each of his brothers. 'They hurt her.'

He said nothing about the violation she'd endured; he didn't have to. He saw the way their faces tightened in understanding.

'If any man laid a hand upon Genevieve, I'd flay the skin from his bones,' Bevan admitted.

'Then you know why I want them punished.' He sat down once more, waiting for Patrick to give his opinion. But the King seemed to be weighing his own thoughts, listening to all that was said.

'How should we approach the chief?' Trahern asked. 'Much as I'd like to simply go in and kill the bastards, I'd rather not cause a war between our tribe and theirs.'

Patrick sat back and seemed to consider the matter. 'The Ó Reilly men have just cause for their accusations. They can bring the matter before the *brehons* and ask for compensation if the men are found guilty. As for Morren—' He stopped and studied Trahern for a moment. 'She may also seek justice. There is no need for your involvement.'

'She's under my protection. I won't let her go alone.' Trahern didn't say anything more, for he couldn't name the feelings he had for Morren. It went deeper than he'd realised. He wanted vengeance for her sake, so she could go on with her life. 'I've promised her that the MacEgan men will offer their support.'

Patrick's expression tightened. 'You can make no such promise, Trahern. If it were Genevieve, Isabel, or any of the other wives, I would not question it. But Morren is not one of us. I'll not risk our men or the peace of our tribe for a stranger.'

'She's not a stranger.' He sent a blistering look at his older brother, unable to believe Patrick would step back and withhold his support.

'She's not your wife, either.' The King's words cut down his argument, making it clear that Patrick would not support any venture that would endanger the tribe.

It was as if his brother had knocked the wind from his lungs, for he'd never anticipated this. MacEgan brothers stood together, always.

'And if she were?' he asked softly.

'Then we would treat her as we would any of our own women. We would defend her.'

'Prepare your men,' Trahern said, rising to his feet. 'I'll wed her during Samhain. And after that, we'll confront the *Lochlannach*.'

He knew he should feel betrayed by Patrick, angry at being pressured into this arrangement. But…he didn't. It was as if Ciara's hold had relaxed upon him. He suspected his betrothed would have understood the need.

But now he had to convince Morren of the necessity. And he hadn't the faintest idea how.

'Did he agree?' Isabel demanded of Patrick, later that morning. 'Will he marry her?'

Her husband led her up the winding spiral stairs to their bedchamber. 'You're an interfering woman, Isabel MacEgan.'

She saw the wicked intent in his eyes and let her *brat* fall to the floor. 'Trahern deserves happiness. And it's time he married. He's not getting any younger.'

'But is Morren Ó Reilly the right woman for him?'

'Are you blind? Haven't you seen the look on his face when he watches her? And the way she can't tear herself from his side? She worried about him all day while he was at Gall Tír.'

'I did see them in the garden last night,' he admitted.

'Oh? And what were they—?' Her words were cut off when her husband pulled her into a deep kiss. A sigh fell from her mouth, and she fitted her body to his. As he lowered her onto their bed, he kissed her until she couldn't catch her breath.

When at last he broke free, he answered, 'That's what they were doing, *a stór*. And it's why I agreed to your idea of pressuring him into the marriage.'

Isabel reached to remove his tunic, never minding that it was the middle of the day. Even after so many years, she'd never stopped loving her husband. 'I'll make certain their wedding day is unforgettable.'

'If she says yes.'

'She'd be a fool not to marry a MacEgan man.' And with that, Isabel pulled him into her arms.

Chapter Seventeen

The first night of Samhain was cold and crisp. As the sun set over the fields, Morren saw a bound sheaf of corn, shaped in the form of a woman. The *Cailleach*, or the Hag, as it was known, was surrounded by young girls, each daring one another to reach out and touch the crone.

Annle, a former healer of the MacEgan tribe, watched over the girls, her wrinkled mouth stretched into a smile. She was the most respected of the elderly women. Nearly seventy years of age, she had watched generation after generation of MacEgans rise up and be succeeded by their sons and grandsons.

She sat upon a chair, observing the children's excitement. With gnarled hands, she helped some of the younger children tie on their masks. Morren wore the bark mask Liam had decorated for her, though it scratched at her face. It wasn't at all attractive, but after the boy's hard work, she wouldn't say anything to hurt his feelings.

Trahern's mask was made of beaten gold, and it was large enough to cover the top half of his face, baring his mouth.

There was something different about him tonight. He appeared distracted, and he'd hardly spoken to her. She wondered if it was because of the time they'd spent together in the garden. Even thinking of it evoked a trembling within her skin, a sense that there was much more he hadn't taught her.

Liam brought forth his carved-turnip lantern, with a candle stub burning inside. 'See?' He showed her the light. 'This will drive off the evil spirits.'

Morren pretended to be frightened, and the boy beamed at her. 'It's quite terrible,' she said.

With a lightness to his step, Liam went to join his cousin Cavan, who had two missing front teeth.

'Let's go,' Cavan urged. 'Sir Anselm promised us cakes.'

The two boys joined the other children, collecting treasures and sweets from the tribe members. They played more fortune-telling games, and a group of the older children competed for apples.

Trahern's brother Connor had hung a rope over a tree branch and mounted a horizontally spinning cross containing two lighted candles and two apples hanging from each of the ends. The older boys leapt into the air, trying to bite the apples off without being burned by the candles.

Trahern had taken his seat at the far side, near one of the fires. He began telling the legend of Nera, a man who had wed the faery king's daughter and saved his clan from the *sídhe*. Morren was about to move closer when she heard Annle speak.

'His mother would have been proud to see him,' the old healer whispered.

Morren drew near and saw that the woman's *brat* had fallen to the ground. Her narrow shoulders were bowed, her frail fingers lined with blue veins. 'A shame, really, that she died so young.'

When Morren reached her side, she lifted the woollen shawl over the old woman, and was rewarded by a warm smile. Annle's eyes were distant, staring at the back of one of the men. 'Trahern looks like his father. Not like the others.'

'What do you mean?'

Annle gave a secretive smile. 'Nothing. Only an old woman's foolishness. Go and enjoy the stories.' Her lips curved into a wrinkled smile. 'He's waiting for you.'

Morren didn't understand the woman's enigmatic response, but she squeezed Annle's hand before she departed. She sat near the fire, listening to Trahern weave his spell over the people.

'Nera warned his people that the *sídhe* were coming to *Rath Cruachan*, intending to attack. He prepared his warriors, but as they readied their weapons, he thought of his wife and newborn son, waiting for him beyond the golden gates of the faery world.'

Trahern's gaze fell upon her, his grey eyes compelling her not to look away. Morren felt her cheeks grow warm, uncertain of whether he was still telling the story or not.

'She meant everything to him. And he would not let her go, despite the betrayal of the others.'

A shiver crossed over her, and she heard the faint cry of Alanna, Genevieve's young infant. Trahern's face softened when he spied the babe, and he continued his tale, weaving the victory of Nera over the immortals and the reunion with his wife and son.

When the story was over, Trahern stood. He waited until the group had dispersed before lifting his mask away.

'Is it heavy?' she asked, pointing to the gold.

'A little. But the children enjoy it when I wear it.' He held the mask in his palm. 'Will you walk with me? There's… something I need to speak with you about.'

No longer was he the smooth, confident storyteller. He appeared uneasy about what he had to say.

She knew he'd spoken with his brothers this morning about Gall Tír. More than likely they wouldn't allow her to go with them. But she wasn't about to be left behind. Not now, not when they were so close.

She joined Trahern, removing her mask and letting it dangle from her fingertips. He took her past the barren fields, towards the channel that divided the mainland from a nearby island. He'd brought a torch with him, and along the way, he asked her to gather brush and wood for a fire. When they'd reached the edge of the cliffs, they worked together to build a small fire, lining it with stones.

'I'm going with you to see the *Lochlannach*,' she insisted, after they sat down beside the flames. 'Whatever happened won't change that.'

Trahern didn't answer for a while, but stared out at the sea. 'My brother refused to send men to help us plead our case.' There was disbelief on his face, but also the sense that he was holding something back.

'We don't need his men,' Morren insisted. 'We can go with the others and demand justice.' She moved to sit beside him and placed her hand on his arm.

'We could. But having the King guarding our backs would make a stronger case.' His hand moved beside hers. 'There is…a way he would help us.'

She waited, but he seemed to struggle with the words. More than once, he looked upon her face, before at last he blurted it out. 'If you married me.'

'What?' The words broke free before she could stop them. Marry him simply to gain soldiers and to strengthen their case before the *Lochlannach*? 'You don't mean that.'

'I didn't expect him to suggest it,' he confessed. 'But he's right. If you were my wife, the MacEgans would become your family. It's a stronger reason to argue before the *Lochlannach*.'

Her mouth nearly dropped open. Had he really said that? He wasn't asking her to marry him because he cared about her or wanted to share his life with her. No, this was about vengeance, once again.

Out of nowhere, anger descended over her. 'No,' she answered. 'I won't marry you.' Every reason for it was wrong. She took slow, deep breaths, trying to push back the frustration within. Marriage had never entered her mind, but if she'd considered it, the last thing she wanted was an offer because his brother had suggested it.

Trahern stared out at the water again. 'I thought you might refuse. But there are other reasons.' His hand closed over hers. 'I could protect you. No man would ever hurt you again.'

She pulled her hand away. 'Do you think that's all that matters to me?' Rising to her feet, she strode to the edge of the cliff. Below, the turbulent water swept over the rocks in pooling waves of foam.

'No. I thought—'

'You didn't think at all.' She whirled and nearly stumbled. He caught her wrists, bringing her away from the edge. 'If I needed a guard, I could hire one. I don't need a husband.'

'You're afraid of marriage.'

'No, I'm angry. I can't believe you'd think so little of me. Or yourself. Let's see…my brother thinks I should get married, so that's reason enough.'

'I don't dance to my brother's tune,' he argued. 'I make my own decisions. And I think we would make a good match.'

He didn't understand. Not at all.

'I don't know that we would.' Morren pushed him away, fury and humiliation making tears spring up in her eyes. But she wouldn't let herself cry.

His hands moved to rest on her shoulders. 'I wouldn't ask you to share my bed, Morren. You know that.'

From deep inside, all the broken dreams seemed to spill out in jagged shards. 'I don't want a shadow marriage, Trahern. I want a husband who will love me or no husband at all.'

He didn't pull back, as she'd expected him to. Instead, his thumbs dipped into her shoulders, stroking at the tension there. 'And you don't believe you could care for a man like me.'

Her head fell back against his chest as his hands loosened the knots in her nape. She struggled over the words, afraid of revealing too much. 'That isn't what I said.'

His hands moved to her hair, gently caressing her. Just the simple touch began to coax a response. She leaned into him and murmured, 'You mean more to me than any man, Trahern. But I know I'll never fill the space Ciara left behind.' She took a breath and then stepped away. 'I won't be a substitute, or an excuse. It's not enough for me.'

The expression on his face was unreadable, his grey eyes revealing nothing.

'I'll walk back with you,' he said at last.

Food and drink were passed around, and the children were asleep inside the huts. Trahern donned his mask once more, as did Morren. The adults were laughing, enjoying the celebration while old Annle regaled them with stories of her own.

He'd lost his mood of celebration, his mind spinning with

discontent. Morren was right. He'd asked her to wed, not because he wanted her as a woman, but as a means of furthering his revenge. He knew he couldn't present a true show of force against the *Lochlannach* without his brother Patrick's support.

He hadn't been thinking about the long term of marriage, or how she would perceive his intentions. She had a right to be angry.

What startled him was his disappointment that she'd refused. He hadn't expected to feel anything about the arrangement. In his mind, he'd envisioned it as a military strategy, a way of accomplishing a goal.

And by thinking of it as such, he wouldn't be betraying Ciara's memory. It disquieted him, for he hadn't been thinking of her quite as much any more. Already he'd begun replacing her with Morren. He didn't even know how or when it had happened.

Guilt filled up within him, for Morren had been right. She'd seen right through his poor excuse of a marriage. And yet he sensed it would have been a good match.

He squeezed Morren's hand, leading her past a few of the onlookers. Gunnar stood on the outskirts, as though he wanted to join with the MacEgan tribesmen, but dared not. Trahern stared hard at the man, suddenly seeing things he hadn't before. The Norseman's height towered over the others, and he sat near the others, intent upon a story Annle was telling.

The older woman was speaking of Trahern's parents and the way his father, Duncan, had struggled to win the love of his mother, Saraid. Trahern moved closer to listen, keeping Morren's hand in his.

'One night, when Saraid was heavy with her fourth child,'

Annle began, 'she discovered a foreign woman wandering outside the ringfort. Like herself, the woman was expecting a babe, and so Saraid invited the woman to stay with them.

'Not a word did the woman speak,' Annle continued, her ancient voice holding them captive. 'And all wondered who she was. Did she come from the land of *Tír na nÓg*? Was she a faery in disguise?'

Gunnar moved forward through the crowd without warning, his attention locked upon Annle. 'What did she look like?'

His question broke through the spell, and a few of the MacEgans were irritated by his interruption.

But Annle only motioned him to sit with the others. Trahern found himself gripping Morren's hand tightly.

It's just a story, he told himself. *Like the thousands of others you've told.* And yet, it wasn't. He sensed it, and couldn't bring himself to walk away.

'The woman looked like you,' Annle admitted to Gunnar. 'She had long golden hair that she wore in a thick braid down to her waist. We thought she had wandered from the settlement at Gall Tír.' She waited for a slight pause, adding, 'But we were wrong.'

Reaching for a drink of mead, Annle waited before continuing her tale. 'It is said that those who offer hospitality to strangers receive the blessings of the *Tuatha Dé Danann*. Saraid knew this, and she befriended the woman. And when the time came, the woman bore her child.' She paused, raising her eyes to meet the crowd. 'At the first light of dawn, both mother and child disappeared. Whether they were mortal or not, no one knows. But after that, the MacEgans were blessed with prosperity.'

The applause from the crowd made the old woman smile

as she took the hand of a young man, letting him escort her back to her home.

Trahern didn't move. He saw the thoughtful look upon Gunnar's face, and then the man turned to stare at him. There was speculation on his face, as though he were trying to discern an uncertain truth.

A sickening portent took root in Trahern's stomach. Against his better judgement, he excused himself from Morren's side and followed Annle.

Her steps were slow, and she leaned upon the young man for balance. Trahern caught up to them and offered, 'I'll walk with her.'

Annle smiled and took his arm. 'And how are you, Trahern? You seem better than the last time we saw you. The children spoke of your stories and how much they enjoyed them.'

He murmured his thanks for the compliment, but slowed his pace. 'Annle, about your story…'

'You want to know if it's true.' Her voice grew hushed, and she stopped walking. The ancient blue eyes seemed to reach inside him. 'What does it matter, Trahern?'

'You know what happened to the woman, don't you?'

Annle began walking again, and he was forced to remain at her side. 'I do.' She gestured for him to open the door to her hut. He did and saw that someone had already brought in hot stones to warm the interior for her. Annle was the oldest woman in the tribe and beloved by all.

'I don't look like my brothers,' he said, when they were inside. 'I always thought I looked like my grandfather. But there's more, isn't there?'

'You've seen the ones who do look like you.' She leaned

heavily upon him as he helped her sit down. 'And it troubles you.'

The Lochlannach.

The coldness bled from Trahern's heart and through his veins, fear snaking up into his throat. 'No. It's not true.'

Annle folded her hands on her lap. 'The *Lochlannach* woman came to us, long ago. She gave birth to a son the very night after Saraid gave birth. But your mother's child was sickly. He came too soon, and there was nothing I could do to save him.'

Annle reached out for Trahern's hand. 'I know you can guess what your mother did. The woman was bleeding, and she died that night. Saraid took you and raised you as her own.'

He wanted to deny it, to give all the reasons why it couldn't be true. But his physical appearance didn't lie. His height and his features were not like his brothers.

You're a Lochlannach, Áron had said. Trahern's jaw tightened, hating the thought that it was true. Even Gunnar had believed he was one of them, from the moment Trahern had tried to kill the man. His eyes had been blinded to the truth, it seemed.

He wanted to drive his fist into a wall, anything to burn off the reckless anger rising inside. But Annle's delicate hand held firm, squeezing his palm.

He forced himself to take a breath. 'You said the woman didn't come from Gall Tír.'

'She wasn't one of the Hardrata tribe,' Annle agreed. 'She'd fled their settlement, begging us for sanctuary.'

'What happened to her, after she died?'

Annle's quiet smile held amusement. 'You know that she

didn't truly disappear. We buried her along the sea cliff, and covered the place with stones.'

The healer took his hand. 'The woman may have given birth to you, but Saraid gave you a home and a family. You may not be a MacEgan by blood, but...' she reached out and touched his heart '...you are here, where it counts.'

Trahern didn't hear the rest of what she said, words of consolation and words trying to explain the lies. He'd always believed that Saraid and Duncan were his parents. And his mother had treated him as though he were born of her own flesh.

'Did my father know?'

Annle nodded. 'He did. But they chose to treat you as their own son, a precious gift in the midst of Saraid's tragedy.' The old healer patted his hand. 'Don't let it bother you, Trahern.'

But it did. Not only would he never know his true parents, but his family ties had been dissolved with a single revelation. He wasn't a MacEgan. And knowing the truth was like a knife slashing through his heart.

He bid farewell to Annle, but he was numb to the celebration going on around him. He saw Connor laughing with his wife, Aileen, and his brother waved.

No. No longer his brother. He was *Lochlannach*, of the same blood as his enemy.

Trahern kept walking, away from the crowd. Right now, he couldn't seem to grasp what had happened or what he should do with the information.

Behind him, he heard quiet footsteps following. He continued back to the castle, knowing who it was. But right now, he didn't know what he could say to Morren.

'Trahern?' she called out to him, when he reached the spiral stairs. 'Is everything all right?'

No, it wasn't. But he could only lift his shoulders in a shrug. 'I just need to be alone for a time.'

Long enough to decide what he should do about Annle's confession. It was as if someone had swept his past clean, destroying his family.

Morren moved closer, concern etched in her eyes. 'Something happened since I spoke with you last. After you left Annle's hut, you looked upset.'

'It has nothing to do with the raiders,' he reassured her. 'You can go and join the others.'

Morren took a step up, passing him until she stood above him on the stairs. She reached out to touch his cheek, her face lined with concern. 'You're still my friend, Trahern. Tell me.'

He wanted to deny her again. He ought to hold his silence, not troubling her with his errant thoughts, yet Morren's calm presence steadied him. She knew him as no other woman did and would not cast any judgement.

'Come.' Trahern took her hand and led her up the winding stairs until they reached the family chambers. He opened one of the doors and invited her inside. Turmoil and uncertainty shadowed his mind as he wondered how to begin. She didn't push for answers, but simply waited.

'Annle told me a story about my mother,' he admitted. 'It bothered me to hear it.

He explained what he'd learned about the infant Saraid had lost and how she had raised him as her own.

'I know she loved me,' he admitted. 'And I grew up believing I had five brothers.'

'You did. Whether or not they are your brothers by birth, you know it's the truth.'

'I should tell them, but a part of me doesn't want to. I'd rather they believed the lie.'

'Just because you don't possess MacEgan blood doesn't change the feelings they have for you. You're their brother and always will be.'

'I don't want to have *Lochlannach* blood running through me. Every time I think of them, I think of Ciara. And you.' He reached up and tucked a strand of hair behind her ear. 'I don't want to be related to my enemy in any way.'

He gripped her hair, lowering his forehead. 'She was fleeing from Gall Tír, Morren. I was likely fathered by one of them.'

She embraced him, wrapping her arms around his back in a gesture of silent comfort. 'Nothing's changed, Trahern. Nothing at all.'

She was wrong. Something had changed, something between them. Though she claimed to be his friend, there was more. He held her tightly, breathing in her scent. He didn't press her for anything further, but he couldn't stop the physical response to her. The closeness of her body against his was a reminder that every time he touched her, he was desecrating Ciara's memory.

He was about to pull away when Morren's hand moved up to the back of his head. The touch of her hands struck him aflame like a match against dry leaves.

He wanted to draw her close and remove the layers between them. Instead, he took her hands and lowered them. Her smile faded, and she pulled them back. 'You're angry with me.'

'No. Angry with myself.'

She hugged her shoulders, shivering slightly. 'You're angry that I refused to wed you.'

He shook his head slowly. 'I promised myself I would never forget Ciara. That I would avenge what happened, even if I died in the attempt.'

Her fingers moved up to touch her mouth, as though holding back what she wanted to say.

'I'm angry at myself because…I've stopped thinking of her.' He raised his eyes to hers, feeling raw and furious for being weak. 'And because I want you, far more than is good for either of us.'

Her shoulders lowered in confusion, but still, she didn't speak.

'Leave, Morren,' he said. 'Now. Before I do something I'll regret.'

He wasn't thinking clearly, the anger and sexual frustration mingling together in a way that made him feel like an animal.

'You're not betraying Ciara,' she whispered, taking a step closer. 'She loved you. And she would want you to go on living.' Before he could argue, she stood on her tiptoes and brought his mouth down to hers.

God above, but he needed this. He needed Morren's gentleness, her soothing warmth. And she seemed to sense it.

Without breaking the kiss, he led her to a chair and sat down, pulling her into his lap. Her breath caught, but still he didn't stop kissing her.

He tasted the seam of her mouth, and she allowed him entrance. But when his tongue touched hers, she emitted a soft gasp.

'You shouldn't have started this,' he murmured, cupping her nape. He shut out the raging voices that told him how wrong this was. He didn't care. Morren had reached out to him, and damned if he'd turn down this moment with her.

He'd kissed her like this before, but she seemed tentative all of a sudden. 'Don't be afraid, Morren.'

'You wouldn't hurt me, I know.' Her whisper was tremulous.

'Never in a thousand years.' He nipped at her mouth again, feeling hazy with desire. 'You know that, don't you?'

'Yes.' She let her hand slide down the back of his tunic, her cool hand exploring his skin. The rippling touch sent a grinding pulse of heat through his groin, and his fingers curled against the seat of the chair.

She sensed it and drew back. 'I didn't mean to cause you pain.'

He gritted his teeth. 'No, it feels good.' To show her he meant it, he loosened the ties of his tunic and lifted it away, baring his skin. He held still, seeing the mixture of fear and curiosity on her face. When she didn't move, he lifted her palms to his chest.

'Go on.' He leaned back, closing his eyes. She'd refuse, no doubt. Even Ciara had preferred to let him do the touching.

But Morren surprised him. Her hands slid over his muscled chest, slowly. Fingertips traced the battle scars from years ago, gently learning the planes of his body. 'When did you get these?'

'Years ago, in the battle against the Normans.' He didn't open his eyes, and it was torment to feel her caressing his skin.

Get her out now, his brain warned. *Stop her before it goes too far.*

'You're strong.' Morren's hands moved over the taut muscles of his stomach. Lower, until they brushed the ties of his trews.

The head of him strained to meet her touch, and he caught her hands. His breathing had grown hoarse as he fought to keep himself under control.

'Morren, stop,' he managed.

She drew her hands back, her lips parted in shock. 'Have I done something wrong?'

He closed his eyes, shaking his head. 'I'm about to do something very wrong, if you don't leave.'

She moved away from his lap, but his harsh words hadn't dimmed the curiosity. 'What…would happen?'

He leaned forward, resting his wrists upon his knees. Heat burned through his skin, his body craving hers. 'I'd remove the gown you're wearing. I'd take off every layer until you were sitting naked upon my lap.'

Her expression grew wary; colour stained her cheeks. She took a step backwards, her hands gripping her arms. 'Then what?'

Her voice held a trace of interest, and he stood up. Her innocent question aroused him even more. Though he didn't want to frighten her, she needed to understand. Advancing towards her, he brought his hands to the curve of her waist, sliding down to her hips.

'I'd put you in that chair, Morren, and I'd kiss every last inch of your skin.' He leaned up, pressing his mouth against her throat. 'Here.'

His hands held her in place while he lowered his head to the curve of her breast. Through the woollen fabric, he breathed a warm breath upon her nipple. It tightened, and he caught the faint shudder of her desire. 'Here,' he whispered.

Then he brought his leg between hers, lifting her weight to

straddle him. Though her gown and his trews kept the barriers between them, he knew she could feel his thick erection against her thigh. 'I'd even kiss you there, Morren.'

The rise and fall of her lungs was quickening, and he sensed that if he touched her intimately, she would be wet. Sleek with desire.

'I'd use my tongue to taste your salt. I'd kiss you until you trembled, lick your folds until you screamed.'

When he leaned back to look at her, her eyes were closed, her cheeks flushed. Her mouth was swollen from his kiss earlier, and he wanted to capture it again, driving her closer to her own fulfilment.

She moved her body against his length, and he sensed how close she was. He pressed her back against the wall, his hands just below her arms. Her breasts strained against the wool, and he lowered his mouth to them once again.

'Then, do you know what I'd do?' he murmured, dangerously close to her nipple. The sensitive nub rose up against his cheek, and the aching pain of arousal was so deep, he was close to losing control.

'What would you do?' she breathed, her breath coming in short gasps.

'I'd lift your skirts and I'd join my body with yours. I'd suckle you here...' his mouth took possession of her breast, dampening the fabric '...and then I'd let you ride me. Slow and deep...' He used his fingers to stroke the other nipple, and her face was tight with need.

'Or hard and fast.' He lifted his leg between hers, rubbing her. Coaxing her to reach for the release she craved. 'I'd give my body to you, Morren. For your pleasure alone.'

Chapter Eighteen

He took her mouth in a fierce kiss, and that was all it took to send her over the edge. Morren gripped his neck, clinging to him in the storm of her release.

It was too much. She trembled as waves of shaking pleasure rocked through her. Her centre felt wet and swollen, craving more.

Trahern groaned, holding her tight, and his face suddenly transformed, before relaxation came over him. Something had happened, and she suspected his frustration wasn't as bad as it was before.

She shuddered, resting her face against his chest. Her hands moved over his skin, tracing a pattern over his muscles, her nails scraping against his taut nipple.

Then, when she realised what she was doing, she pulled back. Embarrassment and shame washed over her. 'I'm sorry. You're right, I should go.'

A coldness seemed to fill the air between them. He released her, remaining silent.

And yet she couldn't stop herself from the babble of words

that came out. 'I know you had other reasons for wanting to wed me. That it wasn't about…love.' Her shoulders lowered, and she bared her most secret shame. 'But even if I'd agreed, I could never be what you wanted.'

'What is it you think I wanted?' There was a steel to his voice, and she turned from him, unable to look.

'You're a man who should have children. I can't give that to you.'

'It was only going to be a temporary marriage,' he told her. 'An arrangement.'

His voice was cold, like the stone walls of the chamber. 'I—I know,' she stammered. 'I just thought that—you would expect me to act as your wife. In all ways.'

She lowered her forehead to the wall, feeling all the world like a fool. He was a man, the same as any other. When she'd thrown herself at him, he'd taken what she'd offered. And she was desperately afraid that he'd want her to share his bed, making love to her.

The thought of any man joining with her body made her feel nervous and sick. She hadn't minded the way Trahern had touched her tonight, for he'd caressed her with words, as much as anything else. It had been so different from the violence she'd experienced.

But he would want more. She didn't believe they could have a celibate marriage, not from the way he'd caressed her.

'I'm not an animal, Morren,' he told her. 'Believe me. I can keep my hands off of you.'

Oh, Heaven above, she'd offended him. It wasn't at all what she'd intended.

Face him, she urged herself. She turned around and saw the irritation in his grey eyes, the palpable frustration. She forced herself to speak. 'I don't think I could…lie there and let it happen again. Not with any man.'

His jaw tightened. 'As I've said, when I offered you a marriage arrangement, I wasn't intending to consummate it.' He let out a breath. 'But you should know that I would never ask you to lie there and endure my touch.' His eyes held an unnamed emotion as he softened his tone. 'I promise you, you'd enjoy it.'

A shiver passed through her. When he'd touched her earlier, she'd felt liquid inside, before the sweet torment had sent a flood of release pulsing within.

She swallowed her fear back. 'Perhaps. But you wouldn't enjoy being with me, if we were to—' Her voice broke off in humiliation. She couldn't even speak the words.

There was not a doubt in her mind that she would freeze up or scream, the way she had with Adham. And she didn't want her fears to damage their friendship.

Trahern took her hand in his. 'I would enjoy every moment of it, Morren.' His thumb slid over her palm, but his words grew careful, his tone even. 'But I'll honour your wishes. We'll finish the matter at Gall Tír, and then I'll take you back to Glen Omrigh.'

Her heart seemed to grow brittle at his suggestion. She didn't want to be brushed aside again. 'That's not what I want.' Her words came out as a whisper, and Trahern took his hand away. Resting it against the wall, he touched his forehead to hers.

'If you want something more—' His mouth nipped at her ear lobe, his tongue swirling over the soft skin. Shivers poured through her, drenching down her breasts and between her thighs. She clung to him for balance, afraid her knees would buckle.

'I'll teach you whatever you want to learn.'

She found it hard to think clearly. Against her better judgement, he was coaxing a response she'd never anticipated. Her body was acting on its own needs, ignoring the common sense of her brain. She'd inadvertently pressed herself closer to him, needing the warmth of his embrace.

But it was still only an arrangement, Morren reminded herself. Not a true marriage. Even if he did somehow drive away the demons of her past, their paths weren't meant to join together.

Closing her eyes, she pushed him back. 'Take me back to the others,' she pleaded. 'Let us enjoy the first night of Samhain among your family.'

Trahern stared at her for a moment, but he gave a nod that he'd heard her. Within minutes, he escorted her down the stairs and outside again. He put on the golden mask once more, and as soon as he did, she sensed the distance widening between them. Her own mask was crumbling apart, so she let it fall to the ground.

The atmosphere had changed during their absence, and it sent a wave of uncertainty through her. Masked men and women paired off, retiring to the shadows. Trahern's hand rested upon her waist, and she caught a glimpse of Connor and Aileen slipping away together. The blond man looked upon his wife with the same expression of desire she'd seen in Trahern's eyes, just moments ago—as if he would lift the world on his shoulders for her.

The fires burned brightly in the night sky, and around the huts turnip lanterns rested upon the doorways. Other men and women ate, drank and laughed together. Morren spied one couple kissing amidst cheers, their hands bound together with three coloured cords.

They must have handfasted, she realised. Bound together in marriage for a year and a day. If they did not suit as husband and wife, both could be free of each other after the trial period.

It was what Trahern had offered her—a temporary union. And though it wasn't threatening in any way, it bothered her. He'd already admitted that after they faced the men of Gall Tír, he would end the marriage.

He didn't even want to try, she realised. That's what troubled her. He treated the suggested union as one easily discarded. Her frustration heightened, for what woman wanted a marriage like that? Yet she couldn't deny the feelings she held for him in her heart. He made her feel safe, almost beloved. It bothered her to let him go.

In the firelight, Trahern's mask gleamed, and though he attempted a smile when his brother Patrick greeted him, she saw the strain beneath it and a hint of guilt. Would he tell Patrick the truth of his birth, that they were not brothers? Or would it matter at all?

They passed by a table of food, and Trahern reached for a loaf of bread. She, in turn, chose a flask of wine. Hunger gnawed at her stomach, and he chose a place for them beside one of the fires. Tearing the loaf in half, he handed her the bread. She tasted it and then took a sip of wine from the flask, passing it to him.

His fingers brushed against hers when he took the flask, and her heartbeat quickened. In the firelight, his hair was a dark colour, still cut close to his scalp. Grey eyes watched over her, and the rest of the world seemed to slip away.

'You look like an ancient god, wearing that,' she teased, pointing towards his mask.

His mouth didn't smile, but he removed the mask and set it aside. 'I'm not a god, Morren. Just a man.'

A man she'd turned away. A soft shiver of regret flowed over her skin at the memory. Trahern had shown her that a man's touch didn't have to be degrading or painful. It could be something beautiful.

All around them, she saw men and women together. Trahern's eyes faltered upon the handfasted couple. Though he said nothing, she sensed something in his gaze. Was it envy?

Confusion tangled up her thoughts, for she saw that her refusal had indeed bothered him. She'd struck down his pride, believing that he'd wanted only to use her in the arranged marriage.

But perhaps that wasn't it at all. In his grey eyes, she saw the loneliness of his life. He'd been a traveller, moving from place to place while his brothers had their own homes and families. Now, he'd lost the only stability he had, without the MacEgan name to call his own.

She ached for his loss, and in that moment, she realised how much she cared about him. Just as he made her feel safe, she wanted to offer him the comfort of her own embrace.

His marriage proposal had been awkward and clumsy. But she sensed that he would have honoured the vows spoken, treating her like a cherished bride. Though it might be an arrangement at first, perhaps it could become something more.

Did she want that? To fall asleep with his arms around her and awaken beside him each morning? The very thought opened up a longing deep within her. She wondered if it were even possible, to push away the darkness of her past and learn what it meant to feel desire.

It was growing late, and she ate the remainder of her food, realising that most of the men and women had retired for the night. She was about to ask Trahern to walk back to the castle with her, when she suddenly heard a noise.

Frowning, she listened, trying to identify what it was. There was a rhythmic, panting sound, coupled with a female moan. A man grunted, and she recognised what she was hearing.

A flash of panic came over her, and Trahern saw it. Images poured through her, and she set down her bread, clenching her knees to her chest.

Just get up and leave, she told herself. *You don't have to listen.* And yet, her feet wouldn't move.

Trahern took her hand, saying, 'He's not hurting her, Morren. Don't be afraid.'

Throaty moans came from the couple, and she threw herself into Trahern's arms, trying to block out the sound. More harsh memories battered at her, threatening to drown her. But through it all, he held her.

He'd become her stronghold, her shelter from the darkness. In his arms, she had what she needed most—a man who understood her pain.

She knelt on the ground with her arms around his neck. Trahern murmured words of reassurance, his wide palms smoothing down her spine. Like a healing touch, she warmed to it.

And in that moment, she realised she needed him, this strong man who had lost so much. In spite of everything, he'd always been there for her. Could she do less for him?

His eyes were intensely focused upon her, as though no one else existed. She brought his arms to her waist, reaching up to his shoulders. Behind him came the satisfied moans of the lovers; after a time, their voices fell into silence.

Her mind drifted back to the handfasted couple she'd seen earlier. A year and a day wasn't so very long to ask. It was enough time to learn whether the arrangement could become a lasting union. Her one hesitation was the prospect of the marriage bed.

'Are you all right?' he asked, releasing her from his embrace.

She nodded, taking a breath. Best to speak her mind and be honest with him about the thoughts troubling her. 'Trahern, if I were to agree to your marriage proposal, I don't want you to despise me.' Her cheeks warmed with embarrassment. 'I can't be…like most women.' When her gaze shifted in the direction of the lovers, he seemed to understand her meaning.

'Do you trust me?' he prompted.

'Yes.'

'Then know that I would never hurt you, nor despise you. No matter what happens.'

She lifted her face until her mouth was a breath away from his. So badly she wanted to believe it. And though it went against her instincts, she found herself saying, 'I'll marry you, Trahern. Until after we've settled the matter of the *Lochlannach*.'

He nodded, but there was no sense of anticipation or joy in his face. She hid her disappointment, wishing there was the hope of something more.

The following afternoon, Trahern found himself pacing. He hadn't seen Morren, not since she'd voiced her desire to handfast. Though he'd behaved as though it were nothing of importance, that wasn't true at all. When she'd agreed to marry him, he'd felt a sense of relief. Not simply because he would gain Patrick's support, but also for his own reasons.

He wanted to be close to Morren, even if it would only be for a short time.

Last night, when she'd taken refuge in his arms, he'd wanted to shield her from the world. When she'd clung to him, it was as if she'd become a physical part of him, one he couldn't let go, even though he had to.

A heaviness rested in his spirit, for, despite his promises not to touch her, he wanted Morren. His body seemed to mock him for the thought. Last night, he'd barely been able to keep control over his lust. He'd desired Morren so badly, his hands had been shaking. And when they'd overheard another couple making love, he'd imagined joining with her, sheathing his hard length within her moist depths.

His mood darkened, for it wasn't wise to let his thoughts go down that path. Thank the saints, their marriage would only be temporary. Keeping his hands off Morren would likely kill him.

It bothered him that she hadn't arrived for the handfasting yet. Queen Isabel and Aileen had gone about their way, saying nothing of the ceremony tonight. Had Morren told them of their plans to wed? Did anyone know?

From the casual behaviour of his family, he doubted it. Trahern had worn his best clothing, a tunic that was a dark shade of red. His sword hung at his waist, and he'd fastened his cloak with a golden brooch shaped like a serpent. He felt like an anxious lad, about to kiss his first woman. The next group of handfastings would take place at sundown, with Father Brían to bless them. And he didn't know if Morren would come to him then or not.

'You look nervous, lad,' came an old woman's voice. It was Annle.

He offered her a smile in greeting, and she motioned him

closer. 'I have something for you. I've kept it all these years, and it may be that you'll want to have it.' Annle pressed a cloth-wrapped packet into his hand. 'It belonged to *her*.'

He didn't need to ask whom she meant. Without elaborating, the old healer hobbled away to join the children. A small boy hugged her leg, before Annle dropped a kiss upon his forehead.

Trahern waited until he was alone before unwrapping the packet. Inside, he found an unusual stone. Upon the stone, it seemed that the spirit of a fish had been captured, carved within the rock. A small section of the stone had broken off, but the image of the fish was clear. Someone had bored a hole into the rock, lacing a strip of leather through it to form a necklace.

He rubbed his thumb over the rough imprint of the fish, wondering what sort of woman his mother had been. Like the stone, it was as though there were a piece missing of himself. A mystery that would never fully resolve.

And deep inside, he feared that the man who had fathered him was one of the *Lochlannach* at Gall Tír. Would he find a man who looked like him, among the enemy?

Lifting the necklace over his head, Trahern tucked it beneath his tunic, where it rested upon his chest. He wished he could have known the woman who had given him life. It felt strange to wear something that had belonged to her.

'Trahern,' a voice called out. 'Are you coming to witness the handfastings?' Connor MacEgan approached, but then stopped short at the sight of Trahern's finery. A cheeky grin spread over the man's face. 'Well, now. You look fetching, don't you?'

Trahern only shrugged, studying the crowds of people for a glimpse of Morren. 'What do you want?'

'What do I want?' Connor repeated. His face twisted, and he uttered a dramatic sigh. 'If you really want to know, sleep is what I'm wanting, brother. A full night of sleep.'

He rubbed at his head, adding, 'Finn came running into our chamber last night, claiming he was afraid of the dark. And not a minute later, Dylan joined him.' Yawning, Connor added, 'Wait until you've children of your own. They're both a blessing and the curse of your existence.'

Trahern said nothing, for he couldn't imagine himself as a father. Not with Morren as his bride, or anyone else. It seemed like an impossible vision, though he wouldn't have minded having sons.

'Don't worry, Trahern,' Connor teased. 'One day you'll know what I mean, if Morren agrees to wed you.'

'She—' Trahern started to answer, but Connor cut him off.

'After all, you're too tall and not nearly as handsome as the rest of us.' Connor reached out to rub his head, and Trahern caught the man's wrist.

'This isn't a laughing matter, Connor.' He knew his brother was only trying to break his foul mood by teasing him. But the jest had the reverse effect. All his life Trahern had been teased about his height. Many a time, he'd used it to his advantage, fighting with Bevan or Connor when they'd insulted him.

But today, it only reminded him that they weren't his true family. There was a reason why they looked nothing alike. It sobered him, making him feel like more of an outsider. He almost wished he'd never heard the truth from Annle. Beneath his tunic, the shell necklace felt harsh upon his skin.

'Have you seen Morren?' he asked Connor.

'She's with the women. She went to speak with Aileen

earlier, but that's all I know.' His brother's eyes gleamed. 'Did she agree to the marriage? You did ask her, didn't you?'

'I did ask,' he said tightly, 'and I think she might.'

Connor's face transformed from surprise into happiness. He slapped him on the back, adding, 'Good. It's about time you opened your eyes and saw what was in front of you.'

'And what do you mean by that?'

'She's good for you, Trahern,' Connor said. 'You're happier with her.' His brother's face turned serious. 'I know this past season has been hard on you. When we saw you at Midsummer's Eve, I'd never seen you like that before.'

'Like what?'

'Enraged,' Connor admitted. 'You looked like you would have taken a dagger to your own throat. Like you cared about nothing any more. Not even us.'

Trahern stared into his brother's face. He'd been so caught up in his grief and his need for revenge that he'd kept everyone away. 'I wanted to die,' he admitted. 'Every time I saw you with Aileen or Patrick with Isabel, I was eaten up with jealousy. All I could think of was what I'd lost with Ciara.'

'It was terrible, seeing you like that.' Connor rested his scarred hand upon Trahern's shoulder. 'We're family, Trahern. And whether you know it or not, your pain was ours.' His dark expression softened. 'If Morren is the cause of bringing you back to us, I can only be grateful to her.'

As they walked toward the inner bailey, Connor's words forced his spirits even lower. For they weren't truly family, were they? His brothers believed that they shared the same parents, when there was no blood between them. All they had were memories.

He held his tongue, not wanting to lose that. Though Morren had claimed his brothers would stand by him, even knowing the truth, he couldn't bring himself to admit it. Not yet, for he didn't want to relinquish the MacEgan name.

In the small courtyard, several couples waited with the priest. Among them, he saw his youngest brother Ewan holding the hand of his new wife, Honora.

Though the pair had been married only a few weeks ago, there was no dimming their happiness. Honora rushed forward and hugged him. 'Ewan told me you were here, Trahern. I'm so glad to see you.' She reached up and rubbed his head, smiling at the new growth of hair. 'You're looking more handsome, I must say.'

He ignored her comment and voiced the question, 'Why is it that women are fascinated with touching my head?'

'Enjoy it,' Ewan urged. 'If women would come up and rub my head, I'd shave it every day.'

'And I'd run them through with a blade,' Honora retorted. 'Watch yourself, MacEgan.'

Ewan kissed his wife. 'You can rub my head whenever you want, *a stór*. Or other things.'

Honora's face turned crimson. 'I can't believe you said that out loud.'

His brother's teasing made him laugh, and with his humour restored, Trahern joined them to watch the handfastings. Couple after couple spoke their promises, and Father Brían blessed the marriages, combining pagan and Christian traditions. It was the way of their family, remembering the past, along with the present.

When the last marriage was completed, he ignored the emptiness of disappointment. Morren hadn't come. He wondered if she'd changed her mind again. Grimacing, he turned away, ignoring the platters of steaming food that were brought forth from the kitchen.

'Trahern,' came a voice. It was Connor's wife, Aileen. Her face was pale, but she took him aside from the others. 'I spoke with Morren this afternoon.'

The devastated expression on her face made him wary. 'Is she all right?'

Aileen's nod was hesitant. 'She told me…everything.' Tears filled up the healer's eyes, and she reached out to take his hands. 'I understand now why you're so protective of her.'

'Where is she?'

'She's coming to join you and Father Brían now.' Aileen reached out and touched his cheek. 'But you should know something, Trahern. Though her body may have fully healed, there are some injuries that haven't. And I doubt if she'll have children.'

'It doesn't matter,' he responded. It was the truth. He didn't own his own land, and he had no need for heirs.

'I bid you happiness,' Aileen said, stepping away. Within moments, he saw Morren arriving to speak with the priest. Her hair was crowned with heather, and she wore a gown he'd never seen before. The forest-green silk was trimmed with fur, the cloth vibrant in colour.

'It's the gown you meant for Morren to have,' Aileen murmured. 'Isabel arranged to purchase the silk, after you sent that lad off with a handful of coins the other morning.'

'It wasn't enough for silk,' he argued.

'No, but Isabel contributed some. She thought there would come an occasion when Morren would need a finer gown. And I see she was right.'

It pleased him to know that he'd contributed to the gown, though he'd only intended to offer Morren something better to wear than her travelling clothes.

'We spent most of the day sewing,' Aileen continued. She

rubbed at her fingers. 'Morren looks beautiful, don't you think?'

Trahern took a step forward, then another. His bride's hair was intertwined with tiny golden balls, which accentuated the fair colour of the strands. 'She does.'

He walked past Aileen to join Morren. He took her hands in his, feeling spellbound by her appearance. 'The gown looks well on you.'

Her cheeks grew pink, and she gave his hands a faint squeeze. 'Thank you.'

Then they turned to the priest, and Trahern grew aware that all of his brothers and wives had come close to hear their vows. As he spoke the words that bound him to Morren, he didn't miss the way Patrick drew Isabel closer. Or the way each of his brothers held his wife, as if to echo the promises made. He was glad for their presence, though the burden of his past weighed down upon him.

Morren's hand squeezed his, her blue eyes soft. Though she appeared uncomfortable with everyone watching them, her lips curved in a faint smile. Whether she meant to reassure him or herself, he didn't know. But when he looked into her eyes, he was startled at the contentment of having her at his side.

Only a few weeks ago, she couldn't have endured the touch of his hand in hers. So much had changed between them. Within her expression, he saw faith and trust. His fingers tightened over hers in a silent promise to take care of her.

When the three cords were wrapped around his wrist and Morren's, the MacEgans applauded with cheers and encouragement to kiss her. Trahern didn't ask permission, but touched his lips to Morren's. They were hesitant, but she accepted his kiss of peace.

'Kiss her longer than that!' Ewan called out.

Trahern started to refuse, not wanting to embarrass his bride. But Morren had already risen up on her tiptoes. Though she was flustered, he saw amusement on her face.

This time when he kissed her, he tilted her face to meet his. He hardly heard the voices around them or the teasing when her unbound hand went around his neck.

When their lips touched, he gave her the kiss a new husband ought to give his wife. Hungry and heated, he captured her mouth, coaxing her to surrender.

Morren rested her hand upon his face, then broke free of the kiss to the sound of loud cheers. Her face was crimson, and Trahern held her waist close.

The remainder of the evening had blurred, and he hardly remembered any of it, though they had shared food and drink. He couldn't take his eyes off of his bride, and at one moment, Morren cast him a smile.

'I'm not going to leave you, Trahern. Our hands are bound together,' she reminded him. 'I couldn't if I wanted to.'

And yet, beneath her words, he sensed a sudden edge, as though something bothered her. He lowered his voice to murmur, 'You seem frightened. What troubles you?'

From the glance she cast towards Aileen, he sensed he knew what it was. 'Let them believe what they want,' he said softly. 'I won't touch you.'

Morren tried to muster a smile, though her face had gone pale. Trahern led her away from the others so they could speak alone about whatever it was.

'I've been thinking about what happened between us last night,' she admitted. 'I turned it over in my mind so many times, I could hardly sleep at all.'

He waited for her to continue, and she lowered her chin. 'You told me what it would be like, if you gave in to your desires.' A faint shiver rocked through her. 'And though it terrifies me, I want to rid myself of the unwanted memories.'

She rested her bound hand upon his heart, staring into his eyes. 'I want to become your wife in body, as well as in name. For however long that is.'

Chapter Nineteen

Later that night after the feasting was over, the King and Queen had offered them a chamber to themselves. Unlike other weddings Morren had attended, there were no women to laugh and undress her. Thankfully, Aileen had kept the other wives away, allowing them privacy.

But now Morren stared at the bed in the centre of the room. It was small, leaving no doubt that she and Trahern would touch each other while they slept.

She bit her lip to keep it from trembling. The fear consumed her so badly, she could hardly move. She didn't know if she could go through with her promise. At the deepest level, she was afraid of losing her courage, of screaming and trying to push him away. Or, worst of all, lying beneath him while he used her body for his own pleasure.

A hard knot formed in her throat, for she didn't want to believe it would be like that. She wanted so badly to let go of the past, to move beyond her fear. But she sensed that she would be nothing but a disappointment to him.

Trahern reached to loosen the cords that bound their hands.

Morren took a breath, willing herself not to cry. To her surprise, he took her in his arms, holding her. His strong arms were like a shield, and she breathed in the welcome scent of a man who cared.

'You're tired, aren't you?' he murmured.

The words were an offer to escape his touch, to simply sleep beside him. But she found herself saying, 'No. I'm all right.'

His hand pressed against her hair, loosening the plaited strands until they fell free around her shoulders. He removed the crown she'd formed of vines and heather. The green fragrance calmed her, reminding her of the hillside where Aileen had helped her find the late-blooming flowers.

'Come and sit,' he bade her, leading her to a wooden bench. A steaming basin of water rested upon the floor, no doubt placed there by the Queen's servants. She recognised sprigs of dried lavender floating in the water, no doubt to soothe her anxiety.

She started to take off her shoes, but Trahern interrupted her. 'Let me.'

He removed the shoes, immersing her bare feet in the water. His large hands washed her skin, massaging the soreness from them. Morren closed her eyes, surrendering to the gentleness of his touch. He poured warm water over her calves, his hands caressing her skin as though she were something precious.

Warmth slid over her, and she looked down into his eyes. He was focused upon her, humbling himself like a servant. When he saw her gaze, his hands grew still.

'Don't fear me, Morren,' he said slowly. 'I'll make no demands of you.' He reached for a cloth and dried her feet. 'As you said last night, nothing's changed.' His face ventured a quiet smile.

She didn't know what she'd expected, but it wasn't this. And then it occurred to her that he'd once planned to marry Ciara. Was he thinking of her and what they'd shared together?

'If you don't want to be with me, I understand,' she managed. Shame poured through her, for even asking this of him.

He was hesitant, choosing his words carefully. 'It's not what I had intended.' He sat down on the bed and took his shoes off. 'I think it's better if I leave you alone.'

An unexpected tangle of frustration balled up in her stomach. She'd steeled herself to do this, to face her greatest fear. The last thing she'd expected was for him to turn her down.

'All right,' she lied. 'That's all right, then.'

Was it so wrong to hope that he'd give in to the flush of desire both of them had felt last night? Why did he have to suddenly behave with honour?

This morn, she'd confessed everything to Aileen. She'd released all the painful nightmares she'd held inside, and the healer had hugged her tightly. Then Aileen had said that Trahern could heal the wounds no one else could see. That if Morren asked anything of him, he would not turn her away.

And yet he had.

'I've hurt your feelings, haven't I?' His deep voice held pity, and it was beginning to irritate her.

She stood up and walked towards the bed. 'No. That's not it.' Before he could say anything patronising, she spilled out her thoughts. 'I wanted to forget about what was done to me. And I thought you could…help me to overcome my fear of… joining with a man.'

Though she could hardly believe she was telling him all of this, she couldn't seem to stop herself. 'You wanted me last night. You told me all the things you wanted to do.'

Her skin was alive with a blend of fear and desire. Trahern was staring at her, as though he didn't know what to say or do. Driven by shame, Morren blurted the rest out. 'I know this isn't a lasting arrangement, but I thought that, maybe, you could—'

She stopped speaking, feeling like an utter fool. 'Forget what I said. It was a bad idea.'

But Trahern hadn't taken his eyes from her. There was definite interest there, but she sensed the conflicted feelings. 'I haven't been with a woman in a very long time, *a chara*.'

'Oh.' It seemed a ridiculous thing to say, but she could think of nothing better.

'I don't want you to hold regrets,' he added.

She let out a sigh, shrugging. 'It doesn't matter.' She tried to convince herself that the words were true. It was just as well, for she probably couldn't have gone through with it. And yet, unexpected regret spread through her.

'Don't look at me like that. I'm trying to do what's right.' His voice was grim, and she tried to force away her hurt feelings.

'I liked it better when you weren't thinking,' she admitted. 'I liked kissing you. It was nice.' She sat beside him on the bed, one foot tucked under her.

'Nice?' There was a dry tone to his voice, as if she'd insulted him.

'Well, yes.' Was he hoping for another compliment? 'You're very good at kissing.'

Trahern eyed her for a moment before he lifted his tunic away, baring hardened skin. She saw the outline of pectoral muscles and a tight stomach. The startling instinct to touch him came over her without warning, but she held her hands back.

He's only undressing because he plans to sleep, she told herself. *Not because he wants something else.*

Her pulse beat wildly, like a primitive drum. His grey eyes studied her, and beneath his gaze she grew flushed. Second thoughts collided with her courage, and now she wished she'd never spoken.

To distract herself from her embarrassment, she removed her overdress, leaving her *léine* on. The form-fitting gown hid every part of her body, and yet she shivered as Trahern watched her. She supposed she'd get warmer when she was beneath the coverlet.

But sleep would be impossible now.

'Come here, Morren,' he murmured, 'and I'll kiss you goodnight.' It was a way of pacifying her and yet setting boundaries.

Before she could say another word, his mouth touched hers lightly. It was more than the brush of their lips, but neither was it the captivating kiss that had stolen her wits yestereve. She leaned in, her hands resting upon his heartbeat.

Trahern shuddered, and she pulled her palms away, afraid she'd trespassed.

'No,' he murmured, putting her hands back. 'It's all right.'

Her hands moved tentatively, unsure of herself. But he fascinated her, with his honed muscles and warm, smooth skin. She trailed her fingers down his chest, over his ribcage to his waist. A breath escaped him, and Trahern's gaze grew heated. He tempted her in ways she didn't understand.

He laid down on his stomach, baring his back to her. 'Lie down beside me,' he offered. A small smile lifted his mouth. 'And if you want to keep touching me, I'll not complain.'

She hesitated, but realised that it would be more comfortable to stretch out on the mattress. There seemed to be no haste on his part, and so she laid down beside him while caressing his back with one hand.

He shivered when she reached his lower spine. Did she truly have that effect upon him? The instinct to taste his skin came over her, and she pressed her lips to the place her hands had just touched. A prickle of gooseflesh rippled over him, and she placed another kiss higher upon his spine.

She stopped, questioning what she was doing. Trahern rolled onto his side, and the look on his face held her captive.

'There's no need to stop.' He placed her hand on his back once again. 'I'll endure it if I must.' The teasing note in his voice made her relax, and this time she massaged his shoulders, growing bolder. With her fingers, she touched the back of his neck, reaching up to the fine hair upon his scalp.

He groaned, and his fingers clenched into the mattress. Encouraged by his response, she soothed the tension and knots from his neck. But when her lips brushed the nape of his neck, he rolled over.

Dark grey eyes caught hers in silent invitation. He cupped her nape, and her hair spilled between them. He drew her atop him, his mouth covering hers.

Like warm rain, his kiss melted through her, sinking down into the secret places of her body. She felt her breasts tighten against her *léine*, feeling heavier and more sensitive.

His hand slid beneath the hem of her gown and up her calves. He kissed her again, his thumb pressing lazy circles over her lower leg. Though the gesture was nothing more than what he'd done before when he'd washed her feet, it conjured an echoing sensation in other places. Her skin grew warmer, the underdress constraining her.

When his touch moved beneath the neckline of the gown

to touch her bare shoulders, she couldn't stop the wave of trembling that came over her.

'I want to take this off,' he said huskily. 'And God help me, I know it's wrong.'

Her throat closed up with shame, and a heavy silence descended between them. 'I shouldn't have asked you.'

He linked his fingers with hers. For a long time, he studied her, searching for answers, it seemed. 'You said you wanted to forget what had happened to you.'

She nodded. Just being near him made her feel desire, and she hadn't forgotten the way he'd evoked such a strong release. 'Aileen said…the best way to forget about that night was to replace it with better memories. And you're the only man I trust.'

His hand moved to her face, stroking a strand of hair behind her ear. 'Are you certain you want to do this?'

She gave a nod, trying to mask her fear.

'You hold all the power, *a mhuirnín*. Any time you want me to stop, speak the word.' His grey eyes held an irrevocable promise. In them, she saw desire, and something she couldn't quite understand.

Though she was terrified of what would happen next, she trusted him. 'Turn around.'

He did, rising from the bed and facing the opposite wall. Morren removed her *léine*, sliding naked beneath the coverlet. The rough wool abraded her bare skin, and she grew cold, both with fear and anticipation. Closing her eyes, she turned to the opposite wall and proclaimed, 'I'm ready.'

A moment later, she felt his weight upon the mattress, and he got under the covers with her. His feet touched hers, and when her hand brushed against his knee, she realised that he, too, was naked. Panic froze her in place, and she gritted her teeth when his palm touched her shoulders.

'Relax, *a mhuirnín*. Lie on your stomach.' When she obeyed, he moved the coverlet down to expose her back. His hands caressed her skin, massaging the back of her neck, just as she had done for him. Warmth permeated her, and he trailed a kiss down her spine.

The softness of his mouth made her think of the other night when he'd promised to kiss every part of her body. Would he? She shivered at the thought. What would it feel like?

Slowly, she rolled onto her side, revealing her breasts to him. His eyes grew hooded, dark with desire. 'I want to touch you,' he whispered. 'And I want to taste you.'

His words were heady, and she took a deep breath, bracing herself for what was to come. She gave a slight nod, but it couldn't have prepared her for the sensation of his thumb and forefinger, teasing the hardened tip of her nipple. Soft and sensual, he caressed the sensitive bud, and she felt an echoing sensation between her thighs. A shudder rocked through her, but it was nothing compared to the delicious warmth of his mouth upon her breast. His sleek tongue darted against the tip, coaxing her to pull him closer. He took her breast into his mouth, suckling one nipple while his hand teased the other. Her breathing quickened, her fingers grasping the softness of his short hair.

'You taste like the sweetest spring berries,' he said against her flesh, and his mouth moved lower to her stomach.

It was like fire, licking at each limb, consuming her with heat. She held on to his neck, shuddering as his palm moved over her hip.

It took the greatest courage of all to lie still when his hand brushed over the mound of curls between her legs. Her knees locked, instinctively trying to remain shut. Trahern didn't argue, but he lowered his hand to rest upon the triangle.

'I've never wanted any woman more than you,' he admitted. 'And there's nothing I want more than to watch you soar with release. I want to see your face and watch you come apart.'

His finger slid to rest upon the flesh just inside the top of her intimate folds. Though she hadn't unclenched her legs at all, she was shocked at the arousing sensation of his finger stroking her.

She found herself leaning into his touch, straining for him to reach the part of her that ached. His mouth covered her nipple once more, tantalising her, and making her shift her thighs together.

It frustrated her, that she needed him to touch somewhere else, and yet he wasn't in the right place. The rhythmic touch of his hand became a torment. Morren lifted her hips, opening to him.

When she did, he lowered his thumb just slightly. Not enough to ease her, but closer.

She arched again, gripping the back of his head.

'Do you feel it?' he asked, his voice growing ragged. His face held the intensity of a warrior upon a battlefield, as though he'd fight to the death for her.

'Yes.' A shiver rocked through her, and she opened her legs a little further. He rewarded her by teasing at the wetness, dipping his hand against her.

It startled her to realise that she wanted to feel his caress there. It was nothing at all like the night she'd been hurt. Trahern was completely attuned to her, his hand coaxing the same dizzying sensation she'd felt on the night he'd pressed his knee against her centre.

She gave a cry when he suddenly found the spot she'd been

yearning for, and instantly she fragmented. A rush of hot shivers broke through her, with shattering waves of delicious heat. He kissed her again, and she clung hard, her body shivering against the pleasure. Her knee eased over his hip, and she felt the length of him pressed close.

Instantly, she stopped moving. His mouth moved to her throat, soothing her. 'It's all right if you want me to stop now.'

She did, for what he'd given her was wonderful, intimate and so pleasurable that she wanted to treasure the memory. But he hadn't experienced the same release. His body was tense, though he tried to mask it.

Morren faced him and touched his cheek, wondering if she dared allow him to go further. She rested her head against his chest, feeling the warmth of his arms around her. His hand idly rubbed her back, and when her breasts pressed against his chest, an answering warmth seemed to unfold from within her womb.

Her leg rested upon his hip, but a moment later, he rolled onto his stomach to keep his erection from touching her. He understood her fear, as no other man could. And he'd put her needs above his own.

If she turned him away now, he would accept it. But she wanted to experience a true marriage with Trahern.

A year and a day, she reminded herself. Perhaps less. The thought of leaving broke her spirit into a thousand pieces.

But for tonight, they had each other. She traced her hand over his closely cut hair, down his strong jaw line. 'Don't hide yourself from me. It's all right.'

The words were a lie, but she was determined to get through this. She would endure what she must, because she wanted him to experience the same thrilling rush.

Trahern nipped at her palm and rolled onto his side. This time, she felt his manhood nestled against her warmth. He adjusted her leg so that the tip of him rested at her entrance.

'Slowly,' she pleaded.

And he listened. Each second seemed to last an eternity, but when his thickness nudged at her, she held herself so tight, it took the greatest control not to cry out.

'Easy,' he breathed. With his mouth, he kissed her lips, his tongue sliding within her mouth, just as his body pressed against her flesh. He used his manhood to coax another response, conjuring a sleek wetness. Another shiver passed over her, and it became easier to join his flesh within hers.

The distraction of his kiss helped, and she let herself enjoy the hot pressure of his mouth. His hand moved down her spine to her bottom, where he gave a gentle squeeze.

To her shock, the motion angled her in such a way that he was fully sheathed. Trahern didn't move, his eyes locked upon her.

'Are you all right?' he managed. Perspiration gleamed upon his forehead, and she saw his struggle not to hurt her.

'Yes.' The intrusion didn't hurt at all. To her surprise, it felt…good to be joined with him.

He started to withdraw, and the friction made her gasp with the startling sensation that seemed to caress her from the inside.

His mouth kissed her nipple once again, and she felt it as surely as if he'd kissed her intimately. Once more, he buried himself in her womb.

With smooth, long strokes, he filled her. But he was taking nothing from her. Nor was he using her for his own fulfilment.

Instead, he was using his body to evoke her pleasure. The

same sense of building urgency came over her again. Each penetration aroused her, his shaft causing her breath to come in quick gasps.

'Will you be all right if I do this?' he asked, moving faster. He brought her beneath him, balancing his weight on both hands. The change in pace made her body rise to meet his.

'More,' she breathed, wanting him to feel the same way she was feeling now. She wanted him to come apart, to see the rush of pleasure in his own expression.

Her encouragement was all he needed. He raised her knees, and with each penetration, she cried out with a keening need. Her hips moved in counterpoint to his, faster and faster. At last, she wrapped both legs around his waist, holding on to him while he surged deep inside.

She felt him the instant he shuddered, his body finally succumbing to the explosion rocking within her. With his last thrust, he sent her past the brink once again, and she trembled in his arms.

His large body covered hers, and she could do nothing but hold him. Tears filled her up inside, and she cried.

For he'd reawakened the part of her that had been lost.

Chapter Twenty

'Are you ready?' Trahern asked quietly.

'Yes.' Morren clung to the reins of her horse, her posture tense. The grey gown she'd chosen was one she'd altered to fit, given by Katla. It moulded to her waist, and she'd braided her hair back from her face, her hood shielding her head. It was bitter cold, and Trahern wished they were anywhere but outside the gates of Gall Tír.

He'd much rather take her back to the chamber they'd shared at Laochre, and warm her, skin to skin. Over the past three days since their handfasting, he'd made love to her during most of the night hours, falling asleep with her hair against his lips, her body nestled beside him.

And each time, he cursed himself for it. He'd never intended for this marriage to be anything but an arrangement. But with each day that passed, he found himself fighting what was happening between them. He'd let himself love a woman once, and Ciara's death had almost destroyed him. Love had weakened him, leaving a monster in its wake. A man without a soul.

He couldn't let it happen again. Already, he'd let Morren get too close to him. The sooner she identified the men and returned home to her clan, the better. He'd come here for justice, to avenge Ciara and the Ó Reilly clan. And he couldn't forget that purpose.

He brought his horse alongside Morren's. 'It will be over in a few hours,' he reassured her. 'We'll find them, and I'll send you back to Laochre.'

She gave a nod, but her cheeks were unnaturally pale. Her knuckles whitened on the reins as she followed him inside.

Leading their group was his brother, King Patrick, surrounded by his retainers. Beside the King rode their youngest brother, Ewan, and his wife, Honora. Trahern was grateful that Honora had come, for unbeknownst to the Hardrata people, she was a skilled warrior who would help him to guard Morren.

His nerves were drawn taut as a bowstring when he helped Morren dismount. She kept her face hooded, to hide her features. The Viking guards were on edge, for the presence of Laochre soldiers evoked a physical threat.

This was not a visit among friends, and they knew it.

Morren clenched his hand, her eyes searching. Her fingers were cold in his, and he leaned in to murmur softly, 'Tell me if you see any of them. Or if you want to leave at any time, Ewan will take you back.'

'I'd rather see this through.' She walked beside him, and one of the Hardrata guards led them to the house of the chief, near the centre of the settlement.

Gunnar remained behind the others, and Trahern saw tension in the man's face. There was something more the *Lochlannach* wasn't telling him. A reason for being here that had nothing to do with the attack on the Ó Reillys. But there was no time to ask why.

Before they reached the chief's hut, Morren's hand suddenly tightened so hard upon his, he thought she was going to break his fingers. He looked to see the source of her anxiety, and one of the men standing nearby abruptly walked away.

He hardly glimpsed the man's face, but he leaned over to his brother Ewan. 'Follow him.'

Ewan had a talent for slipping away, unnoticed. And Trahern had no doubt his brother would find the guilty man. More than all else, Trahern wanted to join in the pursuit, but he had to speak with the chief. He forced himself to remain patient as they entered the chief's dwelling.

Vigus Hardrata sat upon an elaborately carved chair upon a dais, one that had been passed down for generations. It had been made by Trahern's grandfather Kieran, as a gift to his sister Aisling, who had wed one of the Hardrata warriors.

The chair was also an unspoken reminder of the ties between them. The chief stood and invited Patrick to sit with him.

'Something has gone wrong,' Vigus began. 'You would not have brought soldiers among us, otherwise.'

Patrick gave a nod of acknowledgement and motioned Trahern to approach the dais. All eyes turned to him as he took Morren's hand. She lowered her hood, revealing her face to the chief. Beneath her serene expression, he saw the bone-deep fear. He sent her a silent look of reassurance that he would keep her safe. Even so, she didn't release his hand.

'This past summer, my wife's home, Glen Omrigh, was attacked by five of your men,' he said. 'They burned homes and killed innocent people.'

'And how do you know they were Hardrata?' the chief asked.

'One of the raiders returned to the Ó Reilly *cashel* seeking the rest of his payment,' Trahern asserted. 'He claimed that Gall Tír was his home before he died.'

The chief betrayed no emotion on his face. 'If what you say is true, we will not let such actions go unpunished.' He leaned forward, steepling his hands. 'But there must be evidence of your claims.' His blue eyes were cold, his grey hair ragged against his bearded face. The chief reminded Trahern of his Great-Uncle Tharand, a stoic man who valued honour above all else.

Trahern reached into the pouch at his waist and poured a handful of coins into his palm. Offering them to the chief, he said, 'Few men would have coins such as these. They are from an ancient hoard.'

One of the *Lochlannach* leaned forward to examine the coins. He whispered into the chief's ear, and the chief's expression darkened. 'A man may possess coins such as these. But it does not make him a murderer.'

'We have witnesses who saw the men,' Trahern continued. 'Those who lost sons and fathers.' His voice hardened. 'Women were violated, and we demand justice.'

'Why did the Ó Reilly chieftain send you in his stead?' Vigus asked.

'Because he is dead,' Trahern responded, 'and cannot speak for those whose voices were silenced.' His anger was rising, and he rested his hand around Morren's shoulders. 'I also speak on behalf of my wife.'

An uneasy silence filled the space. His brother Patrick intervened, saying, 'As leader of the Hardrata, you are likely aware of which men left the *longphort* last summer.'

The chief gave a slight nod. 'But they deserve to be questioned.'

Patrick inclined his head. 'And we are here to witness their confession.' The threat of war hung between the men like an invisible blade. 'Bring them here and let them speak.'

The chief whispered to his servant, his expression furious. 'It is true that several of our men left, to visit one of the tribes in the west. One did not return.'

Gunnar stepped forward at that moment. He extended a knife, hilt first. 'I believe this belonged to the raider. It hung at his side.'

Trahern shot a look at Gunnar. He recalled Gunnar removing the blade, and it was definite evidence against the intruder they'd captured.

The chief examined the blade, and his grim mood heightened. 'This did belong to Illugi, the man who did not return.'

A hint of satisfaction passed over Gunnar's face before he nodded at Trahern, as if to confirm his support. Trahern was grateful for it. He'd known that the coins were not enough to support his claims, but Gunnar's proof was undeniable.

Vigus rose from his chair. 'The four men will face their trial this afternoon. You may observe, if that is your wish.'

The noise of a man struggling resounded from behind them. Trahern saw his brother Ewan coming forward with his captive, the man Morren had identified earlier.

'Release me,' the *Lochlannach* demanded. But when he saw the chief staring at him, he froze. His gaze flickered over the visitors, stopping upon Morren. She raised her chin and confronted him.

Like the face of Death, she stared at him, willing him to acknowledge his guilt.

'She lies!' the man proclaimed. 'Whatever she told you, Vigus, I have done nothing to her.'

The chief ignored the man's protestations and signalled to

another servant. 'Bind Brael, and prepare him to face his trial by fire.'

Rage lined the chief's face, and Vigus stared at Brael. 'The woman gave no accusations at all. You proclaimed your guilt when you tried to deny it.' With a wave of dismissal, he commanded, 'Take him.'

Morren buried her face against Trahern during the trial. Heated coals were set upon the ground until they glowed red-hot. One of the men broke down and confessed his guilt, which earned him the punishment of exile. The Hardrata people turned their backs upon him, treating him as though he no longer existed.

Icy fear slashed through her. They were just going to let him go? With no other penalty than to become an outlaw? Her hands trembled as she watched him, but as he passed the group of Ó Reilly men, she saw Áron Ó Reilly seize the raider. Áron took his dagger and slit the outlaw's throat before anyone could stop him.

The Ó Reilly met Trahern's gaze. 'For Ciara.'

The Hardrata people pretended as though they'd seen nothing. Morren covered her mouth with her hands, horrified at what she'd just witnessed.

Trahern pulled her close and whispered in her ear, 'An outlaw may be killed with no consequences. It's why the others haven't confessed their guilt.'

Though she could hardly bear to watch, she was unable to tear her gaze away. One by one, the remaining raiders were forced to walk across the glowing coals. Their screams pierced through her consciousness, though Morren tried to block out the sound.

It was a brutal trial, where it was believed that God would

protect the innocent. A man whose flesh did not burn would be allowed to go free. But in this instance, she knew that each of the men was guilty.

Another raider stumbled when he walked across the coals, and his clothing caught on fire. He cried out for help and tried to run. Within moments, the fire consumed him, and his screams fell silent.

It was then that Morren caught the last raider staring at her. His features had haunted her through her nightmares. He'd been the first man to attack her, and she'd never forgotten him. His cold gaze ripped through her with hatred. Though he had accepted his trial and punishment, there was no remorse upon his face—only anger that he'd been caught.

She learned from the chief that his name was Egill Hardrata, a mercenary who'd been punished for lesser crimes once before. But Egill remained silent throughout the questioning, his face defiant. Neither he, nor the other surviving raider, would admit who had paid them to attack.

Egill and the other raider stumbled toward the gates, their feet bleeding and charred from the coals. But when Áron Ó Reilly attacked, Egill dodged the blow and tripped the Ó Reilly man, stealing the blade away.

It was as if he'd ignored the pain of his wounded feet. As if nothing could penetrate the shield of indifference he'd cloaked around himself.

The last rays of the afternoon sun were dying, the evening slipping free of its shadows. Even when both men were gone, Morren couldn't seem to release the rigid tension in her shoulders. Aye, it was doubtful that either of the raiders would survive without shelter or food, now that it was nearly winter. But their faces would remain imprinted upon her memory—the faces of her nightmare.

Morren wasn't aware she was weeping until Trahern's hand brushed across her cheek, wiping the tears away. 'It's over, *a stór*,' he murmured. 'They won't trouble you again.'

She knew it, but right now, everything within her was so tired. 'I wish we could leave now,' she pleaded. She'd had enough of torture and death.

Trahern lifted her hood over her hair, trying to protect her from the cold wind. 'It's late, Morren. I'll have Ewan take you back to Laochre in the morning.'

'What about you?' He spoke as if he wasn't coming with them. She shivered, not knowing his intentions.

Trahern's hand went to his sword hilt, his gaze focused on the outlaws' path. 'Patrick is staying behind to speak with the chief.' He eyed Áron, who had mounted his horse and was preparing to follow the outlaws. 'And I have unfinished business, *a stór*.'

Though he'd implied that he would protect Áron and bring him back, she suspected there was much more that he meant to do.

'I'm going with you,' Gunnar demanded.

Trahern stared at the *Lochlannach* and shook his head. 'This isn't your fight.' He strode toward the horses, adding, 'Áron Ó Reilly is past talking. He wants the blood of those men, and I don't want him going after them alone.'

He saw no reason for Gunnar to join them. For that matter, he didn't understand why the Norseman had come on this journey. From the time they'd left the Ó Reilly *cashel*, Gunnar had kept his reasons to himself.

Trahern stopped short, suddenly wanting the answers. He turned on the *Lochlannach*, demanding, 'You never did say why you came to Gall Tír.'

Gunnar evaded the question. 'I've reasons of my own.'

'If you want to come with us, you'd better share those reasons.'

The Norseman stared at him, as if shifting the decision in his mind. 'My mother was taken,' he said at last. 'When I was a young boy, we lost her. One moment she was holding my hand, and the next, she was stolen away on horseback.'

He expelled a breath, admitting, 'I've always wondered what happened to her. We looked among all the surrounding clans and settlements. But she was gone.'

'You think the people of Gall Tír took her.'

He lifted his shoulders in a shrug. 'I've never known. But when I saw your face, I had my suspicions.'

A coldness pierced through Trahern, when he understood what Gunnar was suggesting. He'd heard Annle's story that night, about the Norse woman who had come to them and borne a child.

'She was pregnant when they took her,' he admitted. 'My father told me about it when I was older.' Regret threaded through Gunnar's voice.

Without speaking, Trahern reached inside his tunic and unfastened the necklace Annle had given him. When he saw the image of the fish, Gunnar's fingers closed over the piece.

'She loved the sea,' he admitted. 'My father gave her that.' From inside a fold of his tunic, Gunnar pulled out a chipped piece of stone. He held it up to the necklace, and the two pieces fit together. 'This is all I have of her.' Gunnar withdrew the stone, his expression resigned. 'I was too young to remember her, but I swore I would find out what happened. I promised my father.'

'Is your father still alive?'

Gunnar shook his head. 'He died a few years ago.'

It was unsettling, realising he would never know the father who had given him life. And yet, Gunnar Dalrata was his blood brother, his true kin, though they had been separated for most of their lives.

'Our mother died after my birth,' Trahern admitted. A sense of sadness crossed over him for the mother he'd never known. 'But she was given sanctuary by the MacEgans. Saraid MacEgan took her in.'

There was a weariness in Gunnar's face, but he accepted it. 'Does the King know?'

Trahern shook his head. 'I'll tell him, soon enough. And the rest of my broth—' He broke off, realising that he could no longer call them that. 'The rest of the MacEgans,' he amended.

Gunnar mounted his horse. 'If you'd like to know about our father, you've only to ask.' A hint of sadness darkened his mood. 'He was a poet and a storyteller. Like yourself.'

They spent the night at Gall Tír, and though Trahern had returned to sleep, he'd remained restless. Morren wrapped her arms around him, trying to warm his cold skin.

'Did you find Áron?' she asked.

'Aye. He's back with the others. We didn't find the raiders, though.'

So they were still alive. And knowing the truth made it even harder for her to sleep. She burrowed closer to Trahern, but when her hand moved down his stomach, he caught her fingertips and squeezed them. 'Not tonight, *a stór.*'

It was the first time he'd turned her away. She was glad he had his back turned, so he wouldn't see her humiliation. Was it because they'd now had their justice? Was he planning to set her aside and send her home again?

A heaviness settled in her stomach, her throat dry. She pulled back from him, turning away to try to sleep. With only a few words, he'd made it clear that the arrangement would soon end.

She'd been naïve to think that he might change his mind. Though Trahern had taught her not to fear a man's touch, the very thought of being with anyone else struck her as wrong. He was the only man she could imagine being intimate with.

Aye, the past few nights had been passionate and loving, but the shadow of the past wasn't entirely gone. Trahern kept her fears at bay, never forcing her to do anything she didn't want. But he was the only man she trusted. The only man she wanted.

And though his body heat warmed her skin this night, she was freezing inside, for already she feared she'd lost him.

As soon as light dawned in the sky, Trahern was gone. Morren rode with Ewan and Honora on the way back to Laochre. Ewan claimed that Trahern would catch up to them, but after two hours of riding, there was no sign of him or the other Ó Reilly men.

King Patrick had remained behind, with his own soldiers, to speak with the Hardrata chief. He intended to ease the peace between their people.

Though Morren knew she was safe enough with Ewan and Honora, not once did she take her eyes from her surroundings, searching for a sign of Trahern.

Half an hour later, it began to snow. Thick and fast, the flakes spread a layer of white upon the grass. It was too early for snow such as this, and Morren blew upon her hands, trying to warm them.

Ewan led them into a grove of trees for shelter. He brought his horse up beside hers, asking, 'Do you want to turn back or wait out the storm?'

Morren hesitated. Though it was wiser to return to Gall Tír, she had no desire to revisit the *longphort*. 'Let's wait and see if it slows down.'

Her face must have shown her worry, for Ewan reached out and caught the reins of her horse. 'Trahern can take care of himself, Morren. He'll join us, soon enough. Don't be afraid for his sake.'

Morren gave a slight nod, though his words didn't reassure her. She didn't trust Egill. The wounded *Lochlannach* raider was merciless, and would not hesitate to strike back at Trahern, given the chance.

They rode into the circle of trees, and Ewan stopped their horses. The dry snow fell swiftly, making it impossible to build a fire. Morren huddled against one of the trees, staring out at the horizon for a glimpse of Trahern. Silently, she prayed that he would return to her.

Near the edge of the trees, Ewan stood with his wife, Honora. His arm slipped about her waist, and he spoke quietly with her. Honora leaned her head against his shoulder, and love seemed to emanate from the couple.

A slight ache of envy slipped within Morren's heart, mingled with worry for her husband. But more than that, she couldn't dispel the anxiety about what would happen when they reached Laochre. He'd always claimed that their marriage would be temporary, in order to gain his brother's support.

Now that they had succeeded in punishing the Viking raiders, would Trahern end their union? The thought of being left behind at Glen Omrigh evoked such a loneliness.

He didn't love her. Not the way he'd loved Ciara. Though they had been intimate every night since their handfasting, she'd sensed him keeping a careful shield around his heart. He would make love to her, showing her new ways to find pleasure with their bodies.

But afterwards, he would lie on his side, facing away from her. She didn't know what to say or do, and so she tended to curl up away from him until sleep took her.

Heaven help her, she didn't want him to set her aside. She wanted to remain married to him. To wake beside him, to love him and know that he would never leave her.

Her hand moved down to her flat stomach. Aileen had said that it was unlikely she'd bear another child. If she were to become pregnant, the chance was strong that she'd miscarry again.

For a moment, she allowed herself to dream of a child. A babe with Trahern's smile and his sharp intelligence. Wistful dreams that could never be. She started to close them away, drawing her cloak tighter against her body.

But then abruptly, her mind demanded, *Why don't you fight for him?*

She stilled, wondering if it were possible. Could she win Trahern's heart for herself? He'd turned her down last night, but she suspected she could get past his defences if she tried hard enough. He was a man worth fighting for. A man she loved. And even if he hadn't forgotten his love for Ciara, she couldn't simply let him walk away from her.

I have to try.

It had grown colder, and her anxieties multiplied. No doubt Trahern was trying to track down Egill and the other raider.

More than likely, they would die of their wounds, whether or not Trahern found them.

She started to walk towards Ewan and Honora when she caught sight of something in the snow—a discolouration of some sort.

Blood.

Whether it was human or animal, she didn't know. 'Ewan, will you come and look at this?' she asked.

The trail continued through the snow, a path leading to the side of a hill. 'What do you think it is?'

Please don't let it be Trahern, she prayed. *Let him be all right*.

Ewan saw the direction of her gaze, but when she reached the outer edge of the trees, he called out, 'Morren! Don't go any further.'

'Why? It's leading away from us. And what if it's Trahern?' Though she obeyed him, remaining in place, she was afraid of what the blood meant.

'I'll go and look.' Ewan unsheathed his sword and started to follow the tracks. Ahead, they heard the sound of muffled voices. 'Honora, guard her,' he ordered his wife. 'Morren, don't leave this grove.'

Once Ewan had left the trees, Morren shivered. He was out in the open, where anyone could attack. It made her uneasy, and she saw the reflection of her fears in Honora's face. The woman was pacing, her hand resting upon the lightweight sword at her side. It was killing her not to follow Ewan.

'I'll be fine,' Morren told her. 'Go and guard his back.'

'But you—'

'He's in more danger than I am. I promise, I won't leave the trees.'

Honora looked torn, but gave a nod and drew her blade. 'I won't be gone for very long.'

Morren watched from within the shelter of the trees as both of them continued toward the hillside, tracking the footprints. The cold wind made the branches shiver, and she huddled against one of the trees, beside an evergreen yew to shelter her from the wind.

'You killed my brother,' came a voice.

She spun and Egill stepped out from behind the yew, staring at her. In his hand he held a knife. Morren tried to voice a scream, but it froze within her throat. Ewan and Honora weren't far away, but she couldn't seem to overcome the suffocating fear.

Egill drew closer, and she stepped backwards. 'They won't have time to help you. I'll slit your throat before they can move.' He held the knife up, fury rigid upon his face. 'I watched him burn because of your accusations. Whoring bitch.'

Morren took another step backwards. If she could reach the clearing, Ewan could help her. But a moment later, Egill grabbed her arm and dragged her to him. She felt the kiss of the blade against her throat.

I'm going to die.

Every moment of the previous attack returned to her, and she felt lightheaded and nauseous. She wanted to fight back, but her limbs wouldn't move. Empty screams locked in her throat, her courage imprisoned.

Egill Hardrata didn't care about anything, save vengeance for his brother. The rigid darkness in him reminded her of Trahern's coldness, only months ago.

She'd been afraid of everything, then. A fragmented shell of a woman with no substance. But Trahern had given her back her strength, teaching her not to be afraid of the darkness. In him, she'd found herself once more. A woman of worth.

I won't be his victim this time, she swore. *Not again.*

Her mind seized upon Egill's weakness, and she used the force of her weight to stomp upon his burned feet. He expelled a cry of pain, his hand slipping against her neck. She felt the stinging slice of the blade, the warmth of blood on her throat.

But she kicked at him again, fighting back against her own fears and seizing control. He wasn't going to take her life, and she wasn't going to die quietly.

Wrenching free of him, she let out a piercing scream that brought Ewan and Honora running. Egill lunged for her, but when he caught her wrist, Morren threw herself to the ground. She rolled over, her palm finding a stone.

Voices shouted, but she heard none of what was said. A knife flashed, and she struck the stone at Egill's face, hearing the crunch of bone. Blood streamed from his wound, and he crumpled to the ground.

It was then that she saw the knife embedded in Egill's back. Standing behind him was Trahern. She didn't know when he'd arrived or how, but her husband caught her up in his arms. Morren clung so tightly, it was as if she became a part of him.

'Are you all right?' he whispered in her ear, still not letting go. 'You're bleeding.'

'I'll be all right.' She used her *brat* to wipe away the smear of blood. 'How did you—?'

'I was tracking him.' His expression turned grim, sobering at the body of the raider. 'Exile or not, I wanted my answers.'

'What about the other outlaw?' Her voice trembled, and

the shock of what had happened was starting to take hold. 'He's still alive.'

'Not any more,' Ewan said, joining them with Honora at his side. 'Áron took care of him.' He pointed in the distance to the path of blood.

'It was the last raider's tracks you saw in the snow,' Ewan explained. 'I found Trahern and the others when I followed the trail of blood.' He glanced at his wife, and Honora coloured with guilt.

Trahern glared at Ewan. 'You should never have left Morren alone. She could have been killed.'

'I'm sorry,' Honora apologised. 'I blame myself for what happened.'

'No,' Morren intervened, sliding her hand around Trahern's waist. 'It was my fault for sending Honora away. I thought it was safe.' She touched her palm to Trahern's cheek, trying to soothe his anger. In truth, it warmed her to know that he'd worried. 'I didn't know Egill was hiding among the yew trees.' Morren pointed to the evergreen where the raider had concealed himself. 'None of us did.'

The glint in Trahern's eyes suggested that there was something else bothering him. Gunnar rejoined them, his own countenance grim.

'What is it?' Morren asked.

Trahern exchanged a glance with Gunnar. 'Before he died, the last raider confessed who hired them to attack the Ó Reilly *cashel.*'

She drew back, afraid of hearing the answer. 'Who?'

'It was Katla,' Gunnar interjected, his voice furious. 'My brother's wife.'

Chapter Twenty-One

Hours later, at Laochre Castle

'We have to go back.' Morren paced across the chamber they shared. 'I left Jilleen with Katla.' Trahern saw the anxiety on her face, the desperate worry for her sister.

'We will,' he reassured her. But not this night. The winter snow had intensified, and he was thankful that they'd made it back to his brother's castle before the worst of the storm had struck. 'As soon as the snow clears, we'll leave.'

She stared out the window, her face visibly upset. 'Do you think it's true? Could Katla really have done such a thing?'

Trahern shook his head. 'I don't know. It doesn't seem so, but how else would he have known her name?'

Katla had taken charge of the Ó Reilly survivors, organising food and shelter. She'd been indignant at Trahern's suspicions, insisting that her family was innocent. Now, he wondered if it had all been an act.

Morren went and sat down on the bed. Her shoulders were lowered, her face pensive. She let her *brat* fall away, and she huddled her knees to her chest. 'I can't let anything happen to Jilleen. I never should have left her.'

There was nothing he could say to alleviate her guilt. And so he remained silent, vowing inwardly that he would make it right somehow.

It was then that his attention centred upon the thin red line marring her throat. Although the cut was light, another inch, and Morren would have been dead. His throat closed up at the thought. He couldn't have endured such a thing. Not again.

He moved over to the bed and sat beside her. She looked lost, and his hand closed over hers. Lightly he stroked her fingers. She lifted her eyes to his, and he didn't like the fear he saw in them. 'I won't let any harm come to Jilleen. I promise you.'

She leaned against him, her arms circling around his waist. 'Trahern, after you take me home—?' Her voice broke off, as though she were uncertain about finishing her question. He waited for her to finish, and she took a breath. 'Are you planning to leave me behind?'

There was disappointment in her tone, mingled with resignation. She believed he would set her aside, ending their brief marriage.

It was what he'd intended. Their marriage had been an arrangement, centred upon bringing the raiders to justice. Now that it was done, he ought to bring her back. And yet the thought of leaving her felt wrong.

Fair strands of hair tumbled around her face, tangled from the long ride earlier. She looked like a woman who had just awakened from sleep, beautifully rumpled.

It reminded him of the first few mornings following their handfasting, when he'd found himself without a coverlet. Morren had bundled herself into her own cocoon, leaving him not a single inch of wool for himself. He'd snatched the covers back, only to end up making love to her, wrapped amid the warmth.

The memory tugged at him. No, he didn't want to leave her behind. But neither did he want to pressure her into a permanent marriage.

'What do you want?' he asked, evading the question. 'Shall I go or stay?'

Her fingertips reached up to his cheek, and she rose onto her knees beside him. 'Today when you were gone, I was afraid.'

She hadn't really answered the question, and he wasn't certain what to think of that. 'I blame myself for leaving you,' he said. 'I trusted my brother, thinking that—'

He stopped, suddenly realising what he'd said. Ewan wasn't truly his brother. Gunnar was. And he hardly knew the man. He didn't know anything about his blood family, nor their other brother Hoskuld, Katla's husband.

An unsettled feeling pricked at him. Too many unanswered questions. Too many unspoken secrets. He needed the answers, needed to learn about his lost family. And he owed the truth to the MacEgans.

'Ewan is still your brother, Trahern.' Morren drew his mouth to hers, breaking off his troubled thoughts. 'And I don't blame anyone for what happened. In the end, you kept me safe.' There was faith in her eyes. 'I never doubted it for a moment.'

'Morren, I won't let anyone harm you.' He caught her nape and leaned in, tasting her lips. 'Not again.'

She pressed herself closer, as though she could fuse her skin to his. 'Stay with me, Trahern. No matter what happens.' Her lips pressed close to his, her arms wrapped about his waist.

In the barest whisper, she said, 'I know I'm not Ciara…but I don't want to end this marriage. Not yet.'

His feelings constricted, knowing the courage it had taken her to speak the words. 'You're not a replacement for Ciara. You never were.'

He brought his mouth to hers, feeling as if all the right words had escaped him. Instead, he used his hands to show her how he felt. His fingers threaded through her fair hair, his thumbs caressing her temples. Like a blind man learning the planes of her face, he touched her.

'When I saw the *Lochlannach* raider trying to kill you…' he lowered his hands down to her shoulders, then to her arms '…I couldn't let it happen. I would have died in your place, Morren. My life for yours.'

He touched his mouth to her lips in a soft kiss. 'I don't want to let you go. I'll stay, for as long as you'll have me as a husband.'

A smile creased her lips. 'We were married on the eve of Samhain. You once told me that anything that occurs on that night will last forever, don't you remember?'

Her reminder of the tale of Oengus, the son of Dagda, evoked an answering smile. 'You're right.'

When she drew him down for another kiss, Trahern felt an unquenchable need to mark her as his own, joining their bodies together. He pulled her atop him, fumbling with her clothing. The gown was caught in the tangle of their limbs, and he fought to free her.

Morren started to laugh when he couldn't seem to get the laces untied. 'You've been defeated by a length of wool.'

'I'm going to get my knife and cut it off you if I can't get these laces loosened.' The words were only half-jesting.

But then she managed to free the garment, and he lifted

it away. The curve of her breasts, the sweet dip of her waist, caught him like a fist between the ribs.

'When I look upon you, I can hardly breathe,' he murmured against her skin. With his mouth, he trailed a path from her ribs to the hidden spot beneath her breast. She shivered, reaching to his own clothing to lift it away. When they were both naked, he rested his weight atop her.

'You're keeping me warm,' she murmured, lifting her mouth to his for another kiss.

'Perhaps you can warm another part of me,' he teased, pressing his length against her hip.

She shivered, but smiled as she kissed him. She opened to him, uttering a soft cry when he used his shaft to tease at the moist centre of her.

He wanted to drive her mad, to push her past the brink until she writhed with desire. His mouth coaxed her nipples into sharp points, and she shuddered with relief when he filled her.

'Trahern,' she breathed, her hands reaching to grasp his hips. He made love to her slowly, savouring the soft depths as he entered and withdrew.

'Do you suppose I could…have another baby?'

The words stopped him cold. He froze in place, not knowing what to say. The idea hadn't even entered his mind. 'I thought Aileen said it wasn't possible.'

Morren eased back, wrapping her legs around his waist in a silent urge for him to continue. 'She never said it wasn't possible. Only that it was unlikely.' She reached up and took his face between her hands. 'There's nothing I'd want more.'

Icy fear snaked through his skin, and he held still within her body. In his mind, he'd believed that she would have no children. After the bleeding and the pain she'd suffered, he'd never considered that she could bear another child.

And what if she did become pregnant? What if his own child died? Would he have to stand back and watch her suffer, watch her grieve once more? Or worse, what if she died in childbirth? It had happened to his own mother, because of him.

'You don't have to stop,' she whispered. He heard the hurt in her voice, but he couldn't have gone on if he'd wanted to.

Too shaken to continue, he withdrew from her body. 'Morren, no. I can't be the cause of you dying.'

'I'm not going to die.' There was anger in her voice, and she sat up, pulling the coverlet to cover her body.

'You almost died a few months ago,' he shot back. 'I was there, remember? I held the body of your son in my hands.'

She flinched as though he'd struck her. Tears welled up in her eyes, and she sat back to stare at him. 'Trahern, you're being unreasonable.'

'Am I? I swore I would never hurt you,' he said. The vehement words poured out of him, 'And I won't. I touched you before, thinking that it was safe. I thought…after your son died, that you could bear no more children.'

'I don't know if I can or not,' she admitted.

'I won't be the cause of your suffering.' The desolate words were a vow. 'If it's a child you want, we can foster Alanna, Genevieve's daughter, when she's old enough.'

'And you'll martyr yourself, having a celibate marriage?' Anger and sexual frustration laced her tone.

'We can give each other pleasure, without the joining.'

'It's not the same.' She drew back from him, lying down and facing the wall.

He'd hurt her feelings. But damn it all, he'd been there that night, watching her suffer. Nothing could have prepared him for the helplessness, not knowing if she would live or die. He wouldn't go through it again.

Trahern ached with longing for her, his shaft stiff and swollen. With one hand, he reached out to touch her silken hip, his fingers sliding toward the cleft between her legs.

Her hand clamped over his. 'No, Trahern. I don't want it. Not without you.'

Her rejection burned through him, and he rolled over to face the opposite side of the chamber. In his mind, he remembered how it had felt to join their bodies together. It had been far more than consummating a marriage. It was a way of giving to her, and he'd loved watching the way her face would tighten with pleasure.

But, God forgive him, he couldn't let her bear a child. He wouldn't cause her pain and suffering, not when it could be prevented.

Somehow, he had to make her understand that.

His brother King Patrick arrived late the following afternoon, despite the snow. Queen Isabel fretted over him, and Trahern asked to meet with him and all of the MacEgan brothers.

'I need to speak with you and our brothers privately,' he said to the king. 'Along with Annle, if you can arrange it.'

'I thought we'd finished with the Gall Tír matter,' Patrick said. 'Is something else wrong?'

Although it wasn't over, Trahern didn't want to discuss Katla's involvement. Patrick had done everything he could, and he preferred to handle the rest on his own. 'That isn't why I need to see all of you.'

'Is it about Morren?'

He shook his head. 'Something else.'

The mention of his wife made him uneasy, for she hadn't spoken to him since last night. When he'd tried to make conversation, she'd answered his questions. But there was sadness in her voice, along with regret.

'Within the hour,' he said. 'In your chamber.'

As soon as he made the request, he felt a sense of emptiness. It was the right thing to do, telling them the truth about his birth mother. And yet he was afraid that Annle would be wrong, that his confession would change the way they saw him.

As he waited, one by one, his brothers arrived. Connor, Ewan, Patrick and Bevan. Each one a warrior, like himself. Patrick, the King of their province, who would put everyone else's needs before his own. Bevan, a stoic warrior, whose actions often said what words could not. Connor, a teasing man who had lost the use of one hand, but was no less a fighter. And Ewan, the youngest of them, who had struggled to find his own strength, but had proven his own worth time and again.

They waited for him to speak, their silent glances trying to reassure him that whatever happened, they would stand together. As they always had.

Annle was the last to arrive. Her wrinkled face was placid, for she knew why he had summoned her here.

'Tell them,' Trahern urged.

The old healer sat down, resting her hands upon one knee. And after she'd finished her story, Trahern's hands tightened into fists. It broke him apart, the truth had to be spoken.

'I'm not one of you,' he said at last. 'Not by blood. I may

have been raised a MacEgan, but Duncan and Saraid were not my parents.'

Patrick's mouth tightened into a line. 'You learned of this a few nights ago. And you said nothing until now.' There was disapproval in his tone, laced with the authority of a king.

Trahern eyed each one of them. 'I could have remained silent about it. Unless Annle had spoken, you wouldn't have known differently. But there has always been honesty between us. And trust.'

Bevan looked as though he wanted to speak, but he closed his mouth again. The scars lining each of his cheeks tightened, and he glanced over at Ewan.

'What do you want us to say?' his youngest brother demanded. 'Do you want us to cast you out? Pretend that all the years don't matter?'

'I don't know what matters to you. All I know is that the life I knew was a lie. I believed that Saraid was my mother.'

'She was,' Annle interrupted. 'In every way, she was. She loved you no differently from any of the others.'

'She might have loved you a little more,' Patrick said. He rubbed at his chin, and Trahern noticed the slight traces of grey in his brother's hair. 'Whenever you scraped a knee or got a bruise, she coddled you. There was more than one time that I wanted to drown you for it.'

An unexpected laugh broke forth. 'You tried.'

'All of us tried to kill each other,' Bevan added. 'Have you forgotten when Liam convinced us that we could fly, if only we concentrated hard enough?'

'I was seven,' Trahern remembered. 'It was Midsummer's Eve, when I was home visiting from fostering.' He'd been so glad to see his family again, he'd spent all day playing with his brothers.

'We climbed the highest tree we could manage.' A pang caught him, as he thought of the eldest MacEgan brother, Liam, who had died in battle years ago. 'Liam told me to close my eyes and flap my arms as hard as I could.'

Bevan grinned. 'You realised he was lying when you hit the third branch. Da beat Liam senseless, and our mother fed him naught but gruel for a week after. I thought she wasn't going to forgive him for it.'

'I nearly didn't forgive him.' He couldn't stop his smile, as he studied each of his brothers. 'I broke my arm that summer.'

Bevan smirked. 'It was funny at the time, watching you flap your arms. Until you got hurt.'

'I thought it was rather funny, too,' Connor admitted with a chagrined look. 'I was glad you jumped first, for I changed my mind about flying after I saw you fall.'

Hundreds of stories and memories bound them together, Trahern realised. And through it all, was the unbreakable bond of brotherhood.

'It doesn't matter, Trahern,' Patrick said quietly. 'Blood or not, you've been my brother, all my life. And always will be.'

It was then that Annle slipped quietly from the room, a faint smile upon her mouth. She'd known. Keeping his birth a secret wasn't meant to deceive others. His parents had known the truth, but it hadn't mattered. Saraid had never once treated him any differently from the others. He'd believed he was a MacEgan, because he was raised as one.

'I don't know what to call myself any more,' Trahern admitted. 'MacEgan or Dalrata.'

'You know the answer to that,' Patrick said. 'Do you believe we'd turn our back on you, after all these years?'

'No.' He understood then, that to take any other name was an insult to them. 'You wouldn't.'

'Good. That's settled.' Ewan stood up and walked to the door. 'There's a good deal of snow on the ground. I'm thinking we should make use of it.'

They left the chamber, and it was as if they were boys again, planning to make fools of themselves in the snow. Before he could join them, Patrick stopped him. 'Are you taking Morren back to her home, or will you remain here?'

He sobered. 'I have to go back with her. And after that, I don't know.'

The remnants of the disagreement he'd had with his wife hung over him. He couldn't think about it now, not when he didn't know what to do about her desire for a child.

'You might want to spend time with the Dalratas over the winter,' Patrick advised. 'It may be wise to get acquainted with your other family.'

'You're right.' Trahern started down the stairs. 'But first, I think Ewan needs a lesson in humility.'

The Queen was coming up the stairs with her maid and overheard their conversation. 'You're not planning to get my husband all wet with snow, are you?'

'Him and the others, yes.' Trahern shrugged at Isabel. 'We'll have a fight in the snow. And when I've finished, you can take the wet clothes off him.'

A flush rose in Isabel's cheeks. 'Well, hurry up, then.' She sent a seductive smile to her husband. 'I'll be waiting for you.'

Patrick eyed her with his own wicked smile. 'And when is the last time you played in the snow, *a stór*?'

She gave a delighted laugh. 'I'll join you.'

* * *

Morren stood in the shadows of the castle, watching the men throwing balls of snow at one another. The swirling storm was beautiful, and when she saw Trahern among his brothers, a wistful smile crossed over her face.

'Come with us,' came Aileen's voice from behind her. The healer had bundled herself in a warm woollen gown, her *brat* wound over her head. 'I'm planning to.'

Honora and Isabel were already among the others, laughing and ducking when snow came their way.

'I don't know if he would want me to join them.' After the way Trahern had turned from her, Morren couldn't seem to let go of the hurt. He'd rejected her, and she hadn't known she could feel so humiliated. Though he'd claimed it was because he didn't want to risk her life, all she could think about was how empty it had felt, with him sleeping on the opposite side of the bed.

'You're his wife,' Aileen countered. 'Of course you should come.' The dark-haired healer reached up and lifted Morren's *brat* around her head and shoulders. 'It will be fun.'

'He's angry with me right now,' Morren confessed.

'And how many times have Connor and I fought?' Aileen retorted. 'We've been married for five years now, and I can't even name all the arguments we've had. He can be as pig-headed as the next man, believing he's right. But you can convince him of your own way, sure enough.'

Morren found herself following Aileen outside. 'He's afraid I'll bear another child.'

Aileen stopped walking. 'Oh. So that's it, then.' She nodded towards them. 'I won't lie to you and say it wouldn't be dangerous. But there's always hope.' The healer offered a warm smile. 'And I think it would do you some good to release your anger in a good snow fight. Knock some sense into Trahern.'

'I don't think it would work.' She eyed the men, who were covered in splattered snow.

'If he's denying you in bed, I'd say you have more than a few reasons to knock him about.' Aileen reached down and formed a tight ball of snow. 'You're a woman. The best form of revenge is to drive him wild with wanting you.'

'But I don't know how.' The very idea of trying to seduce Trahern, though it fascinated her, made her feel like an awkward girl of thirteen. Was she supposed to strip off her clothing? Throw herself at him?

'Deny him,' Aileen said. 'Use your body to tell him that he can look, but he can't touch. Believe me, it won't take more than a few hours to convince him to be with you. MacEgan men are hot-blooded. I know that, well enough.' She handed Morren the snow ball. 'Go and teach him a lesson.'

Morren sent Aileen a hopeful smile. 'I just might.'

Chapter Twenty-Two

A slushy shower of snow struck him on the back of the neck. Trahern spun, ready to fire his own packed ball. When he saw Morren standing behind him, he was taken aback.

'Did you just—?' His words were cut off when she hurled another ball at him, striking at his shoulder. 'Now that was a mistake, Morren.' He strode forward, hurling the ball at her shoulder. It exploded on impact, dousing her with wet snow.

'I'm not a bit sorry for it.' Her mouth curved upwards, and he realised that she was using the snow fight as a means of releasing her anger and frustration.

When another snowball struck him, he whirled and saw Ewan was the guilty party. Before he could return the blow, Morren had struck Ewan across the face with another snowball.

'Good shot,' he murmured.

She sent him a conspiratorial smile. As the fight continued with his brothers, Morren proved that her arm was as good as she'd boasted. Even when his brothers ran to try to avoid her, she managed to nick them with the snow.

Gunnar joined them, and his *Lochlannach* brother proved to have as strong an aim as Morren. The three of them allied together against Connor, Aileen, Patrick and Isabel. Ewan and Honora kept switching sides.

After nearly an hour, all of them were soaked, and freezing.

'Lucky bastard,' Gunnar muttered. 'At least you've a woman to warm your bed tonight. I'll be sleeping in the Great Chamber on the floor with nothing but the dogs.'

Trahern knocked him on the shoulder. 'Don't worry, brother. If you kiss them sweetly, the right dog might snuggle up to you.'

Gunnar swore at him in the *Lochlannach* tongue, but his meaning was more than clear.

Morren started to walk up the stairs, but Trahern shadowed her. Though it seemed that she was less angry with him, he didn't know what else to say to her. He tried to think up arguments that would make sense to her, rational ways of explaining why they should not be intimate with each other.

But every last word fled his brain when he saw her stand on the far side of the room, removing her gown. She moved slowly, peeling off the damp wool and lifting it away. The *léine* underdress was next to go, baring her long legs and taut bottom.

His mouth went dry when he saw her naked. She ran her hands through her long golden hair, squeezing water from the ends. And when she turned to face him, the damp locks framed her tight nipples.

Sweet Jesu. Was she trying to kill him, then?

Yes. Yes, she was. With slow, sure steps, she walked towards the bed and got beneath the coverlet. Trahern gritted his teeth and removed his own wet clothing, laying it out to dry. His teeth chattered as he slid into the bed beside her. The raw need to touch, to be with Morren, coursed through him. His shaft was rigid with desire, his hands clenching the mattress.

Abruptly, she turned to face him. Though she huddled beneath the coverlet, she offered a faint smile. 'That was fun.'

It had been, but he could think of more fun things they could be doing right now. He gave a nod. 'It was.'

'Patrick said it would be clear enough that we can leave tomorrow for Glen Omrigh.'

'Yes.' He could hardly trust himself to speak more than a word or two. It was tormenting him, knowing that her smooth naked skin was just inches away from his touch.

'I'm a little cold,' she said suddenly. Before he could say another word, she turned her back to him and nestled her bottom against his erection. She brought his arms around her, and his fingertips brushed against the curve of her breasts. 'You don't mind keeping me warm, do you?'

He bit his tongue to keep from growling when she nudged her bottom higher, bringing his manhood against the seam of her legs. If she opened to him, it would be effortless to slide within her.

'I know what you're doing,' he said. 'It's not going to work.'

'I don't know what you mean,' she said. 'You yourself said that there was nothing wrong with giving each other pleasure in other ways.' Her hand reached around, her fingers closing around his heated length.

With one firm stroke, she took apart all the reasons for not touching her. He forced her to turn, and took her mouth. Her leg lifted around his hip, in wordless invitation. The kiss drowned out his protests, the warmth of her skin pushing away all thoughts of self-control.

He needed her, this woman who had become such a part of his life. Tonight, when she'd thrown snowballs at him, he'd forgotten about their disagreements. He'd seen only the breathtaking woman, with the infectious smile. The woman who meant everything to him. The woman he loved.

'I'm sorry,' Morren whispered, breaking the kiss. 'I didn't mean to make you uncomfortable.' She reached down to touch him again, and he couldn't stop the groan that escaped him. 'If you'd rather just…touch each other, I suppose that's all right.' Her mouth moved to his throat, kissing the skin while her hand moved in rhythm upon his erection.

Though the pleasure coursing through him was undeniable, he wanted her to feel the same. He reached around to the hooded fold of her womanhood, stoking the fire of her own release. Her breathing grew heavier, and her hand moved faster upon him. Trahern shuddered, and when she suddenly arched against him, her body breaking free with racking tremors, his own seed came spurting forth.

He held her afterwards, his heart pounding. She was right. It wasn't the same at all.

The uncertainty and feeling of loneliness overshadowed the satisfying release. There was something more fulfilling about being inside her, feeling her legs tangled up in his.

But God help him, how could he risk her life? He couldn't, plain and simple. To join with her was a selfish act, and he refused to endanger her in any way.

No matter how much he wanted her.

It took over a fortnight to reach Glen Omrigh. Storms and the winter cold made travelling nearly impossible, and they'd had to stop numerous times with neighbouring clans.

Morren had braved the journey as best she could, but in the past few days, she'd worried about Jilleen to the point where the mere thought of home made her physically nauseous. Her stomach lurched, and she picked at her food, terrified of what could have happened to her sister.

They approached the *cashel*, and Morren was gratified to see that the fields had been ploughed and prepared for planting next spring. If they could get enough grain, they might be able to slowly build back their supplies.

Once they arrived within Glen Omrigh, she saw that the *cashel* was completely rebuilt. The comforting smoke of peat fires rose from the stone cottages with freshly thatched roofs. The palisade wall was built of stone, and she saw the familiar faces of friends waiting.

Her mouth was sour with fear, but Trahern rode alongside her. His presence brought her comfort in the midst of her inner turmoil. Though not once had he made love to her since their time at Laochre, he'd slept with her in his arms. It was something, though not at all what she'd wanted. She prayed that time would wear down his resolve.

When they reached the interior, she found Jilleen outside, talking with a group of girls. As soon as her sister caught sight of them, she raced forward, her face beaming with excitement.

Morren dismounted and caught Jilleen in her arms. She wanted to cry, so grateful was she, to see her sister unharmed. 'I'm glad to see you.'

Behind them, she saw Gunnar and Trahern. Both stood observing the *cashel*, their faces guarded. 'Where is Katla?' she asked Jilleen.

'She's inside with Hoskuld. I was helping her make soup, just now.' Jilleen added, 'Do you and…the others…want to come inside?' She glanced over at Trahern and Gunnar, her face curious.

Morren motioned to the two men, and she admitted, 'Trahern is my husband now.'

A delighted smile spread over her sister's face. 'I'm so happy for you. I had hoped that he might take care of you.'

Jilleen took Morren's hand and led her inside. Trahern and Gunnar followed, and once they were inside, the meaty scent of mutton stew filled the small hut. Though it should have been enticing, the heavy odour made Morren feel even more sick.

'Why, Morren!' Katla exclaimed, wiping her hands upon her apron. 'I never thought to see you so soon. Come in, come in!'

The woman's warm welcome didn't appear false, and she shut the door behind Gunnar and Trahern. 'Hoskuld is visiting with Dagmar this morn, but he should return soon. Sit, all of you, and you can have some of this stew. I've enough for everyone, thankfully.'

Trahern exchanged a glance with Gunnar and withdrew a pouch at his waist. 'We came to speak with you about this.' He poured a small handful of the foreign coins into his palm, showing them to Katla.

The woman's face faltered, and she paled as she set bowls before them. 'I've never seen coins like that before.'

Her tone was too hurried, but her eyes spoke of guilt. Morren left her bowl of stew untouched.

Jilleen stared at Katla. 'Those are the coins we found in the *souterrain*, used to pay the raiders.'

Katla moved back to the pot of stew, stirring it, though it likely needed none of her attentions.

'He knew your name,' Morren said softly. 'Egill Hardrata spoke of you.'

Katla didn't move. The spoon clattered against the iron edge of the pot, and she didn't face them.

'Why, damn you?' Gunnar demanded, striding forward and grasping her arm. 'Tell me why he would know your name!'

'What would you have me say?' she whispered. Katla's head turned back, and tears streamed down her face.

'You hired them to destroy the Ó Reilly tribe. Isn't that right?' Trahern stood and walked towards her, using his height to intimidate her. 'Their homes burned, lives lost. The woman I intended to marry was killed. Because of you.'

Katla covered her face, sobbing now. 'I never wanted this to happen.'

'Then what did you intend?' Trahern's face was stony, his tone unforgiving.

'They acted of their own accord. I never hired them for that,' she insisted.

Her hysteria was so strong, Morren almost believed her. She tried a different tack. 'How would you have even met those men?' she asked. 'They live so far away.'

'They came here to trade last spring,' Katla said, her voice breaking on a sob.

'Did Dagmar—?' Trahern began, but Morren cut him off.

'No.' She stared at Trahern, shaking her head. 'Let her finish.'

An unexpected memory came to her, one she'd put aside for so many months. 'You had a daughter, didn't you? She was about Jilleen's age?'

Katla's face tightened into sobbing. She nodded once, then buried her face in her hands.

'Our chief spoke with her a time or two,' Morren remembered. 'I remember when a few of you came to see us. He seemed fond of her.' Understanding pushed past her own fury, for she realised what Katla had done.

'Our chief was too old for her, wasn't he?' Morren whispered. 'He gave her more attention than he should.'

'He hurt her,' Katla wept. 'My daughter, who had never done anything wrong. She was just back from fostering, and we'd had so little time together. That bastard took her innocence, and he threatened to kill her if she ever told anyone. But she did. She told me, her mother, knowing that I would make it right.'

Katla's hands clenched into fists. 'I found her body lying in the field a few days later. And I swore I would kill him for what he did to my child.' Her eyes glittered with wildness, and Morren reached for Trahern's hand. His steady palm granted her comfort.

'After Dagmar met with the raiders, I came to them in secret with coins I took from my grandfather's hoard. I begged them to kill the chief. I told them they would find the rest of the coins in the Ó Reilly *souterrain* when they completed their task.' Her sobs caught in her throat. 'That way, they would have to go there. But I never thought they would kill innocent people. They acted of their own will, burning the homes and taking other lives.' She sat down, resting her head between her hands.

'I thought about ending my own life, after I learned what they'd done. But then, who would look after Hoskuld and our other children?' She raised reddened eyes to look at each one of them. 'All I can do is atone for it. I can't ever forgive myself. And I won't ask you to.'

Morren reached out for her sister, Jilleen, and hugged her tightly. Then she glanced at Trahern, whose face was unreadable.

'I believe you,' he said at last. 'It does not release you from your guilt, but I understand why.'

'I don't want to be exiled,' Katla said. 'But I always knew I would have to meet my punishment.'

Hoskuld returned at that moment. At the sight of her husband, Katla paled. Gunnar relayed the tale, explaining to his brother what had happened.

'Why didn't you tell me any of this?' Hoskuld demanded. 'You *knew* who had harmed her, and you didn't trust me to avenge our own daughter?'

'I wanted to protect you,' she cried. 'You might have started a war if you went after their chief. I believed I could escape notice and the raiders would take the blame if they ever found out.' She tried to throw herself into her husband's arms, but Hoskuld stood with his arms at his side, his anger palpable.

Morren looked up at Trahern, trying to sense his own reaction. There was uncertainty on his face.

'What you did was wrong,' Trahern said to Katla finally. 'And I want to speak to Gunnar and Hoskuld with the chief, before any decision is made.'

Morren studied Katla's reddened face. It was not the face of a murderer. She was a grieving mother, who'd wanted to avenge her daughter's death. And she would have to live with that guilt for the rest of her days.

'I believe her,' Morren said to Trahern. 'It was the raiders' fault.' Morren said to Trahern. 'The destruction they wrought was their decision, and they have paid for it with their lives. I don't believe Katla should suffer the same.'

Trahern gave a nod. Glancing at the other men, he said, 'Send for Dagmar.'

When Dagmar arrived the following day, the chief listened to Katla's confession. A mixture of fury and embarrassment crossed his face. After several hours of deliberation, they made a quiet decision. Katla would be allowed to live, but she would dwell among the Ó Reillys, so that she would never forget what she'd done. They would tell no one of her involvement, so long as she paid restitution every day for the rest of her life.

'You will work alongside them,' Dagmar pronounced. 'You will dedicate yourself to rebuilding what was lost. And you may not return to live among us.' To Hoskuld, he added, 'I hold you responsible for ensuring that your wife obeys.'

It was an exile, but not a death sentence. Trahern felt that the penalty was a fair one, and his respect for Dagmar increased. Though it still felt strange to think that these men were his kinsmen, his former antipathy had lessened.

After he and Gunnar left the chief's dwelling, his brother turned to him. 'The Ó Reillys need a new leader. Have you thought about joining them as their chief?'

He stared at his brother. 'I'm not an Ó Reilly.'

'No, but we are merging many of the Dalrata with them. A man who can call himself both Irish and *Lochlannach* would be a strong representative. Unless you think yourself unable to lead?'

Gunnar's goading challenge wasn't lost on him. Trahern had never considered leading a clan of his own, for he'd always thought of himself as a MacEgan. But he was also Dalrata, by birth. It was strange, to realise that he had two families now. He was possibly the only man who could bridge the two sides, bringing them together.

'If the Dalrata and the Ó Reillys can accept me, I'll stay.' Though he wasn't certain he wanted the responsibility of becoming the new chief, he didn't doubt that he could lead the people, if they chose him.

'Will you tell Hoskuld that we're brothers?' Trahern asked. He hadn't spoken a word of his heritage to the man, not knowing how it would be received.

Gunnar nodded. 'He'll want to know. It might give him some consolation, after all that Katla has done.'

It was time to lay bare the truth. When Trahern faced Gunnar, eye to eye, he saw the image of himself. But this time, it no longer bothered him. Instead, he found acceptance in his blood family. 'Brothers should stand together,' he said at last.

'They should.' Gunnar gripped Trahern's forearm in support. With a nod towards Morren, he added, 'And I think it would please your wife, knowing she can remain here with her sister.'

Apprehensive thoughts clouded Trahern's mind, for his marriage had weakened over the past few weeks. The celibacy was beginning to wear down on both of them. Though he'd slept with Morren, occasionally touching her, there was an emptiness that cast its shadow.

'I'll see what Morren thinks.' He released his brother's hand, walking alongside him. 'What about you? Where will you go?'

Gunnar flashed him a wicked grin. 'I'll build a hut of my own here and fill it with beautiful women.' His brother gave him a slight shove. 'And speaking of women, I think you should tend to your own.'

Morren had been walking towards them when she stopped and rested her hand on one of the huts, her face blanching. In seconds, Trahern was at her side. 'What is it, *a stór*?'

She rested her hands over her midsection. 'It hurts, Trahern.' Pale and terrified, she stared into his eyes. 'Like before.' Abruptly, she doubled over, in such pain, her meaning suddenly crystallised.

'When did you have your last woman's flow?' he demanded. *Oh Jesu, please, not this. Not again.*

She shook her head. 'I haven't. Not since before our handfasting.'

And he knew. God help him, she was carrying his child. Possibly she might lose the babe, if he didn't do something to help her.

No words could express the fear he felt right now.

Chapter Twenty-Three

Trahern lifted her into his arms, taking long strides to the nearest hut. Morren struggled against the cramping pain, and she voiced silent prayers for the life of their child.

Be well, she pleaded. *Don't leave us.*

Trahern set her down upon a pallet, and once she laid down, some of the pain started to clear. She kept her knees raised, and took a steadying breath. It was better, a little more bearable. And it didn't seem that she'd been bleeding.

Her husband, however, looked as though he were going to faint. His dark hair had filled in, along with the traces of a beard. Like a fierce angel, he watched over her.

'It's not so bad now,' she admitted. 'The pain caught me without any warning.'

'How long have you known?' His voice sounded leaden, as though he expected her to die.

'I didn't know, truly. I've only missed one flow, and that can happen.' She reached out for his hand, needing his touch. 'But it's a blessing I could only dream of.'

'I am never touching you again,' he swore. 'This is my fault.'

He looked so serious, she realised he meant it. 'Trahern, this is everything I wanted. To bear a child for the man I—' She broke off, her face reddening. They had endured so much together. He'd been at her side, during the most heart-wrenching moments and in the better times. She couldn't imagine being with anyone else.

'For the man I love,' she finished.

Trahern sat down beside her, taking her hand. 'Morren, I would give anything to spare you this pain.' The fear upon his face made it clear that he did care about her.

She eased to a seated position, leaning against him. 'I know you would. But if it's true, that I have a second chance at being a mother, I want it.'

He moved beside her, supporting her in his arms. In his eyes, she saw the fear of losing her. She ventured a smile. 'You gave me this precious gift, Trahern. I'm grateful for it.'

He held her so tightly, as though she would disappear from his embrace. 'No matter what happens, I won't leave you.' His hand stroked her shoulder, his mouth brushing against her temple. 'I'll never leave you, even if the worst happens again. I love you, Morren.'

She drew back, her blue eyes meeting his. The fear of losing this child was a bond they shared, but she held fast to hope.

'I'm going to be all right, Trahern. I believe that.' The cramping was no longer the same as her earlier miscarriage. This was more like the onset of her monthly discomfort.

'I pray you're right.' He kept her in his arms, holding her near. 'Is there anything I can do to help you? Summon the healer, perhaps?'

She shook her head. 'The only thing I want right now is to

have our marriage back the way it was. I won't live like this any more. It's hurting both of us.'

The truth was, she could see the strain it wrought upon him, trying to stay away from her. Each night in his arms, she could feel his desire, and she sensed his pain. She knew why he was withholding himself, and it bothered her, knowing she was the cause.

He remained silent, and she pressed further, touching her forehead to his. 'I need you. Not just in spirit, but also in body.'

Trahern's face was haggard, torn with the need to touch her and the conflicting need to keep her safe. She raised her mouth to his, kissing him. 'I love you, Trahern. And I know you'll take care of both of us.'

'You mean everything to me.' He kissed her as though he were afraid she'd shatter in his arms. As though he loved her with every part of himself.

And it was enough.

The seasons passed, winter turning into spring. As the seedlings began to rise from the fertile ground, so too did Morren blossom. Trahern watched over her with a vigilance that never failed. Her rounded stomach grew with each month, and somehow, she held on to the babe she wanted so badly.

He hardly slept any more, the worry building up inside of him. Later that summer, he sent for Aileen, Connor's wife. If anyone could help Morren survive the birth, it was she.

'You look terrible,' Connor remarked, grimacing at the sight. 'Has it been that bad, being chieftain of the Ó Reillys?'

'It's not as difficult as I thought it would be.' He'd accepted his new place without much thought. The Ó Reilly survivors and several of the Dalrata Vikings had merged together, forming a new clan that was a blend of traditions. 'Hoskuld and Gunnar have helped.' He'd found that his new brothers had no lack of advice to share, and they frequently offered their opinions—whether he'd wanted them or not.

Trahern hid a smile at the thought.

'Did you have enough supplies to endure the winter?' Connor asked.

'We did.' Trahern pointed toward a section of the fields. 'We found a hoard of coins buried there, a fortnight ago.' He walked alongside his brother to the *cashel* entrance. 'It seems that the former Ó Reilly chief was the cause of all the unrest with St Michael's Abbey. He was collecting tithes from his kinsmen, blaming the abbot for greed, when he was the one stealing from his own people.'

Trahern grimaced and shook his head in disgust, 'He told the abbot that the Dalrata people stole the tithes.'

'Leaving him free to take everything,' Connor predicted.

'Aye. But at least we found the coins. We were able to buy more grain, and it made it easier to rebuild.' They entered the gates, and the familiar sounds of activity surrounded them. 'It's like taking care of a large family,' Trahern admitted. 'Handling disputes and ensuring that everyone has what they need.'

'Like being a father,' Connor suggested, a slight hint of amusement on his face. 'And I believe you'll be a good one.'

Trahern had tried not to think of the child. For now, he merely wanted his wife to survive the birth. 'How do you stand it?' he asked suddenly. 'I think about Morren giving birth, and I'd cut off my arm to take the pain away from her.'

'I won't lie to you,' Connor said, 'there's nothing in the world that makes me more tense than watching Aileen in labour. You think of all the things that could happen to them. And somehow, when you hold your child in your arms, you forget about all else.' A soft smile crossed his brother's face. 'It's like holding a piece of the love you share. You see yourself and her in the child's face.'

Connor clapped him on the back, but there was no denying the emotion on his face. 'You'll survive it, brother. Only a few hours longer.'

'A few hours?' He stared hard at Connor, not knowing what he meant.

'Aye. Usually the first takes a bit longer, but—'

'She's going to give birth *today*? Why in the name of Belenus didn't anyone say anything to me?' He wanted to knock the knowing grin right off Connor's face.

'Perhaps because you'd overreact? Didn't you notice that Aileen hasn't left Morren's side today?'

'She was talking with her and grinding medicines,' he argued. 'Neither of them said anything about the babe coming.'

He broke away from Connor, running towards the hut he shared with Morren.

She was sitting up, her face tight as she breathed slowly. 'That's it,' Aileen soothed.

When Morren opened her eyes, she sent him a slight smile. 'Hello, Trahern.'

'Were you planning to tell me,' he demanded, 'or were you going to simply suffer in silence?'

'I wouldn't say that the last pain was particularly silent,' she admitted. 'But I didn't want you to be afraid. It's going well, actually.'

He glared at Aileen, who shrugged. 'She's right. I would say that the babe will be here by this evening—' She was interrupted when Morren closed her eyes again, her palms digging into the coverlet. Her breathing quickened, and he didn't miss the pain upon her face.

'Connor,' Aileen said, 'take Trahern away.'

'I'm not going anywhere.' He moved to rub his wife's shoulders, trying to offer comfort.

'Don't touch me!' Morren snapped.

In spite of herself, Aileen laughed. 'Don't take it personally, Trahern, but when you're about to give birth, the last thing you want is a man touching you.'

'I'm sorry,' Morren apologised. But a wave of pain passed over her, and she squeezed his hand so tightly, he thought she might crack his fingers in half.

'I won't do this to you again, *a mhuirnín*,' he promised. 'You have my word, you'll never have to suffer this pain any more.'

When she opened her eyes again, she sent him a furious glare. 'If I bear a healthy child, so help me, you will not withhold yourself from me again. You will share my bed whenever I want you to.'

Connor and Aileen were laughing at him, and he sent them a blistering look. 'Morren, I don't think—'

Another pain washed over her, and she swore at him. 'Aye, this was your fault, and when I've recovered from it, I am going to have my way with you. Stop being such a saint, and be a damned husband!' Her last words rose up with another pain, and Aileen went to examine her.

'It's not going to be as long as we thought,' the healer said. 'Trahern, help to support her.'

The next few hours were the worst he'd ever endured. When Morren pushed, crying out, he told her how much he loved her. With each wrenching pain, he relived those moments when he'd delivered her stillborn son. He remembered how badly she'd bled, and how he'd held her all night, telling her stories.

He whispered the story of Lugh once again, and of Dagda. The tales flowed through him, as he fought with her for this fragile newborn life.

And when Morren gave birth to their son, there were no words at all. Only the most all-encompassing joy he'd ever known. Aileen placed the newborn child upon Morren's bare stomach, and he marvelled at the tiny perfection.

'He's wonderful,' Morren wept. 'And he's ours.' Happiness filled her up, and he touched the child's downy head, his fingers brushing against hers.

Thankfulness replaced the fear in his heart. As he kissed Morren softly, he marvelled that any man could be this happy.

The harvest came, and autumn darkened the foliage across the land. Morren walked up the forest hillside, back to the hunter's cottage. Trahern took their son Iain into his arms, when she arrived at the small earthen mound that he'd covered with stones. She'd planted heather upon the earth, and the flowers had bloomed throughout the summer.

Kneeling beside the small grave, she voiced a prayer for her lost child. For long moments, she thought of him, wondering if he would have been like young Iain. Would his eyes have been the same quiet grey, his mouth as soft as a rosebud?

Bittersweet tears filled her eyes as she rose to her feet. 'I miss him, though I never knew him.'

'He led me to you,' Trahern said, pulling her into his arms. 'The greatest gift he could have given.'

With a sleeping Iain between them, she kissed him, and his mouth covered hers with the intensity of a man who loved her more than life.

'Let's go inside,' she said. 'Iain can sleep, and I'm going to show you how much I love you.' She opened the door for him, and waited while he arranged a place for the babe. When he turned around, she let her overdress and *léine* fall to the floor, opening her arms to him.

Trahern closed the distance, removing his own clothing. Skin to skin, he held her, pulling her onto the bed. Without words his hands spoke of all his feelings, telling her how much he loved her.

And when their bodies joined at last, she gave a breathless sigh. 'I love you, Trahern.'

He moved slowly within her, as if in reverence. 'You're mine, Morren. As I am yours, for now and always.'

She took his face between her palms, her heart spilling over for this man.

'Always,' she promised.

* * * * *

Read on for a further dramatic tale
by
Michelle Willingham

VOYAGE OF AN IRISH WARRIOR

This was first published on the eHarlequin.com website

VOYAGE OF AN IRISH WARRIOR

Michelle Willingham

Chapter One

Ireland, 1180

Cool spring air rippled the sea, and Brenna Ó Neill pulled her *brat* around her shoulders for warmth. She stood with her bare feet in the sand, waiting for her betrothed husband's ship.

It had become a ritual she'd kept in the four months since she'd promised herself to Aimon—walking along the shoreline in the hopes that he might return. He'd gone on a trading journey that was meant to last a few weeks. Weeks had turned into months, and despite all their best efforts, the fishermen hadn't found a trace of the vessel.

She raised a hand to shield her eyes against the setting sun, her heart as cold as the lapping waves. Likely the ship had sunk. Perhaps it was her curse to bear, her punishment for choosing the wrong man. And now, she'd lost them both.

As the sun cast its last golden spears upon the shimmering black water, Brenna caught a glimpse of something approaching on the horizon. There were no billowing sails to mark it as a ship. And yet, the massive hulk floated closer, like a ruined fortress. Her heartbeat quickened, afraid of what she might find.

The wood was charred black, with hardly a single mast standing. But there could be no doubt it was Aimon's ship. Her hands gripped her skirts, dread rising up inside her. Were there any survivors?

A lone figure steered it toward the strand, but the ship was eerily quiet on the water. From her vantage point, she couldn't see who it was. As the minutes passed, the sky shifted to dark violet, the sun disappearing.

Voices shouted from the ringfort behind her, and within minutes a small crowd gathered on the shore. Torches flared, and as the vessel drew closer, the excited voices faded into silence. The ship's scarred exterior foretold the deaths of many. But which men lived?

One of the survivors trudged through the shallow water, three men following him. Brenna stepped into the edge of the sea, trying to see who they were. When they reached the shore, Aimon was not among them.

But Quin MacEgan was.

Brenna couldn't breathe when he strode toward her, like a warrior come to claim his conquest. Hardened and fierce, he said nothing to his tribesmen, ignoring everyone else but her. His dark blond hair hung against his bearded face, while green eyes locked with her own.

Quin stopped walking when he stood an arm's length from her. In his eyes, she saw the shadowed longing, mingled with pain. His clothes hung in rags, while dirt and blood caked his face. "He's dead, Brenna."

The harsh words cut through her, and hot tears welled up in her eyes. It was only the ice frozen around her heart that kept her standing. Kept her from crying out with raw anger and guilt. Aimon had gone on this voyage for her, in the hopes of increasing his holdings. Now, his dreams of wealth and glory had ended in death.

As a single drop rolled down her cheek, Brenna knew that she was weeping from guilt instead of loss. Weeping because the man she had denied as her bridegroom was standing before her.

Quin took her hand in his. Warm and alive, she let their fingers lace together as he pulled her away from the others. She didn't voice a single protest when he took her back to the hut she'd planned to share with Aimon.

When at last they were alone, she let herself shatter, grieving for her betrothed. Quin's arms caught fast around her, his strength granting her comfort. Brenna clung to him while he murmured that it would be all right.

But it wasn't going to be all right. At last, she broke free from his embrace. "You can't stay here." She crossed the room and opened the door, waiting for him to leave. "I made my choice not to marry you."

But Quin didn't move. "You might have made your choice, Brenna. But it was the wrong one." Closing the door behind him, he took a step closer. "And I intend to change your mind."

Chapter Two

Críost, he was so tired. Quin hadn't slept in days, while he'd fought to keep the ship from sinking. It was God's miracle that they'd made it back alive, after the foreign raiders had stolen their wool and silver, killing most of the men.

He drank in the sight of Brenna, even knowing that she was ready to shove him outside. Her brown hair was braided back from her face, the strands tinted red against the firelight. Stormy gray eyes glared at him with anger.

"This is Aimon's home, and I'm not about to dishonor his memory by letting you stay. He wouldn't have wanted that."

It bothered him that she was building Aimon into a saint. "You never really knew him, did you? You agreed to marry him a fortnight after you said no to me."

"I knew him well enough," she murmured. Then her expression sharpened. "Were you hoping he would die?"

"I tried to save him." Quin bit back the arguments, for she would never understand. He'd tried to save Aimon for *her.* And the failure haunted him still.

"I don't believe you," she whispered, sinking down upon a

wooden stool. She rested her elbows upon her knees, lowering her head.

He kept silent, afraid of saying the wrong thing. He'd have walked upon shards of glass for Brenna, for even a single tear shed on his behalf. The need to touch her, to ease her grief, overshadowed his exhaustion. More than food or water, he thirsted for her.

He took a step forward. Then another, kneeling down beside her on the cold earthen floor. Though he wanted to slide the lock of hair over her shoulder, revealing the smooth tear-stained cheek, he kept his hands at his sides. "I'm not going to leave you this time, Brenna."

"I won't marry you." She turned to him, her face pale. "My reasons haven't changed."

"You were afraid of what there was between us."

"No." She looked down at her hands again, unable to face him. But her face colored with embarrassment.

Quin touched his knuckles to her delicate cheek, leaning in until his nose touched hers. The hushed scent of spring clung to her hair, and he closed his eyes, savoring the closeness. He was alive, here with her. He rested his palm upon her cheek, waiting to see if she would pull away.

Instead, her hand covered his. "Quin, you want something I cannot give."

"For now, all I want is this." He leaned in and claimed her mouth in a heated kiss.

Chapter Three

Brenna yielded to him, her arms grasping his shoulders for balance. Sensual and overpowering, Quin pressed her body against the door frame. He trapped her in place, plundering her lips like a conqueror. Hot and hungry, he kissed her like he'd been starving for her these past four months.

Quin had been her closest friend, her protector for the past three years. And though he meant everything to her, he'd awakened a desire inside that she couldn't fight. The feelings he aroused within her were terrifying. She felt herself slipping away, becoming a woman she didn't want to be. And so, she'd pushed him away.

His tongue slid against the seam of her mouth, coaxing her to surrender. She tried to hold herself back, but it wasn't worth the fight. He plundered her mouth, and desire poured through her, down sensitive breasts, spiraling to the intimate place between her thighs.

Quin's hands twined in her hair, both palms cupping her face while he kissed her. *Danu,* she had missed him. She'd sent him away, believing that once he'd left, she could lock away her feelings. Now that he was back, she couldn't stop herself from pulling him close, falling under his spell. Like a candle flaring to life, she felt wanton, her instincts roaring into desperate need.

I won't do this, she told herself. *I can't.*

Brenna pulled away, turning her face aside. Her heart was aching, even as it pulsed within her chest. "Leave me alone, Quin."

Quin's green eyes stared into hers, his gaze unfathomable. "You're running away again."

Yes, she was. But he would never understand why she kept herself from him. Why she'd chosen Aimon—an awkward, quiet man who had never kindled a single spark of desire. She'd needed someone who would never expect passion from her. A man who would give her a respectable marriage, allowing her to start again.

Her foster parents had tried to shield her from the stories whispered about her, but they couldn't protect her all the time. Everyone knew where she came from. What she was.

Her throat ached with tightness, but Brenna opened the door. "I want you to go."

"For now."

In his eyes, she saw determination that matched her own. And when Quin closed the door behind him, she sank down onto the floor. Her mouth was swollen, her body awakened into a temptation she couldn't face.

Be glad that he's gone, she told herself. Instead, the emptiness seemed to swallow her.

Chapter Four

The moon illuminated a pool of light upon the burned ship. Quin sloshed through the seawater toward the broken vessel, his mood as black as the wood. He climbed aboard, never minding his soaked trews. Inside the boat, four inches of standing water kept the interior wet. The damage was extensive, and Quin didn't know if the boat could be repaired.

Over the next hour, he studied every inch of the remains, trying not to think about Brenna. The kiss they'd shared had left him frustrated and aching for her. He'd savored the taste of her, and the sweet softness of her breasts pressing against him while his hands palmed her spine.

Though she denied it, he sensed the fettered desire buried deep inside of her. It abraded his pride, for never once had Brenna admitted any feelings toward him. He'd tried to transform their friendship into love, but she'd fled from his arms at the first stirrings of physical desire.

And now, all he had was a stolen kiss. He didn't know if it was enough to rebuild anything between them.

Quin reached out to touch a charred beam, and saw the

traces of blood upon the wood. The blood of his kinsmen and closest friends. Some were dead, and others had been taken captive. He didn't know if the Moors had intended to sell them as slaves or seek a ransom. But he had to get them back. Somehow, he had to fix this ship and gather a crew of men to seek out the survivors.

A noise alerted him, and he saw Dermot approaching. Quin helped him board the vessel, and in exchange, his friend offered a small cloth-wrapped bundle of food. "I didn't see you at the welcome feast."

"I didn't go." But Quin opened the bundle and found wrapped venison and bread, along with a horn of ale. He devoured the food, the first true meal he'd had in nearly four months. "I wanted to see about the ship's repairs."

"In the dark?" Dermot shook his head. "Quin, let it go. The ship brought us back, and that's all that matters."

"It didn't bring all of us back. Or were you planning to forget about the captives?"

"I haven't forgotten," Dermot said quietly. "But we should speak with the king. He'll want to send men of his own. And we'll need a new ship."

The pointed tone wasn't lost on Quin. But he'd built this ship with his own hands, steaming the planks and fitting them to the frame. Letting it go was like releasing a piece of himself. He knew Dermot was right about speaking to his cousin, King Patrick. Without question, Patrick would offer his assistance.

Dermot rested both hands on the side of the boat, his expression grim. "We shouldn't have left the men."

"We had no choice," Quin responded, handing back the cloth. "The damned ship was on fire."

From the way Dermot studied him, Quin wondered if the

men blamed him for slicing the ropes that tethered their boat to the raiders' vessel. He'd made the decision to leave the others behind, to save what men he *could*.

How many raiders he'd killed that night, he didn't know. The nightmare of blood, fire and death haunted him still. But they'd managed to break free, steering the boat out into the open water.

"We're going to get them back," he stated. "I won't let them die."

"None of us will," Dermot reassured him. "Once we have the king's support, we'll go back."

Changing the subject, his kinsman ventured a smug grin. "I saw you with Brenna. Did she offer you a proper homecoming, then?"

The idle remark ripped apart his temper. "Don't speak ill of her," Quin warned.

Dermot raised both hands in surrender. "Peace, Quin. It was teasing, nothing more."

"I'm going to wed her. You'd best keep your teasing to yourself."

"But…she's a—"

"I'd suggest you don't finish that sentence." He knew what others said about Brenna, but it wasn't true.

Dermot rephrased. "I meant, she isolates herself from everyone. And she was betrothed to Aimon."

Quin crossed his arms. "Not anymore." He'd made the mistake of letting her go, once before. It wouldn't happen again.

Chapter Five

⦿⦿⦿⦿⦿⦿⦿⦿

Brenna rose to her feet, needing a distraction. At the opposite end of the hut, she gathered a length of wool and a spindle. The mindless task of spinning eased her, while she thought of what to do next. Neither this hut nor the land belonged to her. Though she doubted the chieftain would force her to leave right away, Aimon's brother would claim it soon enough.

She could go back to her mother's house, but it held such terrible memories, she didn't know if she could bring herself to enter. The thought made her ill.

The creamy wool twisted beneath her fingers, transforming from a mass of fleece into thin, even thread. She imagined the vibrant colors she would dye, weaving the strands into cloth. Perhaps crimson or green.

A noise outside her hut caught her attention, but no one knocked. Brenna set aside the spindle and wool, waiting. But there was no longer any sound at all. Had she imagined it?

Feeling foolish, she opened the door. Lying on the ground across her threshold was Quin, his cloak thrown carelessly over his body.

"What are you doing?" she demanded.

He rolled over and lifted his head. "Sleeping. Or at least, that's what I intended before you came and woke me up."

"You can't, Quin." What did he think he was doing? What would everyone think of her, if they saw him sleeping outside her hut? "Go back to your own place."

"I haven't a place of my own," he reminded her. "The others won't care if I'm gone. Like as not, they'll appreciate the extra space." She remembered that he slept in a common hut with several of the other unmarried men. Or sometimes in a covered shelter, barely large enough to hold the boat he was working on.

Her answer was to shut the door. No. She couldn't possibly let him behave like this, like a child who refused to give up until he got his own way.

Don't think about him. Let him remain outside and uncomfortable. It's what he deserves.

But an hour later when the strong winds began, she put her spindle aside. Surely he had left by now. Cautiously, she opened the door a crack. Quin was leaning against her hut, holding his cloak over his head. He sat upon the ground, his knees propped up. The darkening sky began to spatter rain, and still he didn't move.

"Would you like to join me?" he offered.

"Thank you, no."

"It's a nice, cool evening." He sent her a smile that slipped beneath her resolve and pricked at her conscience.

"Why are you doing this?"

He stared at her, and the intensity of his gaze made her long to shut the door again. He was looking at her like he had nothing better in the world to do, than to study her face. "You know why I'm here."

She did. Longing and guilt intertwined, even as she knew it would be a mistake to let him in. When the lightning slashed the sky, she opened the door wider. "Come inside. And stay away from me."

Quin entered the space, rain clinging to his skin. His outer clothing was wet, but he didn't look at all miserable. No, he looked like a man who had achieved his victory, and was more than pleased about it.

After she closed the door, he dropped his cloak upon the ground. Brenna crossed to the other side of the hut. Though she picked up her spindle, her fingers were shaking. Quin raked a hand through his wet hair, and chose a wooden stool to sit upon. "Thank you, Brenna."

She nodded, pretending not to look at him. Though she stared at the wool in her hands, she was fully aware of every motion he made. He stood, trying to peel back the wet clothing. "May I warm myself by the fire?"

She shrugged, but moved to the opposite end. He went over to the peat coals and held out his hands. A moment later, he peeled off the soaked tunic, baring sun-darkened skin. His broad shoulders were ridged with firm muscles, and his chest held the strength of a man who spent his hours bending pieces of wood into the form of a ship.

"You're embarrassing me," he said huskily. But she saw the amusement in his face, for he knew she'd been watching.

"Put on one of Aimon's tunics," she advised. Covering her eyes with her hands, she waited. "Tell me when you've finished."

In front of her, she heard him moving. Heard the rustle of clothing and footsteps coming closer.

"Keep your eyes closed," he murmured.

Brenna felt his presence behind her. Though he didn't move,

her skin flushed. She kept her hands closed over her eyes, even as she heard him kneel behind her.

His hands caressed her shoulders, then her nape. She could hardly breathe, her skin half-shuddering with anticipation. It felt so good to be with him, and she hated herself for holding still. Letting him touch.

I'm betraying Aimon's memory, she thought to herself. But then, they'd had no memories at all. Though they had been friends, not once had Aimon kissed her. Not the way Quin had.

His fingers dug into her scalp, massaging her hair and moving to her temples. When her hands fell into her lap, he pressed them back over her eyes. "Don't look, Brenna. I'm not nearly finished."

Chapter Six

Quin touched her gently, soothing the fragile skin of her temples. Past the scar that never should have been there. Brenna might have died from the attack. Even now, it infuriated him to see it.

The fools had tried to stone her. Though it had happened three years ago, he remembered it with vivid clarity.

He'd gone out hunting that day, tracking a deer. Brenna had stood only a few paces away from his hiding place in the forest, picking blackberries. She was alone, as she always was. He hadn't seen or spoken to her since he'd returned from his fostering, for she rarely left her home.

Like an angel, she'd lifted her face to the sun, as though trying to absorb it into her heart. Her clear skin appeared luminous, her gray eyes filled with ever-present sadness. Wild brown hair tumbled down her shoulders, touched with fiery red strands.

When had she grown this beautiful? The first stirrings of interest had caught him, and he'd remained hidden, fascinated by her.

He didn't know how long he'd watched her picking berries, but he heard the light tread of footsteps approaching. A flicker of movement caught his eye, and he spied two boys, Owen and Ulat, striding forward. Both held leather pouches slung across their shoulders.

Troublemakers, both of them, though they were only fourteen. The chieftain had warned them, more than once, to stay out of mischief. Quin was about to move forward when he saw Owen hurl the first stone.

It struck Brenna on the temple, and Ulat followed with another rock that nicked her cheek. She cried out, covering her head with her hands. Blood streamed down her face, and Quin charged from his hiding place. The instinct to protect her dominated any sense of self-preservation. Ignoring the flying stones, he sheltered her with his own body.

"Whore's daughter!" Ulat taunted. But when he threw another stone, Quin caught it and sent it flying back.

A moment later, he nocked an arrow to his bow. "Get back," he warned, pulling the bowstring tight. "Or that will be the last stone you ever throw."

Ulat stared at him, as though determining whether or not he was serious. Quin shot an arrow into the ground at the boy's feet, as an added warning. With another arrow prepared, he waited for them to make a move.

Never had he felt such a vicious rage against mere boys. But his threat worked. They dropped the stones and fled. Quin kept his bow drawn tight until they disappeared from the forest.

Brenna was crouched upon the ground, her head hanging low. Blood streamed from her temples, and she wept at his feet. He lifted her into his arms, ignoring her protests. "I'm taking you home."

She weighed hardly anything at all, and when he saw what they'd done to her, his fury at the boys magnified. Cursing, he blamed himself for not anticipating the attack.

No one was inside the dwelling when he arrived with Brenna. Quin laid her down upon a fur-lined pallet, filling a bowl with cold water.

"Don't," she whispered, clutching her head. "You must leave. My mother mustn't find you here."

A knot swelled up on her forehead, and he held a damp cloth to the gash at her temple. "They hurt you."

She took the cloth from him, meeting his gaze with her own. "I'll be fine. But you have to go."

"I'm going to tell the chieftain. He'll see to it that the boys are punished."

Brenna shook her head. "This wasn't the first time. Likely, it won't be the last."

"You're wrong." He leaned in, letting her see the rigid anger coursing inside of him. "I can promise you, Brenna. This will be the last time anyone tries to hurt you."

Whether it was her innocent beauty or her lack of protection that lured him, he didn't know. But he couldn't allow Brenna to endure taunts and physical attacks, merely because of her mother.

"I'll send the healer," he offered.

"Don't bother. It's nothing." Though she tried to venture a smile, it didn't meet her eyes.

He took Brenna's hand in his. The skin was calloused, rough from spinning and weaving. "I'm going to take care of you."

And he had. For the next three years, he'd kept a close watch over her, letting all the men in the ringfort know that he was her protector.

Then, one morning he'd found a wrapped parcel. At first he thought it was a blanket, but when he finished unfolding the triangular shape, he realized it was a sail for his boat. Made of the finest cloth, he tested its strength. It would hold steady against the strongest winds, carrying his boat as far as he dared travel.

She'd made it for him. She'd known that, of any gift, it was the greatest treasure she could have given.

And on that day, he'd promised himself that Brenna Ó Neill would belong to him.

Chapter Seven

"I blame myself for this scar," Quin said, his knuckles grazing the edge. "They hurt you."

His voice was so close to her ear, she shivered. She could feel the warmth of his breath against her skin. If she turned her head a few inches, his mouth would rest upon hers.

Temptation and resolution warred inside, and she opened her eyes, rising to her feet once more. "Boys do foolish things sometimes."

"So do men." He moved in front of her, smoothing her hair behind one ear. He sent her a roguish smile that would charm the wool off a sheep. "If you'd prefer, I can go back outside to sleep."

She shook her head. "They already know you're here. I don't suppose the gossip can get any worse."

He returned to the fire, studying the flames. "I'm not here to make others think badly of you."

"They already think the worst. That I'll be just like my mother, welcoming any man into my bed." When she had returned home after her fostering, she'd spent countless nights sleeping in the forest while her mother had entertained men. On the rare occasions when she'd come back too soon, she'd seen the lust in their eyes. For her.

Brenna crossed her arms over her breasts, shuddering at the thought. Thank God they'd left her alone after her mother's death. Whether it was Quin's doing or the chieftain's, she didn't know. But she'd tried to remain invisible to the rest of the clan.

"It was your choice to isolate yourself from everyone in the ringfort," Quin continued. "No one blames you."

Brenna moved over to her weaving loom, adjusting the threads. "They've teased me for as long as I can remember. I don't need them."

"They need your skills." He pointed to the loom and the multicolored threads she'd woven. Though she hadn't intended to make a pattern on the woolen cloth, she hadn't been able to resist the bright colors.

She began weaving, to give herself an excuse not to speak. For a long moment, Quin watched her.

"Why, Brenna? Why did you say yes to him, and not to me?"

Because Aimon was safe. Because he would never make me feel any sort of desire for him.

Her silence prompted him to crouch beside her on one knee. "I would have given you anything you'd ever wanted."

"Not everything." She passed blue thread through the loom, keeping the weaving tight and even.

From the corner of her eye, she saw his expression grow tight. She'd made him angry, but he would never understand the fear locked deep inside. If she ever let go of the rigid control over her body, she might become like her mother, losing herself in the need for pleasure.

"I'm going to see the king tomorrow," he said, rising to his feet and walking away. "I want you to come with me."

She was about to refuse, but curiosity caught her. "Why?"

"There were captives taken from our ship. I'm going to ask for men, to help bring them back."

Captives? She nearly asked if Aimon was among them, but his taut features made her hold back. Quin had never been one to tell lies.

"Where were they taken? And by whom?"

"I don't know. The Moors often sell men into slavery in Al-Andalus. If we have any hope of finding them, we'll need a new ship." He shook his head with regret. "My ship wouldn't make the passage without sinking."

She set down her shuttle, her heart hastening. "Why do you want me to come with you?"

"Because this isn't your home. And I want to bring you to my cousin's ringfort, to keep you safe while I'm gone."

He rested his hand against the door. "I'm asking you to wed me. Whatever Aimon promised you, I'll grant the same. Even if it means never touching you."

His statement stunned her, and she met his green eyes with uncertainty. He was offering her a home and the vow of his protection, though she'd refused him once before.

"What is your answer, Brenna?"

Chapter Eight

He could see that she was going to say no. It was written upon her face, and Quin cursed himself for speaking on impulse. It speared his pride, for he'd offered her everything he had.

"You couldn't make such a vow," she said flatly. "Not to touch me."

He forced himself to remain still. "I could. If it meant sharing my life with you, I would do it."

"I don't believe you."

"Shall I prove it?" He walked in front of her and placed both hands behind his back. "Do whatever you wish. I won't move."

Her lips drew into a suspicious line. But she set down her weaving and drew closer. Closer still, until she stood a single palm's distance from him. He could smell the light aroma of the soap she'd used in her hair, and her gray eyes remained wary.

It was torment. And when she stepped so close that their bodies touched, he could feel the warmth of her skin against his own. The curve of her full breasts tantalized him, and he couldn't stop his physical response.

She froze, suddenly aware that his body was straining for hers.

"Not my fault," he said with a wry smile. "I've no control over that reaction." But to his surprise, she didn't move away.

"I won't blame you for that. But what I want to know is whether or not you're able to keep your word." She touched his hair, bringing her palm to his face. "I don't think you can."

He closed his eyes, gripping his fists at his side while she traced the line of his jaw, over his mouth. It was unbelievably arousing, having to stand motionless while she tempted him. Quin shivered when her thumbs rubbed the corners of his mouth, and her nose touched his.

If he dared to touch her, he'd lose her. That, and that alone, was what kept him from moving a single muscle.

"I admire your restraint," she said at last, stepping away. "I didn't expect it."

"I keep my vows, Brenna." He moved toward the door. "I'm leaving at dawn for Laochre, to speak with the king. If you decide to come..."

"I can't answer you yet. Too much has happened. With Aimon gone, I can't think clearly." She turned her back on him, her shoulders lowered.

"Why did you choose him?" Quin asked quietly. She'd never told him, and he wondered what her feelings had been for Aimon.

She turned back. "Because he was safe. I knew we would be comfortable together."

"I would have kept you safe, Brenna."

"You don't understand." She rested her hand over her heart. "When I'm with you, I lose myself."

Shame covered her face, and it suddenly became clear. She didn't want any part of her mother's past, nor anything that would cast her in the same light. No desire, no lust. Nothing but simple companionship. She wanted a marriage based on friendship, not love.

"If we married, would it make any difference to you?"

She shook her head. "Every time I touch you or kiss you, I'm reminded of how my mother chose to live her life. I can't let it happen to me."

He didn't know what to say. He'd never really understood how a woman of her beauty and intensity would blame herself for another woman's sins.

"It doesn't have to be that way," he murmured. "I want you, Brenna, more than I've wanted any other woman. For me, there is only you. And there's no sin in that."

"I'm afraid," she whispered.

"Handfast with me, for a year and a day. And if you're unhappy, you can leave me at any time."

She crossed her arms over her chest, uncertainty reigning over her face. "Quin, I don't know."

He leaned one hand against the wall. "You can break free of the past, Brenna. If you'll try."

Chapter Nine

Dawn slipped beneath her door frame, whispering rays of sunlight filtering inside the hut. Brenna sat up, drawing her knees to her chest. She didn't know what to say to Quin today, now that she'd had several hours to think about his offer.

Though he'd proven that he could keep his promise not to touch her, she hadn't missed the tortured expression on his face. It bothered her, knowing she'd caused it.

Danu, she didn't know what to do. She'd moved into Aimon's hut after she'd promised to wed him. The walls seemed to taunt her now, reminding her of her disloyalty to Aimon.

She couldn't stay here anymore. It held too many memories of the quiet man she'd once thought of as her friend. With a heavy sigh, she began packing her belongings, though she didn't know where she would go now.

A low knock sounded at the door. She expelled a sigh, not knowing what to say to Quin. He'd ended up sleeping outside last night and would expect an answer. But what could she say?

With reluctance, she opened the door. To her surprise, the chieftain, Lughan Ó Neill, stood before her, his face grim. There was no sign of Quin nearby.

"May I come in, Brenna?"

She gave a nod, holding the door wider. Lughan spied her packing efforts and took a seat upon a bench. "I was sorry to hear about Aimon."

Fresh hurt rose up inside, and she held onto her waist, keeping the sorrow buried. "So was I."

"His brother Pól asked me to speak with you."

"I know what you're going to say." Though she knew it was rude, she returned to her packing. "I have to leave this hut."

"Pól has granted you several days," the chieftain offered. "But yes. As the second-born son of the family, this hut now falls to him. He's invited you to stay with them, if that is your wish."

The idea of being surrounded by Aimon's family was akin to being smothered. She had no right to be here, not when they had never married. "It's all right. Tell him I won't burden him by staying. He'll want to keep his wife and family here."

"I'll find a place for you with another member of the clan," Lughan offered gently. "You needn't return to your mother's hut."

She rubbed her arms and shook her head. "Don't trouble yourself."

"You are a member of this clan." Lughan's voice grew sharp, and her cheeks warmed when she realized she'd insulted him. "And therefore, my responsibility. I'll let no one go homeless, nor hungry here."

"Did Quin speak with you?" she interrupted. Had he told Lughan of his intentions or his desire to wed her?

At her query, the chieftain relaxed. "Aye, he did. This

morning, he asked for men and horses. He will act as my representative to King Patrick of Laochre, and we'll get the captives back, God willing."

Brenna's spirits sank a little, for she'd expected Quin to say something to Lughan about taking her with him. *Why would he?* her conscience chided. *You've given him no reason to believe you'll say yes.*

Even so, she was reluctant to travel with a group of men. Likely Quin hadn't thought of that or what people would say to hear of it.

Just then, the door swung open. Quin's hair was wet, his skin gleaming as though he'd just washed. His green eyes admired her as though she'd just risen from his bed. Her body warmed at his attentions. *"Dia dhuit ar maidin."*

The chieftain returned the morning greeting. "Have you chosen the men to accompany you to Laochre?"

"I have. But their wives want to go, as well. I'd forgotten that the queen is hosting an *aenach* just before the Feast of Imbolc."

Lughan laughed. "They don't trust their husbands, do they?"

Quin caught her gaze, and Brenna couldn't bring herself to look away. Handfasting was commonplace at festivals, and this *aenach* would be no exception. Imbolc marked the beginning of spring and the coming of a fertile year. No doubt the wives intended to keep their husbands from roaming.

She eyed Quin once more. Handsome and strong, there was no doubt he could capture the attention of any maiden he desired. In her mind, she envisioned him embracing another woman, kissing her and laying her down upon a pallet. The jealous thoughts made her fists dig into the clothing she was packing.

To the chieftain, Quin added, "I invited Brenna to come and meet my cousins. With your permission, she may want a change in her surroundings, after what's happened."

The chieftain turned to her. "Well?"

Her tongue felt frozen in her mouth. Quin's expression was steady, not demanding anything of her. She could go or stay. It was entirely her choice.

Though her lips formed the word *no,* to her surprise, she blurted out, "Yes. If the women are going on this journey, then I will join them."

She only hoped she wouldn't come to regret it.

of grass. Surrounded by trees, the stone ring appeared in the center, as if touched by magic. "Look at what I've found."

Interest transformed Brenna's face, and she walked forward to examine it. The granite stones were just above her height, and spiral carvings marked it. Quin ran his fingers over one of the stones. "Do you suppose they held ancient rituals in a place like this, long ago?"

She gave a tentative smile, reaching out to touch. "Perhaps."

Exploring the surface with her hands, she stopped when she reached his palm. The smile faded into more apprehension. But Quin didn't move his hand. Instead, he stared into her eyes, letting her see all the caged desire he felt. Right now he wanted to remove the blue gown she wore, sliding the wool from her shoulders until she stood bared before him. He wanted her with a visceral need, as though she were a part of him that had gone missing.

"Quin," she breathed. Her hand reached out to touch his, but even so, he saw the regret in her eyes. She'd already given up on him. And no matter how hard he tried to reshape her future, she was still caught in the past.

Chapter Eleven

"You aren't your mother, Brenna," he said. "Whatever choices she made have nothing to do with you."

She drew her hand back as if he'd struck her. "I know that. But I'll never be the kind of woman you want, either."

She couldn't have been more wrong. Beneath her shield of fear was a woman of compassion, a woman who understood him as no other had. "I've wanted you for three years, Brenna." He guided her back to press against the granite, while he rested both hands on either side of her shoulders. "Nothing's changed."

Though he gave her every opportunity to escape the embrace, she startled him by resting her cheek against his chest. "I don't know if that's true anymore."

Quin drew her close, a measure of hope dawning. It was the first time she'd willingly come to him.

"You were right. I did choose Aimon because I was afraid to marry you." She touched his face, and in her gray eyes he saw the hurt. "You deserve better than a woman like me."

"You're the woman I want, Brenna."

She stepped out of his embrace and walked toward another standing stone. For a time she stood with her back to him. "But you don't understand me. I've never told you anything about what it was like."

"Tell me now."

Her shoulders lowered with shame. "I don't know who my father was. Even when I was a girl, my mother would often leave and follow the Norman soldiers. Once, she took me to their camp with her."

Quin's chest tightened at the thought of a young girl exposed to such a place. "Did anyone harm you?"

She shook her head. "But I saw what she did with them. And I ran away." When she looked back at him, he saw the tears spilling over her face. "If it weren't for my fostering, I'd never have known a family."

"But you did." He moved behind her, resting his hands upon her shoulders. "And they took you away from her for years."

"I wanted to stay with them." She wiped the tears away. "I felt safe there."

"You're safe with me," he swore. "And you'll have your own family one day. Your own children, if you'll let me give them to you."

She stared back at him, her face stricken. "I don't know if I'll ever be able to let any man touch me. Not in that way."

He brought her palms to his heartbeat, and she let them rest, though he felt the tremor in her hands. "Do I frighten you?"

"What I feel for you frightens me."

Her words dissolved the last of his good intentions. Right now, he wanted to comfort her, to show her that he would never ask more of her than she could give.

Quin took her hands in his and brought them around his

waist. "Don't ever be afraid when you're with me." He took her face in his hands. "You're mine, Brenna. As I am yours. Ever since the day you wove the sail for me. Since the day I first kissed you."

She lifted her eyes to his, filled with such pain. "I don't want to live like this anymore. Help me to not be afraid."

Chapter Twelve

Though Brenna suspected Quin was going to kiss her, he didn't. Not yet.

Instead, he removed his tunic, letting it fall to the ground. The strong planes of his arms were unyielding and firm, like the ships he created. His stomach was ridged with tight lines, and she spied a white scar near his ribs.

Though she tried to put on a brave face, he sensed her apprehension. "I'm offering myself to you, Brenna. There's nothing to fear."

He lifted her hands to his chest, letting her touch him. With her fingers outspread, Brenna explored his chest and shoulders, running her hands over the taut muscles. And though her heartbeat quickened, an unexpected languor seemed to spread over her, as though her body were fully attuned to him.

When Quin reached for the ties on her gown, she hesitated. In the cool evening air, gooseflesh rose over her arms. Anxiety welled up, and she reached out to stop him.

But Quin eased the gown away until he bared her breasts. Brenna longed to cover herself, but he pulled her body to his, skin to skin. Her breasts were small, her nipples tight against the heat of his chest.

His hands moved up the side of her arms, grazing her sensitive skin. Between her legs, she grew damp, and he slid his thigh within them, to support her weight.

"You're everything to me, Brenna," he murmured, bending his mouth to her throat. "There's nothing to be afraid of."

He supported her against the cool standing stone, while his other hand moved to touch her breast. Shyness struck her at the vulnerable position. No man had ever seen her exposed like this, and she desperately wanted to hide herself from his gaze.

"You're like silk," he whispered. "So incredibly soft." His thumb caressed the tip, coaxing an unexpected response that pierced her to the core. Gentle, and wicked, he stroked her aroused nipple until she twisted from the deepening sensations.

When his mouth covered her breast, she couldn't stop the moan that escaped. His tongue caressed her, his mouth suckling in a way that made her press her womanhood against his knee. A shuddering gasp erupted from her throat, and she no longer knew if she wanted to break free or draw closer.

Brenna hardly felt the cold anymore, as the wildness rose up once more, like a fever she couldn't control. Between her legs, she craved him. Needed him. She ached, and when he shifted his thigh to caress her intimately, it was too much. The drowning desire was killing her, and Brenna used all of her strength to shove him away.

"I can't do this. You have to stop."

Chapter Thirteen

They hardly spoke to one another on the rest of the journey. Though Quin had taken her back to the camp without question, she knew she'd offended him. His stance was rigid, like a man enduring physical frustration.

Misery dogged her, even when they reached Laochre the following day. Brenna wondered if she should have succumbed to his touch, no matter that she'd grown uncomfortable. But she couldn't bring herself to speak of it.

When they arrived at Laochre, she saw that the king had used a Norman design for his castle, similar to the holdings she'd seen in the northeast. With large square towers and walls greater than a man's height, she didn't doubt that King Patrick had the wealth and means to bring back the captives from Iberia.

She craned her neck as they passed through the gate, spying an impish boy smiling down at her from the murder hole. Within the inner bailey, a small group of women were practicing archery. They were guided by another woman with dark hair, cropped to her shoulders. To her shock, Brenna spied a sword belt around the woman's waist.

"That's Honora MacEgan," Quin answered, nodding toward the woman. It was the first time he'd spoken to her in half a day. "She married my cousin Ewan this past summer."

"A female warrior?"

Quin shrugged. "Patrick saw it as a way to increase our forces. Only the women who choose to fight are asked to train with Honora. It's not required."

Brenna studied the women. They wore modified men's clothing, but their long braided hair gave evidence to their sex. Lean and strong, she saw an air of undeniable confidence. There were several men, presumably engaged in repairing a stone wall, who openly flirted with them.

Instead of being embarrassed, the women appeared to enjoy the attention. One sent a taunting smile to the men before pulling back her bow. She held the weapon tight, showing off the honed strength in her arms, before loosing an arrow into the center.

A pang of envy caught Brenna. To be admired instead of scorned was something she'd not experienced before. And these women made her all too aware of her own insecurities.

Moments later, Quin lifted her down from her horse, bringing her to meet Ewan MacEgan. The dark-haired warrior greeted her, and Brenna noticed the similarity in the men's green eyes. Ewan had a more muscular build, in contrast to Quin's taller form, but both men were undeniably strong.

"We received word about the captives," Ewan said. "Tonight we'll meet with King Patrick and discuss our strategy."

"Will you be wanting women to go and fight?" a female voice interrupted. Honora MacEgan joined her husband, and he kissed her in greeting.

"*A stór,* there's only one woman I'm wanting. And not for a fight." Ewan sent his wife a mischievous smile, and Honora grinned.

Brenna found herself warming to the couple, seeing the devotion between them. She looked back at Quin, but his expression was strained.

It was her fault, though he'd not spoken one word of blame. Once again, she'd let her fear of desire control her, and she was tired of that coming between them. Time and again, she'd pushed Quin away, as if she didn't believe she had the right to happiness.

You're not your mother, he'd said. And she wasn't, not at all. There was only one man she wanted in her life. The man who had stood by her all these years.

"I'll arrange for a place for both of you to sleep," Ewan was saying. His expression narrowed, as if trying to determine whether or not to separate them.

Brenna took a deep breath and turned to Honora. "Might I ask for your help?"

Ewan's wife turned curious. "Of course."

Though her heartbeat clamored in her chest, Brenna took Quin's hand in hers. Though shyness made it difficult to speak, she wanted Quin to know her answer.

Steeling her courage, she forced the words out. "Quin and I are promised to one another. I would like to handfast with him tonight, before he leaves on the voyage."

Chapter Fourteen

After the disastrous evening he'd spent with her in the woods, Brenna's acceptance was the last thing Quin expected.

He'd been so distracted, thinking of her during his meeting, that he'd hardly heard a word spoken by his cousin, the king.

"You may take a dozen men," King Patrick offered. "Along with horses and two ships."

He'd bowed, but Patrick stopped him. "Quin, how many captives were taken?"

"Six," he admitted, offering the names of the men.

"And how do you intend to find them?" The king's expression grew wary, as though he didn't believe it could be done.

"I'll return the ship to where we were attacked, off the coast of Iberia. We'll search along the coastline and find whatever survivors we can. I suspect the Moors wanted to sell the men."

"And if you don't find them?"

"We will," Quin insisted.

"But you can't remain at sea forever," Patrick remarked. "Especially not if you're leaving a wife behind."

Quin colored at the reminder, while his nerves grew anxious. Though Brenna had agreed to handfast with him, he wondered if she might still change her mind.

"You have until Midsummer's Eve," the king commanded. "If you haven't located the men by then, I'll expect your return."

Quin nodded and departed the king's chambers. Though he looked for Brenna, Honora and Queen Isabel had taken her away to prepare for the handfasting. He spent the remainder of the afternoon and early evening pacing.

When the moon rose over the castle, the king's men escorted him outside the grounds to a smaller circle of stone huts. There, he saw his cousins and friends gathering near a small bonfire.

In front of the fire stood Brenna, her hair crowned with purple heather. She wore a moss-colored gown that accentuated the red tints within her brown hair. Though she tried to smile at him, he noticed her white pallor and the way she clenched her hands together. She didn't like being the center of attention.

Queen Isabel and Honora stood nearby, their faces bright with anticipation. Flowers decorated the huts, and from the delicious smells of roasting meat, he knew Isabel had spent the afternoon preparing for the ceremony. His cousin's wife loved nothing better than to organize feasts and celebrations.

As he reached Brenna's side, he took her hand and brought it to his lips. She gripped his fingers, her mouth compressed with fear.

"Are you certain this is what you want?" he asked, beneath his breath.

She managed a nod, and as the priest blessed their union, binding their hands together, he never took his eyes from Brenna. Her cool fingers warmed in his, and when he kissed her, it was hardly more than a whisper upon her lips.

As the feasting and drinking progressed, he saw that his new wife was becoming more and more overwhelmed. The queen had set aside one of the huts for him and Brenna, decorated with more flowers.

"You've had enough of this, haven't you?" he whispered into Brenna's ear.

"No, I'm fine. Really."

Quin ignored her, lifting her into his arms despite the ribald comments and cheers. Brenna's face turned crimson, but her arms stayed around his neck. As he took her into the bridal hut, everything else seemed to slip away except for her.

And tonight, he wasn't about to let her go.

Chapter Fifteen

Brenna sat down upon a wooden bench, her heart racing so fast, she was afraid she'd faint. But it was done now. She'd spoken her vow to Quin, and tonight he would become her husband in body, as well as in name.

It terrified her, though she trusted him.

He barred the door, retreating toward the fire. Minutes stretched, and still he didn't speak. The silence nearly suffocated her, and at last she approached him, touching his arm. Quin spun without warning.

"*Críost,* I wasn't expecting that. I'm sorry." He ran a hand through his hair, venturing a smile. There was a shadow beneath it, and she knew her behavior the other night had caused his wariness.

"Are you tired?" She clasped her hands together, not knowing what else to say.

"No." He didn't face her, and so she touched his shoulder again. His muscles were knotted, rigid as she caressed him. She marveled that she was able to reach out to him, without any fear of him pushing her away.

"Why did you say yes to the handfasting, Brenna?" he asked, pulling her into his arms. He stroked the line of her hair, down to her jaw.

"Because I'd rather be with you, than alone." She closed her eyes, inhaling the warm male scent of him. His lazy caresses against her hair were making her relax. Though she hadn't touched any wine or ale, it was as if she'd drunk a dozen cups. Her hands moved up to his tunic, slipping beneath the rough wool.

Quin tilted her face up to look at him. "I'm leaving for Iberia tomorrow morning. We've only this night together."

She knew it, and it only strengthened her resolve to endure the physical intimacy that lay ahead. To answer his unspoken question, she stood on her tiptoes and offered a kiss. Like a blessing, his mouth came down upon hers. His tongue probed at her, and she opened to him, trying not to be afraid of the arousal rising up within her.

There's nothing to fear, she reminded herself. And when she thought of the night she'd pushed him away, she realized that no matter what happened, Quin would never make demands of her.

In his green eyes she saw the raw need, the tight control over his body. He was rigid against her stomach, and knowing that she had caused such an arousal was humbling.

"I won't run from you this time," she promised.

He didn't smile. Instead, he removed his tunic and trews, standing before her naked. Powerful and strong, the beauty of his body was unlike anything she'd expected. The urge to touch him came over her, but she made no move toward him.

Instead, she loosened the ties of her gown. Her pulse pounded as she removed her own clothing, standing bare before him.

Chapter Sixteen

"You're the most beautiful woman I've ever seen," Quin murmured. His words washed over her like an invisible caress.

She waited for him to touch her, and when at last he drew her body against his, she shivered with gratefulness. His wide hands moved down her spine, tracing every inch of her. He cupped her bottom, and when she spread her legs slightly, his hands slipped between her thighs.

A shudder caught her when his fingertips dipped into the moisture at her center. The brief touch staggered her, and when she stepped away from him, he let her go.

"Lie down on the pallet," he ordered. With knees shaking, Brenna obeyed. The pallet was lined with soft furs, and the sensation against her bare skin was heady. Quin strode toward her, his erection bobbing forward. He knelt beside her, and Brenna clenched the furs in anticipation.

"Not yet, *a stór*," he whispered. He spread her hair out, down to cover her breasts. Using the long strands, he rubbed them against her nipples. The silky sensation puckered her breasts, and after that he exposed them to the air. A shimmering breath of desire caught her, and she tried to pull him down atop her.

Her attempt to rush him met with failure. Quin's dark gaze swept over her body, and he sent her a slow smile.

"We've only one first time together, *a stór,*" he whispered. "And I intend to make it last all night."

Brenna gave a faint nod, and he leaned over her, kissing her lips…her throat…down to her breasts. As his mouth tasted the hardened nipples, he ran a hand across her ribs and stomach, down to her thighs. She instinctively tightened her legs together, even as her mind ordered her body to relax.

This was Quin. He'd promised to take care of her. To guard her with his very life. And though he hadn't said it, she sensed that he might love her.

She exhaled a gasp when his hand moved behind her knees, his mouth lowering to her mound. He stopped to look at her, his green eyes heated with desire. "Tell me if anything bothers you. I'll stop."

The promise was not made lightly. She knew he was referring to the other night, when she'd lost her courage.

"Don't stop," she whispered, pulling his head down for another kiss. He met her mouth roughly, like a man on the brink of losing himself. He pulled her knee up, lifting it over his hip as he kissed her. Against her wetness, she felt his length caressing her. When he moved his shaft, rubbing her intimately, she trembled.

But he didn't join their bodies together. Instead, he drew back and lifted her other knee. Moving lower, his mouth nipped at her inner thigh. Then across the other. Brenna tried to close her legs, but he held them apart.

"Trust me, *a stór.* I only want to kiss you again."

She waited for him to cover her body with his, but instead of taking her mouth, his tongue slid over her woman's flesh. Wet and sleek, he covered her, setting her senses on fire.

"Quin," she gasped, unable to stop the intensity from building. She fought him back, trying not to let the fierce pleasure consume her. But when his mouth nipped at the hooded flesh above her center, sucking hard, her body trembled.

"Do you feel it?" he murmured against her body. His tongue licked her, penetrating gently. "Don't resist what's happening to you. Let go, Brenna."

"I can't," she whispered, even as his mouth coaxed her to an even higher point of pleasure. It was almost painful, the burgeoning sensation that wound her tight.

"You can." With his thumb, he entered her body while he worked her with his mouth. She was almost sobbing, her legs shaking.

"No. I need you to stop."

Chapter Seventeen

Quin withdrew his hand abruptly. It was hard to breathe, her lungs catching in quick gasps. Brenna's eyes flooded up with shame, for even at this she was a failure. Whatever it was he wanted, she couldn't give to him.

She wanted to weep, for she'd let him down once again. Quin studied her, his face unreadable. She half expected him to leave the hut in disgust. But right now she felt ready to break apart. It angered her that she couldn't be the sort of wife he wanted or needed.

After all these years, she still couldn't bury the past. But instead of anger, she saw strained patience upon his face. A strange smile flickered over his mouth. "I shouldn't have rushed you like that," he said. "You weren't ready."

He stretched out beside her, his body still heavily aroused. His manhood rested against his stomach, thick and hard.

"I'm sorry, Quin. I thought—"

"No. It's all right," he reassured her. "There will be time enough for this."

But there wasn't. He would be leaving with his men in a few

hours. She reached out to hold him, resting her cheek upon his chest. Though she'd been uneasy about being naked around Quin, she was starting to grow accustomed to the intimacy. Her hand moved over his skin, stroking a pattern. His eyes were closed, but she didn't think he was sleeping.

Her gaze turned to his manhood, and she wondered what it would feel like in her hand. Would it be hard and rough? She reached out tentatively with a single finger. Quin spasmed when she touched him.

"Sorry."

She pulled her hand back, but he shook his head. "You can touch me all you want, *a stór*. My body belongs to you now."

The idea intrigued her. Perhaps she might be a failure in lovemaking, but she knew there were ways to bring a man pleasure. She cupped the base of him, running her fingers along his length. A sharp exhalation erupted from his mouth and she took her hand back again.

"No, Brenna. It feels good." He opened his eyes and she saw the ferocity of his need. "Straddle me while you touch."

She felt awkward, but positioned herself atop his hips as she explored the length and head of him. Quin was moving his body in a rhythm in counter to her strokes, and her hand grew wet where she fisted his length. To her surprise, she realized that her own body was beginning to respond in the same way.

Her wetness ached to be filled. She wanted to feel him inside her, to satiate the hunger. Slowly, she raised herself up and he met her gaze when she positioned him at her entrance.

"Brenna," Quin breathed, his face taut as she slid against him. Her body took the place of her hand, sheathing him.

Though it was tight, it didn't hurt as much as she'd thought it would. He was adjusting her hips, lifting her slightly and when she sank down, a jolt of warmth pooled inside her.

It was like before, the spicy arousal starting to build. But this time, she was able to control the sensations. Experimentally, she lifted up until only the tip of him remained inside. When she slid down again, an answering shudder pulsed in her womanhood.

It felt…good to be joined with him. And as she began to move up and down, she saw the same reactions upon *his* face. She was giving him the same torturous pleasure he'd tried to give her. And the power, knowing that she was making him feel so good, only drove her to ride him faster.

Flesh to flesh, hardness to softness, she increased her pace, her excitement rising. Quin sat up, changing their position so that she sat with her legs around his waist. His mouth fastened over her breast once more, sucking and tasting the nipple. Brenna almost stopped, but Quin urged her to keep taking him inside, impaling her with his shaft.

The wildness of mounting him, over and over, suddenly took hold. She gripped the back of his head, forcing him to endure the sensation until his face tightened in pleasure. Seeing the ecstasy and fulfillment broke apart her control, and a frenzied climax erupted within. He gripped her hard as she shattered, both legs still wrapped around his waist.

Even when he laid her back down, keeping his body joined with hers, aftershocks rippled through her.

When at last she managed to open her eyes, Quin wasn't smiling.

Chapter Eighteen

Never in all his dreams had he ever imagined a night like this. Even when he was spent inside her, Quin couldn't let go of Brenna. He held her close, stroking her spine and the luscious curve of her bottom.

"How do you feel, *a stór?*"

She raised her head to look at him. "Not afraid anymore."

"Thank God." But even as he withdrew from her, he didn't let go. It was as if he could make her a part of him by holding her skin to his. He'd known that she was a passionate woman, but he'd never expected that she needed to be in control to find her own release.

He kissed her cheek and throat again, his hands kneading the soft flesh that led to the sweetness between her legs. Brenna rolled over, her hands poised against his chest. "What are you doing, Quin?"

He sent her a wicked smile. "Making up for lost time. And ensuring that you'll miss me when I'm gone." He penetrated her with his fingers, feeling the warm wetness of her arousal.

Though it was too soon for him to make love to her again, he wanted her to experience yet another awakening.

Brenna answered his smile, but it was quickly replaced by a sweet moan. She shuddered against his fingers, and he found the place that deepened her arousal. Her hips arched and flexed in rhythm and he exerted pressure, loving the sensation of her wetness around his thumb and fingers.

"Will you think of me when I'm gone, Brenna?" he teased, penetrating her again. He stroked her into a frenzy until she gripped him hard, biting back a scream. Ripples of fulfillment overtook her, and Quin reveled in the shocked pleasure on her face.

She pulled him down for a deep kiss. "I wish you didn't have to go. And I wish I'd said yes to you, so much sooner than this."

"I'll come back to you, Brenna. I swear it."

Dawn broke through their night of lovemaking. And when he boarded the ship, Brenna stood on the sand watching. A harsh aching took hold of him, seeing her standing on the shoreline, apart from the others. As the waves took the vessel out to sea, he didn't take his eyes from her.

His wife. His reason to return.

And yet, as the wind took hold of the sail, taking him farther away, he feared he would not see her again.

Chapter Nineteen

Laochre had become a second home to Brenna. When Queen Isabel had learned of her weaving skills, she'd set her to work creating tapestries for the castle. In time, some of the younger children came to watch, and Brenna found herself instructing the girls. No one treated her differently here, and as Quin's wife she found a new home with the MacEgans.

But still, she missed him.

She waited along the sand each night, waiting for his ship to return. But month after month passed, and there was no sign of them. Midsummer's Eve came and went, and Brenna feared the worst.

Another month went by, and she was at her loom when Liam MacEgan came running in. "Brenna! The ship is here!"

She practically threw the skeins of wool across the room, racing toward the shoreline behind the young boy. Already men were sloshing through the water, running to their loved ones. All six captives had been found, and Brenna smiled with thanks that Quin had succeeded.

She waited, her heart trembling within her chest as the last man disembarked from the boat. He moved slower than the others, and she raised her hand to her throat when she saw who it was.

Aimon.

A low buzzing rang through her ears, confusion sweeping through her. But Aimon was dead. Quin had said so himself.

Had he lied to her? She couldn't believe he would betray her like that.

She didn't want to believe it, but within moments Aimon stood before her. His blond hair was longer, and no longer was he the calm, placid man she'd known. Fury permeated every feature, his brown eyes narrowed upon her.

"I thought you were dead," Brenna whispered. She didn't know what to feel right now, for Quin had not emerged from the ship.

Aimon's hardened gaze showed not an ounce of sympathy for her plight. "I was wounded. Not dead." He gripped her wrist while several of the MacEgan tribe members watched. "But I hear that you didn't wait for me."

She hardly heard what he was saying, so sickened was she to think of what had happened. And where was Quin? Was he hurt as well?

Before she could ask, Aimon jerked her forward and Brenna stumbled to the ground. Her hands pressed into the sand, her eyes stinging as she stared up at him. One of the MacEgan men, Ruarc, stepped forward to help her, but Aimon sent the man a furious look.

"I spent the last few months fighting to stay alive. For her." Blistering anger ridged Aimon's face. "She was never anything but a whore's daughter. Lucky that any man would want to wed her."

He spat upon the ground. "Blood will tell, won't it, Brenna? For you've become a whore yourself."

The shocked faces of the MacEgans made her skin flush. She hadn't told any of them about her mother, and Aimon couldn't have humiliated her any more.

Honora MacEgan stepped forward and helped her rise to her feet. With her arm around Brenna, the woman glared at Aimon, her hand poised upon her sword. "That's enough. Brenna is wed to Quin now. She's one of us."

Dermot approached her, his face sober. In a low voice, he offered, "We didn't know Aimon was alive, Brenna. None of us did."

She met his gaze with her own fear, but managed a nod. "Where is Quin now?"

"He gave himself to the Moors," Dermot admitted, "in order to set Aimon free."

Brenna's heart splintered, for she knew he'd done it on her behalf. Hot tears slid over her cheeks, and Aimon's mouth curled into a snarl. "It would serve her right if he's dead."

Chapter Twenty

Summer waned into autumn, and Brenna slipped into a despondency. Though Isabel and Honora tried to coax her into taking part in the tribe's activities, she'd retreated into isolation.

Exhaustion and fear were her constant companions now. But that night, she'd risen to her feet once again, her shoulders heavy with despair as she'd walked to the shore.

A whore, Aimon had called her. Though the insult meant nothing to the MacEgans and they'd exiled him back to the Ó Neill clan, the word bothered her. For the truth was, she'd gone back into Quin's arms without grieving for Aimon at all. She *had* betrayed him, not only with her body, but with her heart as well.

She'd loved Quin, with every part of her spirit. From the moment he'd rescued her from the boys in the blackberry bushes, to the night he'd helped her overcome her fears of lovemaking, she'd given herself to him. And now, she needed him more than ever.

The moonlight slid over the small channel leading to the

sea, the waves quiet and calm. There were no ships to bring him home, and though the king had sent men to search for him, there had been no sign that Quin was alive.

Brenna stood carefully, familiar tears pricking at the corners of her eyes. Only a tiny boat lay upon the water, a fisherman bringing in his catch for the night. Once again, she would return to her hut alone.

But something held her feet in place. A familiar shape caught her eye, and she looked back at the small boat. The oars cut through the water at a swift pace, faster than a fisherman would ever move.

Fragile hope caught within her. When the moon emerged from behind a cloud, she started to weep.

Quin threw the oars aside, running through the water until he reached her side. Strong arms encompassed her, and she gripped him hard. He'd grown thinner, but he was alive and whole. It was enough.

"I love you," she whispered, drawing his mouth to hers. Quin kissed her, their tongues tangled in a fervent reunion. Holding him in her arms once more mended all the broken pieces of her heart.

When he ended the kiss, Quin cupped her jaw. "I swear to you, I didn't know that Aimon lived," he insisted. "I saw him struck down in battle."

"Padraig told me what happened." Brenna covered his hand with hers. "And I vowed I would wait for you, no matter how long it took for you to be free."

"I've thought of you every moment for the past season," he swore. "And to find you waiting for me—" His voice broke off, and he drew back.

In wonder, his hand moved down her body to the rounded stomach beneath her gown. The new life growing inside her seemed to sense Quin's presence, and a slight tremor rippled through her skin as the babe kicked. Quin's hand moved over the child in a light caress, and he enclosed her in an embrace once more.

He touched her stomach again, unable to stop his smile. "When will our child be born?"

"In winter."

Quin appeared awed by the forthcoming birth, and he leaned down to kiss her once again. "I love you, Brenna. Now and always."

"I love you, too, Quin." Their hands linked together as they walked along the sand. Brenna kissed his palm in a silent prayer of thanksgiving. "Welcome home."

HISTORICAL

SECRET LIFE OF A SCANDALOUS DEBUTANTE
by Bronwyn Scott

Beldon Stratten is the perfect English gentleman and he's looking for a perfectly bland, respectable wife. Exotic Lilya Stefanov is anything but bland. Beneath her evening gowns and polished etiquette lies a dangerous secret—and a scandalous sensuality...

Regency

ONE ILLICIT NIGHT
by Sophia James

After one uncharacteristically wicked night, Eleanor Bracewell-Lowen now leads a safe and prudent life. On his return to London, Lord Cristo Wellingham looks different from the man she knew so briefly in Paris. His touch invites passion, but this is a man who could destroy her good name with just one glance...

Regency

THE GOVERNESS AND THE SHEIKH
by Marguerite Kaye

Sheikh Prince Jamil al-Nazarri commands his kingdom effortlessly...less so his difficult little daughter! He hires an English governess hoping she'll instil some much-needed discipline... But Lady Cassandra Armstrong is the most unconventional—and alluring—governess Jamil has ever seen!

On sale from 3rd June 2011
Don't miss out!

HISTORICAL

PIRATE'S DAUGHTER, REBEL WIFE
by June Francis

Bridget McDonald is in fear for her life—and her virtue—on board a slave ship. She's rescued by rugged Captain Henry Mariner. Despite her reserve towards him, he knows there is no other option... The only way to protect her is to marry her!

HIS BORDER BRIDE
by Blythe Gifford

Gavin Fitzjohn is the illegitimate son of an English prince and a Scotswoman. A rebel without a country, he has darkness in his soul. Clare Carr, daughter of a Scottish border lord, can recite the laws of chivalry, and knows Gavin has broken every one. Yet still Clare is gripped by desire for this royal rogue...

QUESTIONS OF HONOUR
by Kate Welsh

Why, in all the years Joshua Wheaton had been away, had he never made contact or acknowledged Abaigeal's news that she carried his baby? Now Abaigeal will look Joshua in the eye as he realises he has a son, and hope to rediscover the honourable man she fell in love with all those years ago...

On sale from 3rd June 2011
Don't miss out!

REGENCY

Collection

*Let these sparklingly seductive delights whirl
you away to the ballrooms—and
bedrooms—of Polite Society!*

Volume 1 – 4th February 2011
Regency Pleasures by Louise Allen

Volume 2 – 4th March 2011
Regency Secrets by Julia Justiss

Volume 3 – 1st April 2011
Regency Rumours by Juliet Landon

Volume 4 – 6th May 2011
Regency Redemption by Christine Merrill

Volume 5 – 3rd June 2011
Regency Debutantes by Margaret McPhee

Volume 6 – 1st July 2011
Regency Improprieties by Diane Gaston

12 volumes in all to collect!

MILLS &
BOON

www.millsandboon.co.uk

REGENCY
Collection

*Let these sparklingly seductive delights whirl
you away to the ballrooms—and
bedrooms—of Polite Society!*

Volume 7 – 5th August 2011
Regency Mistresses by Mary Brendan

Volume 8 – 2nd September 2011
Regency Rebels by Deb Marlowe

Volume 9 – 7th October 2011
Regency Scandals by Sophia James

Volume 10 – 4th November 2011
Regency Marriages by Elizabeth Rolls

Volume 11 – 2nd December 2011
Regency Innocents by Annie Burrows

Volume 12 – 6th January 2012
Regency Sins by Bronwyn Scott

12 volumes in all to collect!

MILLS &
BOON

www.millsandboon.co.uk

0511_BOTM

MILLS & BOON

are proud to present our...

Book of the Month

Come to Me
by Linda Winstead Jones

from Mills & Boon® Intrigue

Lizzie needs PI Sam's help in looking for her lost
half-sister. Sam's always had a crush on Lizzie.
But moving in on his former partner's daughter
would be *oh-so-wrong*...

Available 15th April

*Something to say about our Book of the Month?
Tell us what you think!*

millsandboon.co.uk/community
facebook.com/romancehq
twitter.com/millsandboonuk

2 FREE BOOKS
AND A SURPRISE GIFT

We would like to take this opportunity to thank you for reading this Mills & Boon® book by offering you the chance to take TWO more specially selected books from the Historical series absolutely FREE! We're also making this offer to introduce you to the benefits of the Mills & Boon® Book Club™—

- **FREE home delivery**
- **FREE gifts and competitions**
- **FREE monthly Newsletter**
- **Exclusive Mills & Boon Book Club offers**
- **Books available before they're in the shops**

Accepting these FREE books and gift places you under no obligation to buy, you may cancel at any time, even after receiving your free books. Simply complete your details below and return the entire page to the address below. You don't even need a stamp!

YES Please send me 2 free Historical books and a surprise gift. I understand that unless you hear from me, I will receive 4 superb new books every month for just £3.99 each, postage and packing free. I am under no obligation to purchase any books and may cancel my subscription at any time. The free books and gift will be mine to keep in any case.

Ms/Mrs/Miss/Mr ———————— Initials ——————

————————————————————————————

Surname ——————————————————————

Address ——————————————————————

————————————————————————————

———————————————— Postcode ——————

E-mail ————————————————————————

Send this whole page to: Mills & Boon Book Club, Free Book Offer, FREEPOST NAT 10298, Richmond, TW9 1BR

Offer valid in UK only and is not available to current Mills & Boon Book Club subscribers to this series. Overseas and Eire please write for details. We reserve the right to refuse an application and applicants must be aged 18 years or over. Only one application per household. Terms and prices subject to change without notice. Offer expires 31st July 2011. As a result of this application, you may receive offers from Harlequin (UK) and other carefully selected companies. If you would prefer not to share in this opportunity please write to The Data Manager, PO Box 676, Richmond, TW9 1WU.

Mills & Boon® is a registered trademark owned by Harlequin (UK) Limited.
The Mills & Boon® Book Club™ is being used as a trademark.